SPARKENBROKE

SPARKENBROKE

BY

CHARLES MORGAN

MACMILLAN AND CO., LIMITED
ST. MARTIN'S STREET, LONDON
1950

First Edition April 1936
Reprinted July 1936, 1938 1946, 1950

PRINTED IN GREAT BRITAIN
BY WESTERN PRINTING SERVICES, LTD., BRISTOL

To

CHRISTOPHER ARNOLD-FORSTER

who lent me courage to seek my goods

and to my father

CHARLES MORGAN

who gave me freedom to ply it

I offer this book

with the gratitude of a son given his chance

and of a friend whose imagination was shared

H.M.S. MONMOUTH, 1914   LONDON, 1919

. . . Now every human soul must have seen the realities of that other world, else could she not have entered into this body. But to recall those things by means of the things of this world is not easy. . . . Few indeed are left who have a ready and sufficient memory; and they, when they behold here any likeness of the things there, are amazed and cannot contain themselves. But what this emotion really is they know not, because their perception is too indistinct.

PLATO: *Phaedrus*.

Trans. ROBERT BRIDGES.

I am certain of nothing but of the holiness of the Heart's affections, and the truth of Imagination. What the Imagination seizes as Beauty must be Truth. . . . The Imagination may be compared to Adam's dream,—he awoke and found it truth.

KEATS : Letter to Bailey, 1817.

... Now every human soul must have seen the realities of that other world, else could she not have entered into this body. But to recall those things by means of the things of this world is not easy. ... Few indeed are left who have a ready and sufficient memory; and they, when they behold here any likeness of the things there, are amazed and cannot contain themselves. But what this emotion really is they know not, because their perception is too indistinct.

PLATO: *Phaedrus.*

Trans. ROBERT BRIDGES.

I am certain of nothing but of the holiness of the Heart's affections, and the truth of Imagination. What the Imagination seizes as Beauty must be Truth. ... The Imagination may be compared to Adam's dream,—he awoke and found it truth.

KEATS: *Letter to Bailey,* 1817.

CONTENTS

CONTENTS

BOOK I

THE SPARKENBROKE MOUND

CHAPTER ONE

SINCE the death of Lord Sparkenbroke, tourists from Chelmouth who would formerly have been content to wander through the corridors of his great house, gazing at its treasures and listening to the mechanical chatter of the guides, have added the church and the churchyard to their pilgrimage, for in the churchyard stands the Sparkenbroke Mound, an open, grassy sepulchre of a type familiar in Wales but rare so far east as Dorset, and through its iron-barred gate Lord Sparkenbroke's coffin may be seen among those of his ancestors.

Though he died of a disease which he had long known might claim him, unusual circumstances attended his death—namely, that he died alone at night in his own tomb, having admitted himself with the key that he always carried. That section of the public to whom a graveyard is a place of terror could not easily believe that it was his frequent habit, when in England, to visit and enter the Sparkenbroke Mound, and it was rumoured that he had done so on this occasion in an agonized premonition of death.

This legend combines with the fame of his writings and the reputed disorder of his life to draw, on Saturday afternoons in summer, a continuous stream of visitors to the burying-ground, and no one who loved him, not his widow, nor his son Richard, nor Dr. George Hardy, approaches the place at that time.

Above the door of the tomb is a scroll on which six lines of conventional verse were long ago inscribed, and above the scroll is another set of verses, composed by Sparkenbroke himself and set up during his lifetime. Although, when he died, no photograph of him was available to the press, he having avoided cameras while he lived, these verses, addressed to the passer-by, have been so often photographed and commented upon that among the group of Saturday visitors there is always one who will contrast the smooth melancholy of the early rhyme, which bids the living pity the dead, with the challenge of Sparkenbroke's sequel:

> *Who mourns? A fool with mortal look*
> *That dares to weep for Sparkenbroke?*
> *Weep thine own exile: not my life.*
> *With Earth for mother, Sleep for wife,*
> *Here in the womb is winter spring.*
> *Who stays? A Fool. Who knocks? A King.*

Even the obscurity of the last line has been cleared away by commentators, and no guide is needed to explain that, in Lord Sparkenbroke's opinion, he who had admittance to death entered into a kingdom.

On their way to the church itself many of the visitors that are townsmen may be heard discussing the genuineness of this sentiment, often humorously, for to them, whose natural earth is the pavement, it seems that death, like poetry and love, may be spoken of only under cover of that laughter which has become a nervous substitute for awe. Unable or unwilling to apprehend Sparkenbroke's positive view of death as re-entry into a continuous reality from which birth and sensuous existence are a divagation, they read into his words an extreme pessimism hardly to be credited. If he had been poor and old and pious, they might have permitted in him a stale yearning for heaven; but he was not pious; he was not old; he had fame, position, women and, seemingly, riches. Why should he wish to die? And, if he did, why didn't he kill himself? So the argument proceeds, swaying uneasily between envy and righteousness. There is seldom any conclusion to it among men except that poets are mad and will say anything. Women, if they are young, incline to a more liberal verdict, Sparkenbroke's reputation, at the safe distance of the

grave, offering to their fancies a pleasing contrast with the
dullness of their own lovers and husbands.

They are quick to discover satirical point in the text
chosen for the tablet on the church wall:

IN MEMORY OF

PIERS TENNIEL

SEVENTH VISCOUNT AND TWELFTH BARON

SPARKENBROKE

OF CHELMOUTH IN THE COUNTY OF DORSET

POET AND STORY-TELLER

BORN JANUARY 22, 1892. DIED JULY 11, 1928

Blessed are the pure in heart: for they shall see God

For them the word pure has but one meaning—not the
gospel's. It is, they think, amusingly inappropriate to
Sparkenbroke's life, and the knowing among them smile
to think how Lady Sparkenbroke was deceived. That the
text may, in its application to an artist, have justice and
truth, however irregular his carnal life, enters the minds
of very few.

In the great house itself tourists are shown Lord
Sparkenbroke's writing-table, his chair and his pen; in the
grounds, the wooded lake in which he swam; and, in
Derry's Wood, as they pass out of the estate on their way
to their motor-coaches, the lodge, called Derry's Cottage,
in which, when he was in England, he spent a great part
of his time. Near to the cottage they find a stream, with
a willow overhanging it, which, they remember—or are
reminded—appears more than once in his works.

The public is admitted only on Saturday afternoons and
on certain holidays, as it has always been. The number of
visitors has increased, not the frequency of their coming.
For long stretches of winter, when there are no bands in
Chelmouth and no excursions through Sparkenbroke
Green, the house is bleak and solitary on its hill, the
orchards and terraces are deserted, and the church is
entered by none but its parishioners. From high windows

looking south, straggling outcrops of brick may now be seen in the valley of the Chel. Little else has changed since Sparkenbroke was a child.

As a boy, he was treated not unkindly but as though he were a visitor in his own home—"a visitor," he said afterwards, "who had been away on a long journey and whom it was not easy to recognize." His half-brother, Stephen, disliked him even then, perhaps because the speeds of their thought were different, Stephen's intelligence being plain, straightforward and regular, while Piers's moved with seeming reluctance to all ends that he might not attain by direct apprehension. Stephen, moreover, had resented his father's passion for Piers's mother, his second wife, and was irritated by her son's resemblance to her—by the gleaming black hair that swept upward from his temples, by the fullness of his lips, the high carriage of his head, the peculiar flexibility of all his movements, by his whole air of easy vitality, like that of a ship in sail before a following wind. The same resemblance to the girl who had deserted him and was dead fascinated Lord Sparkenbroke. He looked at his younger son continually and in silence, as though he were a pane of glass through which the past was visible; he patted his shoulder sometimes and began to speak, then turned away in stiff embarrassment.

Piers remembered his mother; she had run away when he was six years old, taking him with her. He remembered the wet decks of the ship, and the train that stood high above the platform, and the porters, like the porters in his French Conversation book, with luggage strapped on their backs. The man who travelled with his mother and himself had a crocodile pocket-book, with a clasp, made of silver snakes, which snapped when he closed it after showing their tickets. Piers remembered that when his mother was asked: are you happy? she had not answered, but her face had glowed and her eyes shone. She had frightened him; she was strange; her voice was not her voice, but quick and vibrant as though she were throwing words away and forgetting them. It was thus he remembered her, throwing out words into the swaying noise of the train, throwing sparks of herself into its glittering speed and darkness. And he remembered having been brought home to England by Mrs. Glazing, who had cried and told him stories and clutched his hand. Her knuckles had been grey through black cotton gloves.

He had not seen his mother again. Two years later she had died. Will she come home to be buried? Piers asked, and when Mrs. Glazing stared at him, unable to reply, he had gone to his father and told how, long ago, he and his mother had been walking through the churchyard. . . . I don't wish to hear it, his father had said. But, Father, she promised that she and I should be buried in the Mound together. His father had answered: I'll tell you something, Piers. Where a man's buried makes no great odds. In my mother's day, she wouldn't have smoking in the house, and my father wouldn't have it in the stables; he was afraid of fire; and on wet afternoons my brother and I used to shelter in the Mound and smoke our pipes among the coffins. So it don't go for much. But Lord Sparkenbroke had been unable to laugh at his own droll story and Piers had gazed at the working of his face.

She had not come. She was buried, they told Piers, outside a town in Italy, called Florence. In Sparkenbroke House she had become a whisper, then a silence; she was more than dead. Even Mrs. Glazing did not speak of her; her portrait was sewn up in canvas; and for a reason connected with her that he did not fully understand, Piers was not allowed, for six years after her running away, to share in the ceremony called the Sparkenbroke Mass. When he was twelve years old he was readmitted to it by an unexplained impulse of his father's.

CHAPTER TWO

THE custom of performing, on the birthday of the heir, a
religious ceremony at the tomb had its origin in days of the
family's allegiance to Rome and was commonly spoken of
as the Sparkenbroke Mass. Little of the ancient form remained, but the ritual, which was conducted at sunset,
still had power upon the imagination, and, of the servants
taking part in it, few attended voluntarily. On Stephen's
seventeenth birthday, the twentieth of September 1904,
they came out from their quarters at dusk. A group,
standing close and awkwardly, gathered within the shadow
of the great staircase. Some wore overcoats and the
women their Sunday hats; at their feet were set three
stable-lamps of which, as yet, but one was lighted. A footman, who had been coming downstairs taper in hand, lit
the banister-lamp above their heads. Its click, as it was shut
again, interrupted for an instant the murmur of their conversation, and, as the flame drew up, their shadow spread
before them on the waxed boards. Soon the Rector would
knock at the central door and enter, followed by his choir
carrying lanterns. He would summon the heir by name,
who, with his father, would lead them to the churchyard.

As they waited, Piers came out of the library and began
to cross the hall. The sound of footsteps had aroused him.
There would be time enough, he had believed, to go up-
stairs before his father and Stephen came out to meet the
Rector. As yet only servants would be in the hall, and
Piers was not afraid of servants.

When he felt their eyes upon him, he moved the more
leisurely, that he might not seem to be in haste, for they

knew that he was forbidden the Sparkenbroke Mass, and he had no wish to invite or to recognise their pity. He was already within a few yards of the stairs when a door on his left-hand opened and Lord Sparkenbroke came into the hall. Seeing his father, and Stephen at his side, Piers halted, it being his intuition not to give an appearance of retreat.

"Well, Piers . . ." Lord Sparkenbroke began; and, though he was seemingly unable to think of more to say, an impulse of kindliness having evaporated, or become inarticulate, within him, he continued to look into the boy's face, which revealed, in the mingled gleam of window and lamp, the refinement of feature and the entranced passivity of his mother's, quickened by a spiritual urgency that was his own. It was a grave, reckless face, the mouth deeply curving, the eyes at once tranquil and illumined.

From contemplation of it Lord Sparkenbroke dragged himself away and was about to pass on; but he hesitated, looking now not at Piers but beyond him; then at Stephen; then again at Piers.

"Where are you going?" he said.

"Upstairs, sir."

Lord Sparkenbroke hesitated again, as though a sense of injustice in the present or of obligation to the past were urging him to bid his son stay, but he said: "Very well," and made with his hand a small, loose gesture of defeat as the boy accepted dismissal.

At the head of the staircase, Piers entered a corridor hung with chandeliers, but lit now, dimly and at long intervals, by lamps set on tables against the wall. From this corridor rose a secondary flight, up which he turned, taking with him one of the chamber-candlesticks that stood in a shell-recess at its foot. But he did not need the candle; a staircase window, admitting the grey twilight, guided him well enough; and in the room to which he went, that had been his nursery and was still his own, there was flame in the grate. Before him were five windows, heavily curtained. Lifting a pair of curtains apart, he passed through, and let them close behind him.

He knelt on the window-seat, tugged at the lower sash until it opened, and, leaning out, waited. Autumn had come early; there was chill in the air.

Beyond the terraces that fell away in front of Sparkenbroke House and the sloping orchards into which they passed, from within the belt of wood that bounded the estate on this side, the church bell tolled. The sound produced in the boy a feeling of mingled exaltation and sadness—of sadness that he should be shut out from a rite to which even servants were admitted, of exaltation because, knowing that the bell's slow measure spoke of death and was fearfully echoed in the minds of all others who heard it, he was unafraid, and curious and eager. For him the bell rang not terror but discovery; he burned for its incomprehensible news which, if he could but distinguish it, might fulfil his consciousness of that life, external to the body, of which he was already more than a little aware.

His home, though a sparse regularity of religious observance had always been maintained in it, was without spiritual tradition. Wherever he made tentative inquiry, attempting to find another who was aware of the phenomena that from time to time pressed urgently upon him, he encountered the same bar—that the word spirit implied, in the minds of those he questioned, only the individual presence of one dead. Sometimes with fear and sometimes with that ribaldry which is fear transformed, it was used in association with rappings and hauntings and professional trance. These things were foreign to Piers. The servants and others who spoke of them to him seemed always to regard spiritual presences as exceptional invaders, invited or uninvited, of this world. We were normally separated from them, he was given to understand, by the grave's barrier, and by time, which was considered as a tape-measure, rolling itself out hour by hour in obedience to the kitchen clock, and becoming at last "eternity"—which, though vaguely spoken of as endless, was still a tape-measure unrolling itself in a straight line. That all those with whom he lived should be circumscribed by this idea gave him the same feeling of isolation that he might have had if he had found none on earth to share the five senses with him. With eyes and ears open, he seemed to live in a community of the blind and deaf.

His own experience was neither even nor continuous. Sometimes he had no world in which to live except that inhabited by the blind and deaf, whose incapacity he then shared. He endured it, not as they did, with apathy, but in hunger for what he had lost, and being, as they were not, a creature of flashing energy, he turned on the world as a wild thing on the bars of its cage. If he had been a man, he might have spent himself in labour or in sensuality or in those creative outbursts which are an artist's release from his chains; as a boy he had recourse to mischief and daring. He took from the stables horses that were beyond his strength and rode them; he went into Chelmouth, nine miles away, and climbed down cliffs on which there was no visible hold for foot or hand; once, at night, without audience or reason, he had leapt from balcony to balcony along the face of Sparkenbroke House. Against him, in these moods, punishment was of no avail. He was as indifferent to pain as to fear.

Sometimes, on the contrary, the spiritual pressure upon him was increased. Such is the nature of the human imagination that this pressure or urgency took on then a partly anthropomorphic form. He glowed in the nearness of a Being who, though it had neither features nor shape, had certain qualities indefinable except in human terms. It had two aspects, perceived simultaneously. First, it was an intensification of Piers himself. He needed no more evidence of its reality than of his own. As he might have said: "I am because I am," so he might have said also: "This Being is because I am," the two statements having the same inward completeness and the same logical inconsequence. The absence of this Being, during the periods of withdrawal that were Piers's agony, had, therefore, the quality not of the desertion of a friend or of any creature separate from himself, but of self-division and self-betrayal, and its approach, its nearness, the sight of its brilliance, the heat of its breath, the leap of its pulse within his own—this supreme and urgent intimacy had the nature of self-realization, in which, if it had been complete, an absolute enfranchisement might have been attained from which there could be no slipping back.

This Being had also a second aspect. Piers felt that if ever he were fully possessed by it, he would be possessed by all that is, and become a part of all that is, as a detached flame becomes a part of a conflagration or a raindrop loses its identity in the sea. The rhythm of life would then never slacken into speculative dreaming; he would be everlastingly active, as he desired to be; the flame in him would not smoulder but burn and ascend; his existence would be a perpetual outpouring of energy without boundaries of time and without imprisonment in a single form. He would not be a boy only, confined within his individuality; he would become the tree he sat under and experience its growth and joy; he would be the earth and the water under the earth; he would be in the wind, and in the nature of birds, and in all living things and in all things called dead.

Since he had no means of expressing these anticipations even within his own mind, nor any ordered understanding of their nature, he could but appear to others, when he was farthest from his ecstasy, as a boy filled with rashness, and to himself, when he was nearest to it, as one upon whom a spell had been cast. But there were many weeks of his life when he was far from both extremes, and he would wonder then—and wondered now, as he knelt in the window—what issue there was for him from this secret ebb and flow of his being. The child in him longed for release. He wished sometimes that he was as others were, blind to his light and darkness, deaf to the tumult of his perceptions. But at the core of his secret lay expectation that some day final acceptance would not be denied him; and though he knew neither fear of death nor pity for the dead, this hunger for fulfilment had in his mind a connexion, the nature of which was undefined, with the idea of mortality. He listened eagerly, therefore, to the tolling of the bell that came up to him from the wood.

After a little while, the Rector and a few choir-boys ordered in pairs ahead of him were to be seen mounting the brow of the orchard. Behind them the tops of the churchyard elms, which not long since had been aglow, were turning from bronze to iron, and the nearer trees were stiffening to that appearance of brittle rigidity which they would later present to a risen moon. Far away, over the elms and beyond the falling country that separated Sparkenbroke from the coast, the sea was visible—more clearly visible than often in full daylight, for the water of Chelmouth Bay had now a brazen sheen on it that cut into the ploughy texture of the land; and, to the east of Chelmouth, the lighthouse on Croom Head, not having yet darkness enough to give flash to its beam, softly pricked, from minute to minute, a tiny aperture in the dusk.

The lamp bobbing at the head of the procession, obscured now and then by the branch of a cherry tree or by a fold in its bearer's cassock, was not needed, and, as if aware of this, presently went out. The boy responsible for it checked at once and knelt down beside it. The straggling line of surpliced figures closed upon him into a knot, and Piers began to drum his fingers at the foolish delay. Come on, come on, he exclaimed in his mind, leave the lamp! Bring it on as it is! and his impatient imagination yielded to him the oily smell of the wick and the blur of voices offering advice. Come on! he repeated, his fist closing in anger, but suddenly he forgot to be angry, for the boys in their surplices were a solid cluster like a white flower. In that instant, the grass, which had hitherto fadingly acquiesced in the approach of dusk, threw out its last green challenge; the whole earth became radiant and the human cluster shone. Its whiteness, intense and paralysed, had the quality of frozen light. All Nature gazed at it for a moment; then moved on towards darkness.

Piers witnessed this miracle of light not as a spectator only. It caused in him a sensation, distinct from admiration or joy, of being penetrated—an experience made familiar by the approach of his ecstasies. He shuddered and became physically cold; then, gradually, warmth flooded him; his palms tingled, his forehead burned, his eyes widened and brightened as though power were being given him to perpetuate the beauty he had seen; but the poet within him was as yet without development; he had not understanding of this power nor craft to apply it, and it passed away, leaving him to make what he could of being Stephen's half-brother and a boy twelve years old.

As the procession advanced, he withdrew from the window and, crossing the dark room, curled himself up on the hearth. Last September he had watched the procession come and go; this year he could not, so violent and confused were the emotions within him; and he began to sing, under his breath, a tune of his own invention. But the tune was meaningless; he had no voice; and, on his hands and knees, he stared into the fire like an animal, repeating aloud but softly: "How am I to say it? How am I to say it?"

The door opened. A candle appeared and the head of Mrs. Glazing, the housekeeper.

"Why, Master Piers, is that you? Quick. Up with you. We've been looking everywhere. Your father wants you at once."

"Me?"

"Yes. His lordship said: 'Go and tell Master Piers he can come with us.'"

Piers sprang up.

"To the Mass? Do you mean to the Mass?" He ran past her to the door. There he stopped, ran back, seized Mrs. Glazing's hand. "Come on," he said, "come quick." He held the door open for her and took her candle. Mastering his impatience to be gone, he lighted her downstairs. Oh, she thought, he's like his mother, he's like his mother. No wonder his lordship can't keep his eyes off him and yet can't bear to have him about. "Now don't you wait for me," she said when they reached the lighted corridor. "Just put the candle in its place. Then you hurry on."

"Aren't you coming?"

"Not to-night."

"Why not?"

But he was gone without her answer.

CHAPTER THREE

THE church stood in a clearing among the trees that
separated the estate from the main road. From the
orchards it was reached by a private path; from the road,
the people of Sparkenbroke Green came to it by a short
bridge of stone over a stream, which, running westward
beside the road, poured itself between low banks into the
river Chel. The graveyard, continuing the orchard's slope,
fell away from north to south, and near its southern
boundary declined sharply before levelling up again to
the brink of the stream. From the steep bank thus caused,
the vault protruded. A visitor approaching it from above,
who did not know the place and expected folk to be
buried underground, would not at once have recognized
it as a tomb. Its roof was grassy so that it appeared to be
but a hummock of the bank itself, but from the level
ground at its foot it was seen to have been excavated and
lined with masonry and provided with a gate. In daylight,
the shelves within and the coffins ranged upon them were
clearly visible. A semicircular tympanum of stone containing a set of verses and surmounted by the Tenniel
arms, indicated that this was the family's burying-place.

It was on the piece of flat earth between the sepulchre
and the stream that the ceremony was performed. The
curious who had come from the village and the servants
from Sparkenbroke House stood upon the outskirts of
this space, retreated against the trees, their faces doubly
illumined by the lamps set upon the ground and by the
surviving day. The choir-boys, divided into two groups,
were on either side of the entrance, their backs to the

tomb. In their midst, framed in the now open gateway, the Rector stood, a grey, narrow-skulled man of fifty years, holding in his hand a book that contained the form of prayer. Lord Sparkenbroke, Stephen and Piers, an isolated group, faced him.

Since he was a little child, in days before his mother had left Sparkenbroke House, Piers had not seen the iron gate opened. The key was kept, with a dozen others, on an encased row of hooks screwed to the wall of his father's room. Ordinarily the case itself was locked, but now and then it stood open, and Piers had often been tempted to take the key of the Mound and admit himself to this place that struck fire in his imagination. He had been tempted the more strongly when he observed that the key of the Mound and the key of the disused entrance to the water garden were hardly to be distinguished; it would be easy, he had thought, having taken what he wanted, to transfer the garden key to the vacant hook and to say, if his theft were discovered, that he had wished to go into the water garden. But since this way of covering his tracks had presented itself to him, only once had he seen the case open; and then he had defeated his own purpose by confiding it to Stephen. He might have known that Stephen would have seen his project as a small boy's escapade and have refused to take part in it. But don't you see, Stephen, it's not a rag! I want to go there. I want to be there. Why?

He couldn't tell Stephen. He might have expected that. But he hadn't expected Stephen's thin blue eyes to close to little streaks as they always did when he was angry or to hear him say: You little swine! Don't you know it's a family place? Poking about among coffins like a tourist! Why not take a pencil and write your name on them? Olive Jones, Swansea. Piers Tenniel, Sparkenbroke. Like that. . . . I don't wonder Father won't let you come to the Mass. You're the only son who hasn't come; you know that, don't you? Even babies in arms have been carried.

Now he was at the Mass. His sleeve and his father's were touching. He was listening to Mr. Hardy's voice.

"Oh merciful Father, who in Thy servant, Stephen Henry O'Gorman Tenniel, didst raise up new seed to them departed, refresh him with Thy Grace that he may bear nobly the arms, which they surrendered only unto Thee, until that day when Thou receivest him also into Thy keeping, and so endow him with Thy Spirit that he may have no enemies but Thine, through Jesus Christ our Lord. Amen."

Piers looked at Stephen, expecting to hate him, but could not hate him now. A breeze had sprung up. The branches were creaking and rustling overhead. The stream was crying out with the melancholy of shallow water at night; the grasses on the bank were rubbing their blades together; and on the summit of the Mound, where he had lain often in the sun, pressing himself to the earth, long grasses stood in the lamplight like a plume.

> Lord, have mercy upon us.
> *Christ, have mercy upon us.*
> Our Father, which art in heaven . . .

Under the influence of the familiar words, his imagination carried him again to the hour when he and his mother had stood beside the sepulchre. It seemed to him necessary that she should return, and he searched for her face in the darkness that he might assure her that her body should be brought home and her prophecy fulfilled. He saw her face clearly, and experienced again, as though it were new, the delight he had had in her company; but when, wishing to prolong this experience, he tried to remember where they went together and what she had said when they turned away from the Mound, the thread of memory snapped and she was gone. He found himself repeating the old rhyme above the door. Though it was not now to be read in the uncertain beam of lamps, it ran in his mind.

> We also moved, as thou dost move,
> With pride of youth and quick in love.
> Have pity then, who drawest near,
> That love and youth are ended here.
> Though in sweet April thou dost shine,
> December waits for thee and thine.

Their smooth melancholy irritated him. He saw no good reason that the living should pity the dead. He would have liked to compose a sequel, not whining but triumphant. When he went to the Rectory, he would remind Mr. Hardy of his promise that they should translate these verses into Latin; and perhaps add others to them, Piers said to himself, for they were too colourless and humble for his mood. And if the Rector won't spend time on the verses, he added, I shall ask George or Helen. He saw them now, side by side, under the elm-tree to his left. George, solid and reliable, was, he felt, though three years older than himself, his own friend rather than Stephen's, and Helen, who was nineteen and almost trained to be a school-mistress, pleased him because she was at once kind, severe, lovable and, in her self-assured precision, a little ridiculous. Even the Rector smiled at his daughter. Helen keeps us all in our places, he said, and it was true that she composed Latin verses as if they were an exercise in arithmetic—a problem with an answer, right or wrong. George would fumble with the verses. The first thing to do, he would say, licking his pencil, is to make sure that we understand them in English before beginning to translate. He would understand them himself but would make heavy weather of expounding them: Well, you see, what it means is . . . or what I imagine it means . . . if you think it out quietly. . . . Helen was quicker. She'd know too. There were no mysteries for her—not even in Catullus. Subject, verb, object, adjective qualifying object—everything plain and straightforward. What it means quite clearly is this, she'd say. She might be right or wrong, but she would tell him what she supposed the verses to mean; the Latin would follow. He liked Helen. A smooth road; neat signposts at each corner; a brisk stride, no loitering.

"Awaken us in the morning, O God, our Creator, as Thou shalt on the last day awaken those that sleep. Sound, though it be from afar, the trumpet of Thy Salvation and give us ears to hear Thee, that, so heralded, Thy peace may shine through our battles and be in this life perfect assurance of the life to come. Amen."

The lips of George and Helen under the elm-tree moved to say amen. Soon afterwards Piers ceased to be aware of them or of their father's voice reading the prayers. If there was such a life as he imagined, where none was dead in the body or in any part of the soul, it existed now, within his reach, if he but knew how to leap into it; within reach of the waiting dead, if they but knew how to break from their coffins and seize it. But they did not hear the stream, nor the creak of the elm-trees overhead, nor the crackle of fallen leaves blown in over the Rector's feet to the stone floor of their tomb. Or did they hear, as he also heard continually, the rumour of a life not yet attainable? While they dreamed, did they too know that they were dreaming?

CHAPTER FOUR

NEXT day, after luncheon, George Hardy went to the top of the Rectory orchard that he might secretly train himself to a pipe. His teeth held it deep and awkwardly, and his face, with its slash of brown hair over a hard, freckled forehead and its eyelids drawn down as he cautiously sheltered his match, had the character of a face carved in wood, lively and solid, by a sculptor eager for bones, and better pleased by a blunt angle than by a curve. Neither his father nor Helen would find him here, the pear-trees happily intervening, and he paced the uppermost path with determination, sending up more smoke from his bowl than he was willing to draw into his mouth.

He was to spend that night as Stephen's guest at Sparkenbroke House; after dinner they would sit for a little while in the library with Stephen's father, talking perhaps of Eton, perhaps of the morrow's cub-hunting; then would go to Stephen's sitting-room and smoke. Stephen, taking a cigar from a high cupboard, would crack it, a trifle conspicuously, between finger and thumb; and, though it was not George's habit to be greatly influenced by others, even his independence was not proof against his desire, at fifteen, to have the good opinion of Sparkenbroke's heir. He had, moreover, a better reason than this for learning to smoke—a reason that was his own, a part of the boy he was and of the man he would become. To smoke appeared to him as a normal and companionable habit that put men at their ease; it would, he thought, be almost part of his professional equipment when he became a doctor; not to smoke was freakish, and freakishness he abhorred in himself because it greatly interested him in others. Except in a tentative hint now and then to Piers Tenniel, who, he imagined, was too young or too self-engrossed to understand, George had never confessed that his wish to be a doctor had an emotional basis; I think it's the job I could do, he said, and allowed his preference to go unexplained; but it had its origin in an affectionate curiosity for the seeming wilfulness of human behaviour. He had observed that, in small things and great, many of those he met were, in the language of his own thoughts, out of plumb. They became angry or apathetic, happy or unhappy, confident or afraid, for reasons that were not reason enough; sometimes, when they were far out of plumb, they became physically ill; always, even in the most rational of them, even in the clearest human glass, there was a little area of cracking and distortion. That is what makes them interesting, he thought, and I suppose it's because I'm without it that I'm dull. People were to him like the angles marked on his school protractor, some leaning to one side of the upright and some to the other. The upright was no better than the rest because it happened to be in the centre, but it was of use as a basis of measurement.

Out of this conception, at once proud and humble, of his place in the world, had arisen his imagining of himself as a doctor; and, if there was freakishness in him at all, it was, by a paradox, his inward insistence upon his own normality, his determination not to permit himself whims and airs, and not to condemn, but to watch, the peculiarity of others. To be patient, to discover good in men, to like and understand them, to smoke a pipe with the world and do his job—this, without elaboration of theory, was George's intuition, and even the detail of his practice was obedient to it. The pipe gripped between his teeth was part of his social discipline, in the same category with the opening of doors to women or the putting on of clean collars. He must learn to smoke now as he had learned, when a child, to dress himself.

The arrival of Piers Tenniel at the five-bar gate which

opened into the orchard from the Chelmouth-Ancaster road was good reason to postpone the exercise of smoking, and George began to tap the bowl against the heel of his boot.

"Just finishing a pipe," he said.

Piers looked at the wad of moist, smouldering tobacco that fell to the ground. "Why do you pretend to like it? Because Stephen does?"

George grinned. "Partly, I suppose."

The younger boy made no comment on this. He had found out what he wanted to know and was no moralist; for all he cared George might smoke till his lips were the colour of Castile soap and his eyes overflowed.

"Stephen," he said, "is trying to grow a moustache."

They walked together down the slope towards the Rectory, crossed the little lawn, rounded the house and, having time to spare before Mr. Hardy would be ready to criticize Piers's Latin prose, loitered on the white-railed bridge by which the front door was approached from the village. When they were together, they spent a great part of their time in silence, but each found in the other's independence a response to his own—Piers, in George's power to be the same in all weathers, a background to his own fantasies, and George, in Piers's brooding and gaiety, something that amused and delighted him.

"George?" Piers said.

"Yes."

"You know I went to the Mound last night? Father let me."

"I know."

"You saw me there?"

"Of course I did."

"And your father—and Helen?"

"We all saw you."

George had the wisdom not to add: "Why?" The subject, he knew, was one on which it was best to allow Piers to take his own way, speaking or nursing his secrets as he would; for to question him about the Sparkenbroke Mound was as useless as to dispute the vast web of stories that was spun in his mind. He would describe the persons of an imaginary tale as if he had lately seen them in the flesh and recognized no clear boundary between his world and theirs, or he would say of the elm-tree, which grew in front of the Mound, that it had joined his army and would fight on his side, or of the stream that it would bring him news, or, with a gleam of terror and desolation, that he had lost them, that yesterday they had gone away, were dead, could recognize him no more. From talk such as this, he would emerge calmly and happily if he was given time. It had always so natural a flow, such narrative innocence, that it gave an impression not of lying, not even of abnormal invention, but of truth inwardly seen; but to dispute his legends with him or seek to know more than he told was to thrust him into lying denial and secretive boasting. George, therefore, asked him nothing of his appearance at the ceremony. Piers would say more of it if he wished to say more, now or at another time; meanwhile it was enough to lean on the rail of the bridge, hearing the water flow beneath them and watching the broken image of the Rectory, a white, rippling blur, held mistily in the surface.

But when Helen came out from the front door to announce that her father was ready to begin Piers's lesson, she said at once what George had forborne to say. A tall, thin girl who had lately put up her hair, she was conscious still of a new, brisk authority. She had charity, self-discipline, good sense. There was no vanity in her but the stern vanity of not being vain, and she would work for others, particularly for children, with all her heart and intelligence. But she had not her brother's intuitive forbearance, and she said in a tone of bright congratulation:

"So they let you come to the Mound last night, after all, Piers. Aren't you glad?"

He said: "What do you mean—'let me'? It's my right. I have always been to the Mound. Every year, since I was a baby. Always."

"But, Piers, that isn't true. You know it isn't." And when Piers had rushed past her into the house, she added to George: "I wonder what good he thinks it does to tell

B

lies like that—lies that everyone knows are lies. It's the same with the stories he makes up. Of course, as long as they are just stories, that's all right, but sometimes——"

"I don't think it's lies," her brother said.

"But about the Mound—that was a lie. So useless, and silly too. I shall speak to him about it later."

George shrugged his shoulders. "I shouldn't. It wasn't a lie to him," and because she loved her brother enough to put off for his sake the stiffness of her seniority, and could feel the warmth of his judgment though her own was opposed to it, she said: "Very well," and felt that she was rewarded when his arm was linked with hers. Opening the door of the study, she put in her head. Piers, flushed and wide-eyed, his hair springing up from his forehead in a crest, was seated, with a book across his knees, on an upright chair beside her father. Sometimes, she thought, he seems to be all head, like a bird, his neck is so long and slender. His eyes came up to hers in challenge, as though he felt himself pursued, but the challenge went out of them, the fear that had darkened him was lifted like a curtain, and he smiled, as though he were recognizing her anew—such a smile of welcome as caused her heart to leap. Having said what she had come to say—that there was tea and supper for him that evening at the Rectory if he cared to stay for either—she went about the house joyfully, not knowing by what power the boy had kindled a light within her.

He had welcomed her coming for the sake of the interruption it had caused; a servant or a wasp would have been as welcome as she; and he had smiled as he did because the mischief was in him.

He had been indolent. Though his prose was written, all his blandishments had not persuaded Mr. Hardy to take it first; and Piers had not glanced at the Tacitus he was now being required to construe. Having then, as in later life, a habit of retrieving his idleness by sudden flashes of energy, he had for ten minutes been translating unseen the passage he should have prepared, and translating it with an elaborate show of preparation. There was delight in the struggle and, above all, in the pretence. While he was translating a sentence, he glanced ahead out of the corner of his eye lest, if the Rector interrupted him with a general question, he should have to confess that he was reading this passage for the first time, breathlessly leaping from phrase to phrase without knowledge of what was to come.

"You see now, Piers," the Rector had said, "how skilfully Tacitus is leading us to his climax?" and at that moment, when all seemed lost, Helen had entered. Her coming had given the desperate translator breathing-space in which to plan a diversion. When she had gone, he began at once:

"Don't you think, sir, Tacitus is like someone writing telegrams?"

"Telegrams?"

"Sharp and quick," said Piers. "Tap, tap, tap. Words left out."

The Rector smiled. "Well, yes—that may be. Probably you feel it more by contrast with the Ciceronian thunder. . . . Now, on you go."

"Is there—" said Piers quickly. "I mean, would you say that in English there was anyone——?"

"What? Corresponding to Tacitus in style?" and the diversion was accomplished, for Mr. Hardy was no dull taskmaster to whom fifty lines were fifty lines; the Latin tongue was as alive to him as his own; his purpose in teaching was that it should acquire and preserve the same vitality in the mind of his pupil; and soon they were out of their chairs, browsing from shelf to shelf, or kneeling on the hearth-rug with a volume of Swift between them. "But you must not liken Swift to Tacitus," Mr. Hardy said. "You must contrast them. Neither wastes a word but their economies differ. If you ask me to define the difference, all my answers wouldn't convey as much to you as your own ear. Tacitus belongs to the silver age of his language and Swift to the golden age of ours."

At first, Piers gave but part of his attention to Mr. Hardy's discourse; it was enough for him that the dry voice should continue and Tacitus be forgotten. How

easily old people could be tricked! You cast a fly that
tempted them and they rose at once; you could play them
for an hour! And Piers's thought ran upon fishing, for
Walton had been spoken of; he saw before his eyes the
low, brown glitter of a trout stream, his father in the midst
with water curling almost to the edge of his waders. Some
day, he thought, I must read *The Compleat Angler*. Mr.
Hardy seemed to have read all there was to read in Greek,
Latin and English. "How old were you, sir, when you read
The Compleat Angler?" But Mr. Hardy did not take that
fly; he would not be led away into discussion of fishing;
and Piers heard him say that the Elizabethan was the
golden age of verse—more than a golden age, an age in
which every man's tongue had a miracle upon it, but
Elizabethan prose was too young, too impetuous, too
elaborate. "They choked themselves, they were so eager—
like a child who has too much to say and tries to say it all
at a gasp. But some day, Piers, read the Queen's own
writing—her messages to Parliament; state documents
have a discipline imposed upon them from without which
was precisely what Elizabethan prose needed; and you'll
find to-day that nothing beats a few judgments in the High
Court or the Courts of Appeal. There again there's an
external discipline imposing form on modern formless-
ness."

Piers thought: he's like a terrier at a hole. The arched
figure, loose but alert, kneeling on the hearth-rug, the
eyes staring at the fire-irons, the grey hair clipped and
mottled, the long bony nose, the taut forearms stretched
out to clasp the knees, all emphasized the Rector's likeness
to a terrier, lean and wiry, crouched before an earth; and
suddenly, when Piers had already begun to smile, the
head was cocked sideways and the resemblance became
irresistible. That he might not laugh, Piers was bound to
interrupt, but the Rector would not listen. "A man and
a language," he said, "take much the same course. At
first, a language is childish and clumsy; it becomes strong
and gives out poetry; it becomes mature and yields its
prose; at last it weakens, it becomes garrulous and

pedantic, and so it dies. Or, if it is preserved here and there, it is preserved consciously—the impetus is gone. . . . Or so I say," he added. "I who read and can't write. If you mean to be a writer, Piers, don't you read too much."

This pang of self-criticism did not endure. Having a theme in his mind, the Rector was bound to pursue it, so quick and urgent was the prompting of his thought, and he said that the beginning of English maturity was in the Prayer Book and the Bible; the need to translate had supplied the external discipline which made such splendour possible; the form was there, in Greek or Latin or Hebrew, enabling the young language to yield masterpieces before its time. "But long after that," he said, "the language remained immature. Some day your own ear will tell you that Tillotson and even Jeremy Taylor were too abundant. Bishop Taylor was rich in gold but the dross wasn't all purged away. Swift and Goldsmith give you the contrast of perfection. Read *The Vicar of Wakefield*, then *Rasselas*, and you'll see why Johnson lives chiefly in Boswell. Johnson was thick with dross, but Goldsmith shines."

"What do you mean?" Piers asked. "'Lives chiefly in Boswell'?" and the Rector, while he explained who Boswell was, gazed at his pupil in delight, greedy for the boyhood to which so many shelves were unexplored. And Piers said with confidence: "I will read Boswell to-morrow, and *Rasselas* afterwards."

"But you haven't read *The Vicar* yet?"

"No."

"So next week," Mr. Hardy said, "you will read *The Vicar of Wakefield* for the first time."

Already there had begun to float in Piers's mind a story that he himself would write about a Vicar or a Rector. The imagining of a pen in his own hand touched with personal fire each word that he heard spoken, and he listened to praises and criticisms of the dead as though they were addressed to him. If he and not Goldsmith had written *The Vicar of Wakefield*, he would go to his father, to Stephen, to Mrs. Glazing with the volume in

his hand and say: I have written *The Vicar of Wakefield*.
Their expression would change when they saw the book,
and he would say: It is not the only one I have written,
and take them into the library, and pull down the ribbed
green books on each of which, under the title, was his
name: Piers Tenniel. "But you remember, Piers," Mr.
Hardy was saying, "that long before Gulliver set out on
his voyages, he prepared himself for them—he learned
navigation and mathematics and doctoring."

"Yes, I know," Piers answered. "But anyone can see
that you must learn navigation if you're going to be an
explorer. I mean, anyone knows what a good sailor is.
But what is a good story-teller? There seem to have been
so many of them and all different."

Mr. Hardy chuckled at that and, standing up, went to
the window by which was his writing-table.

"There was a Frenchman once who said: 'I see but
one rule: to be *clear*.' How does that do for you?"

"Who was he?"

"Stendhal."

"Would Goldsmith have said that too?"

"I think he would."

"Then—I mean—were they alike, Goldsmith and
Stendhal?"

"Not in the least—except that they were clear."

"Then I don't see that it helps much," Piers said.

Mr. Hardy looked at him, his face up to the window-
light, and thought: The boy will remember what I say now
and all my reading has not taught me what to say; and
the pride of scholarship fell away from him.

"To be an artist," he said, "is like being a follower of
Jesus. One man cannot teach another, but Jesus taught
those who followed him that each might understand with
his own understanding. He taught first to be single-minded;
he would not have one man bury his father or another
bid farewell to his friends. 'No man, having put his hand
to the plough, and looking back, is fit for the kingdom
of God.' But 'Everyone that hath forsaken houses, or
brethren, or sisters, or father, or mother, or wife, or

children, or lands, for my name's sake, shall receive an hundredfold.' That is his hardest teaching, Piers. Can you follow it to write a book?"

The boy did not answer. His lips tightened and he asked: "What else did he say?" A question which, by its calm acceptance of Christ's demand, stirred in the Rector an ironic impulse to break down a resolution too simple. The pride of controversy rose in him, and looking for confusion in the boy he thrust upon him the Christian paradox.

"Jesus said: 'Forsake all. Let the dead bury their dead.' He said also: 'Love thy neighbour as thyself.' "

Piers answered: "I see that," as though for him the paradox were resolved.

"What do you mean—you see that?"

"I see what he meant," Piers repeated.

"But do you see how to live in accordance with his meaning?"

A silence fell between them, such a silence as divides two planes of imagination, and Mr. Hardy remembered having said once, in an address on the fanatical single-mindedness of saints and artists, that, hard though it was for plain men to think of them as anything but cruel and selfish, they were not to be so considered if their passion was genuine; they obeyed both the commandments of Jesus—to love their God and their neighbour—for the absolute and the universal were identical, an absolute love of God comprehended a love of his creation. It had seemed to him then an ingenious resolution of the paradox; the audience of priests to whom it was delivered had praised it; but it had flattered his mind without engrossing his heart; and now, when he began to repeat it to this boy, whose whole being was enchanted by the speed of his perceptions, its slow refinements froze upon his lips and he faltered. To conceal his faltering he pulled out his watch. The time for their lesson was almost ended. "We have neglected Tacitus so long," he said, "that we must postpone him until to-morrow. Would you like, in the time we have left, to——"

"Could we see," Piers cried, "how Goldsmith begins?"

"But we can't begin to read *The Vicar* now. Helen will be ringing the bell for tea in eight minutes."

"Just the beginning," Piers said. "The first words—that's all."

He could not contain his eagerness, and when they had read the opening sentences he jumped up from the floor and said:

"It is like someone telling a story—not writing it!"

"It is like an angel telling a story," the Rector answered. "Goldsmith was plain. He had none of Lamb's whimsies and none of the lovely weakness of Steele. Lamb can be imitated; Steele was imitated by Thackeray; it is conceivable that even Landor's deliberate majesty might be copied. But no one can imitate Goldsmith. Swift had more substance and energy. There are people who say he was greater than Goldsmith. I suppose he was. And yet—'greater'? One can't compare one perfection with another. Since they died the language has been growing old."

He had spoken with the easy pride of conservative melancholy. "The language has been growing old" was a phrase that rounded off his theme comfortably on the eighteenth century; in the dining-room, Helen was ringing her little silver bell.

"Do you mean old—dying?" Piers said.

"It isn't quite dead yet."

"But do you mean that it's no good writing any more? You don't mean that?"

The grave urgency of the question spoke the boy's mind. He could not endure that there should be no more voyages for Gulliver; he would not have tombstones of the eighteenth century shut him in; he would be a writer of a new golden age, not of a decline. And the Rector, suddenly ashamed of what he had said in face of so passionate a hope, answered that perhaps he himself was growing old. "I have read too much," he repeated. "In art nothing is certain except that the impossible will happen continually. Shelley will appear, and, for a little while, send Pope and

Dryden to an upper shelf. And if Shelley can spring out of the eighteenth century——"

"Like moving mountains," Piers said.

"What?"

"I mean—if you believe—if you believe enough. I . . ."

"You must start home," the Rector said, "unless you will stay to tea with us."

"I'll run," Piers answered. "I shan't be late. I'll go the short way through the churchyard." And suddenly: "Why did Jesus say: 'Let the dead bury their dead'?"

CHAPTER FIVE

DAY was still up, for the time was not yet five o'clock, but in the wood above the churchyard the undergrowth was already webbed with darkness, and Piers, who had been running, paused there. They think I'm a little boy, he said to himself, and that nothing matters until I am grown up, but it's not true. His future was big within him. He knew that because he wanted one thing so much, and had no other comparable want, he would attain it; and to express a joy that he could express in no other way, he began to run up the hill again. Coming into the open, he saw Stephen approaching him.

"Why are you running like a madman?"

"Getting . . . home . . . to tea."

"Well, do you want your tea—or this?" And the key to the Mound was twirling on Stephen's finger.

"Where did you get it?"

"Where it hangs. Father left the case open. He's gone over to Smirth's Green to meet a horse-dealer. . . . Do you want it?"

"Yes. Give it me."

"Oh no, you don't!" Stephen withdrew his hand and retreated a pace. "What will you give me for it?"

"What do you want?"

"Your locket."

"My mother's?"

Stephen nodded, smiling, twirling the key.

Piers drew breath. "You can have it, but——"

"But what?"

"When you're dead, I'll have it back."

32

Stephen came nearer to him. "I don't want your locket. Why should I?"

"Why did you ask for it, then?"

"To see what you'd say."

Piers did not stay to argue; he had one purpose. "Give me the key then," he said.

"What do you want it for?"

Piers was silent.

"Tell me what you want it for," Stephen said, "and you can have it."

"I can't tell you."

"Why not?"

"I can't. . . . I can't, Stephen."

"Why? Don't you know?"

"Yes, I know; but not in words."

"You'll have to tell if you want the key."

"I want it because—in the Mound—I shall find . . ."

Unable to answer, tormented by his expectation, Piers clenched his fists and threw himself upon Stephen. His wrists were caught and held.

Stephen said: "If you'd had a knife you'd have killed me! You're mad, Piers. You're raving mad. You had better go into the Mound and see for yourself there's nothing there."

"I don't want to go if you come too," Piers answered.

"Why not?"

"I want to go alone."

Stephen considered this, and, an idea entering his mind, he said, with seeming good-humour: "I'll leave you alone if that's what you want. I'll let you in and leave you. But I'll stick to the key, that's all. You'd only lose it."

They went down into the wood, saying no more to each other. It seemed to Piers that what had happened was miraculous and fore-ordained. All that he desired would come to pass. That he was about to enter the Mound seemed to him a confirmation of the earlier assurance that the future had made to him. His joy abounded, and he saw his half-brother as his instrument, compelled to do his bidding.

At the entrance to the Mound, when the gate was back and his way stood open, he hesitated, and Stephen, supposing that he was afraid, taunted him. But he was not afraid. He was stopped by the torrent of his imagination as though it were a wall of light advancing against him from within the sepulchre; for he knew that to go forward now was to leave behind for ever the shadowy links that held him to his father, to Stephen, to the world, and to accept, as his own, a plane of reality different from theirs of which there could be no renouncement. Knowing that he was summoned and must go, he was yet torn by the agony of departure, for things experienced have in them a comfort that is heavy, like a cloud, upon the glory of things guessed at. Therefore, standing upon the ridge of brick that was the gate-socket, he was beset by the torment of one that cannot leap, though it be to safety, or accept, though bliss dwell in acceptance; and there arose within him the cry of his own likeness, and still he delayed. But when he was gone in, and the iron gate was slammed behind him and locked, then he was at peace. The clash of iron and Stephen's voice shouting from a distance did not say to him that he was imprisoned. Ribbons of daylight, that fell through the gate, were bent upward, by the vaulting, into long spirals ascending; the coffins, touched by them, shone. In the ribbed darkness, Piers drew breath and was still. His body became cold and light. Under his hands a wind was moving and under his feet.

CHAPTER SIX

GEORGE HARDY, carrying the heavy suit-case that contained what clothes he would need for the evening and for cub-hunting next morning, walked through the churchyard an hour later with no thought that anything unusual had happened there. His way did not take him past the face of the tomb; his mind was occupied by the weight of the burden he carried, for the leather handle was cramping his fingers; no sound reached him but that of his own footsteps and the soft evening sounds of the wood.

At Sparkenbroke House a footman took his bag from him and led him to his room, which was next to Stephen's sitting-room.

"Is Mr. Stephen in?"

"I'll inquire, sir. He took a toss from a new horse of his lordship's about an hour ago."

"Not hurt?"

"Oh no, sir. I believe not. Just a bruise or two. He went round to the stables afterwards with his lordship. Maybe he's there still. I'll send over and tell him you're here."

Soon after the footman had gone, the youth who was Stephen's valet came in, laid hands on George's shabby suit-case and began to open it.

"I think I'll unpack myself," said George with hesitation.

"Very good, sir. Shall I bring your hot water now?"

It was as yet early to dress for dinner, but George did not know how else to occupy himself. While the hot water was being fetched, he looked into the sitting-room, hoping

35

to find Stephen there. It was empty. In his bedroom again, he looked anxiously at his watch, fearing that he had come before his time.

When the valet reappeared, he said: "Do you know whether Mr. Piers is in?"

"I don't know, I'm sure, sir. Perhaps he's gone down to the Rectory and will be staying to supper there."

"He wasn't at the Rectory when I came away. I didn't meet him on the way up. But perhaps he went down through Derry's Wood. Then we should have missed each other."

The valet folded a towel over the hot-water can. "Is there anything more you require, sir?"

George began to change his clothes. Finding a hole in the toe of each of his socks, he spread them out flat and concealed them under the paper lining of a drawer. If Stephen had been here, he would have been given a bath, but in this wing of Sparkenbroke House the water for baths had to be carried and George had not courage to demand it. Perhaps, if he waited, Stephen would come; he hoped so, for Stephen could be a good host, who enjoyed sending servants scurrying for the comfort of his guests, and George, though he cared little for any comfort except a bath, enjoyed watching him. But Stephen did not come; time passed; and George began to imagine that he had been hurt. What shall I do then? he wondered. Would it be better to go home again? But that would be impossible. There's nothing for it, he thought. If Stephen's laid up and Piers is at the Rectory, Lord Sparkenbroke and I shall dine alone. The prospect alarmed him; he scrubbed his face with a rough towel to quiet his alarm; but none of George's shynesses endured long—he had too plain and energetic a mind, too small a share of vanity—and soon he was thinking that it might be interesting to dine with Lord Sparkenbroke. There was always a subject that would draw a man out. In this case—horses. No one knew more of horses. And nothing pleased George more than to hear a man talk on his own subject. He loved facts; if the talk were of horseflesh, he would have them in abundance; and, already imagining the dinner-table, he was interested and grateful; questions that he wanted to ask jumped to his mind. Other people, even Stephen, were afraid of Lord Sparkenbroke. He had heard his own father say: "Poor Sparkenbroke's gone dry," and he felt sorry for his host. Piers's mother made him go dry, I expect. Running away. . . . Well, yes, I dare say she was years younger. Still . . . George's feeling was against her. I dare say she had a rough time too, he thought, reluctant to condemn. But his intuition was against her. The issue was plain; she had broken her word; she hadn't done her job; and when it was your own wife who let you down——

"Sorry I wasn't here when you came," Stephen said from the doorway.

"What happened? You're not hurt?"

"Oh no. Father was bringing home a new mare. I met him—just at the edge of the church wood. He made me take her down to the hurdles and try her. She had me off before I was properly on her back. I missed the stirrup, she gave a twist like an eel, and I was pitched on to my shoulder. At father's feet, too. He's in the hell of a mood. Says I was careless. He wanted me to mount again."

"Didn't you?"

Stephen shook his head.

"Why not?"

"I—well—various reasons. Anyhow, why should he expect everyone to be as keen on horses as himself? Horses. Horses. Horses. And he's sly," Stephen added, his voice rising sharply to the pitch of anger or fear.

"Sly!" George exclaimed. The word, and Stephen's tone, astonished him.

"Yes—sly!" Stephen repeated, almost shouting now. "I walked back with him. I went to the stables with him. Then to his room and——"

"But why? If he's in a bad mood isn't it best to leave him to it? Why did you go——"

"Why! Why! Why! For reasons of my own. That's why."

He was sitting on the bed, his head down, his hands now in, now out of, his pockets.

"What's wrong?" George asked.

Stephen looked up and hesitated. His lips opened to speak but he pressed them together again.

"Nothing," he said, and with no other word went from the room to dress.

"Where is Piers?" Lord Sparkenbroke asked, looking across the corner of the dinner-table at Stephen, but Stephen seemed not to have heard and it was the butler who said: "Taking supper at the Rectory, I believe, m'lord."

"That right, George?"

George, replying that he knew his sister had invited Piers to supper, satisfied his host and would himself have been satisfied if he had not, in that moment, seen with what anxiety Stephen hung upon his answer and how his lips moved in a secretive smile when the answer was given. Has Stephen played some trick on Piers? he thought, and after dinner, as they walked behind Lord Sparkenbroke towards the library, he said in Stephen's ear, expecting a laughing confidence in return: "What have you done with Piers? Shut him in his room?"

"Done with him? Nothing. He's at the Rectory, isn't he?" The corridor through which they were passing was a long one. In it was the door, now open, of Lord Sparkenbroke's private room. As they approached it, Stephen halted, glanced at his father's disappearing figure, and thrust George forward with his hand.

"You go on to the library. Keep him occupied. I'll follow in a minute."

"But why? What's the game? I——"

"Go on. Go on," Stephen said in fierce entreaty, his dark head moving quickly, and his fingers increasing their pressure on George's arm. "Keep him in there for a minute. It's my one chance. Go on, I tell you."

Understanding nothing but glad to be a sharer in what seemed to be adventure, George nodded gaily and made haste into the library.

"Where's Stephen?"

"He's on his way, sir."

Lord Sparkenbroke nipped a cigar, threw up his feet on to a leather settee and asked no more. "Sit down, boy, sit down. Take your coffee if you want it."

George sat down, plucked up courage and launched into conversation.

"Was she a good mare, sir, the one you bought this afternoon?"

"Too good for Stephen by a long chalk."

There was silence. The long black legs shifted on the settee; the cigar was held in air and the firmness of its ash inspected; then the head and the doubtful, inquisitive eyes came round. Like a handsome grey rat, George thought, and, fearing that he was to be asked again why Stephen delayed, he struggled to think of something to say and failed. To his surprise, he was asked quietly how old he was; he replied that he was fifteen.

"Three years older than Piers?"

"Not quite three, sir."

"You see much of him?"

"Not much to-day, sir," George said, unwilling to account for Piers's movements until he knew in what way Stephen was committed.

"I don't mean to-day. I mean generally. He's pretty much in and out of your home, isn't he? D'you count him a friend of yours—or is he too young?"

"Oh no, he's not too young. Some ways he's older than me. Some ways he's older than Stephen."

"So I thought. And you're friends? You talk together. What about?"

"Just ordinary things," said George, playing for safety.

"What ordinary things?"

"Well, sir, there's his Latin. And there's doctoring— I'm going to be a doctor when I'm older, you see, and——"

"So you talk about the future? What is Piers's idea of his?"

"Father thinks he's going a long way, sir."

"I don't want to know what the Rector thinks. What does Piers think and what do you think yourself?"

"I think Father's right," George answered stubbornly.
Then, on an impulse that broke down his caution, he
added: "Piers was frightfully proud you let him go last
night."

"To the tomb?"

"Yes."

"Why?"

The fire of questions had sharpened. George stumbled
dully away from them, content that he should be thought
stupid if he might so avoid betrayal of Piers's confidence;
and he could say with truth that he didn't know why Piers
had been proud, why he set so much store by this ceremony.

"I don't know, sir. It's just that——"

"Well?"

"It's just that it means more to him than it would to
most people." Aware of the inadequacy of that and searching for a truth that eluded him, he added: "You see, sir,
Piers is like that. Most of us think first of one thing, then
of another. We wander about. But Piers doesn't. Father
says he has the—the concentration of some kinds of
madmen."

"Did your father say that?"

"Well, yes, sir. But Piers isn't a bit mad," George added
hastily, knowing himself to be in deep water. "That's what
made Father think he'd go a long way."

"So the boy's mad—eh?" said Lord Sparkenbroke, with
a difficult smile.

"Oh no, sir, I didn't mean——"

"Or a genius, is that it?"

George was clutching his knees and staring at the
carpet. "I don't know about that, sir. But he goes on and
on, if you see what I mean. Every bit of him concentrated
on one thing. Sometimes people who didn't know him
would think him impatient because he can flare up so
suddenly. But really he's more patient than any of us. On
and on and on, imagining the thing he wants until at last it
happens to him. It's like——"

George was so deeply absorbed in his struggle to express

his thoughts that he did not hear the door open and close behind him.

"What the devil's the matter with you, Stephen?"

"Nothing's the matter, sir. Why?"

"You stand there looking as if someone had hit you on the head. Come here—into the light . . . Have you been drinking? . . . You can't have been."

"No, sir," Stephen answered, allowing a glint of his teeth to appear.

"Seen a ghost, then? Committed a murder? . . . Or are you ill?"

Stephen grasped at that. "I felt a bit groggy as we were coming out of dinner. I went back for a drink of water," he said. "I'm better now," and he sat down.

"Teach you to keep in the saddle," Lord Sparkenbroke said, and Stephen had not the fire to defend himself.

By the experience of two earlier visits, George knew that the period spent with Lord Sparkenbroke after dinner might not be a genial one. His host might speak a little of Eton—a subject that he and his son had distantly in common—or of the morrow's cub-hunting, but in the midst of a sentence he would break off abruptly, his thought having carried him elsewhere, and if George and Stephen, accepting his detachment, began to speak to each other, he would rouse himself enough to throw in a comment that broke down their conversation and left them in silence again. To-night even Eton and cub-hunting were unproductive. The few words spoken served only to add weight to the silences they interrupted, and George, looking across to Stephen for some message of the eyes that should at least make a joke of their discomfiture, received no answer to his signals.

But they were dismissed at last and went to Stephen's sitting-room. Now he'll tell me, George thought, fingering in his pocket the pipe that he would courageously take out when Stephen settled down to a cigar; but this evening Stephen took no cigar, settled down to nothing, moved between chair, window and fireplace, staying in no position long, and, when George questioned him, replied:

"What has got it into your head that there's some game on? There's none that I know of."

"Then why did you send me into the library ahead of you?"

"I went back for some water."

"What did you mean: 'It's my one chance'?"

"I didn't say that."

"Stephen, you did."

Stephen was ordinarily a better liar; it was plain that he was not giving thought even to his lies; and the poise of George's mind shifted suddenly. Unsuspicious, not given to alarms, he had been hitherto little affected by Stephen's behaviour; at dinner, he had wondered, with a momentary consciousness of something unusual, whether Piers was indeed at the Rectory, but the moment had passed; and even when they had left Lord Sparkenbroke and Stephen had continued to withhold confidence, pretending that there was none withheld, George had been no more than a little hurt, or nettled, to find himself shut out. Stephen, he supposed, had his reasons, which would soon appear, and he had been prepared to wait, more interested than disturbed by postponement. Now, while he was comfortably leaning down to the scuttle to put more coal on the fire, he became aware for the first time that fear was in the room. Round the grate was a low brass fender on which, a moment earlier, he had been toasting his feet. At its corners were the heads of lions, their jaws agape, and it was from one of these heads that his idea of terror, projected upon a material object, shone back. The lion's features appeared to change, to become mobile, to be contorted, in the fire-shadow, by an impact of fear from within the room, and George, turning violently to face whatever there might be to face, discovered that upon all lifeless things, the prints on the wall, the shelves of books sleeping behind their grille of shadow, the fluting on the table-legs, the same impact had fallen. They shook and were made alive; they shook in his mind, and yet were still, as though he were seeing them through a curtain of watered silk; and he knew, before his eyes informed him,

that Stephen's resistance was done. But he was not prepared, even by the current of fear that had passed through
him, for the abjectness of the change in Stephen. The
shock of it lifted a paralysis from his own will; as though
the hurt he saw were physical, he sprang up, eager to
give help.

There was in Stephen's appearance an element of the
ridiculous that made the heart sick. He was perched in
the window-seat, one knee drawn up and clasped by his
hands. His dress—the white collar and shirt-front, the
trousers flattened to their crease, the small, pointed,
beribboned pumps—was new and neat; nothing in it was
irregular except the upward drag of the sleeves and a
linen cuff projected too far and straining at its link; in all
else it was the dress of a mannikin, carefully ironed; but
the face had fallen loose. The mouth was lying slack and
soft as though it were bruised. The cheeks were flabby,
the lips twitched, the eyes were pouched. The expression
was that of an ugly child prematurely aged.

George needed courage to touch him. Never before had
he seen a human being sapped and made gross by terror;
it needed all his strength of will to grip the tautened arm
and jerk Stephen into recognition. "What is it?" he said.
"Stephen—for God's sake—" And suddenly, thinking
that he perceived the cause, he felt his throat contract and
little arrows of pain leap under his finger-nails and down
the backs of his hands. "What have you done?" he said,
stooping down to Stephen's face. "Is he dead?"

"I don't know. I shut him in. In the Mound."

"How?"

"I shut him in. Locked him in. I can't get the key."

Now that Stephen had begun to talk, it was hard to get
from him anything but wild repetition. "I can't get the
key," he repeated again and again, and it was clear that he
had persuaded himself that the key, even if it could be
obtained, would now be useless.

"But why? Why, Stephen? You must get the key. Where
is it?"

It had dropped from his pocket when he fell from the

mare. Lord Sparkenbroke had picked it up. What's this? he had said, and Stephen, humiliated by his fall, frightened, swift to lie, had answered that it was the key to the water-garden. His father had put it in his pocket. "He has it still. Must have. It wasn't in his bedroom after he dressed. It's not hung in the case, though the case is still unlocked."

To relate the facts gave Stephen control of himself. He was afraid now of his father—a fear that could be grappled with; and George said:

"You must go to him for the key."

"I can't. I can't now. I've waited so long. I can't. . . ."

"You must. We'll go together. Come on. Now."

"No," Stephen answered. "I can't. You don't know him."

George continued steadily: "It's late. Someone—Mrs. Glazing—someone will notice Piers isn't home. Father seldom lets him stay after half-past nine. And anyhow, Stephen, you can't leave him there. You can't. You must come. If you won't go, I will."

Stephen stood up. "All right," he said, "I'll come," but, as they drew near the door, he stopped, a shudder passed through his body, a breathy, sucking cry rose from his throat, and George, checked also, saw that the door was opening. Lord Sparkenbroke stood before them, his head inclined a little towards his right shoulder, the pupils of his eyes contracted by the light of the room and of a candelabrum carried in his hand.

"Where is Piers?"

George answered: "We were coming to tell you, sir."

"Where is he? Stephen . . ."

Stephen tried to speak out but could say only: "It's in your pocket. I meant to go back. I should have gone in ten minutes—less." It was George who told the truth. He had expected an outburst of rage, and Stephen, struggling to anticipate it, cried out again: "I should have gone back, I——"

"You! What do you matter?" his father said. "You are ugly and a coward. . . . Come. George, you come. He can come or not as he pleases. . . . Quickly. We won't rouse the servants. They can keep out of this."

They went downstairs; to the stables for a lamp; over the terraces, through the orchard, down towards the church wood. George, on Lord Sparkenbroke's track, watching the sectors of yellow light swing and revolve over the grasses at his feet, heard Stephen, behind him, say: "George!" and repeat it, and repeat it, imploring companionship. George made no response, not because he was pitiless but because he was absorbed. The emotions of this journey through the darkness were falling upon his mind with soft, lulling evenness, as snow falls upon the earth. The heat, the yellowness of Stephen's room, the shimmer of anguish that had at once shaken and intensified his vision there, the white cuff stiff in its sleeve, the lion agape, though they were the prelude to his present experience, and its origin, were becoming detached from it in his thought. As he approached the wood, a heavy cloud rolled back from the moon; pear branches became an engraving upon the light; their trunks threw out ribbons of shadow that curved, a deep plum-colour, on the tufty ground; and George, dropping away from the anguish and responsibility through which he had passed, found relief in his boyhood, yielded himself to the instant, was enraptured by the adventurousness of this night-descent. He felt important and brave. Had not Lord Sparkenbroke chosen him as his companion? Because he was so young, he looked gravely at his excitement and nursed his privilege. He heard the creak of the lamp, sniffed in the autumn of the wood, and, for a moment, forgot all else.

Within the border of the wood, Lord Sparkenbroke stopped. The lamp was silent; its radiance slept fierily on dew and bramble; Stephen's footsteps crashed on, then ceased. No sound came from the tomb. An awakened bird rose in haste's confusion, a tumult of wings, and leafy branches whispered to each other when it was gone. The lamp-beams revolved again and Lord Sparkenbroke went forward.

It was then George discovered that he had formed within him no picture of what they might find. Piers was shut up; he would be waiting; when the gate of the Mound was opened, he would walk out, and then— But if he was waiting, why did he make no sound? Perhaps he was tired of crying out; perhaps he was asleep; and George, quickening his pace until the lamp was playing upon his knees, said: "Shall I call out to him, sir, to let him know we are coming?"

The lamp halted.

"Yes. Call."

George put both hands to his mouth.

"Piers!"

And again: "Piers!"

There was no answer, and Stephen, who had come up, said without meaning in his voice: "Perhaps he can't hear," and added, with pitiable longing for any action that should readmit him: "Shall I shout? Shall I?"

His father turned upon him. "Shout? Don't you understand that he could hear us talking . . . if he can hear anything?"

It was said in a tone that George had never heard from this harsh, rigid man. The anger of its intention failed when the first word was spoken; the rest had tenderness and self-reproach and despair—despair so profound that the speaker seemed to be drained of his energy by it; his footsteps, as he went on, were those of a very old peasant, weary of all his purposes. At the edge of the clearing before the Mound, he faltered, and George, coming up at his side, heard him say to himself: "Yes. I remember now. That elm." He did not know that he had spoken, and when George asked: "Shall I take the lamp, sir?" stood actionless, seeming to have forgotten the end for which he had come or to have abandoned it.

"The key, sir. In your pocket."

He took out the key and gave it to George, who fitted it into the lock.

"It turns easily," Stephen said, but no one regarded him. As the door opened, Lord Sparkenbroke held up the lamp, his head thrust forward, his knees bent.

At the farther end of the tomb Piers was standing erect,

his body stiff and seemingly propped by the wall, the muscles of his throat taut, his eyes wide. So pale was his face, crowned by his tongued and crested hair, that the light in which he stood appeared to emanate from him, and George was dazzled by what he saw.

Soon the eyelids moved and drooped, the head rocked sickly, the bliss of communication faded. The dulled body, from which the spirit seemed to have gone out, lurched forward into Lord Sparkenbroke's arms, who received it with a thick, gasping cry as though he had been struck. Both his arms were wrapped round the boy; the lamp was broken at his feet; and it was by the moon they saw Piers when he was laid out on the turf, blades of grass, that stood up about his ears and temples, throwing narrow whip-lines of shadow across his cheeks.

Stephen was beside him, a hand thrust under his shirt. At the movement of life beneath his fingers, he began to nod his head, speechless; he nodded his head and ran his tongue over his lips; he said: "Yes . . . yes . . . yes . . . yes . . ." in the panting rhythm of breath itself and fell away, staring.

Lord Sparkenbroke raised Piers's shoulders from the ground. "Water," he said, "the stream," and Stephen leapt up, began to run, stopped. "There's nothing to carry it in!" and George, pointing to the steep ridge above the sepulchre, said: "Up the bank. A flower-vase from the Cottam grave," and Stephen was gone.

They waited.

"We could carry him," George said.

Lord Sparkenbroke made no answer. He was speaking to the burden he held, seeming to entreat it. Without looking up, he said:

"How much will he remember?"

George received only the words.

"Couldn't we carry him to the Rectory, sir? It's as near," he persisted. "And downhill."

"But he won't be able to tell," Lord Sparkenbroke continued, pursuing his own thought. "No one can, after an experience of this kind. . . . Look!"

Piers was opening his eyes. Having recognized them, he asked where he was.

"The elm," Lord Sparkenbroke said. "Do you hear the stream?"

Moving his head a little, "The elm," Piers repeated. "And that's the stream, isn't it? Let me get up. Let me get up, George. Why are you holding me down?"

"I'm not holding you."

Piers began to struggle with his hands. His father urged him to be quiet, to rest; there was water coming.

"Yes," Piers answered, acquiescing with the queer smiling reserve with which grown people sometimes acquiesce in the commands of children. Then: "Father?"

"What is it? Better not talk, Piers."

"Father, if a man owns a bit of land, is it true that he owns all the earth under it and the sky above?"

"Yes."

"I see." The answer seemed to content him. There was a long silence until Stephen was heard returning from the stream. George took the jar from his wet hands.

"Water," he said. "Can you get hold of it yourself?"

Piers's eyes moved. He looked at Stephen. "I remember now," he said. "Stephen thought he had shut me up in the Mound." The rapture from which he had come threw up its last flame in him and perished. His face darkened, as though now for the first time he understood to what he had returned, and he began with the groping gesture of the blind to feel the earth with his hands.

BOOK II

DERRY'S WOOD

CHAPTER ONE

MORE than twenty-one years later, on a summer's morning
of 1926, George Hardy drove up to Sparkenbroke House
in a small battered car. He was admitted at once and found
his own way to the room that had been Stephen's long ago.
In it Piers's son, with his nurse beside him, was sitting up
in bed, playing with soldiers that he had set out on a
backgammon board opened across his knees.

"All right, Miss Kelm?"

"Quite, doctor, I think. Seems very bright, doesn't he?
Normal all day yesterday."

"I'll make sure."

Richard was well enough to laugh and wriggle under the
stethoscope.

"But you'd better go steady for a bit," George said.
"If you get excited and jump about, you'll have a hot
forehead again."

"I say, Dr. George, you know to-morrow I must be
quite better, mustn't I?"

"You will be. But why 'to-morrow'?"

"It's my birthday. An' it's the Mass. An' Spark will
be home."

George, who had heard nothing of Piers's return from
Italy, looked to the nurse for information. "Is Lord
Sparkenbroke coming back?"

"Richard says so. He's been saying so for days."

"Well, you see," Richard began, "I shall be six. Last
year he came back for my birthday. Don't you remember?
Mummy said he came in a train all night from London
so's to be here on my birthday morning. He'd come from

Italy. He didn't go to bed at all. In the morning, early, he went down to the churchyard. Then breakfast time—he came in."

The long speech had been delivered slowly with Richard's struggling emphasis. He feared, with glances of anxiety at the two faces looking down upon him, that he was failing to communicate his pride and joy in this god-like father of his who had swept across Europe to visit him on his birthday morning.

"He's such a *grand* man!" he said. "Isn't he, Dr. George? He'll come, I know. Mummy said——" But a troubled recollection of his mother's face caused him to hesitate.

"What did Mummy say?" Miss Kelm inquired.

"She said—well, you see—I'll tell you what she said. . . ." His mouth was straightened by his reluctance. "Mummy said—*p'raps* he'd come. She hoped so. But you see . . ." He stumbled. "Oh, Dr. George, please don't go! Not yet!"

"But I have to see your mother first and then go home for lunch. I'm going into Chelmouth this afternoon."

"What for?"

"More people who are ill."

"Tell me a story first."

George sat down beside the cot. "A short one, then. What's it to be about?"

"A *Dol*-phin," Richard said, curling himself into the delights of audience. "A Dolphin who had three sons. Come on."

"Once upon a time," George began.

"Come *on*!" said Richard.

"There was a dolphin who lived in Italy, and he had one son."

"Three," said Richard.

"One," said George, "to start with."

He had little power to deny children what they asked of him, but that morning the dolphin story could have no successor. He left the nursery and went downstairs, but not in haste, for to be in haste appeared to him a form of weakness. Men who shot their wrist-watches in the face of providence, women, like restless monkeys, who were for ever snatching at the tail of their engagements, had lost touch with the reason of existence. What good was there in life if you hadn't time to smell the flowers as you passed, or, when a pony came whinnying across a meadow, to allow it to nuzzle in your hand? But he found himself wondering how long Lady Sparkenbroke would hold him. Not long; Richard was cured; there was little to discuss; and she was a sensible woman, not a chatterer. She had respect for other people's time—almost too much respect, he thought; if she were less considerate, less disciplined and reasonable, her husband's rare descents from Italy might be more frequent and she the happier.

The great corridors of Sparkenbroke House were alive with the June sunshine. Though he had been familiar with them since his childhood, or perhaps because they thus retained for him the air of gigantic splendour that they would have presented to a dwarf, George could not escape from a feeling of awe as he passed through them. Why, in heaven's name, had anyone, even in the days of George the First, wanted to build a house of these dimensions? You could tack a cutter along the first-floor landing and hold a cattle-market in the hall. On any stair two grenadiers might have slept comfortably on mattresses laid end to end; and down the well of the staircase, painting the walls with long streaks of crimson and blue and gold, shafts of sun fell long and steep. Even the old rugs, thrust away by Lady Sparkenbroke's methodical order into the remoter corridors, yielded their riches to-day, and George, as he began his journey across the hall, saw everywhere, among distant gleam and shadow, little pools of colour giving a sub-dued answer to the high sparkle of armorial window-glass.

Lady Sparkenbroke was, he knew, in the morning-room that she had chosen as the place in which to do the work of household and estate. Here, at a desk beside tall windows that opened on to the terrace, she saw Chatfield, her husband's agent, reviewing his estimates, criticizing

and aiding his administration, commanding his policy—
"as well she may," said Chatfield, who had respect for
her judgment and liking for her tact. "It's her money
that keeps us going." And here, until Christmas 1925,
Mrs. Glazing, who had combined the duties of housekeeper and secretary and was deeply familiar not only
with the internal economy of the house but with the
complexities of the family money, had worked with
Sparkenbroke's wife. For six years they had worked together, first as willing teacher and eager pupil, then as
collaborators. Now Mrs. Glazing was gone, a pensioner,
into retirement. Etty Sparkenbroke had not attempted to
replace her, preferring to save her salary and assume her
burdens. A young girl, called a secretary but little more
than a typist, sat in Mrs. Glazing's chair.

Lady Sparkenbroke was leaning against the frame of the
open window. Her eyes were on a letter in her hand and
she continued to dictate a reply to it. When George
appeared at her table, her body, a girl's still, swung towards him, and her face, which carried more than her
thirty years in the gentle resoluteness of the mouth and
the experience of the eyes, was turned to his with a movement at once graceful and abrupt—graceful in the throat's
strong ripple, the head's easy poise, abrupt only in the
directness of her look, which, to one who knew her less
well than he, might have seemed a challenge.

"Good. I'm glad you've come, George," she said,
giving him her hand. "Sit there for a moment. Smoke if
you like. Let me finish this one letter. Then we'll talk."

He would have liked to tell her at once that the boy was,
in effect, well again, and that there was no need to interrupt her, but he sat down and waited. There, he thought,
admiring the depth of her chest, her carriage, the fall of
her hips, is a woman who ought never to need a doctor.
She has natural health and she's too active to lose it,
unless— Her wrists, he saw, were too thin, her finger-
nails dry and brittle, and he wondered whether, beneath
her self-control, she was unhappy, as all the world said her
husband gave her cause to be.

That Sparkenbroke had married her for Kaid's money George didn't believe. Lord knows, he might have done if he'd thought of it, he said to himself; Piers's impulses admit few scruples; but he wouldn't have thought of it in those terms, his mind doesn't run on merchant-bankers' daughters or the saving of estates. George remembered Etty Sparkenbroke as she had been at the time of her marriage, her slow, vigorous grace, her dark eyes, the quick colour in her cheeks, the mobility that her love's brilliance had given to the firm moulding of her lips. To-day she was no less handsome, but was changed—not indeed by time, for it had had little physical effect upon her, but by an air of self-mastery which had displaced the spontaneous ease of seven years ago.

No doubt, George thought, Piers took more than he gave—that's his prerogative; women surrender to him without condition—as well blame him for writing poetry that I can't write. But it would be odd if a man who can live on bread and cheese and at the same time treat his bankers as if they were the widow's cruse—it would be very odd if he were brought to the altar by allowances from the Kaid trustees. There appeared in George's mind a stupid saying that bad men love good women. Nonsense, he said to himself, but it may be that a rash man, when he's all at sea, is grateful for a steady woman. We all run to our nurse when we're in trouble.

Piers had been deep in trouble then. His name was being bandied about; newspapers and women gave him no peace and he gave no peace to himself. She gave it him; or, rather, she stood by him while he found it again. The rest were hungry for him, hot and greedy; she loved him, steady and calm. . . . And cold? George added, knowing that here, probably, was an answer, one way or the other, to the questions that Lady Sparkenbroke's appearance had provoked in him. More women were made ill by unhappiness than by any other cause. If their unhappiness was an unhappiness of love, they would sometimes bitterly cure themselves by falling out of love with love itself; they had a queer power of self-sterilization

C

which left them competent, even-minded, healthy, dead. And sometimes, though less easily than men, they could compensate themselves, throw out a new shoot, like a creeper baffled by a gap in a wall, and grow emotionally in a new direction. But if they neither compensated nor sterilized themselves, they became sick women, whatever their physique.

No doctoring's any good for that, he thought, and the symptoms of it—well, in the flabby sort of women it's tears and indigestion and self-pity, but in a woman of character, with pride in her soul, it's precisely the brisk, rigid self-discipline, a bit harder and more cheerful every day, which—and he was surprised to discover how little, until this morning, he had known, or considered, Lady Sparkenbroke's mind. He was shocked; for, to him, the mind was the root of diagnosis. True, she had never been seriously a patient of his; the Kaids had called in the panjandrums of Great Ormond Street when the heir was born; his services had been limited to the after-care of a normal confinement. Nor was she a woman to use the local doctor, or indeed any doctor, as a confessor. There was a reticent dignity in her friendliness that spilled no confidences and invited no theories. He had never known how deeply she had been affected by the swift cooling of Piers's sentiment for her or how far she was able to be content with the affection, the honour, the almost fearful gratitude that remained. If she was unhappy, she had given no sign of bitterness; if hungry, she had never betrayed it. It had always been easy to assume that she was not by nature passionate and that her life was in her child, in the estate, in her husband's achievement as an artist, which, though remote from her understanding, was quick in her admiration. But I've been duller than I should be, George reflected. Even this morning, if she hadn't been standing up in the light and fiddling with that paper, I might not have noticed her wrists and her finger-nails.

CHAPTER TWO

THE letter done, she surprised him by sending her secretary away. "But you needn't be afraid I shall keep you," she said, ordering the papers on her desk. "This is your day for Chelmouth, isn't it? I know you're busy. But I've done enough for this morning. I'll come part of the way to the village with you if I may. . . . Did you walk up, or have you the car here?"

"I have the car."

"Peters shall drive it to the church gates and hand it over to you there. We could walk down over the terraces and through the churchyard. That won't delay you too long?"

The tone was deliberately careless, as though she wanted nothing but a little fresh air and, perhaps, his company, but there was something in her manner, or an intuition in him, that had authority. He said without hesitation that he would like the walk. She rang the bell, gave orders for his car, and went out through the window, he following. They walked in silence for a little while. When he spoke of Richard, she answered: "That's all right then. I'm glad," and said no more until, having crossed the lawns and entered the lower orchards, they were on a level with the belfry of the church. Here she paused and, with a shyness, a visible effort, unaccustomed in her, said:

"I want your help if you'll give it me."

The severity—or, rather, the assurance—of her demeanour fell away as she spoke. Her eyes, ordinarily so easy in their encounters, looked at him now with conscious frankness as though she had said: I musn't be afraid to look him

57

in the face, and had compelled herself. The need for that compulsion awoke George abruptly to the crisis of her mood. His emotion of tenderness towards her, because her pride was manifestly in trouble, must have been reflected in his face, for she flushed and her eyes hardened.

"Of course I'll help you," he answered. "In what way?"

Already she was in retreat from confidence, gathering her pride.

"Oh," she said, "it's not as serious as all that. I oughtn't to have dragged you out here."

"But, Lady Sparkenbroke——"

"Lady Sparkenbroke? George, why do you never call me by my name? I grant you don't often call me Lady Sparkenbroke. Usually you avoid calling me anything at all."

He said plainly: "I don't know. I find it difficult—not to you particularly, I mean. I'm not easy on Christian names. Old-fashioned, I suppose. Besides," he added, "it's easier to call a woman by her name if you hear her continually called by it. But Spark seldom calls you Henrietta—it's generally Etty or some nickname."

"Etty will do very well," she said, smiling at his long explanations and moving on between the fruit-trees. "But tell me. I've often wondered. Sometimes you call Piers 'Spark.' Why that?"

"Everyone does—except you."

"But it can't be an old nickname. He hadn't the title when you were boys. He wasn't even the heir until Stephen was killed at Messines."

"No, he was Piers to me then. 'Spark' is fairly new, I suppose. I think I've caught it from Richard. It's his name for his father."

"The London name too," she said quickly. "I've never been able to acquire it." And she added: "Do you know, when we were engaged, to call him Piers seemed in some odd way to set him apart for me? I think he liked it then—for that reason. Probably it only irritates him now."

He held open for her the private gate by which the church was approached from the north. The little grey building with its high tower stood, amid a cluster of grave-

stones, in a clearing of the wood. To the south the ground
fell away steeply, and, when they had rounded the east end
and stood by the porch, the sea and the great sloping
landscape that George had surveyed from Richard's
window were again partly visible over the trees, but the
road and the southern gate by which the parishioners of
Sparkenbroke Green came to church were concealed.

"You know the village phrase for dying?" George said.
"They say: 'Old So-and-so will soon be going up the hill.'
At least, they used to say it, but it's rare now."

"Because the churchyard's on a hill?"

"I imagine so. The saying's local. I've never heard it
elsewhere."

"You're full of Sparkenbroke lore, aren't you?"

"But Etty," he said, "there's nothing wonderful in
that. It's where I live and work." He was proud of having
used her name. That ice was broken, and he looked for
her approval which, with a smile at his cheerful clumsiness,
she gave. They had drifted away from the subject, whatever it might be, which had led her to say that she wanted
his help and he was determined not to compel her to it.
Perhaps she would speak of it again to-day, perhaps not
until many days had passed; she must come to it of her
own will. At the outset, a little human blindness was
reassuring to women of her mettle, who would call up
all their prides to resist professional inquiry. If a patient
must undress, he thought, let her undress herself; see
nothing until she is ready; and he strolled away from her
down the slope of the churchyard as if he had all day to
waste. On the grassy roof of the Mound, he began to tap
stray ash from his pipe into the palm of his hand; then
sat down. She followed, seemingly as careless as he,
listening to the June morning.

"Piers used to spend hours here when he was a boy,"
he said.

"He would still if people didn't come into the churchyard and stare at him. Now, when he's in England, he
spends most of his time in the lodge in Derry's Wood,"
she replied, and added: "Often he sleeps there."

There had been no need to tell him that Piers worked in Derry's Wood; he knew it as well as she; and the emphasis in his mind lay, in consequence, on her final sentence from which all emphasis had by her been carefully lifted.

"But not always?"

"Oh, by no means." It was sharply said. An upward glance discovered on her lips an ironic, continuing smile. "He comes to the House of course when he feels inclined."

This lightly toned commonplace, which might have been no more than an intimation of her willingness that her husband should come and go as he pleased, was quick with a different emotion. If she had said: he comes to my bed when it suits him because, now and then, my body interests him still, she would not have indicated more clearly the dark swoop of her thought; yet there had been in her irony not condemnation of him but a puzzled, tentative criticism of herself, as if she had asked: in what way have I failed him? and George, seeing how sad her expression was when at last she seated herself on the grass, was surprised, and a little irritated, by her humility. It would do Piers good, he thought, if she locked her door; but it's useless, he added on the instant, the doctor disciplining the man in him, it's useless to think on those lines. I can call him a sensualist or a cad; I might even persuade her to say it of him; but she would no more believe it than I; she knows as well as I do that Plain Sensualist and Plain Cad don't exist; they are ciphers of the moralists, angry noises, no more; and if she locked her door she wouldn't shut out her loneliness; she would shut in her pride.

"You specialize in the mind," she said.

"No. I'm a general practitioner. I specialize in nothing."

"But when you were in London, before you came back here?"

"The body through the mind; the mind through the body. It's the only intelligent way of approach."

She nodded. "That's why I wanted to consult you. . . . Oh no, I'm not ill. I'm perfectly fit."

"Will you hold out your hand? Are your finger-nails always like that? Look at me." He pulled down the lid of her right eye. "Sleeping?"

"Not well," she admitted. "But I'm not consulting you as a doctor."

How afraid she was of help—of a sacrifice of her integrity in asking it! She was, too, he hazarded, one of those women who had a distaste for all consideration of their own bodies, who imagined themselves always dressed, walking in the open, sitting in a chair, performing the ordinary duties of life that the world might see; who, so to speak, snubbed their secret selves whenever they appeared. Such women would not go to a doctor until pain made them helpless; they put on one garment before they removed another, fearing the most private nakedness, and, if they were naked of necessity, they remained still. For the same reason the physical act of love was often to them an extreme agony of delight; they fainted under it, they died a death, they surrendered in each humiliation a new virginity, and were delivered, or expelled, from a new prison. Was it for this Piers took her, that he might be the occasion and witness of her ecstatic deaths? This, even if it were true, she could not be told, for it could be true only in relation to a state in herself of which she did not recognize the existence; and he answered simply: "Very well. The doctor has gone home, but here I am still," and waited. It was she that must speak.

She surprised him by asking: "You are very fond of Piers?"

"I always have been."

"I believe you are. I wonder why."

"Surely that's not surprising to you."

"Because I'm his wife? My feeling for him has no link with yours. . . . Yes, it is very surprising to me that a man of your kind should like him."

"Of my kind?"

"You have the masculine codes—held pretty firmly."

"They suit me, that's all, as it suits me to get up at

seven in the morning and to drink a pint of water. But I
don't judge others by them."

She hesitated. "You are a normal human being," she
said.

"Is there such a thing?"

A frown darkened her eyes. "You're making it harder,
George, not easier. I know you mean to be kind."

"But I——"

"No," she said firmly. "I'll say what I have to say. I
mean this: that Piers's special faults—if they are faults—
are peculiarly those which you condemn."

"Do I? If I do, Etty, it's a failure in me. It's not my job
to condemn."

"As a doctor? I'm not speaking of that. But isn't it true
that for you—I don't know how to put it . . . ."

He twisted a long blade of grass over one of his fingers.
"I can say it for you," he answered. "You mean that I
have allowed regularity of life to become for me a virtue in
itself. I believe that people should keep engagements, fulfil
contracts, work rigidly by the moral clock. And you mean
that I appear to have very little sympathy for—what
would you like them to be called?—the sins of the flesh?
Is that what you mean?"

She nodded. "Roughly. But you confess it as if it
were a crime. It isn't. It is in fact the practical way of
living. The other ways don't pay; they don't work. Piers
himself admits it. He says," she added with a smile, "that
even nowadays the sins of the flesh always end in tears and
taxis. He speaks with authority."

George smiled at that. "It may be the practical way of
living and it may pay. I think it does," he admitted. "But
still, I'm not very proud of myself. You see, I happen not
to be tempted."

"By the sins of the flesh?"

"Very little."

She smiled. " 'Let not him that girdeth on his harness . . .' "

"Etty," he said, "I'm pretty sure of myself and for a
good reason."

She mocked him again. "What is the good reason?"

"I was in love once. We were to have been married. She died. I like other women—perhaps the better for what happened—but I don't . . . particularly . . . see them."

"I should have remembered," she said. "Piers told me that. Still, the effect it's had on you is rare."

"It's the way I'm made," he answered stubbornly. "No virtue in me. And if it leads me to condemn the temptations of others, it's very far from a virtue. Besides—"

"Besides—what?"

"The sins of the flesh are not what Jesus condemned."

"Sometimes," she answered, "you're very like a large boy. That's what's good about you." And she added with awkward, hesitant affection: "I don't think you need be afraid of spiritual pride, do you? . . . Or *do* you?"

"It's you who are helping me, not I you," he replied, leaving her question answerless, "and though you won't have me as your doctor, I'm not your patient. Tell me this: if you think as I do about—regularity of life, why don't you condemn?"

"I do bitterly—other people. I'm harsh and rigid. But not him."

"Why not? Don't say: because you love him or because he's your husband. That's not an answer."

She pondered, gathering her words. "The value in him isn't diminished by what—he throws away." She drew breath swiftly; her thought had lit a flame in her. Now the words would come. "I don't mean," she said, "that he's an artist and that women are a stimulus to his art. Even that may have a bit of truth in it, but for the most part it's just a slack, ugly catchword used by a thousand little scribblers and dabblers to make their greed sound splendid."

George said: "It was probably true of Goethe."

"Anyhow it's not what matters to me," she continued, seeing her own way clear. "The point is there's something in Piers that makes him see women as no one else does. On the surface, he may appear callous and sensual. If he were just that I should hate him."

"How does he see them?" George asked.

"Ah!" she said, "if I knew that! I don't know what he sees. I don't know what he's looking for. And for that reason I don't know what it is he fails to find. And yet," she continued, "I do know that to be—to be——"

She could not speak and she looked at George, with dry eyes, helplessly. She lowered her head; then threw it up so suddenly that her hair flowed back from her temples. "I do know that to be searched by him is like being searched by a god," she said quietly.

Here, in spite of the firmness of her language, was precisely the touch of emotional extravagance that he had not expected in her, and he disliked it—disliked it the more because it was opposed to her character as he had understood it. "Searched by a god" indeed! Words . . . She didn't know what she was talking about.

"Which god?" he said, and had not spoken before he knew that he had been cruel; but with the same quietness of tone that she had used before, she said:

"That's what I thought you might be able to tell me. Who is his god? What is it he wants?" She repeated: "What is it he wants so profoundly that every other motive is unreal—just as unreal in relation to our codes, our regularities of life, as they would be in a god?"

George answered that he had never known Piers care for anything consistently except the perfecting of his work. "Once I asked him why. I've never really grasped the artist's point of view, the mad, unsparing ruthlessness—unsparing of himself and of everyone else. I asked him *why* it mattered so desperately—in relation to what good? Was it to make men happier or better? And if it was 'done to the glory of God,' what precisely did that mean? He said: 'In relation to nothing. It's an end, not a means.' He cursed me as what he called 'a late Tolstoyan.' He said: 'In relation to nothing on earth. Can't you see, that's the whole point, George? It's only another way of saying: "to the glory of God."'"

"Go on," she said.

"It was almost the last talk I had with him before he

went to Italy this time," George answered. "I can remember it pretty clearly. I was sitting in my own little room at the Rectory, late at night, reading. The window was open and Piers came in. It's odd the effect he has—anyhow on me. He's more alive than anyone else in the world. Not physically. In a way, he's frail. His fever in Gallipoli nearly finished him. Exactly how much his heart is damaged I'm never sure. These attacks of his aren't necessarily the result of a crocked heart. There have been angina patients that seem to have cured themselves, and, what's more, there have been angina post-mortems that have discovered no lesion of any kind. The thing has odd effects on him. He'll work or ride or travel until you'd say he had ten men's strength—then, suddenly, he tires, like a woman; endure and endure, no saving himself—then, suddenly, there's nothing left. . . . You'll have to keep an eye on him."

She smiled. "Can anyone do that?"

"Well," said George, observing with embarrassment that he had been talking less to her than to himself, "we shall have to try. But there's nothing much that anyone can do to check a man who carries his own stimulants inside him. That night it was like that. He was worn out, pale with exhaustion; but he drew on his will, as he always does; instead of becoming slack and heavy he whipped his body with his mind. He was brittle and fiery like a——"

"Like a child," she said, "awakened suddenly out of a thrilling dream."

"Sometimes it frightens me," George answered. "The tension's too high, you know."

"I know. But it's worth being frightened that way."

He looked at her gravely and with admiration. "It was partly my fault. I challenged him. First about his art. Then about his God."

"And he answered *you*," she said.

"Yes," George admitted. "But not for my sake. Something I had said provoked him. It was just chance."

"What had you said?"

"Seeing how excited he was, I tried to warn him—not

for the first time—to keep calm. I'm pretty sure, though others disagree, that high emotion is among the causes of these attacks, and I reminded him of John Hunter's saying—he had angina irregularly for twenty years and died in an attack of it—that it put him at the mercy of any ruffian who chose to annoy him. 'Oh, yes,' said Piers, 'I know that story. It's the bright anecdote of every text-book.' Then his voice changed and he said: 'I'll tell you something else about your text-books, George. They are all wrong in one thing. They say that in an attack you have an agonized sense of imminent death. It's much more than that—much worse and much better. It's not a feeling that you're going to die but that you *have* died. That's the point, the whole point—anyhow with me.' And I told him," George continued, "what I have always noticed about the look on a dead man's face. People are not necessarily happy and content or tranquil when death comes, but they are detached. What they see claims them, and it seems to be an absolute claim."

Her eyes moved to him. "Death," she repeated. "Yes. That always stirs him. But he's not afraid of it. And he doesn't long for it—not, at any rate, as a way of escape. I mean, he doesn't sentimentalize it. He looks to it, I think, as a kind of—as a——"

"An achievement," George suggested.

"More. More than that. As a—a final masterpiece, as though it were of his own making, a book, a poem that would, in some mysterious way, take the place of all his work. . . . He talked to me a little once—years ago. Not much. I remember thinking: here's something that means more to him than his art and yet *is* his art—a consummation of it. . . . Did you talk to him about death deliberately, George, to draw him out?"

"No."

She shook her head, unbelieving. "You are more than a good doctor, if death fascinates you."

"No," he answered. "But when a patient goes out of reach, isn't it natural to wonder what has become of him? Of course you can say he's opening his eyes on a new

world—heaven or hell or what you please. That isn't how
it strikes me. The most significant fact about dying men
is that they seldom appear to be in the least surprised. And
there's another fact. You watch a man die that you've
known all your life and, quite suddenly, in the moment of
death he becomes a stranger. He's not finding something
new; he's falling back on something old, something
familiar to him in the way that his childhood would be
familiar if he could re-enter it. It seems always to have
existed within him and to have been rediscovered now.
And it takes the *whole* of him into itself. His sins, his
anxieties, his ambitions, his friends all fall away and
he's left—alone. Single-minded at last. Unassailable. . . .
'Single-minded' was the word Piers clung to, and
remembered much later in the evening. We went on to
talk of his art. I questioned him as I've told you. I
pressed him further. He had said art was an absolute
end; its values weren't relative to any earthly good. I
said I accepted that from him, the artist. That's what it
was to him. But it couldn't ever be its justification to the
world. Though he might not care for the effect, it remained true that art had effect on the world. And the
world was in a mess. 'High heaven and earth ail from
the prime foundation.' If he said that art was practised
to the glory of God he must say to what god. . . . Isn't
that common sense?" he asked, pulling himself out of his
memories of that evening with Sparkenbroke and looking
to the woman at his side for reassurance.

She rose from the grass and, standing a yard away with
her back to him, gazed over the edge of the Mound into
the branches of the elm.

"Yes," she said. "That's common sense. Did Piers
ride away from it?"

George doubted her tone. "Ride away?"

"I don't mean 'shirk it.' He never shirks—in his own
mind. But there are some things that can't be said in
terms of common sense."

"As you know," George answered, "I'm a sceptic—
theologically. I know enough of facts to guess that they

are misleading; still, I can't go beyond them; outside
their circle I stop and say simply that I don't know. My
job, as I see it, is to come back and reject or verify old
facts and establish new ones as best I can. So I dare say
I'm not the most suitable person in the world to hand on
Piers's ideas to you. Still . . . He said that God was
imagination or, at any rate, that imagination was the
evidence of God of which he personally was aware. I
could see that the idea had been smouldering in his mind
for ages; now he fairly blazed with it. 'The Kingdom of
God is within you,' might, he said, have been written to
express it. And so much fitted in. Imagination is in-
escapable. We can kill our bodies, but, as long as the
body survives, there's no suicide of the imagination—no
repelling it, no getting away. We sleep and it continues.
I said: 'But if we die, Piers,' and he turned on me. ' "Per-
chance to dream!" ' he answered. He was excited and
trembling. Then his voice dropped—tone and pace.
'There's the *effect* of art,' he said, 'the effect on the world
you were asking for, George. And much more than that—
its whole relationship to morals, or, rather, its everlasting
distinction from morals. The curse of man, and the reason
that civilization after civilization breaks down and rots,
is that he allows imagination to stagnate and congeal.
He lets the stream freeze over. Art fluidifies it again.
A story isn't good because it gives men pleasure or in-
structs them or imposes an opinion on them or leads to
the reform of a moral or social evil. And it isn't good
because it does a reader's imagining for him: that's a
photographer's job, not an artist's. It is good because it
re-enables a man to imagine for himself. It unfreezes the
river. After that the river flows on in its own course, god-
like or devilish——' "

"Or devilish?" Lady Sparkenbroke broke in.

"That was my trouble," George answered. "When he
said it, I interrupted him just as you have interrupted me.
But it's the root of Piers's idea. The divine essence of
man, which art and death liberate, isn't necessarily 'good';
it has two aspects, godlike and devilish; their contest is

the drama of the spirit. Art gets the curtain up—that's all, and that, to Piers, is everything. What happens afterwards is a moralist's affair, not an artist's. The principle is the Dionysiac principle of release. . . . Do you understand now in what way, as an artist, he's a fanatic? It's a very different story from the old one of 'Art for Art's sake.' He hates that and repudiates it. . . . Oh, he was alive that night!" George cried. "To listen to him and watch him was like warming your hands at a fire!"

"Go on," she said, turning from the edge of the Mound and kneeling on the grass at a little distance from him. "Go on. I'm beginning to understand."

"I can't go on," he answered. "That's where I stop. I accept the idea from him because I believe in him. And, while he's there, I feel it—or seem to. But I don't feel it in myself."

"The work of art feels it," she said.

"What do you mean?"

"And the woman feels it," she went on, swept forward by her own perception. "The woman feels it. That's his power over women. He is looking in them for the same power of release," she added, her eyes bent upon her rigidly clasped hands. "Seen from that point of view, one woman's like another, I suppose, until she's proved to be useless, as one material for a work of art is like another."

He looked at her shrewdly. Her breast was moving quickly; she had been speaking, as an actor would say, out of her part.

"Is he coming back?" George asked.

She nodded. "Some time to-night or early to-morrow. A wireless came this morning."

"Richard will be pleased. He's expecting him."

She had not told Richard. "One's never sure of Piers. He may stop in London."

"Isn't it the Sparkenbroke Mass to-morrow?"

"Yes."

"Then he'll come. He doesn't often miss it."

"But it's not anniversaries he comes for," she said,

"neither Richard's birthday nor anything else. At least, I doubt it. But after he's been away for months in Italy, suddenly he seems to become hungry for this place."

"For Sparkenbroke?"

"More than that, for *this* place, where we are now. This graveyard. . . . Then he comes back. He says: 'I found I couldn't write any more in Italy.' This place releases him. Releases," she said again, and checked at the word. "Is there a connexion there, too?"

"I think there is."

"Poetry," she said, "and death—and love."

He nodded. "I think so."

"That they are the same? It's a kind of madness, George —by our measure—isn't it?" She sighed and smiled, not unhappily. "I suppose I ought to have married some quite sane ordinary man. This is like being given a great house full of miracles and dungeons and magic rooms and places of torture—and not having the keys to it. Sometimes the doors lighten, as if they were made of glass; then they darken and thicken again, and I'm shut out. And though you've known him all these years, I believe you understand no more than I do. Do you?"

"Understand?" he answered. "Probably not. I've always given him a place apart in my mind; he doesn't fit my rules; and that's the trouble. . . . The key to every man is his supreme want. There are people who haven't got a supreme want clearly marked, just as there are children who grow up without knowing clearly what they mean to do with their lives if they have the chance. They are the muddled majority of mankind—doing jobs that don't mean anything to them and 'amusing' themselves, or seeking to be amused, because they don't know what to do with their leisure. But even in them you can discover a supreme want if you dig patiently enough. And Piers ought to be easier. His supreme want is, for him at any rate, definite enough. There's never been a more desperately urgent man. But he's out of my range. I know the facts but they don't lead me to him. I know that his art holds out to him something—some promise or expectation—

that makes him, by our standards, mad with eagerness.
You know that love——"

"The sexual act itself," she said. "At least, I think so."

"Very well. But what connects the two expectations?
And what connects them to his expectation of death? That
night, before we separated, as we were walking together
through the Rectory orchard, he said to me abruptly, out
of a long silence, that art was the most profound of all the
intimations of immortality. Beneath the impact of a work
of art, he said, we undergo a kind of conversion. Our
stiffness breaks, we flow again; we are aware, as at no other
time, of a continuity in ourselves, as though we were given
eyes to look up and down the river far beyond the little
section of it that is our life in this world."

"Your words or his?" she asked.

"His," George answered, "almost word for word. 'A
work of art,' he said, 'yields a recognition, which seems
almost a remembrance, of what was before birth and what
shall be after death.' His arm was in mine; his face came
round suddenly. It was morning dusk. The garden was
whitening for daybreak. There was life in the hedge. I
could see his eyes shining. 'Isn't that,' he said, 'what you
yourself have seen in the faces of dying men? Everything
runs together to-night, George, doesn't it? Everything de-
clares itself, like a woman who throws back her veil.' Of
course," George added, "he has told you the story of the
Mound?"

"The story of it?"

"As it affects him personally."

"Never."

"I mean," George said, "what happened when he was
twelve years old?"

"Nothing."

He gazed at her incredulously. "Has no one ever told
you? Not even Mrs. Glazing? That he was shut in the
Mound by Stephen?"

"Shut in!"

That Piers had withheld this knowledge from her, and
had, seemingly, bound Mrs. Glazing to withhold it, so

increased its significance in George's eyes that he himself hesitated. But her face persuaded him, and, as they walked together down the slope of the churchyard into the flat space where the elm-tree stood before the face of the sepulchre, he began to tell her how, when he himself was a boy, he had come up to spend a night at Sparkenbroke House, for he and Stephen were to set out cub-hunting next morning before the moon was down. As he told the story, she stood with the sun upon her, baffled and attentive. "But why did he want to go into the Mound?" she interrupted. "It's not natural in a boy." And, as he continued his tale, describing his walk through the orchard at old Sparkenbroke's heels and their coming at last to the tomb, and their taking Piers from it, she cried: "But why was he happy? In what way was he happy? Have you asked him?"

"Yes. I have asked him."

"You mean that he won't tell or that he can't?"

George lifted his shoulders. "It was here we brought him out," he said, finding it easier to press on with his narrative than to speculate concerning it, "here—under this elm. He looked like a water-sprite. I think he was abnormally long and thin for a boy, but that night played tricks with him—with all of us, for that matter. His father was kneeling there—about where you're standing—with Piers's head and shoulders propped up by his knee; even he was seeing visions in his own queer way. And I was here, at Piers's side, calmer than any of them, I believe. Not that what I'd seen hadn't shaken me, but after the first blaze of it I wasn't frightened. I knew Piers better than they did and I knew inside me that what had happened to him was —well, his own sort of miracle. Necessary to him. Happy, too. I've seen women like that after bearing a child—one or two women, not more. . . . Then Stephen came running up with water. Poor Stephen, all dressed-up in his evening suit, slopped with mud where he'd clambered down the bank, and so desperate to *do* something to make amends that he ran with the water and spilt most of it over his hands. I remember that. His hands were cold and wet; I touched them. . . . Well, that's the story anyhow."

She said: "I'm glad you told me." Then, because she was confused and silence pressed upon her confusion, she added: "Was he ill afterwards?"

"Piers? No."

A paralysis had fallen upon their conversation. They felt awkward, dull, embarrassed, having spoken more openly than was their custom and reached no conclusion.

"Well," George said again, "there's the story. You have the facts"; and she made a little gesture with her hands as if to say, hopelessly: and of what use are they to either of us? But she said aloud with a compelled smile: "I suppose you didn't go cub-hunting that morning after all?"

"No."

"There's your car," she said, raising her voice. "I hope I haven't made you late."

She walked with him from the elm a few paces, then stopped, and, as he drove away, he asked himself whether her resolution allowed her to cry when she was alone or whether even her solitudes were armoured.

CHAPTER THREE

GEORGE'S buoyant spirit and his saving capacity, as a
doctor, to allow each hour to fall away when it was done,
enabled him to forget Lady Sparkenbroke before the car
had moved a hundred yards. The tension of her life led
him to consider the quietness of his own, and to be
thankful that he and his father and sister lived without
hungers or disturbance. To his father old age was coming
early; but his mind was composed, neither its energies nor
its acceptances were impaired, and beneath the shrewdness
and mannered intolerance of a scholar, sharp to criticize
the contemporary world, was a timeless, equable grace of
spirit that shone the more brightly in him as he grew older.
He was very far from being without fault; his temper was
quick, he was stubborn in his intellectual prides, he did
not suffer the half-educated gladly, though he had a
Christian hope of fools. I am too hot, too keen, he said
once, I haven't the steady talent of virtue—a phrase that
Sparkenbroke had heard and remembered. A phrase I
shall steal, he had said, as I've always stolen shamelessly
from your father since he began to teach me Latin and
Greek—and it's true, bless him, that he hasn't the talent
of virtue; that's why I can learn from him; but he has the
genius of innocence; when he teaches, he makes the
curtain go up.

And what did he mean by that, George thought—"to
make the curtain go up"? It was a saying that he had heard
Piers use on other occasions; of poetry, which he would
distinguish thus from verse; of women, that in this they
failed him continually; even of death and its promise. It

74

was a phrase used lightly as slang is used; but George, a little proud of his wary treatment of mental processes, was not to be hoodwinked by that, for slang was often the shorthand of a prolific mind, a formula of which the proofs were in meditation, and he was on the edge of perceiving that here, perhaps, was the key to her husband that Etty Sparkenbroke had sought, when a sharp down-hill turn into the Chelmouth road at Sparkenbroke Cross recalled his attention to wheel and brake. I suppose, he said to himself as the car began to roll gently towards the Rectory, that Helen has the talent of virtue; her profession as a teacher is taken from her, she's an invalid, all her activity is denied her, and she is more than patient, more than uncomplaining. She has written off that part of life's debt to her on which she set most store; it is cancelled, put away, she doesn't dwell upon it; and that is harder than to be patient. There are few women with more character than she. But Piers has always been bored by her. She has "the steady talent of virtue" he would say, and, imagining the tone in which he would say this, George was angry, for he loved his sister. Piers is bored by her, he repeated, because she can give him nothing that he wants, and he was indignant against Piers's selfishness. But why? he added. Piers had never spoken unkindly of her; when he remembers, he brings her gifts from Italy; and are we not all bored by people who have nothing to give us? Piers wants much and finds it seldom; I am more easily satisfied; that is the difference between us; and he resumed his even-minded habit, bringing up his car, with smooth precision, in the place where it could be most easily turned. As he climbed out, he looked at the clock on the dashboard and checked it by his watch. By two o'clock he must be in his consulting-room at Chelmouth; there was little time to spare; and his mind, so orderly and accurate that a note-book was almost superfluous to him, began to consider, with the interest of a well-occupied man whose profession is his life, the tasks of the afternoon.

On the bridge leading to the front door he found his sister propped against the rail, a stick in her hand.

The kick of a horse, received while she was helping a child to mount, had so injured her that for eight months she had been crippled. From this injury she had recovered, but meanwhile other symptoms had appeared. Sometimes her gait was unsteady and her speech would halt between syllables. At first, George had supposed that this weakness was a prolonged consequence of her having been bedridden, but it had not corrected itself, and at last he had been compelled to recognise that the extreme feebleness of the legs by which she was from time to time visited had an origin independent of the horse's kick. He observed that, when she stretched out her hand to lift a thimble or a pair of scissors from the table, she would sometimes helplessly miss her aim, and that always her picking-up was erratic. Once she said to him in a puzzled voice: "Do you know, George, it's very odd, but now and then for a little while—it doesn't last I'm glad to say—I see things double. What does that mean, if one's not drunk?" He had known what this and the other evidences meant—inflammatory patches in which the myelin sheaths of the nerve fibre were destroyed—and he had begun to study disseminated sclerosis again. In the end she had come to understand that her career of teaching was done.

"Can I get well?"

"Never completely, Helen. It's a thing that goes up and down. There will probably be long periods, six months and more, in which you are enormously better."

"How long shall I live?"

"Indefinitely," he had said. Perhaps, he had thought, six years or more.

Now, as she waited for him on the bridge, she had an appearance, not of frailty, but of being dried and sapless, as though she had spent a great part of her life in the East; her skin was brown, and, though her hair dully retained its former colour, her eyebrows lay thick and salty on her forehead, giving to her expression the peering quickness of a great bird's. She was waiting for him; her head and stick moved as if she would advance; but the action was slow and not completed.

The sight of her on the bridge recalled to George the day on which she had come out from the house to summon Piers to his lesson. I had been humouring my first pipe, he thought. The smell of it came back to him, sharper than the smell of any tobacco smoke to-day, and the scene flooded in upon him—the sound of the water, Piers's voice, the wild sensation of being young, of being a boy, of life in flux. For a moment, the evenness of his present existence, which had seemed wise and desirable as he drove down from the churchyard, rose up before him like a cloud, and, though he slammed the door of his car and called out to Helen as if no spirits from the past had invaded him, he could not banish the scene of his boyhood, could not rid himself of the thought that what had then lain in the future —his work in London, his hopes and disappointments, the passionate singleness of mind that had made the war an exaltation—was gone, and with it an irrecoverable part of himself. And a good riddance, he tried to say; to be young is like riding an unbroken horse; it gets you nowhere unless it runs away with you and then——

"And what on earth are you doing here?" he asked aloud, for a long chair in the garden was now Helen's accustomed place; but while she answered, leaning on his arm as they went back to the house, he remembered how astonished she had been by Piers's saying that he had always attended the Mass, how he had rushed past her, leaving her indignant at this "lie." He remembered her appearance as it had been then. Her youth's eager severity, which would have given the world, when it deserved as much, six marks out of ten, was lost now in the guarded tolerance of middle age. What lies before her? he thought. Perhaps some day she may even be strong enough to travel a little; and he said: "You're getting on, Helen. This time last year you couldn't have walked to the bridge. Florence and Pisa may not be so far off after all," but it was said to encourage her; he did not believe that this old desire of hers to visit Tuscany would ever be fulfilled; and she answered: "Next year, I expect," in a tone so energetically hopeful that he knew she herself had almost put hope away.

"I hobbled out to the bridge, George, to be sure of not missing you as you passed. You're so late, I thought you might go straight into Chelmouth without stopping for food," and she reminded him that a former pupil of hers, Mary Leward, was arriving at Chelmouth station with her father that afternoon. He had said he would meet them.

"If I could . . ." he put in.

"Of course," she answered. "The train isn't until 4.50. You will be through your work by then."

"Probably. But even so, Helen, why must they be met? Can't they find their own way? Where are they staying?"

"At the Sparkenbroke Hotel. Too expensive for them, I should have thought, but that's what Mary writes."

"Well," said George, "there'll be the hotel bus and a hotel porter with more gold lace than an admiral. No need for me." And, seeing that Helen was unpersuaded, he threw in: "Besides, do young women like being met at railway stations not without dust and heat?"

"How considerate you are!" Helen answered, mocking him. "If you knew a little more about young women, you'd know that it's the plain ones whom railway stations affect. Mary has nothing to conceal. She's eighteen."

"Old enough to look after herself."

"Yes, George. But this is her first real holiday for years. Since her mother died she has run the house for her father. A little house. Most of the work herself. And now she's engaged."

"Engaged?"

"To some young man. Rich. He plays cricket I believe."

It was said in a tone of reproof that made George smile.

"Come," he said, "men will be husbands you know, and girls will marry 'em."

"At eighteen? Its seems rather disgust—well, rather silly, anyhow. Just when she's growing up and might make something of herself."

George gave no answer.

"But she's a dear," Helen added. "This trip to Chelmouth is really her first little freedom—and I suppose it's the last. She's as excited about it as a child. I want her to enjoy it."

"And you think that the sight of my face on the platform——?"

"Well," said Helen, with the air of one who throws in the Old Guard, "let's leave it. If you can't you can't. But it would be kind to welcome them. I'd have gone myself if I could."

To that there was no counter. "All right," said George. "Don't you worry. . . . And what's that?" On the table in the hall a bouquet was lying.

"For her," Helen said.

"For me to present—on the platform? Why don't women feel the embarrassment of flowers? I'd rather carry a baby."

For Helen's sake he would have consented, but she was merciful. On his way to the station he might leave the flowers at the hotel; Mary would find them in her bedroom; and such was George's pleasure in his reprieve that Helen began to laugh at him and they went into the dining-room together, happy that for all their differences a quarrel between them was impossible. At the table the Rector was munching an apple.

"Take some of these in your pocket, George. You haven't time for much. What kept you?"

"Lady Sparkenbroke."

"Not ill?"

"No. . . . Piers is coming back. Are you going to read the Service at the Mound to-morrow? You oughtn't to. The evenings can be cool."

"Yes," his father answered. "I know. But I'm going."

"Why?"

"Piers wouldn't like it if I didn't."

"Do you care so much," said Helen, "what he likes or dislikes?"

"Yes, my dear, I do. . . . He's doing work I want to see done. I had a letter from him. He said he had begun a long poem on the coming of the Holy Face to Lucca. I've heard no more of it. That project may have died. Still there's the novel on Tristan and Iseult. For him to turn from modern subjects to that—and to write of it as he will write of it. . . . Besides I saw the opening chapters. The odd thing about them was that they seemed to be written not so much of a material world that is past as of a spiritual world that is coming. That is the way to treat the great legends. They are deathless. . . . They are deathless and universal—or they're nothing," the Rector repeated. "I know something about legends. I want a finger in both those pies. I hope he'll come."

"He is coming," George repeated.

"Yes, yes, I heard you. I mean—will he come here—to see me?"

"You can be sure he will," Helen remarked, "if he wants anything."

The Rector leaned forward in his chair. "And why not? That's what scholarship is for. Dry leaves for imagination to light and genius to fan. That's what I want. . . . Ah, Helen, you always treat him as the bad boy of the class. You don't know your man. If I was sure I could help him——"

"You can," George answered. "You can help, he said, because you haven't the 'talent of virtue' but——"

"My phrase! my phrase!" the Rector cried, waving a spoon in air. "He's stolen it. . . . That's good!"

"He said," George continued, "that, when you taught, you could make the curtain go up."

There was silence. Spoon and apple went down on the table.

"Say that again, boy."

George repeated it. "Now, Father," he added, "you had better interpret."

"No good," the old man said with a smile. "You and Helen haven't the ears to hear—have you now?—not even when Piers translates the neo-platonic into the *patois*. But don't you forget it was I who taught Sparkenbroke grammar. Put that in my epitaph."

George's work in Chelmouth took less time than he

had expected. His consulting-room was hot and a patient had left her scent upon its air; to drive home at once tempted him. Outside his window in Regency Crescent, beyond the sloping patch of green and the railing backed by a low hedge, his car was standing. Shabby, for a doctor. Still, patients weren't put off by it; they laughed when he told them he kept it shabby to make them pay their fees; and he had more of them in Chelmouth than he could do with if he wasn't to neglect the villages. His job was in the villages. I might drive over to Barling after tea, he thought, and look at Medwall's leg. Then: but I shall be back too late if I wait for the 4.50. Get them to the hotel. Be polite. Flowers. Messages. Damn.

He seldom came to this room more than twice a week. There were few books in it, and they, with exceptions, were not his. He took one at random, sat down, and began to read. It was Morris's *Birds* and held him.

The church clock across the square struck a triple chime; a quarter to five. I shall be late if the train isn't, and in the car, threading his way through the clangour of the tramway-cross where a brown, wiry boy with eyes like a starling's stood on the pavement-edge with spade and bucket, he remembered that, in childhood, there is personality in a bucket; it is a proud, adventurous bucket with a legend and a future, just as a spade is a friendly, faithful spade, though a trifle dull because made of wood. An iron spade would be better. But it is dangerous, like all desirable things: when you are older, an iron spade: when you are older—everything. Eighteen, he had long supposed, when it lay in a remote future, to be the age of final emancipation, the age at which you became, not a man among men as you had been hitherto a boy among boys, but suddenly a god, free, all doors open, absolute master.

The train was in when he reached the platform. Small luggage was being handed down, and already there was a group round the van. George was left alone to stare at the engine, feeling, because it interested him so little, that youth had gone out of him. Every railway station has its

own smell; years do not change it. Ancaster smelt of asphalt
and the boards of waiting-rooms—a chill, school-going
smell—but Chelmouth had the scent of spick and span,
of varnish, of the paste of bill-stickers and, one would
swear, of tarry rope and the sea. Under the influence of
memories which presented themselves to him as actual
perception, George felt his grudging reluctance to waste
time with these strangers fall from him. He wanted suddenly to find them, to look after them, to take them out
into the sun, to hear them exclaim as he drove them through
the golden air: Look, there's the sea. Bathing to-morrow!
The flowers were in the car, for there had been no time
to leave them at the hotel. The girl would be pleased
when she saw them. Women were affected beyond his
understanding, beyond even the beauty of the thing itself,
by a gift of flowers. Oh, how lovely! how lovely! she
would cry, and put her face into them. Poor things, they
need water. At once . . . I'll give them water at once.

A picture of her, standing by his car and behaving
in this way, rose so sharply in his mind that he was
astonished by it, for what voice she had he didn't know,
and in his imagining there could be no face—yet there
had been no absence of a face. He had asked before
he left the Rectory how he should distinguish the elderly
man and the girl whom he was to meet. If you keep
your eyes on the hotel porter you'll see them go up to
him, Helen had answered, but you won't mistake Mary
—even you. When he had asked how tall she was and
whether her hair was dark or light, he had been told that
he must answer that for himself. In some lights her hair
was golden, but that isn't how one knows her, Helen had
added. She is like no one else you have seen. But George,
being a man of common sense, had determined to keep
his eye on the hotel porter, and was soon rewarded by
seeing, in the little knot of travellers that surrounded the
gold-laced cap, a man in a fawn raincoat with a young
girl at his side—a man at once sad and aggressive, with
laced boots, finely crackled beneath a cautious polish, and
a blue, starched cuff fallen about his wrist. His eyes moved

uneasily, then settled on the porter whose attention he had failed to attract and, seemingly, dared not compel. He waited in an attitude of irritated patience, his arms pressed to his sides, his head up like a penguin's. In one hand he held a small gladstone bag on which his name, D. W. Leward, was impressed. George hesitated, looking from him to the girl—a squat girl in blue serge with a sallow, high-cheeked face and a large medallion of butterfly-wing on a chest more abundant than her years. The sight of her confused him, but, going up to the man, he introduced himself and explained why he had come. Mr. Leward answered with a nervous distrust which thawed suddenly when he had had time to understand that a show of affability and good-will was required of him. Then he held out his free hand, allowed his teeth to appear under his moustache, and said: "Ah yes. Dr. Hardy. . . . Of course. . . . My daughter was speaking of your sister not five minutes ago. . . . She's over there, waiting for the trunks." He took a couple of paces towards the group at the luggage van and prodded a girl between the shoulders.

"Wake up, Mary; here's Miss Hardy's brother come to meet us."

The girl turned, her body first, because her father's thumb was at her shoulder-blades, then completely, so that there was for an instant, before she faced him, a lithe swing of her hips and a backward toss of her head swift and boyish in their vitality. George, thankful that after all it was not the butterfly medallion he had come to meet, thought, while she was moving: What a lovely child! and looked at her.

He continued to look at her without embarrassment that any bystander might have observed. He took her hand and, remembering the shyness of the very young, talked to cover her shyness. But he was pierced by an emotion so sweet, so painful, so charged with wild, stabbing remembrance of loves that were dead in him and of imagined loves unborn, that he could say nothing more illuminating than that he had believed *that* girl—the one in blue serge

—to be the Miss Leward he was to meet. She looked at the blue serge, then back to him, seemingly not aware of any particular point in what he had said. "Did you?" she answered. "Because she was standing next to Father, I expect." Then: "What's the bathing like? Is it warm? Where's the tide in the morning—in or out?" Such a light in her face—as though she were looking from a window on to a scene that entranced her. He felt suddenly happy and enlightened, as though, by her, the stain were being lifted from his experience of mankind and he reprieved of his distrusts. It added to his delight that in her face was no recognition of his wonder—only a friendly puzzlement because he couldn't for the life of him remember whether after breakfast the tide would be up or down.

Mary had seen a man enter into conversation with her father, and, having no interest in him, had kept her eyes on the luggage-van, hoping that he would soon go and leave them free to make their way out of the station. Twice before, in her childhood, she had been at Chelmouth, in lodgings. She remembered the long curve of the esplanade; the churning barrel-organ of the blind man, the smell of his dog, the clink of her penny in his tin mug; she remembered the bandstand, the scarlet uniforms, the gleam of brass, the gaiety of the throng that moved always to and fro, the cool, salty breezes that had made her hungry. She wanted to drive away from the station and re-discover all her memories. Her holiday sparkled before her. Extravagant or not, she would enjoy it. She wanted to begin—not to loiter on a railway platform with middle-aged acquaintance.

When her father compelled her to turn round, she had felt the stranger's hand tighten on hers and seen his face alter. Her attention, which had been but little given to this encounter, swung in on him suddenly. His expression was illumined by an extraordinary calm, as though for an instant confusions had left him and his mind become single. She did not know how to interpret what she saw, but she smiled intuitively to welcome its generosity and warmth, its freedom from that glint of acquisitiveness to which, in men, her beauty had accustomed her. It's as if he were going to change into something before my eyes, she thought, but she was glad to find that, in talk, he was simple and undemanding, not taxing her with compliments or with parades of wit. She liked conversation to be dull at first; she liked to feel the ground of acquaintance under her feet, and to know that she was being helped, not waited upon or challenged. Dr. Hardy put her at ease, talking of her journey a little, of his sister a little, of nothing much, unafraid of commonplace which, she felt with friendly sympathy, was as necessary to him as to her.

They drove to the hotel in his car, she sitting between him and her father, holding the flowers he had given her. He asked whether she drove and, when she explained that she had just learned, wishing to please Peter, he glanced at her with a grave, light smile as though he thought she was, without knowing it, talking nonsense.

"Peter Darkin, you know. I'm engaged to him."

"Yes, I know."

"Son of Sir Wilmot Darkin," her father said. "Old friend of mine. Fine cricketer too. Likely for Kent, they say."

"So my sister told me." Then, turning again to her, George asked: "He's not here yet?"

"Not until the day after to-morrow. Thursday—that's right isn't it, Father?"

"You ought to know, my dear."

They had entered the garden of the hotel and were drawing up at the steps. Over tea, George talked to her father, arranging that they should all drive out to the Rectory on Saturday. After luncheon they would go over Sparkenbroke House, which was open to the public on Saturday afternoons.

"Only on Saturdays?"

"If you had come a week earlier, I could have taken you over at any time," he said. "Lady Sparkenbroke doesn't mind. But Sparkenbroke comes home from Italy to-night or to-morrow morning."

"Do you know him very well?" Mary asked.

"I've known him all my life. His half-brother and I were more of an age but I was pretty close with Piers and am still when we meet, which isn't often nowadays. As close as anyone can be with one who—anyhow we go on where we left off."

She put down her cup. "What's he like?"

George tugged at his ear. "Like? I don't think he goes into two words."

"No," she said. "It was only that I've been reading some of his poems, and I felt that to someone—someone who knew him as well as you do—he couldn't be the ogre people say he is."

"Do they say that? A doctor, if he's interested in the mind as well as in the body, doesn't believe much in ogres." Then, looking at her, he added: "Men of genius—or women of great beauty—aren't altogether to be envied. They are more helpless than ordinary people—like a ship in a storm with too much sail set. And you can't help genius or beauty. You're not within reach of them. You watch, that's all."

Though he said what he felt, there was neither self-pity nor the vanity of opinion in what he said. As he turned away to speak to her father, who had been complaining to the waiter that the cakes were stale, she knew that his expression at their first encounter had sprung from the same impulse as his words, and liked and trusted him.

"Well, Miss Leward," he said, "I shall be in Chelmouth on Saturday morning. I'll call here about a quarter to one. Then, if Mr. Darkin has his two-seater, we can all go out to the Rectory without crowding."

She thanked him, and for his having come to meet them. She sent messages to his sister.

"Oh, and the flowers! They did come to life, you know, almost at once when they had a drink."

"I'll tell her," he said. "And you must come out to us all the time you can spare. You'll do Helen all the good in the world. There's not much life in Sparkenbroke Green, and she seldom moves beyond her lawn."

He wrote Saturday's engagement in his diary and was gone.

"I like Dr. Hardy," Mary said.

"Well—yes," her father replied.

"So doubtful?"

Mr. Leward did not always answer his daughter's questions. "I don't think, my dear, I should talk about Lord Sparkenbroke too much," he advised, and added with the pale joviality of a cautious man on a holiday who would not seem repressive: "Just a hint, you know."

"Not talk about him? But why?"

"It's not—well—it's not a very *safe* subject in mixed company."

"But with Dr. Hardy . . ."

"Well, Mary, you may be wiser than your old father. And it won't be much longer that I shall be responsible for you. But in hotels and places it doesn't do for a young girl like you to talk about whatever comes into her head and take men at their face-value. I dare say Dr. Hardy's all right. No doubt he is. Still, when you're engaged, you can't be too careful not to cause little misunderstandings. I didn't altogether care for the way he looked and talked. There are many country doctors who wouldn't be quite so keen to profess friendship with a man like Sparkenbroke. . . . It's not a pleasant reputation you know. . . . You can't be too much on your guard, my dear, one way and another."

With that, he went upstairs. After dinner, he decided that they would not go out. They sat, side by side, in a corner of the lounge, listening to the hotel orchestra.

"Couldn't we go in and watch them dancing?"

"And stand about looking as if you wanted to dance?"

"But I do."

"Peter will be here on Thursday," he said conclusively. She opened her book. "I think this is the best corner of the lounge," he added with a small, silent yawn. "Out of the draught."

D

CHAPTER FOUR

MARY was very little on her guard. She was not unaware of her power over men; indeed, during the past year, she had begun to feel sorry for them because, in the manner of their staring at her, they were so helplessly alike; but she had a habit of forgetting her power, being more interested in the upbringing of her puppy, in the plantains that interfered with the tennis lawn at home, and, recently, in poetry. Poetry surprised her. At first you didn't like it; except when it sang a song, you didn't, at first, like it at all; it was nothing except a kind of rumble and sometimes it wasn't even that. Then, suddenly, you liked it; it came to you like skating. To start with you were terribly proud because you could do it, but soon you didn't feel proud at all, but happy because you could shut yourself up in it —like going into a cathedral or a garden or a very cool, empty room out of a street with trams. No one she knew felt like that about poetry; at least, they didn't tell her about it and she didn't tell them.

She tried to tell Peter about it on Thursday night because she felt that she ought to share everything with the man she was to marry. They were sitting, between dances, in one of the window-seats of the ballroom.

"Well," he said, "what have you been doing with yourself since you came here?"

"Swimming," she answered. "Walking a bit. Taking Father to listen to the band. Watching him play billiards. And reading." She looked up. "It is *lovely*, Peter. Do you think you'll enjoy yourself too?"

"With you? You bet I shall. What an infant you are!"

"I didn't mean *me*. I meant Chelmouth—staying here. It is the kind of place you like, isn't it?"

He smiled at his hostess. "What gave you the idea?"

"Of what?"

"Coming here."

"It was Father's idea. You see we'd been before, when I was small."

"This hotel?"

"No. Rooms."

And though she had wished to forget Warlingham and to think this evening of nothing but dancing; though she had hoped Peter would ask her what she had been reading and give her a chance to tell him, under the music, how wonderful the bits about the owl and the rabbit were in *The Eve of St. Agnes*, the anxieties of her home invaded her.

Her father had said one day that, she having been to stay with Peter's family at Darrington Park, Peter must be invited to stay with them, and had added swiftly, as though the project had long been in his mind: But not here. We can't entertain him in this house. You would have to wait on him. Before she could answer, he had continued: We will go to Chelmouth in June and stay at the hotel and ask him there. Swimming, tennis, golf, dances in the evening—that will give you both something to do. From a drawer he had taken out a mauve prospectus with the name of the Grand Hotel Sparkenbroke stamped on it in silver.

But, she had said, can we afford to stay at a hotel like that?

He had answered that there was some money put by.

Invested money? But, Father, you have said so often that one mustn't ever "sell capital for current needs."

He smiled thinly at this echo of himself. This was the time to spend, he said, and, the barriers down, he spent lavishly, giving her for new clothes more money than she commonly spent on them in two years. You see, he said, we can adjust it, and she had guessed that he was cheating his private accounts as he sometimes cheated at patience.

He was standing now, propped against the door of the ballroom. She smiled at him as she and Peter swept past in the next dance. Though he nodded, the nod was an anxious one and his eyes followed them.

"I think I'll sit out one with Father," she said. "He looks such a miserable old thing. And worried."

"What's he worried about?"

She wondered. Was it money? Or just that he couldn't dance and—

"Peter!" she said. "I found a poem you'd like."

"A what?"

"A poem about cricket."

"Oh."

He did not want to talk while he danced. His mind was differently occupied.

"But it's a real poem," she said. "Not just a cricketing rhyme. It's by Francis Thompson."

He did not answer and she thought: Peter's right, one oughtn't to talk. To dance well was pleasure enough; to dance well was to forget everything, your weight, your body, your partner, to swing brilliantly on air, suspended by threads of music and light; and she yielded herself to it, a smile sleeping between her lips. A coolness that seemed an undercurrent of music drifted in from the sea, and even when she was not dancing the enchantment of rhythm dwelt in her. To begin a new dance was to continue the last, and soon, if a voice spoke at her shoulder, she opened her mind as one opens the door of a lighted room and looks out into the night. Once, in such a moment of recall, she had become aware of Peter, and been frightened, as though she had awakened from sleep to find him staring into her face; but the warning had slipped away with her flying thoughts. When dancing was over and they had said good-night to her father, she felt nothing, as Peter walked with her down the passage to her room, but the delightful burden of sleep upon her lids.

"Sleepy too?" she said.

He did not answer. He seized her hand and she let it lie in his. Because she was happy she would have swung their hands to and fro, but was checked by a stiffening of his arm.

At her door, he kissed her; she had lifted her face to be kissed. "Breakfast at any time," she said, her fingers on the handle, but he did not go. He came forward, took hold of her body and, with blind, plunging head, began to kiss her. For an instant, not yet perceiving by what force he was driven, she would have responded, but her little response was lost, and she herself blinded, as though she were being beaten upon by fists in darkness. Her breath came again, a long, crying breath; she struggled and broke free. He stood over her, dazed and rooted, his shoulders up, the electric light glowing through the angry pink of his ears.

"Well," he said. "Well? You didn't fight when we were dancing."

The strength was out of him. When she began to open the door, he shuffled but did not advance. The door being shut, his footsteps moved off, heavily, as though he were old.

Inside, alone, she kicked off her shoes, and, with the mechanism of shock, began to undress. In mid-floor, a part of her clothing fallen from her, she became still suddenly, like iron awake, her eyes fixed, the loop of a ribbon stiff over her thumb. When she moved again and finished her undressing, she was cold. In spite of her father's protests against the folly of it, she had brought with her from home an oil painting, a small landscape with figures, that had been lent her by the artist. She gazed at it now, shivering, unable to understand why it had once had power to make her happy.

She lay down upon her bed, prepared to think herself into wisdom and calmness. It must have been my fault, too; I drift away so foolishly; I wasn't thinking of him while we were dancing, but he thought I was and so— With her face burrowed into her pillow, she decided that men were different from women. She would not be angry with Peter or repel him even in her thought.

She wished to believe that what had frightened her was
a part of love itself which she had feared because she did
not understand it. Because I don't love him yet, she added.
Not *love* him. He knows that. I did tell him, I did tell him;
but she felt that, perhaps, she was behaving wrongly, was
being unfair, and she plunged for reassurance into the past.
Other men had proposed to her; she had refused them. They
had proposed with a rashness and violence that had transformed them suddenly from acquaintances into strangers
—as though they had been drinking, she had thought; and
she had said no as she would have said it to a madman
who invited her to throw herself from a cliff. Of these
men she had not spoken to her father, but, because Sir
Wilmot Darkin was an old friend of his, she had told
him of Peter, expecting him to say of this, as he did of so
much else: Plenty of time to think of that kind of thing
when you are older. Instead, looking at her in a new way,
eager and envious, over the pouches of his eyes, he had said:
Well, what of it?

I refused—of course. And perceiving, in the twist of
his mouth, that he was angry with her, she had added:
I hardly know him, do I? Just that week at Darrington
last summer. In London once or twice with his sister or
Lady Darkin. Then Darrington again this Christmas. You
see——

I've known his father long enough. Since pretty early
consular days—in Italy—must be more than twenty
years ago. You can take the credentials from me. Don't
you like the boy?

Yes, I do, but——

She had been surprised to hear herself giving reasons
for not entering into a marriage that she had never contemplated. Besides, she had said, they are in a different
class from ours.

How—different? Don't you believe it. Darkin may
give himself airs now he has a handle to his name, and
he may live at Darrington Park instead of on a pension
at Denescroft, Warlingham, Surrey, but it doesn't come
to much.

I mean: we are poor.

Well? The young man wants you, doesn't he?

The unexpected hardness of her father's voice had pierced her, and, remembering it, she was pierced again, and screwed a corner of her sheet between her fingers. It had been in January; behind her father's head there had been ridges of snow on the window-frame and the room had been filled with a harsh, glinting light. Ceasing to look at her, he had stooped down to make the hearth tidy, and, when she took the brush from him, he had said: Of course, you must follow your heart. You mustn't be guided by me.

But her heart had told her nothing decisive. She had enjoyed playing tennis with Peter and swimming with him in the bathing-pool at Darrington; if they had already these tastes in common, they would find others. She liked him; she was very fond of him when he laughed like a great boy and made her feel that she was the elder and the wiser of the two. Dear Peter, she thought. But I don't love you, Peter. I don't love you. You know that? she had said when again he asked her to marry him.

That will come.

Will it? Are you sure?

Sure. You're so young.

That's why. I don't know what love is.

He had stared at her, his face puzzled and alarmed. I say, Mary, don't you—I mean, don't you know—at all? I mean—children and——

Yes, she had answered. I have been told that. That isn't what I mean. I mean—love.

Well?

In the mind.

Oh—in the mind!

He had flicked a squash-ball into the air with his thumb.

Three days later, when at last she had been persuaded to say yes, she would marry him, she had added breathlessly, before he could kiss her: When I'm nineteen, I will.

He had kissed her and held her, deaf to the condition.

Afterwards he remembered it. She didn't mean that they must wait until next year?

January.

But why?

That's part of the promise, Peter.

But why—why for God's sake? It's not sense.

Because—I've told you—I don't love you—yet.

Twining the sheet across her knuckles, she remembered the words and spoke them again in her mind as if he were present and she trying still to persuade him. In the morning she would go to him and say—but in the morning would it not be better to say nothing? Everything would be easier when morning came; they would swim, and talk about the things that interested him. He was clever, in his own way. He wasn't just an athlete; he was interested in motor-cars and aeroplanes, and clever with his hands. He would be pleased when she told him that she had gone twice a week to the garage in Warlingham to learn about the inside of a car, and she resolved to ask him whether there was not some way in which one could do without gear-changes. Perhaps Peter himself would become an inventor and the difference that now lay between them be forgotten in the work they would do together. She began to plan their life, thinking that they would always look for the good in each other and that she would learn to love him in whatever way brought him happiness and peace.

Such was the power of youth and the sea air that her eyelids began to close. She knew that, if she did not at once turn off the light at her side, it would be burning still when she awoke in the morning; and, stretching out her hand towards the switch, she remembered the gas-bracket which hung over the dressing-table in her bedroom at home and contrasted its inconvenience and its tulip-shaped glass with this silken lamp now within reach of her pillow. I'm a child to be so pleased by staying in a hotel, she said under the darkness, and again she tried to think of Peter and of love; but only the private delights of her holiday appeared through her sleepiness, and she re-

membered that to-morrow she would eat meals she had
not ordered, be waited upon by servants for whom she was
not responsible, and read—if neither Peter nor her father
had made too many plans for her—without counting the
hours. If she finished her book she could wander through
Chelmouth on her way to change it, perhaps along the
front where the band would be playing, perhaps up the
hill and through Regency Crescent into the Old Town.
There she would look down on to the boats and barges
laid up in the estuary of the Chel, and walk on to the
harbour itself, where one of the steamers might be landing
passengers.

On the way home she would go to the Circulating
Library and buy one of Lord Sparkenbroke's novels in
a cheap edition, or another volume of his poems. Ought
she to spend three-and-six? After all, she had fourteen
pounds of her own in the post office and Lord Sparkenbroke's novels seemed always to be out of the Circulating Library in Angel Square. She would buy one
of them—*The House of Glasbury*, or *The Open Room*, or
Grant's Fortune, or, perhaps, *Elizabeth Farrant*, which,
Dr. Hardy said, had a part of its scene in Chelmouth
and a part in his own village, Sparkenbroke Green.
She would buy *Elizabeth Farrant* and make it last, reading it very slowly; it would be a memento of her holiday;
and she thought: I must read some of it to-morrow
so that when Dr. Hardy comes next day to take us to
Sparkenbroke I shall be able to recognize the places it
describes. Would Peter dislike being taken, as a tourist,
to Sparkenbroke House? Already he had given signs of
being irritated by the name of Sparkenbroke. Sparkenbroke Hotel. Sparkenbroke Arms. Sparkenbroke Grotto.
Everything in Chelmouth seems to be Sparkenbroke! he
had exclaimed. I've not much use for an English landowner who spends nine-tenths of his time abroad—
slacking in Italy. By all accounts, though he may be a
damned fine writer, he's a pretty bad hat. He *is* a fine
writer, she had answered, but Peter would not discuss
him. Now, now, he had said, patting her, don't let's waste

our time arguing, and he had begun to kiss her, holding her more and more closely, which was his way of ending all discussions except those on cricket and golf.

At the Rectory and among the tourists at Sparkenbroke House, he won't be able to kiss me, she thought, and, perceiving a renewed failure in herself, she wondered how long must pass before she was as he wished her to be. Why was love so different in two people and why so different from what she had read of and imagined? Dear Peter, she said. Until to-night, he had been very patient with her; she understood that now. In the morning, she would not let him feel guilty. She was fortunate and foolish, and there was time to learn before January.

January! Her mind leapt to quick alarm, as though, in counting the months, she were taking the measure of a locked room. But her pillow's softness assured her that she need not fear, for love, when she understood it, would make everything easy. January was far off. She was so young that all the months were years to her; no consequence was eternal. Life was fluid still, for it is passion fixes it, as death the face at last. To her, love was a distant miracle that would redeem her youth and fulfil it, a mild Jesus to come, servant to her hope; not a Christ to storm and break her.

CHAPTER FIVE

THREE nights in Chelmouth had not changed her habit of awaking at seven, and she looked at her watch for the satisfaction there was in defying it. Here she might breakfast when she would. To read in bed at this hour was to do what was impossible at Warlingham. For this reason she reached out an arm for her volume of Sparkenbroke's verses and settled down to feel her leisure, but she was too alive for any book, too eager for the day, and presently was at her window, leaning out. As she moved about her room, brushing out her hair and choosing the clothes she would put on, she smiled because the sun glittered on the brushes Peter had given her and because she had time to waste. Even her bath amused her. The towels were larger and heavier than those she docketed in her father's linen cupboard; they pleased her because she had no concern in the mending of them; and she discovered a dozen occasions for turning the bright taps on and off, remembering, while the water jetted from them, the scarce, reluctant flow of those at home. She was accustomed to a sick, flaky enamel and to window-panes of coloured glass; for years she had bathed in water tinged with rusty shadow. Here, when she moved, a luminous green curled about her and, if she lay still, considering the powder of bubbles on her limbs, she was entranced by the refracted streaks of sunshine below the surface of the water.

When at last she was dressed and crossing the hall, having on a cotton frock sprigged with cornflower blue that had not been worn before, so quick a sense of well-being and independence tingled in her that she threw up her

head and turned from her course, deciding suddenly that
she would go for a walk before breakfast. It was the
pleasanter to change her mind arbitrarily because to do so
was contrary to her habit. She had too much character
to have the character of wilfulness; in small things and
in great, she did her job and kept her word; this, in her,
was not submissiveness, but pride. Therefore, if she
had promised to breakfast at nine, she would have kept
no one waiting; but this morning she was bound by no
promises, and, as she went through the hall, where a
draught from the doors tightened the cornflower sprigs
over her and flooded her for an instant with a naked
coolness and joy, those among whom she passed—the
reception clerk at his desk, the cashier at his ledger, the
page with his lips parted to shout for "Number Sev-en-ty-
sev'n," even the old gentleman, with the legs of a groom
and the back of a grey crow, who was pecking at the
financial columns of *The Times*—were lifted out of their
occupations by her vitality. They gazed at her going, and,
for the fragment of time that gives a poet his poem, gazed,
after she was gone, at the place where she had been.

"*Sev*'nty-sev'n!" said the page.

"Six and five-eighths!" the old man protested to his
newspaper.

Ninety-four, hundred and eight, hundred and twenty-
one, said the cashier in his mind, and, writing down the
figure one, carried six to the pounds.

Soon afterwards, Number Ninety-Six appeared before
the telephone-box, which was within earshot of the re-
ception-desk.

"Just ring up to my daughter's room—ninety-one—and
make sure she's awake. These young people . . . She's
generally down before this."

"She'll miss her bathe if she doesn't get a move on,"
said the young man behind him.

The clerk leaned forward.

"The lady went out just now, Mr. Leward."

"Out! . . . Do you hear that, Peter?"

"Yes, I heard. Where did she go?"

"That I couldn't say, sir, I'm sure."

"What on earth does she want to go out for at this hour? It will be ten before she starts breakfast. Half the morning will be gone," Peter continued; then, recovering himself in part from his impatience, he added: "I'll go out and see if I can find her."

But she, following a little wooded path that led seaward from the hotel grounds, had halted in a clearing from which she might look down upon the beach as from a box in a playhouse, and had remained in its curtained solitude. Peter went into the town and came back unsuccessful in his quest but not empty-handed. To his own surprise he had bought for her a leather-bound pocket edition of Lord Sparkenbroke's works.

After an anxious glance into the dining-room, he sat down in the hall to wait for her, the parcel on his knee.

The trouble of last night would be forgotten in her gratitude. Nothing delighted a girl as much as being given a present to compensate her for having been in the wrong. And she had been in the wrong; after all, they were engaged; he didn't want to be rough with her, but what was the good of being engaged and asking him down here, and pretending that this was the kind of hotel in which she and her father could ordinarily afford to stay, if she meant to behave as though they were friends and no more? She loved him; if she didn't, she wouldn't have promised to marry him. And suddenly, the thought an attack upon his sentiment, he asked himself whether she had supposed last night that he had been leading up to— She couldn't have thought that—not of him. She must know by now that, for him as for her, marriage was— was a solemn—was a—his thought stumbled over the phrase "one flesh" and was dazzled by so sweeping an imagining of her beauty that he twisted in his chair and the parcel of Sparkenbroke fell to the floor.

The page-boy picked it up, for which he disliked the page-boy. I suppose a fellow like Sparkenbroke would know how to treat her, Peter's thoughts continued. Anyhow, he'd imagine he knew; he's had experience enough;

but experience of that kind—well, I'll keep clear of it. He was glad he had kept clear of it, not only because his abstinence gave an edge to appetite, but for her sake. "The lady's coming now, sir," said the page-boy, and Peter's fingers tightened on the string of his parcel. For her sake, he repeated, and stood up, but she was in one of her dreaming moods and did not see him. With a sharp glance at the page, who had no eyes but for the cornflower sprigs, he followed her into the breakfast-room.

"Well," he said, "where have you been?"

"I've found a hiding-place," she answered.

"From me?"

"Peter . . ." She stretched out her hand across the table.

"You were angry with me about last night."

She shook her head and began to pour out coffee.

"Yes, you were. . . . Mary, don't you understand that when two people——" But he had discretion enough not to press this lecture now. "I went into the town to look for you," he said. "And I bought these. I thought you might like them. You've talked about the man so much." He sawed at the string with a table-knife.

"Oh, Peter," she exclaimed with one of the volumes in her hands, "that was lovely of you. Specially lovely."

"Why 'specially'?"

"Well, you don't approve of Sparkenbroke, do you?"

"I don't know anything about him except what people say. And that's not to his credit. You can't know much about him yourself—his work, I mean."

"I shall now," she answered. "Besides, I've got the first volume of verse upstairs, and I've read some of the later work in anthologies and odd places. And I found *Grant's Fortune* in Miss Hardy's room at school. She didn't lend it to me. I stole it."

"Stole it?"

"Until I had finished it. You needn't be shocked, Peter. She'd have lent it to me if I'd asked her. But just at that time Lord Sparkenbroke was in all the newspapers and——"

"He generally is—or was. He manages it pretty well."

"Manages what?"

"Publicity."

"Do you really believe that?"

Peter hesitated. "Oh well, perhaps not. . . . I'll give him the benefit of the doubt if you want me to. I wish you'd go on with your breakfast instead of reading."

"I wasn't really reading," she said, turning a page. "I was only looking, and thinking about what I'm going to read. It was lovely of you, Peter. And generous."

"They didn't cost so much," he said with complacence.

Her eyes came up to him. "I didn't mean generous in that way."

"Oh, you mean last night!" he said. "That's all right. Let's forget about it."

She flashed at his dull forgiveness, but she said quietly: "I meant—only that you hate poets."

"Nothing of the kind. They make no odds to me."

"But you resent genius, Peter. A lot of men do. It's a kind of bad form, isn't it?"

"What I resent," he said, "is your idea that because a man can write he can behave as badly as he pleases and get away with it. I suppose with Sparkenbroke it's in the blood. His mother was no good."

"No good?"

"Didn't you know? She ran away with some man and lived abroad. She's dead now. When she ran away, she stole the child and took him with her. Old Sparkenbroke got him back. . . . That shows how much you know. I haven't read it myself, but *The Open Room* is supposed to be about his boyhood and the woman in it is his own mother. He's always making a song and dance about her because he was kept in Sparkenbroke House and she was never allowed to come there. I believe his poems are full of her if you read between the lines. Anything's copy I suppose to a man of that sort."

His forehead was flushed with indignation, and his light hair, growing back in smooth waves, borrowed a sharpened yellow from the contrast. Mary felt that there was something unnatural and incomprehensible in his anger; it coarsened his good looks and alarmed her. His world was, for him, frighteningly complete. That she should wish to enlarge the boundaries of her own seemed to him an affectation.

"It's not that I think what Lord Sparkenbroke has done is right, Peter," she said. "But I'm afraid of judging. It's no use pretending that there's only our sort of people in the world. I want to grow. Not shut out his work because of him."

"Oh, I know," he said. "Women are always like that about artists. Always forgiving and damned proud of it. No rule of right and wrong."

"Peter," she said, "why are you so angry? Why did you give me the books if you felt like that about Lord Sparkenbroke?"

The quietness of her voice checked his temper. "I'm sorry," he answered. "After last night, you'll laugh at me, I suppose. You can if you like. But the truth is I'm a bit of a Puritan. Anyhow there *are* standards where women are concerned. And Sparkenbroke's the kind of man that get's my goat. . . . What's more, his poetry doesn't appeal to me. I tried some in the shop. Couldn't get any swing in it."

"What did you try?"

"One of those." He touched a volume. "He seems to like dying—anyhow to envy those who do. That's what beats me. Look at that. . . . *The Caged Bird.* . . . Read it."

He pushed the book towards her and she read silently:

> *Last night I flew into the tree of death;*
> *Sudden an outer wind did me sustain;*
> *And I, from feathered poppet on its swing,*
> *Wrapt in my element, was bird again.*

She looked up. "That's an obsession with him," she said.

"What is?"

"The idea of something—some ecstasy that for him—" She hesitated. "That is the equivalent of death," she said at last, surprised at her own unaccustomed words. "It's everywhere in his early book."

"Is that it? I thought there seemed to be a lot about graveyards. A pretty old song with poets, isn't it?"

"It may be. But not with him. He doesn't moan about death. He writes about it as other men do about love. Almost as if they were the same thing. You'd think he'd known it himself, and lost it, and was looking for it everywhere."

Peter was gazing at her. "You are queer," he said, his voice hot with admiration. "Do you know, your eyes were all fiery when you were saying that? I don't care what you say, if you look like a—well, I don't know what you did look like when you were saying it. . . . I wonder what you'd think of me if I could write a love poem? Would you love me more?"

She smiled.

"I can't, you know," he said cheerfully. "Do you think you want to marry a man who doesn't see love and death as the same thing—and isn't a poet?"

"I'll try," she said, as they moved away from the table together. She was delighted that he was in good-humour again, for she blamed her own unwisdom in having ruffled him. In the hall he stopped, and she saw with surprise that he had become suddenly embarrassed and serious.

"I'd have a shot if it would please you," he said.

"At what?"

"At writing a love poem. It's chiefly knack, I expect. . . . Shall I?"

That morning they swam together. She was too eager a swimmer not to enjoy herself, but beneath her pleasure in the touch and sparkle of the water, the blaze of the sun, the sense she had of a brilliant freshness and gaiety in the world, was an unease of companionship. Her exhilaration, that would have been happiness if she had shared it, could not be shared with Peter; nor his, she supposed, with her. She lay on the sand, letting the sun shine into her blood, thinking with a smile what fun it had been when there were bathing-machines, and horses that

dragged them creaking into the waves. The rattle of
chains, the thud of the ladder as it was let down, the gaps
between the floor-planks through which appeared the
scud of shallow foam, the door-chinks that streaked the
floor with pencillings of sun—she was remembering them
all, the salty smell, the discomfort, the adventure of her
bathes in childhood. Gone now—the great cart-horses
that made cloppetty-squelches in the sand and the shouting, barefoot boys; Chelmouth, a conservative place,
must have seen almost the last of them; and, opening her
eyes, blinking into the sudden glare, she saw Peter standing
over her, staring at her wetness with an intent frown on his
face—a red face, dried now, but trickled over by little
rivulets from the yellow hair that the water had darkened.
It was as if she were seeing him for the first time—the
blunt heaviness of him, the full, curling lips, the arched
nostrils, the brow fleshily overhung; and, wondering what
to say, eager to share the morning with him, she sat up and
patted the sand, inviting him to sit beside her.

"Oughtn't you to put on a wrap or something? You'll
be cold."

"Peter, I'm toasting!"

"Well, you know, people stare," he said jealously.
"Lying about like that."

After a little while, she said: "Let's go into the water
again. I'll race you to the raft if you give me ten strokes."

"I doubt whether I ought to be in the water too much.
It spoils your eye, you know."

"Your eye?"

"Batting."

"But you won't be playing cricket for days."

He fished a piece of dried orange-peel out of the sand
and cracked it with his fingers. "Well, I'm not sure. I
promised to put through a call between twelve and one.
When he heard I'd be down here, Glazeby wanted me for
Tuesday. I'd drive over Monday afternoon and be back
here on Wednesday evening. It's a question whether he
can fix it; his side was made up. It's not far away. Only
just beyond Ancaster. You might come over and watch."

She felt herself divided from him. This morning she
had been in a mood to shut out from her all but this
morning—to rejoice with him if he would, to draw nearer
to him in understanding if he would, to say: this is our
day, let us make it—somehow—happily, memorably ours.
But he was dead to her mood, her willingness. He was
dully on edge, restless, overcast. She was all wrong for
him—all wrong—why?

Or he for her.

"Peter, dear, tell me what's wrong?"

"Wrong? Nothing."

"You're on edge. You haven't enjoyed this morning."

He turned angrily. "I want to kiss you—that's all. You
wouldn't come out by the cliff path. You would come
straight into this mob. You drive a man mad."

He was resentful and suffering, greedily beseeching.
Her heart was hardened against him. It was hardened
against her will to conciliate him. She looked into her
own mind and found herself pitiless—like stone, as though
his hurt did not belong to her.

They went to their huts to dress, and left the beach.
Mary, who had a sense of the spiritual darkness of all
quarrels, did what she could now to make amends. A
grudging silence was to her intolerable. She was so warm
in charity with the world, so well-assured that life was
no cheat if you gave your hand to it, that she had none
of the timid prides of dispute. If Peter was wrong, it was
his mood; if she, it was her folly; if both—it was past.
But he was stubborn, allowing her neither to forgive nor
to win forgiveness.

"I'll telephone here," he said, stopping at a post office.
"I may miss him if we go on to the hotel."

"I'll wait," she answered. But he told her he might be
some time getting through. She hesitated, looked at him,
received no response. "Shall I go on then?"

"You may as well."

She turned away from the sea-front into the town, her
deepest imagining of herself challenged by the darting

thought, new in its implication, that she was, after all,
not yet married to the stranger whose white flannels had
vanished behind the swing-door of the post office. To
her, though marriage itself was mistily far off, beyond
the summer, beyond the protecting autumn, betrothal
had, in theory, the finality of marriage. Those who broke
engagements belonged, with those who betrayed marriages,
to a world in which she did not recognize herself, a newspaper world, as remote from all that she inwardly accounted
real as the world of the very rich or the desperate poor
or the criminal. She expected life to be simple, and
believed that it was naturally so. You made your decisions
and stood by them; your friends, and were loyal to them;
you did not twist and turn. Neither love nor hatred had
touched her; she had not felt upon her the near, hot
breath of any hound of the spirit, nor screamed in the
snare. To betray was to betray. To fail was to fail.

Never complain, Miss Hardy had said at school.
Make no excuses—except for others. Face the consequences; you are the cause of them.

From Peter and responsibility to him Mary's thoughts
sped away, on a gust of relief, to George Hardy, with
whom, she told herself, she had been friends at first
sight. He, like his sister, would face consequences without
flinching, but he would not add: you are the cause of
them. Feeling that, if she were to meet him now, his
companionship would steady her, she looked up and
down the street as though his hard-set, lively figure might
appear. Even when this fancy had passed, she remained
ill at ease, lonely, unaccountably expectant. Of what? She
was standing at the pavement's edge, and an errand-boy's
bicycle, propped against the curb, slipped and clattered
at her feet. It seemed the first of a sequence of happenings with which she was familiar; not the clash of the metal
but the sound's familiarity startled her, and she began at
once to cross the street, thinking: I must go back to the
hotel soon; but, seeing before her a little side-lane,
Merton's Passage, that climbed the slope on which Chelmouth was built, she made towards it.

In Merton's Passage she was at a loss; she hesitated, as though she had missed a trail, and was about to turn back. What is it that makes you feel that you've done something, or been somewhere, before? Suddenly the feeling goes, she thought, and there you are, like a fool, in Merton's Passage, wondering what on earth brought you there. But I'll look at that book-shop before I go. She might find a cheap guide to the district; old second-hand guides were often the best; and she went up the hill a few paces to where, under a shabby, fringed awning, troughs of books leaned against a shop-front.

She found no guide-book and soon forgot that she was seeking one, for she had come upon a volume of which she had not heard before, the *Liber Amoris* of Hazlitt, and, drawn by the name, she stumbled into its network of brilliance and torment, of profound suffering and vain self-pity, knowing not what to make of it, but held to the page. Held until, suddenly, the analysis having no key in her experience, she could read no more. She closed the book, but had it still in her hands, pressed against her, when she became aware, at the edge of her glance, that she was being watched by two men—a knotted little fellow in shirt-sleeves, with a grey parrot-tuft, looped, melancholy eyes, and silver watch-chain, and, at his side, not yet fully emerged from the interior shadow, a taller and younger figure, from which the impression that she received was less of static appearance than of movement, attack, penetration. She knew only that he was very dark—"blackness" was the form in her mind—and that he was leaning against the door-post, his head stooped under the lintel.

Suddenly remembering that her own head was bare, she saw it with burning imagination, as though she were spectator of herself. The depths of her hair were tawny dark; so it swung in to the temples and so was slashed at fall and curve; but its surfaces, its brilliant planes, its upward leap and splendour, were now, in the eye of the sun, of light's own texture. She blazed with pride; and was ashamed. Joy sprang in her like a fountain, and she was afraid of her joy. She would not look up, but pressed close into the threadbare shadow of the awning, which sparkled her hands and breast with fine arrows of sun.

Looking at the shopkeeper but not beyond him, she said: "Have you a guide—I mean, something about Sparkenbroke House?" The loops at the man's eyes began to draw and pucker; she thought he would laugh at her; but a hand from behind grasped his arm warningly, the two exchanged a glance, and the shopkeeper said: "You won't find one there, miss. They're mostly snapped up when they come second-hand. But if you'll step inside, I'll see if I can pick one out."

She obeyed him and stood within, her back to the door, the customer behind her. She knew that he would speak, but he did not; there was no sound but the creak of the shopman's ladder and the soft slide and clack of books being taken from and returned to upper shelves. The voices of passers-by drifted in through the open door. He's gone into the street, she thought; there's no one behind me; and she was glad—he frightened her, black against the door, staring at her hair; he was hateful, staring; she was glad he was gone; and she was desolate in the ebb, crying in her heart for the stiff, dark wave that had formed over her and swept her to so fierce a speed and let her drop. And now I'm lying to myself, she said. He is there. She hated him, and stood still.

"I'm afraid there's nothing on Sparkenbroke worth reading," he said.

She turned, and saw before her a man, not young, for he was of the generation that had been young during the war, nor sturdily matured as Dr. Hardy was, but of an indefinable age, separate from hers but not cut off. He was less dark than she had supposed, for though the hair, lying away from the forehead, was so deeply black that the amber of the window-glare was held distinctly, and not diffused, in its lights, the face had none of the thick shadowiness that may clog the features of very dark men. The eyebrows were bold, delicate lines, carried outward in fine continuation beyond the eyes; the nose and upper

planes of the cheeks had, amid the general warmth of the
skin, an exceptional pallor, being clear-drawn to the bone;
the sharp, sculptured indenting of the upper lip, the deep
shadow of the lower, the compact mobility of the mouth
itself, and, above all, the lustre of the eyes, deeply caverned
by the brow, gave to the face that strange character of
contradicted nobility, of beauty frustrate without but
inwardly burning, that appears sometimes in the young
men, at once spiritual and dissolute, whose vitality shines
down from the canvases of the seventeenth century.

To Mary it was a face out of its time, foreign to her experience, and she fell back upon commonplace for defence.

"Oh," she said, "I'm sorry. I believe it's a very interesting place."

"I believe it is."

"If you haven't seen it," she told him, because she did
not wish to seem afraid or ill-humoured, "to-morrow is
tourists' day you know—Saturdays from two to six."

"Are you going to-morrow?" he asked.

"Not to-morrow," and she added, stumbling over this
unaccountable lie. "At least, I'm not sure. Our plans aren't
quite fixed."

"Better in the woods," he said.

"The woods?"

"If you go over Sparkenbroke House, what do you want
to see there? Architecture? Or the pictures? . . . Or the
mirrors?"

"Why, is there anything special about the mirrors?"
Without knowing why, she felt that this must have been an
ignorant question, for a smile had begun to appear on his
face, and she hurried on: "No: what I like is to imagine
people living there. Think of coming down to breakfast,
alone, in a room as big as a church, and having to walk a
quarter of a mile if you forget a handkerchief."

"Perhaps," he said, "noblemen don't need handkerchiefs and have breakfast in bed."

"I should hate that. It wastes the day. Besides, in a big
house, the trays would have to be carried so far, everything
would be cold."

"That's true. . . . So if you were Lady Sparkenbroke," he added, "his lordship would get up for breakfast?"

"What do you mean?"

"He might prefer to go without."

"Why?"

She was lost, not hearing what he said, her thoughts adrift, and, to bring her back, he changed his tone, telling her that there was an old steel engraving of Sparkenbroke House in the picture-shop at the corner of King William Street. He talked so quietly and lovingly of pictures that she was reassured, and stayed while he told her of Italy, making canvases that she had never seen glow in her mind. "I'm going to Italy," she said. "Next year." But she found that there were two Italies; one that she would visit with Peter, which, though sunnier and bluer than Chelmouth, did not greatly differ from it in kind, and another that filled her, as she contemplated it, with golden, new excitement. Her body ached as though an unspeakable delight were slipping away from her. "It must be lovely," she said. "Lovely. . . ." Then, awaking: "I wonder where the shopman is? I ought to go." She looked at her watch. "Oh, I *must* go."

When she was gone, the bookseller emerged.

"Who's your client, Sigberry?"

"Couldn't say, I'm sure, m'lord. Visitor I expect."

CHAPTER SIX

SATURDAY brought so hot a morning that, after breakfast, Miss Hardy's couch was carried on to that part of the lawn where the Rectory's shadow fell, and there her brother came to her before he set out for Chelmouth. Didn't she think that, when their guests came, they might feed in the open air?

"It makes work," she said. "But for once, George, you shall be spoiled."

He answered with a laugh: "She's your guest, you know."

His sister's eyebrows went up. "She was; but since you went to meet them at the station I've begun to think of her almost as your adopted child. Have you ever before made a special journey into Chelmouth to bring out ice?"

"They're going to be good ices. I've superintended the mixture," he answered. "Cook and Joanna think I'm mad. Father will like them."

"Ought he to at his age?"

George nodded. "The very old and the very young ought to be spoiled."

"Which am I?" his sister asked. "You spoil me."

He took off his hat and, standing beyond the shade, felt the sun on his forehead. Above the solid, square, white-washed house, an isolated cloud was floating, fat and snowy, like the puff of a bursting shell. "It's a good world," he said. Then, picking up her hand: "It is a good world still, isn't it, Helen? For you, I mean?"

"But I'm getting better, George! Last summer, I couldn't walk round the garden as I can now."

She lay still when he was gone, her hands folded over

her book, thinking: When I'm dead and Father's gone too, George will be alone. The house, that had been a farm, was their own; it would not pass with the living; and she wondered whether George would stay in it. Was he genuinely content to practise in Sparkenbroke Green and the near countryside? He might go to Chelmouth if he would; already he had patients and a consulting-room there; or he might go back to London. Was it for her sake and her father's that he stayed? Was it for their sake or because Sybil Chantery had died before he could marry her that he remained unmarried? Or was he, in his heart of hearts, content, as he seemed? Resigned or content?—she didn't know, though she knew him so well. Not "resigned"—that was too grey a word to describe him—but she knew of her own knowledge that acceptance may borrow the colours of happiness, sometimes even deceiving the wearer, and yet be different from happiness itself. He was younger than she. All her life, until life brought her down, she had had the habit of safeguarding him, and all her life she had had a horror of the warping of active men by the old and the sick. Her precise, reasonable spirit rebelled against it. She loathed untidiness, confusion, misunderstanding; she couldn't endure that any of life's rooms should be cluttered up with self-sacrifice. But she was uncertain of George's mind. Since the war, his ambition had gone—or been changed. But I don't want money or fame, he had said to her. And I hate towns. I want to do my work here—*here*, in this place. It stands for what lasts and what I care for. The faster the world grows and the more it fights and kills and shouts and grabs, the more valuable what's left of the country becomes—and the people in it. You needn't think I'm pining for Harley Street. And I shan't go to sleep with Chelmouth Hospital to keep me awake. It may be true, she thought, for him—or he may think it is: which isn't quite the same thing, for illusions about ourselves pass—and then where are we?

But the girl's a child, she said. Anyhow, he thinks she is. There's not a grown woman on earth that would set George fussing about ices and lemonade. She closed her eyes, resting actively and with determination, thinking deliberately of the slackness of each limb, for that, if one could not fall asleep, was the way to rest with profit. When the guests came, she would be a lively, intelligent woman, not to be pitied or passed over, but to be received by the living as one of themselves.

Because this impulse was strong in her, she was not an easy hostess to the company that came to her lawn. Her aim as schoolmistress had been not to impose teaching but to meet each child on its own ground, discovered to it by herself. The same purpose survived in her conversation, of which also she chose the ground. At school she had chosen well, having a genius to discern what interested children; but among their elders, though the vigour of her choice was unabated, a weaker intuition guided her. Peter and Mr. Leward were stubborn. Mr. Leward was considerate with cushions; he handed dishes to her and spoke a little of Italian salads; but in spite of his consular experience he had no interest in political changes under the Fascists; Italy was to him a place to be consul in, an office-building from which he had retired; what interests he had had outside that office she couldn't for the life of her discover. The price of bathing-huts on the beach at Chelmouth was, he said, a swindle, not that he was a swimmer, but his daughter was; and at his own church at home they were giving up the old tunes to the hymns. "Sometimes," she said, "the newer ones are an improvement." But even that subject he would not discuss with her; he deferred and conceded, because she was a woman, because she was an invalid, and she left him to tell anecdotes to her old father who, having an everlasting curiosity for the human species, encouraged him. Peter, she hoped, would be more productive because he was young. But when she spoke to him, his eyes moved to her cushion or her left shoulder—or was it to some tree or swinging thing behind her head? Perhaps the cat was on a branch of the sycamore? She looked; there was no cat; he was staring through her or beyond her because, for him, she and her conversation didn't exist. His mind—what mind he has!—was bent on one object only, on Mary; and, except when a vague, reluctant politeness diverted him, his eyes followed his mind.

Surveying his property, Miss Hardy thought; then, instantly, she whipped her bitterness to heel. She must beware of anger against a young man in love; it would sour her; it was "a bad sign"; and she tried to tolerate Peter and to discover sympathy with an idyll. But that this was no idyll might be read in Mary's eyes, which would not answer her lover's; nor did her avoidance seem to have even the twist of shyness in it. Watching the girl, who was listening to George's quiet, plodding conversation, Miss Hardy was surprised, for, at first encounter, the glow and impulse of Mary's beauty had troubled her. She had thought, under her smile of welcome: The child's in love. She's alight with it. I'll get no sense from her. By determination an open-minded woman, she recognized passion as a natural phenomenon which, though it made young girls embarrassing while it lasted, was no good reason for condemning them; they outgrew it, their minds returned to normal courses, and they became companionable again. But she had liked Mary better than any of her pupils; she had looked forward eagerly to her coming this afternoon, imagining her as the girl she had been, lovely, clear-minded, cool; and to perceive that she was changed, that her mind was dazzled with new ardours, had been disappointing. She won't be really interested in anything but *that*, she had thought. I shall get no kind of sense out of her.

This had been her first impression. Now, she was eager to revise it, and, seeing Peter shut out, to take Mary back into favour. With her little breasts, her throat not yet fully rounded, the tilt of her head as she listened, the steady inquiry of her eyes, she was still, in many ways, a child; and this man was nothing to her after all—except, of course, the husband who would provide for her; and yet there was in her that quiver of vitality which Miss Hardy knew well how to recognize, that air of intense expectation, half joy, half fear, with which childhood and

feminine absolutism are abandoned. Did she love this
large, blond youth? If not, what had happened to her?
Was it, after all, passion, frozen to self-consciousness,
which, in the company of others, chilled her towards
Peter? Miss Hardy looked from the girl to him. He had,
in repose, the stolid, pink solemnity, the clotted dreami-
ness, of frivolous young men who, being physically
obsessed, feel, for the first time, their minds gorged with
the excess of a single thought. His state was plain. But
Mary's?

Miss Hardy let the weight of her head drop back upon
her cushions. Her first impression had not been wrong.
The girl was in love. You could see it in the movement of
her limbs when she rose from table; you could hear it in
her voice; you might suppose that, from instant to instant,
the world was being freshly created for her—as it seemed
to be momently re-created for birds flying in the sun. She
was spell-bound—though she might be but half aware of
it—and spell-bound, presumably, by that blurred adorer.
Was it possible? Nature, Miss Hardy said within her,
when she applies herself to human beings, loses her taste;
a wry humour is substituted for it. And when, after
luncheon, George was taking the guests away to Sparkenbroke House, a disconcerting thought appeared. If I were
as beautiful as Mary, she said, I couldn't bear to submit
myself to any man. I should create my own wilderness—a
world of schoolmistresses with no children to teach! But
the truth is, she added with a smile, moving her silent lips
so that her father looked at her with curiosity, that, because I wouldn't submit, Nature has taken good care not
to make me beautiful; and I don't blame her. She must
garland her victims for the sacrifice; that's part of the joke.
Not to see it, is scarcely to be a woman.

CHAPTER SEVEN

IT was George Hardy's pride that he could do his own work and use his own leisure. He was never bored, or tormented by desire for the impossible. In his profession and his daily existence, he took risks when they were necessary, was delighted by victory and steadfast in loss; but he would no longer stake his all. There had been two revolutions in his life, the first when he fell in love, the second when the girl died; and two were enough.

He had not then played his grief to any emotional gallery, even the most secret. He had neither cried out against fate nor yielded himself to extravagant renunciations, but he had become set. Having loved once, he had retired from that emotional stage on which his part was done, and had settled down to be a generous, unembittered spectator of it.

The practice of sane living consisted not in fighting temptation—for such resistance, as often as not, created new temptations and was a cause of mental disease—but in teaching one's mind how to hold its tongue. But how is the mind to be taught? By lack of encouragement, he would have said. Treat it as you would treat a bore with a fixed idea. When it speaks dangerously of women, speak instantly of something else; don't pause to argue; change the subject, engage actively in another. To George it seemed plain enough, for he had no belief in man's helplessness or the intervention of gods. To be a martyr or a self-conscious ascetic was unnecessary. You no more fell in love without wishing, or being emotionally prepared, to do so, than you saw the traffic in a street without first

looking out of a window that gave upon the street. On the
subject of women, his mind seemed to have mastered long
ago the lesson he had wished it to receive. It told him of
much to laugh at in them and of more to admire; it showed
him their gaiety, their suffering, the unending delights of
their unreason; it instructed him in their beauty, but did
not invite him to covet it. This treaty with his mind
seemed to him the more satisfactory because it was not
built upon moral subtleties, which he distrusted, but
dictated by facts. He had no wish to marry; he was not an
adolescent or a sensualist; he had loved once; he was no
believer in magic. The conclusion that followed was comfortably final.

At his first encounter with Mary, he had struggled to
maintain it, issuing fresh commands to his impulse. She's
a child, he had said, and she is engaged to be married;
facts from which a safe conclusion should have sprung
naturally, ratifying his treaty, leaving him in peace. With
an urgency at which he could now smile in retrospect, he
had thrown up paternal walls against himself, but all of
them, though their foundations were in fact, had become
transparent, and, looking through them, he saw his own
life, which he had not hitherto known to be barren,
breaking into flower because this girl was alive. As he
walked beside her up the orchard, his eyes turned to the
colour of her cheek and the little curve of shadow in the
corner of her mouth, which presented themselves to him
as inventions of Nature made for her, not as variants of
what he had seen before in other faces. He tried to kill his
obsession by thinking of the skeleton beneath the girl's
flesh, then by mocking the extravagance of this remedy in
a man who, at thirty-seven, was at any rate old enough to
know when he was becoming ridiculous; but he failed to
laugh at himself with effect; her beauty would not be
repelled, it was invincible, it flowed back upon him as a
scent flows back upon the memory, filling him with an
emotion which, though he could still bid his mind call it
tenderness, had power to isolate her among women, so
that her voice was new, her movement new, and even the

folding of shade and sunlight upon her a new pattern. To
be loved by her would be to enter into a new life.

This recognition blazed and died. He returned doggedly
to facts. He could never be loved by her, and when she
dragged a grass from the hedgerow and held it up for him
to admire, he said that he couldn't remember its name,
though its name was standing up in his mind, for he felt
himself to be as far away from her as from a girl who had
been young before he was born or would come to youth
when he was forgotten.

The curl of shadow at the corner of her mouth moved
and vanished. She was smiling at his vagueness, at the
shake of his head. "Do try to remember. I love being with
people who really know the country." Even her smile at
his expense, a phrase or a tone suggesting that his companionship was pleasing to her, spurred him to the absurd
hopes and delusions that he remembered from his very
early manhood, and he caught himself repeating the self-
taunting, the self-enchanting phrase: "Is it possible?"
which is the music of all impossible loves. It's not that
I'm old in her eyes, he said, checking again the wild
swerve of his thought; her eyes don't see me at all; she is so
little aware of me that she is not aware even that I am
making a fool of myself. To her I am friendly, solid, kind.
I am the useful fellow who can tell her the names of
grasses or answer questions about Sparkenbroke House.

Her father and Peter lagged behind; it would be a relief
to draw them into conversation; and while they were all
climbing the slope of the orchard, he succeeded in this well
enough. Even when they had gone out through the five-bar
gate and were continuing the ascent to the cross-roads, the
little group could still be held together. "The house lies
up there," he said, brandishing his arm and walking back
a few paces that Mr. Leward might not feel he was being
neglected by his host. "There—almost on the crest of the
hill—beyond the church spire and the row of elms that
you see looking out above that hedge. . . . You can't see the
house, of course, from here," he added lamely, aware that,
against his custom, he had been talking for the sake of

talking. "The church copse and Derry's Wood hide it."
Mr. Leward gave little response; Peter none; and George
found, when he turned from them and began to walk
forward again, that Mary, having drawn a few paces ahead,
was now more clearly than ever in his view. As he came
level, she looked up, seeming to welcome his reappearance
at her side, and again he was stirred, as though her friendly
glance had the significance of an enchantment. "Father is
always slow on a hill," she said. "I expect you are used to
them. A country doctor must keep almost as fit as a
country postman."

"Unless he's lazy and uses a car."

"But you told me—do you remember, while we were
driving to the hotel?—you said you often did your local
round on foot or on a bicycle."

"You laughed at the bicycle. Sounds old-fashioned,
doesn't it?"

She looked at him swiftly, wondering, he knew, whether
she had hurt him. "Do you know," she said, "it was that,
first of all, made me like you."

"The bicycle?"

"Well, the idea of it. . . . And walking. It seemed to fit
you."

"Slow and sure?"

"Don't you like that?"

"If you do." And to save her from reply, he added at
random: "Lady Sparkenbroke laughs at me about that
bicycle."

They had reached the Cross and were turned into the
main road eastward. Between them and the wood on their
left ran the church stream, brown but translucent. On
their right, the hedgerow ceased abruptly, laying open
the valley to the south, the distant blur of Chelmouth, the
shining disc of the sea.

"Is she quite old?" Mary asked.

"Old?" He had forgotten Lady Sparkenbroke. "Thirty
or thereabouts."

"That's what I meant. . . . Peter says Lord Sparkenbroke married her for her money. That isn't true?"

E

"They were very fond of each other."

"But she *is* very rich? I mean, it's she who keeps the estate together?"

"She's Malcolm Kaid's only daughter."

"Who is Malcolm Kaid?"

"The Heavy Industries Combine."

"Peter said she was American."

"Her mother was."

Her questions, leading, he supposed, to some fixed point in her own mind, set him, in his lack of comprehension, away from her again.

"Why did you ask all that?"

Her answer delighted and reassured him. "I was wondering," she said, "whether any of his poems had been written to her—the happy ones. It must be terrible, if she's not happy now, to have the poems standing there with all the meaning gone out of them. . . . If she ever——"

"Go on," he said.

"I was going to say: if she ever really loved him. But you're on his side, aren't you? I oughtn't to have asked you all those questions."

"Why—'on his side'?"

"His friend, I mean. So naturally, against her, you stand by him."

"I'm a friend of both. At least, I hope so. I liked your speaking of her as you did."

She would have said more, but Peter shouted from behind: "Isn't that the short-cut through the churchyard? Why don't we go in over that bridge?" and George answered, yes, that was the way, and turned back.

"Had you forgotten it?" she said.

"For a moment I had."

They passed over the bridge and through the gate beyond it. Their path led uphill to the east of the church, skirting the graveyard. "Straight up into the wood?" Mr. Leward asked, and he set out, with Peter following. But Mary stood still, gazing at a great elm that rose, in open ground, between her and the Sparkenbroke tomb.

"Is this the place—he writes of?"

George, alive to the quickness of her perception, replied cautiously: "That's the Mound."

"That means everything to him—doesn't it?"

"It means a great deal."

"Why does it mean so much?" As he was silent, she continued: "You could tell me—couldn't you?—if you wanted to."

"There is an inscription on the tomb," he replied stolidly. "You can read it if you like."

The sun was shining on the entrance, and even from the distance at which they were standing it was possible to see parts of the coffins laid upon shelves within. She advanced as far as the elm-tree, then stopped.

"You can read it here," George said, standing by the tomb and pointing with his stick to the carved tympanum above the gate. "It's an old set of verses. Pretty in a way— anyhow I've always liked them, though Sparkenbroke despises them."

She did not wish to approach, but his waiting compelled her, and she took her place at his side, gazing into the interior of the tomb. He read the inscription:

> *"We also moved, as thou dost move,*
> *With pride of youth and quick in love.*
> *Have pity then, who drawest near,*
> *That love and youth are ended here.*
> *Though in sweet April thou dost shine,*
> *December waits for thee and thine."*

"Why does Lord Sparkenbroke despise that?" she asked.

"The weak jingle of the last line infuriates him. And anyhow, he says, the sentiment is false—the dead don't need to ask pity from the living."

"Does he mean that it's better to be dead?"

"Not in the sense you have in mind; not because he hates life. He sees death as one of the fulfilments—if you understand that. I'm not sure that I do. There are some other verses that—" But this sentence he broke away from abruptly. "Probably the whole place makes you miserable. An open vault upsets some people. Does it frighten you?"

"It makes me imagine," she said quietly; then, with impetuous attack: "Doesn't it you?"

He looked at her sharply, knowing that she was contrasting his stolidity with the Sparkenbroke she had created for herself. "I go as far as facts take me," he said, "but I'm not the dour materialist you suppose. I'm human enough to wonder a bit. But what is beyond the ascertained facts is the affair of poets—and I'm not a poet. I wish I were."

"Do you really wish that?"

"Yes—why not?"

"People don't usually. Peter doesn't. My father doesn't."

"Perhaps they don't say so." And he added with an emphasis of passion: "Sometimes, not to be a poet is like being changed suddenly into a dumb animal. You must make allowances for dumb animals, you know."

But she was not thinking of him. Even her little flame of anger against his rationalism had died down. She was not thinking of him at all, and as they went forward in the track of Peter and her father she thought that she no longer wished to visit Sparkenbroke House with the tourists. She did not wish to be indoors, admiring furniture, pictures, tapestries—inanimate things; and she said: "Need we go to the house at all? Couldn't they go on alone? I'd like to wander about in the woods where everything's alive. Helen said there were all kinds of little streams running through the woods here. Let's go and find them? Do say yes. Father would be angry and Peter too, but—couldn't we?"

"My dear, I can't. Besides——"

"Oh," she cried, "why is it always safe to say no? People always say: no, and miss things. Who'd care tomorrow whether I'd gone to Sparkenbroke House or not? And I should have had this afternoon. I should remember it always."

"I should, if I came," he said.

But she was too eager in her own purpose to give more than a flash of attention to his words, too far carried away from her normal sense of obligation to reflect for more than an ineffectual instant that to leave her father without knowledge of her whereabouts was an act of wilfulness that she could not defend. The light that Miss Hardy had seen and wondered at was burning in her. To enjoy these hours in freedom, to escape from Peter, to be alone—as she would, in effect, be alone, though Dr. Hardy walked at her side—presented itself to her as a necessity, and the girl she had been until yesterday and would be again, the girl who kept her word and despised, in herself and in others, the extravagances of mood, had now no part in her.

"Look at it!" she pleaded, and her arm's movement invited him to all the woods, to the streaks of gold on the tree-trunks, the receding darknesses thin-bladed with light, the imagined streams. He looked about him and at her, wondering by what wild impulse she was driven; and suddenly, made repentant of her urgency by what she saw in his eyes, she said: "Are you angry with me?"

He shook his head, unable to speak, seeing her as she had been under the elm, upright and young as a lily of the valley, her beauty quickened by the imagining of death within her, her eyes grave and fiery, her youth deepened by an intuitive wisdom, not the wisdom of age; seeing her again in the glitter of her new impulse, pleading that he should be truant with her in the woods. He yielded himself for an instant to imagination of that truancy. If he consented and put away from him the appointments he must keep that afternoon, he would become for an hour, for two hours, for three, for all of life that remained to him, the companion of her enchanted mood. To her, he would seem to have no share in it; he would be the great dog that goes with a child upon its escapade, to be returned to and played with now and then, to be forgotten meanwhile; and he would be able to express none of the passion within him—a dumb animal indeed. But he would share more of her mood than she knew.

"My God," he brought out, "angry!" and, as they encountered a steep ascent, he felt her hand glide in upon his arm.

"You pretend to be an old bear," she said.

At the farther edge of the church wood, whence the house itself was to be seen, he called to Mr. Leward and Peter. Being far away among the sloping orchards, they did not hear him and he would have called again.

"No," she said. "I don't want them to wait for me. I'll catch them up before they reach the house," and it appeared to her now that this was what she intended.

"Very well," George replied. They stood face to face, she on higher ground, he looking up at her. He said: "There's work I must do. I'll be getting back now. Come down to the Rectory when you're tired. Anyhow for tea. You'll find Helen there."

"Can't the work wait? Couldn't you come—even to the House?"

He hesitated an instant. "Better not," he answered, and moved down hill away from her.

She watched him go; presently she heard him, as she supposed, running. Running? she said, and her heart quickened in the alarm of understanding, her cheeks flushed at the blunder of not having sooner understood.

That he should love her filled her with a pity that was not pity for him personally but a desolation of heart at the frustration of human purposes in a world brilliant with joys; and, as the sound of his footsteps died in the wood, her pity was turned to a joy of which she did not distinguish the source. She felt that she had never been so happy as she was now and might never be so happy again. She looked about her for origin of the songs within her and found none. The sun was spread upon the foliage like a glaze; the breeze had dropped and in the wood was silence. Dr. Hardy! she thought, her surprise deepening, and she sat down among the grasses.

White clouds were gleaming above the trees; they hung without movement on the sky; and, as she raised her head to look at them, the sun warmed her throat. She put up her hand to her throat, then allowed her body to sink back upon the warm slope of the orchard. There she lay extended, wondering with happy confidence what time would bring to her, the days and years stretching before her like a meadow, like a wood full of light and the song of birds. I suppose I shall grow old! but she did not believe it; and soon I shall be married, she said, but the word had no meaning for her, it was spoken of another girl than herself. Suddenly she remembered that, missing her, Peter and her father would return by this way. It seemed that she heard their voices above her in the orchard, and she lay still, hoping that they might pass by. No one came; there had been no voices; but they will come soon, and, springing up, she made for the cover of the wood. The path by which she entered it led back to the graveyard, and there she stood before the tomb, twisting in her fingers, until they were cut by it, the long grass which near to the wall had escaped the scythe, and hearing again Dr. Hardy's voice as he read the verses. She repeated them silently now, accepting their address to herself as though they were indeed being spoken to her from within the iron gate:

> *We also moved, as thou dost move,*
> *With pride of youth and quick in love . . .*

and she remembered how Dr. Hardy had begun to say that there were other verses. What verses? Perhaps they were by Lord Sparkenbroke himself, for Dr. Hardy had been speaking of him; perhaps they were in some volume of his that she had not read; but she began to look for them as though she expected to find them on the tomb itself. Round the semicircular panel that held the verses she had read was a moulding pierced at its centre by an armorial shield. This moulding had seemed to complete the height of the door, and not until now had she perceived that above it was another area of stone, overshadowed by leafy sprays curling down from the edge of the Mound itself. Here was another inscription which, though moss had already blunted the outlines of it, was evidently not more than a few years old. Through the lace of thorn and tendril, she could read it:

> *Who mourns? A fool with mortal look*
> *That dares to weep for Sparkenbroke?*
> *Weep thine own exile: not my life.*
> *With Earth for mother, Sleep for wife,*
> *Here in the womb is winter spring.*
> *Who stays? A Fool. Who knocks? A King.*
>   *S.*

Not until she had read it a second time and a third, remembering how Dr. Hardy had said that to Sparkenbroke
death was one of the fulfilments, did she penetrate the
meaning of the last line. Then, seeing the initial "S" in the
corner, she understood by whom the verses had been
composed, and she turned away with the chill of exaltation
upon her, feeling that she had entered, or partly entered,
into a secret which Dr. Hardy and Sparkenbroke himself—
though he had set up his verses where all might read them
—had wished to conceal from her. The light of escape
which had illumined her as she came from the orchard to
the wood was overshadowed; she felt that she was where
she had no right to be; a childish panic seized her lest
some passer-by should find her in this place, and look
curiously at her, and question her. What passer-by? What
had she to fear? To the west of the clearing was a green
bridle-path that led to a part of the wood unknown to her,
and she entered it swiftly, glad to have left behind her the
sun-streaked dust of autumn on the shelves of the tomb.

CHAPTER EIGHT

MARY could not have told what it was—the little panic at the tomb, or the solemn avenue of trees inviting her, or the forking of her path so that she must choose which way she would go—that set her thinking with shame of how unreasonable and selfish she had been. Her father would blame her, but not more than she blamed herself. There were excuses she might make but she would make none of them. She would tell the truth—that an impulse had driven her which she could not explain and that while she walked up the bridle-path she had been—she had been—but how could she say to her father that she had been under a spell? Peter would be angry already and such nonsense would make him angrier. At the thought of his sullen anger, that would thicken the neck in his collar, she rebelled again; but this time she looked upon her rebellious self with reproof. She had behaved badly and must make what amends she could. To return through the graveyard would take too long, and through the graveyard she would not return. Perhaps there was a shorter way to Sparkenbroke House? One of the branches of her path led on westward; it would take her to the cross-roads and the Rectory if she pursued it; the other struck up through the wood, curling to the right, leading out, perhaps, into the orchards and terraces. At its curve stood a cottage, shrouded in trees. She would knock and ask her way. Perhaps the way might be so short that, if she made haste, her father and Peter would not be angry with her after all. How much time had passed since Dr. Hardy called to them, how far ahead of her they were, her thought did not measure.

At the cottage, though it appeared to be inhabited, she obtained no answer to her knocking. Here also the path divided, and it seemed to her that she should take the branch to the right; but so anxious had she become to check her impulse, to behave reasonably, that she hesitated and listened, as though listening would help her. Away to her left she heard the trickle of water, the brush of leaves and a low crackle of twigs. The man who lives in the cottage, she thought, is over there—beyond the fold in the ground; that was his footstep; I had better ask him; and, the wood's silence forbidding her to call aloud, she turned hastily in the direction from which the sounds had come. She listened as she walked, hoping that another crackle of footsteps might guide her, but there was nothing to hear—only the light shifting of the leaves overhead and the buried sound of the stream. Suddenly the lap of water came up out of the earth and she found herself beside a little water-course, now very shallow and pebbly, that ran between tufted banks, as a river between high mountains. She followed its curves, wondering if there was not some approach by which she might come near the water and allow it to run over her hand; but the banks were steep; she saw no such approach, and was searching for it, with the enchantment of ripples dancing in her mind, when she became aware that she was not alone, and stood, unmoving, while the man who lay under the ash-tree cried out, not raising his head: "Go away! For God's sake. This isn't your place!"—then saw her and was silent.

She did not move or answer but stood before him like a scolded child, the colour hot in her cheeks. As he came towards her, a little breeze turned the leaves above him, and out of the leaves golden discs of sunlight were shaken down upon his head and shoulders and about his feet. Like the upthrown reflection of water, they flowed and shook upon the plane of his cheek and upon the muscles of his arm outstretched, giving to the flesh a warm transparency and to the whiteness of the inner arm the brilliance of white opal. "How was I to know it was you?"

she heard him say, and soon, when he had brought her to his tree and she was sitting on the upper part of the bank and he below her, he added in the same tone of mocking friendliness:

"Of course, I ought to have known."

"But how could you?" she asked.

"You were bound to come."

"Because, in the shop, I said: 'Saturday'?"

"Because, for me," he answered, "the gods always provide. Lately they've been inattentive. Now they are prodigal."

"But ought I—ought we to be here?" she inquired. "I mean, is this part of the wood private?"

"I expect it is. Didn't you see the notices?"

"No."

"Then the gods certainly blinded you."

"But you——"

"Oh, they blinded me to more warnings than that long enough ago."

After an interval, she persisted: "But if someone finds us here—a keeper or someone?"

"Then we'll become invisible. There's no difficulty about it. Listen. Do you hear anything?"

"Water and leaves."

"Again," he said. "Listen. Footsteps coming down through the wood. Nearer and louder. Crackling the twigs. And now, look—there are two men standing where you stood, and they can't see us because we have made ourselves invisible. . . . Is that a foolish game?"

She shook her head. No fantasy seemed foolish to her in that instant; though her intellect was slow upon his tracks, her intuition ran with him and before him, for this encounter seemed to her part of a series of happenings whose end was already known, or had once been known by her, like the end of a legend heard long ago and since forgotten. Watching him seated on the ground, his body taut, his head thrown up, she felt her little armour of adult stiffness fall away. The thought, which had risen in her mind, that he was as much a trespasser as she, though still true within her knowledge, appeared to her now as one of those truths of childhood that are not to be relied on; they seem to be true, but in a moment their truth will dissolve; for, in childhood, all truth, even the plainest, is everlastingly in flux; understanding shifts and the old truth vanishes, like a bubble, with a soft snap of the mind. And as he had not so much conceded her right to be here as swept away all question of right, enfranchising her by his gladness, so did she, touched by something childlike and fiery that she saw in him, something at once desperate and superb, let slip her reckoning of circumstance and acknowledge within her that where he would be he was master, even of sounds unheard and sights imagined, creating his own world as certainly as he created a world for her.

By swift reversions of thought swiftly annulled, she kept touch with the world to which she was accustomed. It gave her present experience the joy of a fabulous escapade to say to herself how very odd it was that she and this stranger had gone through none of the formalities that she would have expected of an encounter by chance. He hasn't asked who I am or where I come from! I don't know why he's here. I haven't said even that I lost my way. She began to remember her father and Peter, but her picture of them faded; the strangeness of her being seated under this ash-tree, listening to the man's voice, possessed her, and she perceived suddenly that he had not asked who she was or where she was going because for the moment he didn't care. He was so much more alive than any human being she had known, that the flow of his thought, like the flow of a stream round jags, was continuous; her coming had not broken it.

"Were you playing that game when I interrupted you?" she asked.

"You didn't interrupt."

Judging by the drop of his tone and the following silence that she had nevertheless intruded upon him, she began to rise, but he checked her.

"Where are you going?"

"I ought to go," she said, and told him, as if she were repeating a lesson, that she had missed the people she had been with and was trying to find a path back to Sparkenbroke House.

"I've been there," he said. "It's not worth the climb."

"But, you see, my father——"

"Isn't it pleasanter here than with tourists in a herd?"

"Yes."

"And this afternoon, when it's gone—shall you have it to live again?"

"No," she said.

"Then stay."

Assuming her obedience, he turned over leisurely and stretched himself out at full length, his arms under his head. "What beats me is how you came here."

"But I'm certain there weren't any warning notices by the way I came. That may have been because——"

"I wasn't thinking of 'warning notices.' I've told you the gods blinded you to them. But the ways of the gods are interesting. I didn't deserve you. And suddenly, out of the path by which no one ever comes——"

His seriousness frightened her, and frightened her the more because it was but half serious.

"You see," she began, still grave and defensive, "I was in the churchyard, and then, instead of going up the hill by the way the others had gone, I thought——"

He would have none of her explanations. "Never break a spell!" he said. "Give the gods credit. We blame them often enough."

"But you were angry when I came."

"Was I?"

"You were. You shouted at me."

"Then why weren't you angry with me? Why didn't you run away? It might have been better if you had. Would you like to run away now?" he added with flashing urgency. "Behind the cottage there's a path that will take you over the orchards to Sparkenbroke House. Or you can cross the stream by that little wooden bridge; go straight on through the wood until you come to a stile. There you can drop into

the main road and in five minutes be at Sparkenbroke
Cross—safe with the charabancs."

"I didn't come by charabanc," she said slowly, and he
looked over his shoulder at her, as though, she thought
with surprise, he imagined that she was laughing at him.
For a moment she wondered whether she had said something foolish; perhaps he was laughing at her. She tucked
her hands under her knees and clasped them there, trying
to think of something to say. But her shyness did not
endure. If this man criticized her at all, his glancing judgments were unrelated to the rules of behaviour set up by
her father, by Peter, by Miss Hardy, and though, elsewhere, she would have struggled, as one did with strangers
at a dance, to preserve a polite continuity of talk, she found
that in this place silence lay calmly. Over the line of her
knees, drawn up, she looked at the dark oval of the head
below her, at the indentation of the neck from which, at
the back, a loose shirt had fallen away, at the muscle of the
upper arm swelling above the elbow-point, and her old
school-bred anxiety not to displease, not to be con-
spicuous, lost its power over her. She gave a sigh of relief
as a soldier does who takes off his pack, and drew in the
summer air upon her lips, tasting it.

Letting her eyes move over the long, slack repose of the
body at her feet, he'd go to sleep if it suited him, she
thought; he'd get up and stride off without a word if it
suited him; and she smiled, for his absolute impulse was
not the timid, measured arrogance of common men. She
yielded to it, not with the grey submission enacted by
schoolmistresses, but with the obedience demanded as
of right by children and the gods; and the delicious
paradox of free obedience crept over her, relaxing all
the tensions of her life in the first lull of self-surrender
and self-release.

It was true that he had forgotten her; their encounter in
Merton's Passage had fallen away from his mind; and to-
day, until her coming, he had been fast shut in by his work.
To be thus enclosed, to be so engrossed by the struggle of

composition that his personal life—his vanity, his desires, his conscious attitude towards the world—released him from its pressure, was his happiness and his special innocence. While he wrote, he felt himself to be without evil. To imagine was to receive absolution, and the brilliant stress of translating into words what his imagination urged upon him emptied his being of its poisons. Even when he had left his desk and come out to the ash-tree, this light of spirit had continued to shine in him. All day he had worked and failed, and he accepted his failure with an absolute humility contrary to all men's knowledge of him, knowing that his story of Tristan had led him astray, that what he had written in the last six hours must be in great part rewritten, that at some point in it, yet to be discovered, his narrative had swerved. He could do no more to it now. He knew intuitively that the passage which baffled him was of the kind that does not reveal its flaw to its author's intellectual examination. He must wait: he must let it dry, and come to it with fresh energy when his sensitiveness to its impressions was not dulled by labour. Meanwhile, as he lay beside the stream, the story of Tristan's journey to Cornwall having been allowed to fall asleep in his mind, there had come to him unsummoned images of another tale, vaguely projected long ago in Italy, the tale of how Nicodemus made the Volto Santo and how that miraculous crucifix came to Lucca across the sea. Watching the sprigs of grass that curled upon his shoes and the earthy grains that fell in a landslide when he moved his foot, he had understood, as he had failed to understand decisively in Italy, that the Volto Santo, the Holy Face, was for him the subject not of a story in prose but of poetic narrative. He had attempted it in both forms and had failed in both. Now, remembering how this crucifix had come across the Mediterranean in a ship unmanned, and presumably steered by angels, and how it had eluded all captors but the Lucchesi for whom it was intended by God, he had perceived that the legend was a true epic comparable even with the voyage of Odysseus. When Genoese seamen, going about their business in the Aegean, sighted the ship that held the

Volto Santo and approached her, she appeared to them to be empty, and at sea, he said to himself, an empty ship is a marvel. They attempted to come alongside, they put off in boats, but always the ship drew away from them. From imagining their astonishment and awe, he had turned his thoughts to the ship herself, had paced her decks, searching her prodigious emptiness, and had exclaimed within him: But she had a crew of angels! and, peering through their invisibility, had perceived them at sheet and tiller. Nor was this all. When Nicodemus discovered that the head of the crucifix had been carved for him while he slept, with what passion must he have gazed at it, believing God himself to have been the sculptor. That God was the artificer of Nature would be to Nicodemus, as to other men, a thought so familiar that it had lost its impact, but when he awoke one morning and hastened, with an artist's undying curiosity, to inspect his work, and found a work of art from the chisel of God, was he, perhaps—jealous? For a moment, before the saint in him accepted the miracle, did the artist resent the interference? It would be delightful to think so. It would be amusing to discover so recognizable a humanity in Nicodemus, and to watch in his eyes jealousy yield to wonder, and wonder to adoration.

There was no end to the riches of the tale, and as scene after scene from it appeared to him he had turned his face to the ground and hidden his eyes in darkness that he might see the more clearly the eyes of Nicodemus and pierce the arched gloom of his cave. While he had been lying thus, he had heard footsteps and by their sound had been driven from his innocence. He had become in the instant proud, resentful of intrusion, full of bitter possessiveness, and had cried out in anger. Even when he had seen the girl, the welcome he gave her had been in the part that he played before the world, and all the words he spoke to her had been spoken in that part—his challenge to her youth, his provocation to her beauty, his gaiety, even his gentleness, being, within his knowledge, external to his secret self and at enmity with it, not humble as the artist in him was humble but deliberately spectacular, not spontaneous but of design.

"You had better learn my foolish game," he said to her at last, turning over and watching her face. "All you have to do is to imagine a pair of eyes looking at you, and, because they don't see you, you are invisible. . . . Or imagine that the trees are bare, the stream frozen, everywhere winter and night; and, suddenly, by your miraculous will and permission, leaves will come, and sunshine, and the touch of the earth that is hot now under your hand. . . . Or imagine there's no stream. It's the beginning of the world; there's no water or earth. . . . Now, you create it. The water flows because you created it. Listen."

"Isn't it really only another way of 'counting up your benefits'?" she said.

"Of what?"

"Of 'counting up your benefits.'" She had spoken, without reckoning of him, from her private thought, and she hastened to add: "But you wouldn't know it, of course; it was in a book I used to have when I was a child. You know—a bit to read every night at bedtime before you say your prayers. It said that everyone took the good things too much for granted. To count them up was a way of giving thanks to God."

"How long ago was that? I mean, the book at bedtime?"

She smiled. "I still read it sometimes. It's by Frances Ridley Havergal. I always read in bed."

"And give thanks to God?"

"When I remember."

"He must be glad of you. Most of us leave him alone until we want something."

She was grateful and proud because what she had said seemed to have interested him so much. It surprised her that he should be interested in Miss Havergal.

"Isn't that what you feel about your imagining game?" she asked.

"That I'm thanking God for his benefits?"

"In a way."

"No," he answered, "not until you told me. You are going to teach me a lot. Do you know that? It was an arrogant game with me. I wasn't thanking God. I was making a god of myself. But there's something I can teach you. Do you know what the playing of that game may lead to? Sit for a long time still: still for so long and in such a way that your imagination annihilates yourself. You cease to exist. Then, slowly, let consciousness return; hearing, feeling, sight slowly return; and you who were dead are alive again. . . . That's the perfection of it. I can't reach it. And if ever I did, it might not be hearing and feeling and sight that returned but something else that came. . . . You don't follow that. Why should you?"

"Yes," she said at once, "I do. 'Annihilating all that's made To a green thought in a green shade.' "

"Hurrah! Do you read Marvell too in bed?"

"But is that what you meant?" she asked.

He smiled at her. "It goes part of the way," he said, "but to reduce the world to a green thought in a green shade is still to be in the senses; the expectation, the dread, of physical sight, physical feeling and hearing still continues in Marvell's leafiness. It isn't enough. It doesn't take you far enough or deep enough," he said, and added, in a low voice: "It doesn't take you near enough."

"Near enough? Do you mean—to God?"

"Near enough to 'dare the final bound.' Do you understand that?"

Instead of answering his question, she turned her eyes to his with inquiry. It seemed to her that, at some other time, in the past or future, this question was asked her and that she answered it. She told him this and he replied that perhaps the phrase was familiar.

"Listen," he said. "There was a girl once who desired more than Marvell could give her. When he had cast the body's vest aside, his soul into the boughs did glide, and there was content to wait, 'till prepared for longer flight.' The world, if he could plunge into its essential quiet, was so beautiful to him that he could acquiesce in it; he was a quietist, not, as this girl was, a passionate mystic to whom all the senses were a leash withholding her from a different world of experience, desired, tasted even, never finally achieved. Marvell says that the mind creates,

> transcending these,
> Far other worlds, and other seas,

but Emily Brontë had herself entered them and been dragged back:

> Then dawns the Invisible; the Unseen its truth reveals;
> My outward sense is gone—

Is gone," he repeated. "Do you understand that? Gone. Even the green thought in the green shade—gone. No sight in the open eyes; no challenge of the brain; an 'unutter'd harmony,' Earth lost, the whole shell of being utterly dissolved:

> My outward sense is gone, my inward essence feels;
> Its wings are almost free—its home, its harbour found;
> Measuring the gulf, it stoops, and dares the final bound.
> O dreadful is the check—intense the agony—
> When the ear begins to hear, and the eye begins to see;
> When the pulse begins to throb—the brain to think again—
> The soul to feel the flesh, and the flesh to feel the chain."

He had reared himself up while he spoke, his body pressed up from the earth by straightened arms. Now he fell back and lay staring into the branches. "Has no one ever given you that to read in bed?"

"Is that what you want?" Mary asked. "What she wanted?"

"I?"

"Don't you remember? You said: 'That's the perfection of it. I can't reach it.' You said: 'I can't reach it.' But you will."

"Why do you say that?"

"I don't know. It's one of the things that come true, I think. Didn't it come true for her?"

"She died," he answered.

"Soon?"

"Very soon."

"I wonder what they wrote on her grave? As I was coming through the churchyard I read something. I didn't really understand it then, though I thought I did:

> Here in the womb is winter spring.
> Who stays? A Fool. Who knocks? A King."

She said the lines not as verses she had read but as if they were a truth that she had seen before her on the grass. Her perceptions, Sparkenbroke said within him, do not come to her by thought; her approach to them is so simple that she does not know she is approaching them or recognize them when they come. It is one of the things that come true, she said, but already she has forgotten what intuition prompted her to say it.

"Have you by any chance read Keats's letters?"

She shook her head. "Never."

"He says in one of them that 'prophecies work out their own fulfilment.' And in the same letter are some verses about a child:

> Awake it from its sleep
> And see if it can keep
> Its eyes upon the blaze.
> Amaze! Amaze!
> It stares, it stares, it stares,
> It dares what no one dares,
> It lifts its little hand into the flame
> Unharm'd . . .

I forget the rest. Read them some day and see if they weren't written for you." Before she could answer, he added:

"You have a memory for verses."

"Not particularly," she replied. "We learnt them at school. We had to. That's how I knew the bit of Marvell."

" 'Repetition'?"

"We didn't have a special name for it. It was just part of 'English Literature,' of course."

"Did you all stand up with your hands behind you and say verses in turn?"

"We stood up. Why?"

"I was picturing you. It must make a poet shout with joy in his grave when he sees English schoolgirls stand up to say his verses aloud. Then he's 'English Literature, of course'! Westminster Abbey is nothing to that."

"But we didn't say it at all well."

"Were you better than the others?"

"Generally, I got fairly good marks," she said. "You see, one gets to know what the mistress wants. Miss Hardy—I mean the daughter of the Rector here—used to take our class. As long as you got the meaning clear and pronounced the final consonants, she gave you marks. She didn't mind much about the sound as long as you didn't sing-song."

"Bless her," he said. "The meaning and the final consonants and no sing-song—of such is the kingdom of heaven—anyhow a fair slice of it. Still—isn't some of the meaning in the sound?"

"I know," she answered. "I used always to think I said it better to myself than I did for Miss Hardy. I hated saying it in class."

"Why?"

"Well, I didn't mind some poems. 'Horatius,' I mean, and 'The Assyrian came down' and things like that. But I hated it when she chose something I was fond of. It was mine, somehow, and standing up there in front of everybody——"

"Like taking your clothes off," he said, with an abrupt challenge that he despised even as he made it.

She neither accepted nor refused his challenge but allowed it to fall away into her silence.

"Did you ever write poetry?" he asked.

"Write it? How could I?"

"Never try?"

"I've wanted to, sometimes." And she added, as though she were speaking to herself: "Because, you see, you can make things come true in that way."

He looked at her with eager swiftness. "Come true? What things?"

"Things you imagine. I mean—of course it's childish, I

suppose. Most people grow out of it as they get older. But didn't you, when you were a child, feel that there were two of you—the one the others knew, rather dull and uninteresting to you, and the other one you told yourself stories about which weren't—just stories? I suppose," she repeated, "one ought to grow out of that. But I haven't. It's so exciting. You see, you can change other people. And after a bit the make-believe is real and the other doesn't matter much. You see——"

She stopped, surprised in her own confession.

"Yes," he said, "I see." He did, indeed, see her with new eyes, and he asked: "Do you happen to remember what it was like before you were born?"

She laughed—a small, quick breath. "How could I?"

"Easily."

She shook her head, not laughing now.

"Is it completely blank?" he asked.

"I don't really *remember* anything," she said.

"But there is something to remember?"

"In a way, I suppose there is."

He knew, before he asked the question, that she would neither answer nor deliberately avoid it. She would pass away from it, not with the stumble of embarrassment or escape, but as if there were a breeze always ready to lift her up from uncertain ground and set her down again safely at a little distance. An intuitive discretion was a part of her innocence. It filled him with delight to watch her, to permit her silences, to wait for the indication of her secrets that her next word might give; and, as he watched her, his imagination, burning suddenly within him, encompassed her. He perceived, with an assurance independent of his will, her face, not as it was now but rising to him in other moods, in other places, seemingly the mirror of an experience already past; and desire sprang up in him with the strength of premonition, his mind presenting to him, in her person, the image of a girl already searched and possessed. But because they were powerful in him, he distrusted such foreshadowings. Lust invents them, he said; better have a girl without excuse and be done with it

—or let her alone. Why pretend that a hunger of the body is a necessity of the soul? What a rationalizing beast is man who for two pins will make a philosophy of a girl's legs; better cut short debate and proceed to the division.

I want the girl and shall have her, he said, if I play my cards, and all the chatter of art that shall dazzle her, the questions I ask, the tenderness I show, and seem to feel, for her, are no more than Othello's tale of his battles, paraded for the same purpose. In the event she will be no different from the rest; and, fearing to soften his own harshness, determined to expect nothing of her or of himself but the recurrent loll of possession, he stifled the hope by which in other women he had been misled that in her body was more for him than heat of the blood. She will be no different from the rest, he told himself; and that he might not be tempted to believe more than this, he watched her lips and eyes while she spoke, and observed, with the delight and weariness of one whose opponent is no match for him, the ease with which her confidence was won.

How easy it was to talk to him and to listen! Even when she did not fully understand, she was not baffled by her lack of understanding but fired by it, as though she had entered a new country. Soon it would be taken from her; and she was surprised to discover that in her mind a dullness had fallen on the expected pleasures of her holiday. Even the idea of dancing passed before her, colourless. The visits to the Rectory to which she had so eagerly looked forward, the glitter of the sea, the light and comfort of the Sparkenbroke Hotel, appeared as part of a life that she had outgrown; but that's my real life, she thought, and I have nothing to be unhappy about. Leaning back on her elbows, she looked up into the trees, away from the face before her, wondering if she would remember it. How soon it faded! I will imagine, she thought, that I am alone; then look down and find him there; but she was denied her playing of this game, for out of a long silence he began to speak and the sound of his voice flowed upon her body. It was as if her flesh were singing; and she exclaimed:

"I was imagining that you weren't there," and laughed in a foolish way that she was ashamed of.

"I hope because you wanted to recreate me?"

"I wanted to look and find you again."

"If you and I," he said, "when we go out of this wood, find that a miracle has happened and everyone else on earth has ceased to exist, what shall we do? People the earth again? Or let it go?"

"We couldn't let it go."

"So we should behave like Adam and Eve? They didn't make a good job of it."

"Still . . ."

"You believe in the human race?"

"It must have been put here for some reason, mustn't it?"

"Yes, but by whom and for what reason? If I were a cripple and you ugly, should we still people the earth?"

"That's different."

"Then it's the body you are preserving, not the mind."

"I don't know," she said. "I don't know. It won't happen."

"No," he answered, "it won't happen," but the idea that two human beings might be alone on earth, free to choose whether humanity should continue or end, fascinated him, and he began to tell her a story of how he and she lived together in a new Eden, how they obtained food, what customs appeared in the spending of their day, how, little by little, the remembrance of the world as it had been slipped from them, and they looked forward only, understanding more and more that they and the animals and all natural things were one, bound in a common inheritance and necessity. The imagining lighted a new energy in him. His mind leapt to the tale. At first he gave to it a sparkle of irony that dazzled and confused her, but soon a different vigour sprang from its plainness; shining images succeeded one another like images in water beneath a racing sky. There was an impulse in the narrative that entranced her. Something in his manner, covetous and over-assured, that had by its reserves chilled her, vanished, and each part of the story, though an act completed in his mind, seemed also a question asked of an experience more profound than his own, into which his imagination adventured with mingled boldness and awe.

"And while we were deciding," he added, with a smile, "whether, in our wisdom, we should scrap Creation or permit it to continue, the gods would watch us with interest and compassion. In the eyes of the gods a man must appear very much as a dumb animal appears in the eyes of men. He can neither speak their language nor with assurance understand it. But he is not always dumb. Three times at least he may understand and, perhaps, speak it: in his love, in his contemplation and in his death. These are his three ecstasies, his three deaths to this world that free him from the living death of the body; and, except the devil corrupt or folly pervert them, they are one death and one life, one transcendence or ecstasy, the reconciliation of suffering and joy."

In the following silence, she lay still. The wedges and spirals and leaf-clippings of sky that shone down through the ash-tree changed their aspect continually. A squirrel had appeared, and her imagination followed it, taking it into her delight of herself, pouring her own being into it; and when the squirrel vanished into the higher shadows of the tree, it did not vanish for her. She felt the rippled darkness of the foliage descend upon her.

"Did you see the squirrel?" she said.

"You ran away with it, didn't you, up into the dark?"

She nodded, breathless.

"How did you do it?"

"Do what?"

"Become the squirrel, the tree. Become the water and the sound of water, and the sky?"

"It's funny," he heard her say, "that you should talk about the water and the tree. There's a poem of Sparkenbroke's that begins like that. I wish I could remember it. I wish I could remember it here." She wrinkled her forehead in an attempt to recall the words, and, failing, threw up her head with a laughing sigh, and rose, and went to the edge of the stream where a willow overhung it.

"How shallow it is! Is it always like that?" and, steadying herself by a branch that swayed and bent but held her, she clambered down the bank and began to test the water's depth with a willow wand thrust down into the stones. "Look," she exclaimed, "how fast it is! Much faster than it seems. It makes a kind of bow-wave like a ship." She dipped her hand and let the water fall from it. She dipped her two hands, scooped the water up, threw it out into the air. She turned her face to him, for he was at her side. "Mightn't this be the water he wrote about?"

"The place is called Derry's Wood."

"Derry's Wood?" She stood up, shaking the drops from her fingers. "That *was* the name: 'Natural Communion: Derry's Wood.' Oh, I wish I could remember it! 'My tree and water . . .'; then something; then . . . 'sleep.'"

He had begun to tremble, and she thought, from his pallor and the fever in his eyes, that he was ill. He stood before her, possessed by an emotion she did not understand; then, in a visible act of courage, his arrogance gone, he said:

> *"My tree and water, how profoundly you sleep!*
> *Though the breeze move and your little green cry out,*
> *How dark is the vigil of the soul you keep,*
> *With my absence folded over you*
> *And my blindness wrapped about.*
>
> *I also am dead, shut from your light.*
> *All things created are dead that are not one.*
> *Soon, my tree and water, shall your night*
> *End, and the new day be begun*
> *Where shall be no old thing under a timeless sun.*
>
> *Soon? O tree and water, how often have I cried:*
> *Behold God in the last impulse ascending*
> *Into his zenith, who shall his flame divide*
> *In the breasts of his universe, bending*
> *Upon earth as a lover upon his bride."*

"There's more," she said.

"No."

"There was!"

"There isn't now. He's just revised it."

"Has he?" she answered. "I didn't know," and she began again to dip in the water, now drawing it up, now permitting its luminous shell-like reflections to climb her wrist.

"You make a solid cup with your hands," he said. "With me, the water trickles and falls."

"I could drink from mine." She bent her head, and drank and laughed, the sun wet upon her mouth.

"Let me drink."

"Like this?"

She held out her hands, brimming. His head was bent below her, he upon his knees. She felt the cool overflow run back upon her wrists; the pressure of his hands, cupped also, supporting hers; his lips' movement which, by rapturous transmission, seemed to lay the touch of feathered wings upon her breasts; and suddenly her hands were parted. The water was spilled. She shook the last drops on to the willow-root, feeling that she was throwing away her life, for a remembrance of her former self was rising to her like a mist from the ground. When she had climbed the bank she remembered how, long ago, she and her father and Peter had been seated together at luncheon on the Rectory lawn—to which she must return. It seemed to her that she would be revisiting a world that had gone from her as her schooldays had gone. After a little while her father would look at his watch, the journey homeward would begin, and this evening, in the hotel——

She looked swiftly at the man beside her, feeling helpless in his presence and that her helplessness was itself a sin. When he was drinking from her hands, all that she knew of herself, her character, her strength of mind, that pride of modest upbringing which she called steadiness, had flowed out from her. She had been turned to water. She had given and received; and the giving and receiving had emptied all other experience of its joy. She wished to reason, but love is without aspects, without form; the imagination cannot observe it, for it is within the imagination as life is within the body; it is an impulse towards fulfilment, not of the self previously known but of the new self that springs into existence with it.

The word "fulfilment" hovered over her mind, and she asked suddenly: "What does it mean to say that death is one of the fulfilments?" So unexpected was her question that he turned fiercely on her, as though he had been trapped.

"Why did you ask that? Because I spoke of Emily Brontë? But it's not your question. Who told you?"

"No one."

" 'Fulfilments' isn't your word."

"It was the man," she answered, her memory supplying her, "who came up here with me. He said that to Lord Sparkenbroke——"

"It was Hardy, the doctor. You came up with him?"

"We had lunch at the Rectory."

"You are staying there?"

"In Chelmouth, in the big hotel."

He let her answers rest in his mind, seeing her anew in their surprise, their submissiveness.

"You are a child still," he said, and she was dumb. "So the doctor told you of Sparkenbroke. I should have liked to hear it. You had better go back to him. Now. Go and ask the doctor and the priest about death's fulfilment. . . . Or shall I tell you again what the fulfilments are? Poetry is one; and love, perhaps—'the beast with two backs'; and death is one, it may be. But if you're a good doctor with his head screwed on, or a priest with a taste for scholarship, or a girl just out of school, then one is flesh rotting in a grave, and one is my corrupt body feeding on your corrupt body, and poetry—well, what is poetry to you?"

"I don't know. I don't know. Why are you angry with me?" she cried, covering her face with her hands.

He drew down her hands.

"Come," he said. "I'll put you on your way," and he led her across the bridge, westward. "What shall you tell them—that you were lost in the forest?"

"Yes."

"And that you met a fool there?"

She looked at him, questioningly. It was a child's look, aslant across her shoulder. After a silence, she asked: "Are you a visitor in Chelmouth, too?"

"No. You see, I own the place."

She laughed. "Of course! And I suppose you own this wood too?"

"Of course."

She laughed again. "Certainly you behave as if you did. The warning notices didn't keep you away."

"No. The advantage of them," he said, "is that they keep other people away."

"But suppose Lord Sparkenbroke came?"

"That," he admitted, "would be devilish awkward. I should have to annihilate him with all that's made. But it would be extremely interesting. I should like to meet him."

"I wonder," she answered. "Do you know—I don't think I should. It might be disappointing after his work. Miss Hardy says it would be. She knows him, you see, because she lives here—and besides——"

"What?"

"I mean—of course I don't believe everything people say. I expect, if you really knew him, it would all seem different. He may be unhappy or—still, I think I'd rather not meet him, though I suppose if I had the chance I would."

"If he told you he was unhappy, I shouldn't believe him if I were you. Probably it's part of his technique."

"His what?"

"To get sympathy. And then he'd talk to you about his books—to dazzle you with his reputation and make you believe that there was no one who could understand his art but you. And then he'd recite a poem to you, and say that you were miracle-minded."

"What does that mean?"

"It's jargon of his for the people who still trail clouds of glory. He would explain to you. And then, probably, he'd begin to blackguard himself."

"But why?"

"I don't know. Perhaps because he liked tormenting himself. Perhaps because he was making mental notes of you for a book to be written some day. Perhaps to make you think that he couldn't be as black as he painted himself. . . . He might want you to redeem him. . . . People make themselves sick for very queer reasons. Have you read the thirteenth chapter of the second book of Samuel?"

"Samuel Two Thirteen. I don't know. What is it?"

"Never mind. Little Red Riding Hood will do as well."

They walked on side by side. Her silence fascinated him, giving him the impression not of darkness and concealment, and not of emptiness, but of an intense whiteness upon which her intuition was writing in mysterious characters unknown to him.

"What book were you looking at in the bookshop when we met?"

"Hazlitt: *Liber Amoris*. I'd never heard of it."

"What brought you there?"

"I was just wandering through the town."

"The gods again," he said. "They are pretty determined. . . . I'm usually in the country during the day." And he added swiftly: "But at night—what do you do in the evenings?"

"Generally we go out and walk a bit. Then we listen to the band—unless we dance in the hotel. It's a nuisance at the band. All the best seats get taken so quickly and then——"

"I shall have to arrange that for you. You didn't know I owned the chairs as well?"

She smiled; this was a joke she understood. "Do you know," she said, "that little bastion place by the bandstand, jutting out on the sea-wall? I go there if I can. You can see the lights of the town from there, piling up on the hill, and the cars and cabs and things twinkling along the front, and the people walking up and down. It's lovely. And then you can turn your head and there's the sea, and the lighthouse on the point. Of course dancing's lovely too. I hate missing either. Sometimes we——"

"We?"

"My father and—the friend staying with us. But he's going off to play cricket."

"And doesn't your father like to read the *Evening Standard* after dinner? Come and show me your bastion one evening." She hesitated. "Anyhow we may meet by chance," he said.

"I've never seen you there. I'm sure I should have noticed."

He looked at her. "Let's leave it to the gods, then. You'd rather that?"

She nodded. They had reached a clearing in the wood. Stooping suddenly to pluck a yellow flowering herb which had been planted there, she said: "Wouldn't that story go into a book?"

"Which story?"

"The one you told me—about the people left alone in the world."

"The essence of it has already 'gone into a book.' "

"Has it?"

"Called *Paradise Lost*. It would always have the same title. But I'll tell you more of my version of it some day, here or in Chelmouth. Shall you come to the Rectory again? Look how close it is. Here's the road. And there are the cross-roads. Beyond the Cross is your Rectory."

They were at the thicket bordering the wood and she leaned out across the stile as he pointed the way. Beneath the thicket was a bank, steep and short. As she began to clamber down it, one hand on the stile, he asked suddenly:

"Why are you clutching that herb?"

"I press flowers," she said, "to remember places by."

"Then it should have been rosemary. Do you know what it is?"

"No. I was wondering. Miss Hardy will tell me. Do you know?"

"Yes," he said. "I know. It's—I'll tell you one of its Greek names. Will that do? Peganon."

"But the English?"

"Throw it away," he said.

"Why?"

"Throw it away," he repeated.

She let it fall into the road.

"Now I'll tell you what it means. It's called the herb of grace on Sundays."

"Then why did I have to throw it away?"

"It has another meaning on week-days."

From the road she looked up to ask what the other meaning was, but he was already gone. She hesitated, stooped, but let the flower lie. A car was approaching from the direction of Ancaster. She stood still and watched it pass. When it was gone she could hear his retreating footsteps snap and crackle through the wood.

CHAPTER NINE

SPARKENBROKE plunged back into the woods without looking behind him; then stopped suddenly, listening to the
many sounds of the wood, the near sounds and the distant,
the startling thrust of a bird through foliage at his side, the
light creaking and sighing of leafy branches far away, and
he said: why can I not receive their beauty or hers simply,
for the delight that is in them, as children receive their
experiences?

All things seen or apprehended began, in the moment of
their contact with him, to lose their intrinsic values and to
acquire new values in their relationship to art, a form of
experience nearer to reality than life's own. How much
easier to suppose, as many did, that sensuous experience
was itself reality and that art was but a representation of
Nature or, at most, a skilled selection from natural phenomena! But he could not escape from his belief that its
selective process was, like a gardener's, creative; it bred
new species, transforming and re-transforming Nature,
until at last life itself became, in certain aspects, a product
of art, and vision subsisted in poetry, and heroism in
heroic tales. Without pictures there could be desire of
male for female, stallions and mares, but without pictures
there could be no beauty in women. And without women,
there might be no art—or none of mine, he thought—for
between men and women there is a tension, an indefinable
quick expectancy, like a harp-string, taut but at rest, and
the quiver of it is among art's primary impulses.

Already, he knew, his meeting with this girl had become
a power within him. During the morning and the early

afternoon there had been a frost upon the stream of his narrative. In her presence he had become slowly aware of new imaginative vitality; the pulse of his thought had quickened until, when she looked up to say good-bye, he had known that his narrative was alive again.

As he went forward now, she became for him less important than the stimulus she had given, and faded from his mind. Derry's Cottage was empty, Bissett, his manservant, having gone up to the House. Sparkenbroke sat down at his table in joy and fear, hungry to write, but knowing how often such impulses failed in the long battle of his prose. He began to read again the pages last written, and discovered instantly the fault in them to which he had been blind. They were giving to the conclusion of an episode too harsh a finality. In the end of each minor scene must be the spring of the next. There must be no beginning, however lightly stressed, that had not within it a linking remembrance—such a remembrance as that which should bind phrase to phrase continually, each rising cadence giving response to the preceding fall. Only now and then, to mark a choice of new direction, would he permit himself such a deliberate pause, or silence, as a composer permits in the flow of music; and the end of the scene that he had written blocked the channel of his narrative like a ship sunk in a fairway; he had been unable to go beyond it, and would, he knew, be checked again if his re-reading entangled his mind in that false, sunken finality. But now, as he approached it, a new buoyancy came to his story; he understood how the episode might be ended without check; he saw clearly the point of sag, and, dropping to the floor the pages that followed it, he began to write anew. His composition was slow, for he cared above all else to give, even to complex thought, a verbal sequence of the utmost lucidity; thought might be dark, but the mirror of language must be clear; the music might be elaborate, but, the more elaborate the music, the more precise must the playing be. A story was not, to him, an aggregate, however rich, of the experiences of life, but a selective pattern having its origin in them and made always with one purpose—to discover the form, which is the poetry, of character, and so relate it to the universal forms of humanity that whoever read was enchanted into perception and joy.

A joy that he was able, in his novels, sometimes to evoke, however dark their theme, because, while he wrote as he was writing now, he had singleness of mind as at no other time, all his conflicts being stilled, all perils forgotten, and his story appearing to him as an absolute and excluding unity. This activity was his only repose; to return from it was to become a different man, arrogant, aloof, passionate, swayed by divided impulse, the creature that bore through the world's admiration and hatred the perilous reputation of Sparkenbroke. It was to this self that he was recalled by his manservant's coming with a reminder that he must dine at the House that evening. Enraged by the interruption, he exclaimed at once that he would not go. Bissett replied stolidly: "Her ladyship particularly asked me to remind you, m'lord."

Sparkenbroke stared at the sheet on which he had been writing. The mood was gone; he could not hope to recapture it; a barren inertness descended upon him; he felt his body, sitting at the table, propped by the chair-back. From this apathy, his mind moved out suddenly, and he began to set down in pencil a coarse outline of verses which, when the pressure creating it ceased, would be screwed up and thrust over the table's edge:

> *Give me the darkness of the flesh, or full light of the spirit.*
> *How shall I endure this prison, whose walls open and close,*
> *Or maintain this silence wherein thy music sounds*
> > *continually,*
> *Or . . .*

His pencil trailed away in a loose line across his page:

> *In my childhood I was beset by angels. Thou didst look*
> > *through mine eyes.*
> *Thy spears threaded my light. They struck, and lo I was in*
> > *thine arms*
> *Suddenly . . .*

He struggled again, the image of a room neither dark nor light half-formed within him:

> Here is my world: I must live in it, having no other place.
> As a man, when night comes, turns inward to his home,
> So would I draw my curtain and be at rest
> Until in the new day I am cast upon thy morning;
> But the curtain of this flesh has not dark to exclude thee.
> Thy beam is the shaft of an eye, my candle dips and
>   surrenders;
> My house is not my house when thou art in it
> My house . . .

He pushed the paper away from him. Bissett, standing motionless beside the table, observed where it fell. Later, he would pick it up, smooth its creases, lay it out to be revised or rejected. If rejected, it would, like the letters that his lordship too often threw whole into the waste-paper basket, be torn into small pieces; there were those who'd give a fiver and more for what the basket contained; there was a man named Cannister in Little Russell Street who had "important American clients"—it gave Bissett satisfaction to think that neither Cannister nor his American clients would ever set eyes on the piece of rubbish lying between his boots.

Sparkenbroke smiled. "You needn't retrieve that lot Bissett. It's no good."

"Very well, m'lord."

But he would retrieve it. One never knew. His lordship himself didn't know.

"Did you say I was writing, Bissett?"

"No, m'lord. You weren't writing—at least, no good was coming of it when I went up to the House, and I thought that, seeing Mr. Crute was dining to-night——"

Sparkenbroke made no answer. Mr. Crute, of Crute and Waterman, represented the Kaid trustees. Poor Etty, she hated her trustees. She wished to give her capital, as she gave her income, to the estate, not lend it on mortgage; and after dinner, when Crute brought out his papers in the library and asked when the next novel would be done and what advance the publishers would pay on it, and snapped the fastening of his attaché-case with his two thumbs, she would look from one to the other of them, her forehead puckered by her distress in finding herself a usurer. But, my dear, thank God you are. Anyhow, Crute is right. He must have his security. Yours is only a life interest. He has to protect Richard. And she would say: Yes, Piers, I know. But all this makes you think of me in the wrong way. He would try to persuade her that this was not true, but it was true; whenever he came to England she and Mr. Crute were waiting for him, and he sat at his table now, dispirited, stiff in his chair, his pencil fallen slack across his knuckles, trying to think of some way in which he might respond to her tentative affection, her terrible, controlled adoration. If for an instant he succeeded, her eyes would fill with hope; she would become younger, and recall the early days of their marriage by some phrase, some endearment, familiar to them then.

"Bissett," he said, "this journey to England hasn't been a success. We must be off to Italy again."

"Very good, m'lord."

"But not yet. I'm not ready yet."

"No, m'lord."

Bissett stood beside the table, watching his master's face. Slowly Sparkenbroke raised his head.

"Well," he exclaimed, "speak your mind. You know me as I know myself. Is it time to go back to Italy yet?"

"You've always said, m'lord, that the time to move from a place is when it drives you, and the time to move to another place is when it drags you. Apart from that, you've said, the drag and the drive, one place is like another."

"Did I say that? You are Plato to my Socrates, Bissett; you put all your own wisdom into my mouth. Anyhow, it's true. For a little longer, I'll not uproot you. We'll stay at Sparkenbroke. And one day it will become intolerable, and Italy will become necessary. Then we'll go . . . Well?" —for Bissett did not move.

"The dinner to-night—you'll dress here, m'lord, and drive up in the car?"

"No. I'll go up to the House now. The boy won't be asleep yet?"

Bissett looked at his watch. "Not for half an hour and more."

Sparkenbroke's face lighted with eagerness. "I'll keep him awake with stories. There's a fate in it, Bissett, d'you know that? If I tell him a good story to-night, I shall write well to-morrow. . . ." And the odd thing is— I believe it, he thought. I shall write well to-morrow— everything with me leads to that. . . . "You shouldn't have become servant to a man with that madness, Bissett." And no woman should marry such a man, he reflected. "With me," he said aloud, "as with poor Midas, every-thing I touch turns into a story until it chokes me. Do you understand that?"

"Yes, m'lord."

Sparkenbroke stared, his eyes grave, the corners of his mouth flickering. "I believe you do," he said. "And you despise it?"

"No, m'lord, there you're wrong."

"Pity it, then?"

"We all have our twists," Bissett said. "And what's a man without his twists? Nothing you'd recognize."

CHAPTER TEN

On Sunday rain fell. Between Peter and her father, head down against the drizzle, Mary walked to church, watching the dun-coloured ridges of atmosphere that seemed, in the cross-light, to move up-wind over the sea. There was gale enough to buffet conversation. Her father shouted across her: "Not much further! It doesn't seem worth taking a cab!"

Peter said: "What about cricket to-morrow?"

Neither replied; neither addressed her; the rim of her umbrella, butting against theirs, described for her an island in which she lived secure.

Would she, after luncheon, be able to go out alone? The more rain, the better; they would settle to billiards, releasing her; and in driving rain, without umbrella, without hat—for she would go bareheaded if she were alone—she would come to terms with herself. But the clouds lifted, then closed in; the billiard-table was taken. They sat in the lounge, bleakly lit by a window of plate-glass, waiting. Perhaps after tea.

"I think I'll risk it," she said, and rose.

"Don't be silly," her father answered.

"If you must go now, I'll come with you," said Peter.

"Yes. Of course, I will."

She sat down again: they played Patience; behind them the lift sighed now and then. They decided that, as it was Sunday, it would be a change not to dress for dinner. During the evening a clergyman with chalky finger-nails came to their table, discussed with Peter the influence of coker-nut matting on leg-breaks, and, inserting his hand between

Mary's lap and the book that lay on it, said, jogging the book playfully, how refreshing it was to find nowadays a beautiful young lady reading poetry. Lord Sparkenbroke! Well, *quot homines tot sententiae!* He closed the volume with the smile of a man fanatically broadminded. The ring she was wearing had, he said, drawn his attention at once. No one more romantic than a clergyman if the truth were known. A charming ring; stones of good augury; might he be permitted to——— Mary pulled off the ring hastily and laid it on the table, guarding her hand. And was this the happy man?

"I am," Peter replied.

She looked at him and at her bare finger.

"I think I'll say good-night," she said. They stood round her, and through the bars of the lift she saw them still in the same position, the clerical baldness, the crook of a finger beckoning to the waiter, the high-shouldered, blond young man with a limp smile.

To be alone in her room, to be in the darkness, to sink down into the core of darkness, leaving far away the stress of her former self, gave her a joy of release so intense that she covered her face in her hands, and so fell asleep; and in the morning awoke suddenly. The air sparkled; hot June had returned; she would be a fool no more; and she made up her mind that, when Peter was gone to his cricket, she would swim. There were white horses to chase her foolishness away; but when the time came, her impulse was gone. The sunshine on the beach was white and hard, the people sitting there on their short, pebbly shadows seemed to have been clipped out of an illustrated poster. In the afternoon, she walked with her father on the cliff to the east of Chelmouth, but when he sat upon a bench, saying that his boots hurt him, her troubled imagination moved away from all that he told her about the dimensions of the rooms in Sparkenbroke House. He estimated the great dining-hall in terms of their conservatory at Warlingham. "You should have been there," he said. "I can't think how you were so careless; you missed a lot." But she was inattentive, slow in her answers, and the stick with which he scraped diagrams in the dust—an old stick that had stood all her life in the china umbrella-stand at home—had for her the strange familiarity of some relic of her childhood found in a cupboard and now seen anew. She was glad when they returned to the hotel. After tea she set out alone and walked to Merton's Passage. Shadows were over it; the awning above the book-shop had been taken in; so had the books. *Liber Amoris* was not in its tray.

In the evening, seated at her father's side in his chosen corner of the lounge, she began to be afraid of her own mood, for when she tried to give an account to herself of her behaviour and to reprove herself for it, her utmost seriousness would be interrupted by a smile that came upon her unawares. It moved her lips and, suddenly, she found it in her heart. She discovered in herself a capacity for delight, held, as it were, in suspense, and unrelated to any present circumstance. Sadness and gaiety had almost an identity in her, so swift was their interchange; and the sight of her father, planted again in his chair, unconscious of this tingling, perilous vitality so near to him, filled her with an aloof wonder, as if she were looking at an old dog on the mat, that he should be thus inert and content. In the same instant, her exaltation broke. She saw herself as she was, sitting beside him.

"You don't seem to be getting on with your book," he said. " Like a sheet of the paper?"

It was as if for two days she had been lying asleep, dead to natural sensation, and had watched herself sleeping. What on earth's the matter with you? Peter had said. Have you seen a ghost? and she had hated him for saying it, hated him so cruelly that afterwards she had asked to be forgiven. What for? he had answered. Why are you so serious all of a sudden? What's wrong with you? and she had felt that there was nothing to do but tell him of her encounter in the wood and how it had been for her—but she could not tell him. What was there to tell? She was entangled in a secret of which the vague, oppressive significance hourly increased. Peter and her father had become strangers to whose company she was incapable of response, and all familiar sights and sounds, the music from the ballroom, her own prettiest dress that had been a symbol of the delights of her holiday, even the tracery of gold and rosebuds on the coffee-cups, which had seemed once to be overlaid with a patina of foreign gaiety, were dead, with the stabbing deadness of inanimate things associated with a vanished life. Her health of mind and body made causeless sentiment repugnant to her, and she struggled fiercely against the sense she had of having fallen adrift and of being a passive spectator of her own drifting. Why had she gone again to Merton's Passage? Had she expected to find him there? She had gone without any expectation; and it was not until she had found the place empty and the remembered book gone from its tray that she had understood how insubstantial her experience in the wood had become, how it was receding into the past out of her reach, almost beyond her credence. His face would not present itself to her mind's eye; nothing remained but the guilt and joy of having been released from herself, and the anguish of being unable to reassume her habit of reason. He must have been mad to talk like that, she tried to tell herself, but to call him mad was no remedy; there was no remedy now in any of the smooth, well-rubbed comments which, she knew, ought to be applied decisively to her folly. She was making herself ridiculous, she must pull herself together.

"Father," she said, "you know about gardens. What is the thing with bluish-green leaves, spotty-mottled, and a yellow flower?"

"What is that, my dear?" said her father, coming out of his newspaper.

She repeated her description, adding to it. Rue, probably, he told her.

"It was in the wood," she said.

"Then it can't have been rue. Unless it was planted there."

"Are you coming out this evening?"

He yawned. "Early to bed. Do you good, too."

"After a little walk, I will."

"Put on a wrap. Oh, an' Mary," he added, yawning again, "I may be gone before you come back. Just knock on my door. And I'll put us both down for early tea."

"But isn't that an extra?"

"No it's not, after all. I asked. Nor coffee." He bowed, over his spectacles, to the gilt and rosebuds.

CHAPTER ELEVEN

THERE, she thought, is the night after all! It came upon her with the rush of surprise, like the scent of a garden that is entered from an airless house; not through gradual perception, adding beam to beam, shadow to shadow, but with single impact, fluid and alight. Music came to her, but not as a distinct recognition; it showered in the air, and the air had music's lilt, which, upon its lightness, bore a melancholy that was the sea; and, out of the following hush, when distant applause fluttered up and died like the turning of leaves in the wind, sprang the arched remoteness of sky. Night was all hers; hers the stream of heaven; for her the little waves slapped and hissed on the beach and the bronze lion at the drinking-fountain held silver in his teeth. For her the thronging people moved to and fro, with their multitudinous shuffle, their flash of voice, white of eye, roped gleam of necklace, their bright knuckles, their wheeling shadows, their comic bulk that loomed, chattered, vanished.

On her right, beyond the asphalt and the ribbon of lawn, was a cab, alone on cobbled rank; its upholstery of glossy leather bulged from dark button-pits in sprays of ruby light. The horse had his head down; a dry munching came from his bag. She stopped, patted him, spoke to him.

"Keb, miss?"

"No, thank you," she said, "not this evening. I just thought I'd talk to your horse."

"Needs exercise, y'know, miss. Nice run down to the harbour. Two bob to you, there *an'* back."

She felt that she ought not to have aroused false

expectations in the cabman for no better reason than that
she had wished to talk to his horse, but her sudden
affection for this particular animal could not be explained. At that instant a priest, foreign, entered the
cab. "Avenue Walpole, forty-seven," he said with precision, and sat erect, staring at her with acute, solemn eyes,
like a greasy parrot. The cabman jumped down to the
horse's head. "Brought me luck anyhow, miss," and she
answered: "I'm glad. Good-night. . . . You'll let him finish
his supper, won't you?" She watched the old horse amble
off and the spokes twinkle.

Perhaps from Brussels, she thought, and in her imagination this priest, fatly bouncing in his cab, drove beneath
the lighted windows of a house in Brussels from which
streamed down the music of dancing. A soldier, his horse
smoking, clattered in with news. The music, the sound of
voices, ceased. She said within her: How long ago! A
hundred years—more—and saw Napoleon, when all was
over, climbing into his carriage, swaying there, his eyes
shut. Before her was the night. The breeze was under
her hair and she alive. She tasted the faint salt on her lips
and plunged into the stream of people. The band, when
she reached it, was playing a heavy, stolid lump of music,
pompous with brass and drums, but it was easy to let the
noise rumble away into the back of her mind; she enjoyed
the light, the scarlet of the bandsmen's uniforms, the pink
and mauve and amber of the fairy lamps festooned from
the roof, and she stood very still, for the ranks of illumined
faces were still, and thought that some day, like Miss
Hardy, she would go to Italy, where songs would come in
through her open window at night.

She would have liked a chair in her own bastion, and,
though all the chairs were taken there as elsewhere, she
walked across in the next interval, and said to the ticket-
man: "There isn't a chair anywhere, I suppose?"

"Why," he said, "d'you think I makes 'em?"

Perhaps he's tired, she thought; I suppose it was a silly
question to ask, and, unperturbed, stood where she was,
wondering whether this bastion, which seemed to be part

of an old fort, had been here a hundred and eleven years
ago. Chelmouth had been fashionable then. At the moment
when, in Brussels, news had broken in upon the Duchess
of Richmond's ball, someone must have been standing
here, looking up towards the town. It had been June;
there had been people passing to and fro; there had been a
girl perhaps who had stood where she was standing now,
and, as though this girl had been her own sister, she felt a
glow of affection for her and wanted to speak to her, as
she had wished to speak to the old horse.

"So this is your bastion?"

He was standing beside her, his face bright and keen,
his uncovered head so darkly lined with shadow that the
hair was thrown into sculptured relief.

"Yes."

"You were thinking very deeply. Is it a secret?"

"Oh no," she said, her fingers tight on the bag she
carried but her voice even, "I was thinking of the battle
of Waterloo."

His eyes flashed with puzzled amusement. Then, swiftly,
he guessed: " 'There was a sound of revelry by night'?
Is that it?"

"Yes," she said slowly, allowing her eyes in wonder
to meet his, for she had forgotten this link in her own
thought. "How did you know that?"

It must be because he had taken her by surprise that
she was talking to him so easily. Now he had moved
away, perhaps to look for chairs, but there were no chairs;
even he couldn't conjure them up; and she had begun to
think how awkward it would be to stand with him in
front of all those people when the ticket-man came up
to her, very close, and said: "Now then, who's made of
glass? No standin' there."

The voice at her side answered abruptly: "Find some
chairs, then. Bring them."

The man had already opened his mouth to answer
when his expression changed. He touched his cap and went
off at a slouching trot to the bandstand, whence, from a
hidden store, he produced two chairs.

"Thank you," she said, hoping that the poor man, smiling and anxious now, would be given a tip. He was given nothing.

"Now some programmes."

He brought them and again was given nothing, but dismissed with a nod. Two chairs, sixpence, and two programmes—tenpence. She looked at her companion, questioningly.

"I told you I owned them," he said.

As long as the music lasted there was no need to talk, and, sighing happily, she lay in her chair, seemingly relaxed, but with the muscles of her shoulders taut, with one hand gripped fast upon the other, holding the instant. When first he had spoken to her, a brilliant cry of recognition, a shining, brittle cry, had pierced her inwardly like the running of crystal swords; the night, the people, the whole circumstance of her life, had vanished as though they had been tipped over the world's edge; and she lay now in the lull of their slow return, remembering from an unaccountable dream that her lips had spoken of the battle of Waterloo, but actively aware only of his nearness and of the miracle that he also was held by her tension, waiting. This she knew, in a secrecy below the surface of her acknowledgments, with an intuition to which the sensitiveness of all her flesh, as though it were tremulous in a delight of airy contacts, was continuous response. She turned her head to look at him, in wonder not so much that he should be at her side as that he should exist. The music stopped. There was a clatter of applause. His eyes laughed suddenly, not at her rapt seriousness, but in her own joy. Far away, in a patch of intense light, she saw the conductor bowing and, upon his roof, the stars flow down in straws of silver, edged with watery gold. A brim of gold shook under her lashes.

"Happy?" he said.

She nodded.

"And you don't want to talk?" She could not; her lips moved; she could not. "Why should you?" he said. "The gods brought you here. They lit the stars, blew away the clouds, quieted the sea." She knew that he was talking in this way, half serious, half fantastic, to give her time. "They sent me here," he continued, "to provide deck-chairs. You are their guest this evening. So you can behave for once just as you like—as long as you don't go away. You can talk and I will listen. Or I will talk while you listen. And they grant you a wish," he added, "which shall be fulfilled."

"You talk and I'll listen," she said.

"But your wish?"

She shook her head. "I haven't one. This is wonderful as it is." Afraid of missing any part of it that her memory might preserve, she turned in her chair to look at the sea. "The little boats," she heard herself say; "isn't it a pity they can't be taken out at night? It isn't allowed, you know. Wouldn't you think it would be quite safe on a still evening?"

"Not," he said, "for a party of drunks."

She considered that and let it pass among the astonish-ments of mankind. "So only the steamer goes out. But that isn't the same. It's crowded. They play a gramophone on deck and that spoils everything, doesn't it?"

"It would," he answered.

"You haven't been?"

"Never."

It entered her mind that she ought not to have asked him whether he had been in the steamer. She looked at him, remembering her fellow voyagers.

"That was stupid of me."

"What?"

"Thinking you might have gone out in the steamer."

"And why shouldn't I?"

"Because," she answered, "I think you do everything differently from other people." Having said so much, she hastened on. "We went one night last week. It was to have been a kind of treat. But rain came on—oh, but there was one lovely thing. They——"

She had wanted him to share her remembered pleasure,

but suddenly she doubted it, became timid of her own voice in his presence, and was silent.

"Tell me," he said.

It seemed foolish and empty now. "It was only something they played on the gramophone."

"What was it?" he asked. For a moment, in his eagerness, he touched her hand, and she, who had been taught to believe that her little adventures in discovery were freakish and of interest to none but herself, was pierced by a sensation of encouragement and hope that went to her heart.

"I'd never heard it before," she replied. "But there was a boy working the gramophone. I asked. He read the name on the record. It was Schubert : *Death and the Maiden*."

"The Quartet?"

"No," she said. "I don't think so. I mean—this was a song. Why did you say 'quartet'?"

"There is one based on the song."

" I see . . . Are you a musician?"

"No."

"But you know it—the song, I mean? You know it! Isn't it wonderful! Or—isn't it?"

" 'Or—isn't it?' " he repeated. "Why do you doubt when you have heard? It's your school, your damnable school. They taught you Schubert there but they didn't teach you that—and so you doubt! Doubt all opinion on art that has been taught to you. Doubt even your own feeling then. You may be trumping up an emotion without knowing it. But this was new. There it was, suddenly, in the midst of nonsense. You weren't sitting in a concert hall waiting to be impressed. There it was, so many notes on a gramophone, played in a tripper steamer; they all heard it and were deaf; they giggled and tried on one another's hats. But you heard it separately, alone. It was being played to you, wasn't it? You were writing it yourself, all fresh."

"Yes," she said, settling her chin in her hand.

He watched her profile, the little upward thrust of her chin, the wrist's abrupt angle.

"That's what an artist writes for," he said, "not schoolmistresses and their little metronome. He writes to enable the dumb to speak."

She said: "Then you *are* a musician?"

"No. I've told you. I own the deck-chairs."

The conductor was tapping his music-stand. Voices dropped; far away the sea hissed on the shingle; music began. He was writing in a note-book on his knee; a boy, sprung from nowhere, was at his side; when she looked again, the boy was gone in the direction of the bandstand and the note-book was put away.

"Who was the boy?"

He leaned towards her, speaking through the music, and when he replied "A messenger of the gods," it was not of his reply she thought nor of the vanished boy but of the fiery intensity with which he had spoken of music—attacking her, but with weapons that struck life into her such as she had never imagined. "There's a man in this band who can really play the violin," he said. "What's more, they can muster a quartette," and the words hung suspended in her mind while the music continued.

"Do you mean," she asked when the opportunity to speak came again, "that's he's a kind of lost genius? Can't anything be done to get him out of the band?"

"He's not Kreisler."

"But if he were given his chance?"

"Still not Kreisler."

"Which is he? Do show me."

"The pale young man with a high peaky forehead and a rim of dark hair running over it—like a black hair-pin. He's Russian. Why are you so interested in him?"

"I thought how terrible it must be to live the same life always—and the wrong life."

"The wrong life?"

It was of herself she had been thinking, of the past fallen away from her, of the future undeclared. "I mean," she said, "perhaps he feels he belongs in Russia. His roots are there. And perhaps, though he may not be able to *play* like Kreisler or to compose at all, he may always be imagining himself as a great, great musician. And he hangs half-way between earth and heaven—and he goes on playing in the band."

"But so do we all—hang half-way between earth and heaven—and we go on playing in the band. You for example."

"I?"

"You hang between what you imagine yourself to have been and what you feel yourself becoming. What do you feel yourself becoming? You have no words for it. Some people say: 'a poet' or 'a saint'; the young Russian says, perhaps, 'Beethoven'; some people imagine themselves completed as a lover or a mother or, quite simply, as Mayor of Chelmouth or Prime Minister of England. It makes no great odds what you call it. What matters is the impulse to become—say, a god. And the impulse is continuous because the object continuously recedes unless a man dries up and settles down to his cage or his bandstand. But as I understand it, the essence of being alive is in the idea of oneself as swinging, imprisoned, between an imagined past and an imagined future, and in the knowledge of wings."

"You mean," she said, "dying."

"Not only that. There are more deaths than one. But when I spoke to you of the fulfilments, I frightened you. There are more deaths than one and more escapes than one. It was you who spoke to me of *Death and the Maiden*."

"But what can—what can the little Russian do if he's not a great musician?"

"Perhaps," he answered, "it's all a matter of degree. The impulse to be a god may be only a muffled impulse in him; it will cease, it will leave him in a kind of content. In many people it's no more than a flash when they are very young; afterwards they forget the need to die continually. They tuck their head under their wing, and sit on their perch and can't understand why others beat themselves against the bars. And when they are bored, they hop into their swing, and swing, amusing themselves, dining out, chattering, playing cards, putting pennies in the slot, forgetting to die or to be reborn. I think genius is the power to die. In love, in poetry—how you will—but to die."

She waited but he said no more. He was shivering and without regard for her. His eyes, though alive and glowing, were set; he was seeing nothing that she saw; and she began to speak, not because she wished to speak, but because words seemed the only way back to the plane of normality from which, suddenly and with a pang of terror, she had felt herself to be exiled.

"What you say," she began with a primness that belonged to a different world, "about the bird in a cage reminds me——" and in that instant she knew within her who had written the poem that she and Peter had read together. She wished in a panic of longing to cancel the words she had already spoken, but the half-finished sentence hung over her. She could not go back. Even less, when his expectation, his slow, ungentle smile, was turned upon her, could she go back, and she continued in an agony of shame:

"It is in a poem."

"Yes." He nodded. "Say it."

"No; oh, please, no!"

"Yes, you shall say it this time."

"Why? Why must I?"

"Because I have never heard it spoken by any human being. It shall be you."

And she said, staring before her:

> " *Last night I flew into the tree of death;*
> *Sudden an outer wind did me sustain;*
> *And I, from gilded poppet on its swing,*
> *Wrapt in my element, was bird again.*"

And afterwards she said: "You wrote it."

"Yes. Am I forgiven?"

"Forgiven?"

"For deceiving you."

"Oh, I've been a fool," she said. "Such a fool! In a way I knew always. Not that you were"—even the name was hard to say—"Lord Sparkenbroke, but that——"

"Now you know," he interrupted, "are you sorry?"

She turned to look at him with so wide a gaze that he leaned back and laughed aloud.

"My dear, I'm not a tomb in Westminster Abbey. Now you shall tell me your name."

"Leward."

"I know that. George Hardy said as much. But he appeared not to think that your other name would interest me."

"Mary," she said. "Why didn't you tell me? Why did you let me be such a fool? In the wood——"

"I did tell you I owned the wood. . . . And if I had told you more, what would you have done? Run away?"

All she had said, the questions she had asked, the whole drift of her imagination, passed through her mind, and she was ashamed. "Let me go now," she said. "It's all done. Please let me go."

"Why?" he answered. "Tell me. What are you ashamed of? I wasn't deliberately playing a trick on you. I wasn't trying to hurt you."

What was in her heart could not be said, but she could say blindly words that in some way represented it: "You are famous. You are a great man. You have everything."

"Nothing that you have."

"I?" and the question had in it a curiosity so gentle and single-minded that the words he had intended to speak appeared to him in their cruelty. But he spoke them, intently watching her face.

"Don't you know that you are beautiful?" And swiftly, as her expression answered his words, he added: "There are other poets. But there is no beauty like yours. Can't we be equals?"

"If it were true," she said, "even then—oh, I'm so happy and so miserable! . . . So happy—as if nothing were true: everything wild and enchanted."

He caught his breath: "'Wild and enchanted!' Those words together. Where did they come from?"

She shook her head, puzzled. "Nowhere. Why?"

"They move together. Soon," he said, "you will write

a poem for me as well as live it." Then, his face alight, he cried: "I will write something for you to remember this evening by."

"Now?" she said.

He smiled. "I didn't mean now. Is that a challenge?"

"Could you? I mean——"

"Something. Give me your programme."

"My programme?" but she handed it to him. On its back, within a border of advertisements, was an empty square, "This Space to Let," and over it he held his pencil. She watched the pencil move, and began to think that, foolish as she had been in failing to recognize him, she was more foolish in fearing him and believing him to be, as people said, wicked. He belonged to a world different from hers, but to condemn him for that reason was but the stupid prejudice of those who had not met him. Was it true, perhaps, that she was of some value to him? The possibility gave a new value to her own life, and she dreamed that there was an emptiness in his existence that she might make less empty. As though she were telling herself a story of another world unfettered by the conditions dividing him from her, she imagined a vague companionship between them without heat, without consequence, as safely included as a tale within the covers of a book. She knew that no harm could come to her while she was happy as she was happy now.

The programme was laid before her.

> " Lovely and fearless, teach my song
> Thy happy light to borrow.
> Then only shall I do no wrong
> And thou not weep to-morrow."

"Is that the kind of rhyme you wanted?" he said. "Or this?"

He took the sheet from her and wrote again:

> " Let not a dream possess thine eyes,
> Know that my song is all of me;
> But, if thy dream in anguish dies,
> What I have taken—all of thee."

" 'Any Artist to any Maiden',", he said.

"May I keep them?"

"As long as you keep them secret."

Did he mean that he was dissatisfied with them? She would have liked to ask what was wrong with them; but she knew suddenly that, though she had read the words and listened to their rhyme and trembled in the thought that she was now holding in her hand for the first time what she would look at again and again, even in her very old age, she did not know at all what the verses were about. She had given no attention to their meaning and she was about to read them again when Sparkenbroke said:

"Lean back in your chair and shut your eyes."

"Why?"

"Because your wish is going to be fulfilled."

She did not understand but obeyed. From above her, when her eyes were shut, came down the thin, soapy smell of the canvas awning to her chair and, presently, the slow movement of Schubert's quartette. "Did you tell them to play this?" she asked without opening her eyes. As she listened, she seemed to slide away into the future, and to feel memories, that were now her present experience, crowd in upon her. She opened her eyes to look at him, wondering if it were true that she was beautiful and hearing the answer like a song within her.

CHAPTER TWELVE

GEORGE had not seen Mary after leaving her in the church wood. He had returned late to the Rectory and found his sister and father at a tea-table from which their guests had already gone. "I was kept," he said with the brisk, cheerful energy that was his corrective for emotion in himself. "Couldn't get away. Did all three of them pack into the young man's car?" Helen told him that Mary had not reached Sparkenbroke House. Such a disappointment for her. Another Saturday, no doubt, it could be arranged.

George did not reply. Lifting the cosy, he tested the warmth of the tea. It was almost cold, but he said it was hot enough, and sat down. Over the rim of his cup he looked at Helen's face, sharply outlined against the wall of the room, composed and tranquil, like the face of a good queen on a coin; then at his father's. The old man was looking straight at him or at the window behind him, and the daylight lay full on that serene countenance, which to George, in his childhood, had been the recognizable part of the face of God. In spite of this resemblance, or perhaps because of it, George sometimes disapproved of his father, and disapproved, to his own surprise, of what he most loved in him—an impish liveliness, inappropriate on Sinai, that prompted him to make fun of his children as though they were the elders and he the child. Nothing pleased George better or embarrassed him more than to be made fun of in this way. Like his sister, and greatly under her influence, he had always been, by self-discipline, too old for his age, but not, as she was, by inclination; to laugh, to be irresponsible, to throw his cap in the air was an unquenchable impulse of his nature and he loved his father for knowing this and reminding him of it, however inconveniently. His difficulty—and his delight—was that he never knew what that old head was brewing or how far those wide eyes had seen; nor was he able to adjust himself to his father's incalculable simplicities, which, in the midst of more than a little pedantry of speech and dry elaboration of scholarship, would dart out like fiery tongues, enabling him to see the creatures of God, men and women, animals, birds, insects, even trees and flowers, as a child might see the assembly of his Noah's Ark, each possessed of a burning individuality but all equal, all beloved, all timeless, to be laughed at, reproved, examined, enjoyed, but not finally judged. He could be angry, even intolerant; he could, in a fit of temper, banish one of the pieces in his Noah's Ark to outer darkness; but the banishment was part of an unreality of which he did not cease to be aware.

"Jam, please, Father."

The pot was pushed towards him.

"Have a good tea, George," said Helen. "I think you ought to have some more made. They've been gone some time now."

George looked at the empty plates. Two of them had the stubs of cigarettes on them; one, on his father's right, had not. She sat there, he said to himself, and saw the bland face of the mantelpiece clock above her head. So vivid was this imagining that he returned, instantly and resolutely, to his bread and jam—instantly, he supposed, but Helen was gone from the room and he had not noticed her going. He and his father were alone; but they were accustomed to companionable silence, and he was free to wonder, while his crust split under his knife, what it felt like to be young as Mary was young. No difficult researches into the past were required of him; the boy he had been was present in him still; only knowledge and circumstance had changed; but he alone—and his father perhaps—knew and felt this immutability; others saw the outer case—and he looked at his broad hands, the loose creases at the finger-joints.

"George, how far did you take her?"

"To the edge of the church wood and the orchard," he answered at once without reflecting that Mary had not been spoken of for twenty minutes. "What are you smiling at?" he added.

His father ceased to smile. "Into sight of the house?"

"Almost."

"Then what has she been doing with herself?"

"I suppose she got lost," said George, who had a dislike of investigations.

"For a man of science," the Rector persisted, "you put up a stubborn resistance to facts. You have said she was almost in sight of the house. I suggest that she contrived to lose herself."

"Why should she? She wanted to see the place."

"But perhaps not in that company. Did you like the young man?"

"Whether I like him isn't here or there. She's engaged to him."

"She is indeed."

"Well?"

"Well?"

They looked at each other over the cake-basket.

"Oh, nonsense," George exclaimed, resisting the temptations of this fanciful theory. Facts were facts; to be engaged was to be engaged. "Two's company," he said. "Much more probable that she was bored by her father."

"That," the Rector said, "might well be."

"And anyhow," George continued, "I don't see that it's any business of ours."

"No. Except that we are men and that she was beautiful and seemed——unhappy? Andromeda was not strictly the business of Perseus?"

His father had a disturbing habit of giving to his statements a questioning lilt, but George had learnt long ago the virtue of holding his tongue.

"She's a child," was all he said.

"A very excited one when she came in to tea."

"Excited?"

"White and silent. I took her away to show her my books. Scarcely a word."

"Perhaps she's not interested in books."

"Perhaps not," his father said.

A child, George continued to call her; her concerns were not his; but the words "white and silent" dwelt in his mind, and on Sunday, when he awoke, he had the disturbing impression that between sleeping and waking his thought had been continuous, though he could recall of the night nothing but the scent and movement of trees. For three days he was happy when he thought of her and angry when he found himself doing so. On the morning of the fourth, he decided vigorously, while looking out of his bedroom window with shaving-brush in hand, that the sun would shine whether she was in the world or not, and came down to breakfast determinedly glad that he was no longer a young man. That he was able to give his full attention to his first patient and to make her cackle with laughter proved to him that he had, during the week-end, been making a pretty fool of himself; to be engaged was to be engaged and Mary was a child. But, in the after-noon, finding himself unexpectedly at leisure, he perceived how great a pity it was that this child should have missed her chance to see Sparkenbroke House. This was Wednes-day; the next visitors' day, Saturday, was far off. Lady Sparkenbroke wouldn't mind if he took her himself, and at three o'clock he was at the reception desk of the hotel asking for Miss Leward.

She came at last. While she was still on the stairs, half hidden by the machinery of the lift and its wire netting, he saw a frock of lilac cotton, a light of hair, a young, springy movement that stung his whole body with an expectation so intense that pain was part of its delight; but when she was to be fully seen, walking across the hall, the pile of the carpet seeming to come to life under each step of hers, he was filled with an overpowering sense of exclusion and coldness, a feeling that he did not belong to the scene he was witnessing, for her gaze passed over him without recognition; she was not knowingly coming to him; he was not in her thoughts, as he had supposed. A moment later, she saw him. An almost haunted watchfulness, an extreme tenseness, went out of her expression; for an instant, bewildered, she hung between two moods; then came to him with the confiding eagerness of a lost child at the sight of a familiar face and took his hand and said:

"Oh, I'm glad it's you! I am glad!"

"Didn't they tell you?"

"Not who it was. The boy had forgotten the name."

"I should have thought they'd have known me here by this time," he grumbled. "Perhaps he's a new boy."

How quickly her breath was coming, as though she had been frightened! To bring her down to earth, he told her of his proposal that she should visit Sparkenbroke House with him.

"But it isn't visitors' day. Shan't we—I mean, shan't we disturb Lord Sparkenbroke?"

"He's never there at this time."

"What would he be doing now?"

"He'd be at Derry's Cottage—or miles away, riding or in the car. You needn't be afraid of him. . . . Would your father like to come?" George added cautiously.

To his delight she said at once: "Let's go alone. He's out. I'll leave a message for him," and she sat down to write it. He had not seen her handwriting except on the letters Helen had received before her coming and then had paid no attention to it; now, wishing to see it—for was it not a part of herself?—and to hold in his hand the paper that had been under hers, he offered to give in the note at the desk, but she withheld it from him, and went to the desk herself.

"Still no letter for me?"

"No, miss. It's half an hour yet to the four o'clock post."

She is expecting a letter from Peter, George thought; why hasn't the fellow written? for he remembered, as he remembered now with a little pang many experiences of his own youth, that letters were worth receiving when you were in love.

"I wish I looked forward to my letters," he said.

She was getting into his car as he said this and looked round at him with such startled eyes that he felt he had stumbled unpardonably into the privacy of her adventure. "Don't you?" she asked out of a dream.

"Mine are mostly from patients," he replied, and added to himself: Father's wrong this time—she is in love, and while he slipped in the gears his thought repeated: She's in love to take the breath away. Looking at her, remembering the young man, he wondered how it was possible; but Nature's very queer, he said, very queer, and he began to reflect on the mysteries of biology until the beauty of the special instance seated at his side put such general speculation out of countenance. How young she is, he said to himself for the thousandth time but with the excitement of fresh discovery, and her mind—though I must say she seemed genuinely glad to come out with me—her mind is naturally full of Peter. No doubt she'd be pleased by a chance to talk about him, and George, with the tact of a Newfoundland who wishes to enter a drawing-room without calling too much attention to his progress, said how pleasant it was to find oneself still near the beginning of the cricket season; it meant that all summer lay ahead; didn't she think that September, when it came —— but the word "cricket" lighted not a spark in her. Perhaps, George thought, cricket is a game that bores her, as it does bore a great many women; perhaps she has had a difference on this very subject with Peter and they are now deliciously occupied in forgiving each other. As an alternative to cricket, and selfishly glad that Peter was not, after all, to be the subject of their conversation, he launched out on the history of Sparkenbroke House, mentioning dutifully the principal treasures contained in it. There was a Rubens, said to be the *largest* Rubens in any private collection—

"Did you say the *largest*?" she asked.

"Yes, so they say." He would have liked to explain that he himself attached no great importance to its size; he had been repeating a fact which, he had thought, might be of interest to her; but to explain this without seeming to patronize her was not easy and he hurried on, saying that he agreed with Piers that the whole place was too big.

"You agree with—who did you say?"

"Piers . . . Sparkenbroke."

"Is there a portrait of him?" she said.

"There's one in the Long Gallery."

"Isn't it strange that he won't ever be photographed? I should have thought a newspaper man would have been bound to catch him some time."

"One did," George replied with a grin. "On the pavement outside Chelmouth railway station. Sparkenbroke knocked the camera out of his hands, smashed it, gave him a bundle of notes and went on."

"Are there really no photographs of him, then?"

"I have some. I took them myself when he was a boy. Would you like to see them?"

"Oh," she exclaimed, "yes, I should. What was he like when he was small? Did you guess then that he would be famous some day?"

"My old father did, I think. . . . There's one of him with his elder brother."

"I didn't know he had a brother?"

"A half-brother, Stephen; he was killed early in the war. The photograph was taken in the Rectory garden. It makes poor Stephen look half asleep, Piers is so alive."

"Yes," she said, lingering on the word.

"Helen," George went on, "Helen says it's the way the sun falls on him, slantwise across his face, and there may be something in that. But still——"

"Helen's funny in some ways," Mary said, throwing towards him a doubtful, sparkling look, before deciding that with him she might risk this criticism of his sister. "Don't you think that sometimes she *won't* see things she does see—if you know what I mean? I remember at school, when I got excited about something—you know, really happy, quite mad about something in the way you do when you're young—she was pleased, too, in a way, but——"

"I know," he answered.

"Do you? I was half afraid to say that to you—at least, I was when I began—because, well, she's your sister and she's a dear. And then I felt somehow you'd know what I meant."

He turned to her with a little laugh of surprised gratitude; a hand dropped from the steering-wheel.

"Well, you see, even before the far-off days when you were young, I was a younger brother at home."

"Yes," she said, her imagination plunging into history, "of course you were. . . . Oh, look," she cried, when the car had passed the Rectory and turned to the right at Sparkenbroke Cross. "There's his churchyard. . . . When we were there, why didn't you tell me about the other part of the rhyme? I found it myself afterwards, you know."

"You came back into the churchyard? Was that how you got lost?"

She did not answer, but presently, echoing her thought aloud, she repeated:

> "*Here in the womb is winter spring.*
> *Who stays? A Fool. Who knocks? A King.*"

And she added: "I can't feel like that. Can you? . . . Don't you think, on a day like this, it makes him feel a king just to be alive?" She turned round in the car, half lifted from her seat. "Oh, look at those clouds racing!"

"I can't," he answered. "I have to drive."

They swung in by the main gates and she became silent. Sparkenbroke House stretched out across its hill. "It *is* big," she said. "Are you sure it's all right?"

"What?"

"Our coming here?"

"Certainly, it is. We'll just go and have a word with Lady Sparkenbroke first. Probably she'll give us tea."

"Oh, but——"

"Nonsense," he said, "she's charming. And think how proud I shall be of having brought you here."

"But need we stay to tea?"

"Not if you don't want to."

"I'd rather tea—at the Rectory or somewhere."

"Bless you," he said. "All right."

Lady Sparkenbroke was in her morning-room, seated on the floor beside a long sofa. On the carpet were spread out papers that had overflowed from a table near by, and these she was studying in company with a small man, long-faced, like an ant-eater, who leaned down between his knees from the sofa's edge and pointed down with a long, sinewy hand to a row of figures. On the floor Lady Sparkenbroke appeared young and slender; the supple-ness of her curve, the quick movement of her head, her air of having been caught off her guard, gave her for a moment the charm of girlhood; but when she stood up, smiling at once to free George from the embarrassment of having interrupted her, there was, in the simplicity of her manner and in her desire to put others at ease in her presence, a grace of maturity. She laughed at herself for having been discovered on the floor. But it was quite time, she exclaimed, that she and Mr. Crute were interrupted; they had been working too long; and Mr. Crute, in the tone of a minister who yields discreetly, but not for long, to his Sovereign's mood, agreed that they would be the better for a rest, and gathered his papers together. "And this is the first time you have seen the house?" she said to Mary. "You couldn't have a better guide than Dr. Hardy. He has known it much longer than I have. Will you let me come with you, George? I'm sure I should learn things I don't know."

Mr. Crute intervened to remind her that he was, most unfortunately, bound to go back to London by the evening train. "Then," she said, "I suppose we must get on, but let me ring for tea now. I'm sure Miss Leward would like some tea, and you can take her round the house afterwards. I wish I could come too!"

She does really wish it, Mary thought with surprise. It must be wretched to be left behind to go over accounts with that little man! What would happen if she said: I won't, and sent him away? I suppose she could. I wonder

if she ever does? and she looked into Lady Sparkenbroke's
face as if she might find there an answer, not to this
question only but to others half formed in her mind which
their encounter had provoked. Lady Sparkenbroke had
been listening to George while he explained with difficulty
that they could not stay to tea, but, as though she had felt
Mary's look of inquiry, she turned now and their eyes met.
Mary at once looked away.

Never before had she been afraid to meet anyone's
regard. She was the more ashamed because, while her
conscience accused her of deception, her reason mocked
her conscience, saying that she had after all done nothing
to be ashamed of, that she was taking with a schoolgirl's
solemnity what Lord Sparkenbroke had already forgotten,
and that her feeling of guilt in his wife's presence was
itself a form of ridiculous self-flattery and delusion.
Probably he wouldn't even write the letter he had promised
—and now, perceiving clearly for the first time how
desperately her heart was set on this letter, she felt within
her a pang of resentment, even of enmity, against her
hostess, as though, incomprehensibly, Lady Sparkenbroke
stood between her and the appeasement that the letter
would bring; and this sensation of malice towards another
was so profoundly contrary to her knowledge of herself
that she was frightened by it. But George was still saying,
tentatively and as though he scarcely hoped to be believed,
that he had given a half-promise to take Miss Leward
back to tea at the Rectory, and when Mary looked again at
Lady Sparkenbroke, feeling that her confusion must have
been apparent to another woman and above all to this
woman, she found only an expression of puzzlement,
kindly and even a little amused, on that handsome face,
and a sad, hesitant smile on those lips. What is she thinking?
Mary asked herself, and, watching the movement of Lady
Sparkenbroke's eyes towards George, found an answer.
She thinks that George is making these excuses to keep
me to himself, and, because she likes George, she is hoping
that she will like me! She is asking herself whether George
is in love with me and whether he will be hurt! And

G

suddenly Mary was flooded with a feeling of gratitude towards Lady Sparkenbroke because, evidently, she liked George so much, and respected him and was amused by him. "I think the Rectory is very selfish," Lady Sparkenbroke said, "keeping you to itself. But perhaps you'll come again. Come *not* on a Saturday and I'll show you my own treasures. I have some that even Dr. Hardy doesn't know about. Are you staying long in Chelmouth?"

Mary replied gratefully, for she understood that Lady Sparkenbroke had shown this friendliness towards her not for George's sake only. She likes me, Mary said, as I like her; we could, I know, be friends; and she said good-bye with a sense of loss. Lady Sparkenbroke came with them into the hall, and there, touching Mary's arm and pointing to a portrait of a girl in a white dress against a background of sky and trees, she said: "Look, do you recognize yourself? George, isn't it a likeness—the Raeburn?"

"The beautiful Miss Darrant," George said. "Yes, now you say so, it is indeed."

"But not so young," Lady Sparkenbroke answered.

Mary gazed at the picture. "Who was she? An ancestor of yours?"

"Of mine? Oh, no. She's my husband's great grandmother—on his mother's side. It's the most beautiful Raeburn I've seen, though he says there is one to equal it in the Mellon collection in New York—a portrait of Miss Urquhart."

She said good-bye again and returned to her morning-room, at the open door of which Mr. Crute could be seen awaiting her.

"I've never been able to understand how old Sparkenbroke came to leave that picture hanging where it is," George said as he led Mary upstairs, and he told her how Piers's mother had run away when he was a child, taking him with her; how, being brought home, he had not seen his mother again; and how sternly his father had rid the house of every remembrancer of her, even putting away

her portrait which hung now in the long gallery beside
Piers's own. "But Miss Darrant was allowed to keep her
place," he added, "perhaps because she had become for
him simply the Raeburn of a girl in a white dress," and
Mary asked him: "Am I really like her?" She was asking
herself, with a tremor of fear: is it true, then, that I am
beautiful? She repeated the word in her mind, for, since
Sparkenbroke had used it, it had become new to her;
"pretty" and "very pretty" were the words that she had
accepted hitherto and acceptance had dulled them. They
were the words her mother had used long ago in warning
her against vanity: There are plenty of other pretty little
girls in the world; it is character, Mary, that tells in the
end; and Peter used them continually when he wished to
crumple her with kisses and let his thumb move down her
spine. They were words that had no power to disturb her,
coins without currency in her emotion; but beauty was a
new treasure poured into her lap. It was as if, having
thought of herself always as one of the people, she had
discovered that she was an hereditary princess. Ambition
to rule was not provoked in her; it was enough that the
idea of beauty, like knowledge of great ancestry, gave her,
as it were, a name.

Her question gave George the best of opportunities
to gaze at her, and he availed himself of it, turning her
to the light that shone obliquely into the room in which
they stood—one of the antechambers through which
the ballroom was approached. As she looked back at
him, the little flicker at the corners of her lips accentuated, as only the smile of extreme youth can accentuate,
the gravity of her face, and her eyes, bright with a
window's miniature, retained still, within the tragic adoration of women for life itself, that untamed steadfastness of
childhood, half doubt, half challenge, which seems, with
the detached passion of tiger or angel, to consider this
world in terms of another, secretly familiar.

"Am I?" she repeated, and he could not answer, for, if
he answered, time, now still, would move forward again,
and her face be lost; the instant, falling into the past,

would become memory, suffering memory's little deaths; and when at last he compelled himself to speak, he felt lonely, as though she had loved him and were dead. But he said cheerfully enough:

"You look as if you had come into a fortune!"

"If I had," she answered, "I wonder what I should do with it?"

"Would you live in a palace like this?" He nodded at the ballroom they were entering, and she asked, gazing at the covering of the Gobelins, why there were sheets even on the wall. He told her, adding that the ceiling was a beautiful one; but in this light, when she looked up, its vaulting receded into an ochre mist, from which the chandeliers, doubly-banked at gallery-level and higher, hung dolefully in their great balloons of brown linen. At the farther end of the room, like sheep penned in a corner of a meadow, were shrouded forms, recognizably of chairs; from the darkness of the south wall, window after window flashed out, in narrowing perspective, from sun-glitter to slim pencilling of light; the doors to the antechambers were open; the great central doors were open too, and through them, across corridor and stairhead, were to be seen the high windows of the staircase casting their thin rays downward to the hall. A gust stirred in the place, the shrouds rippled, and, following with her eyes a wisp of paper that danced away from her feet over the floor's cloudy mirror, Mary saw, in the great doorway where an instant earlier had been only the cold shine of corridor and baluster, a child. She touched George's arm; her fingers tightened upon it; and the little boy, welcomed by him, sprang to life and ran forward, to hesitate at five yards distance from the strange lady. "This is Richard," George said, leading him up, but the boy was prepared now to give Mary his own greeting, without shifting his eyes from her face.

"Are you seeing the house?"

"Yes," Mary answered. "I'm Dr. Hardy's friend. He brought me."

"I see. . . ." And he went straight to his point. "Would

you like to see Daddy's room, where he works? He's not there now."

"I should very much. Will you take me?"

He led the way.

"Couldn't we go through the Long Gallery, Richard?" George asked.

His own had been a shorter way, up a flight of stairs on the lowest step of which he was already standing, and although, turning back, he made his concession, he was impatient of delays, except at his father's portrait. "That's Spark," he said, "and that's his mother, you see. She was in Florence. Now she's in the Mound. He brought her home," and, taking Mary's hand, he drew her on.

"That is the door of his room," he announced, and stopped that they might consider it before he approached. "Now you can see," he said, opening the door. "Sometimes he's here."

"But doesn't he work more often in the cottage down in the woods?"

"Sometimes he's here," the boy repeated. "Do you like it?" He stared, almost with anxiety, at the whitewashed walls, the couch, the chair, the table—the cell-like austerity of the place. "I do," he added, "it's so little. Sometimes, when he comes up, he tells me stories here instead of in bed. And we make plans. Some day, when he's in Italy, I shall go too. Have you been to Italy?"

"Never."

"Have you, Dr. George?"

"Not yet."

"What do you think this is?" Richard asked Mary, patting a high desk of plain oak built against the wall under the room's single window. "Guess. Don't tell her, Dr. George," and he explained that here his father stood to write when he could sit no longer at the table.

"And now," he said, when they had admired the bare little room, "perhaps we must go."

In the corridor he bade them farewell abruptly and vanished up his own stair.

George hesitated. "More?" he said. "Or have you had enough? Tired?"

She shook her head and drew breath, trembling. "Not tired. But I'd like to go now."

"Then back we go to the Rectory for tea."

"Isn't it late?"

"Five. Thereabouts. There's always tea." Seeing that she hesitated, he added: "What is it? My dear, you're pale. Has this great barrack got on your nerves?"

"I'd like to walk," she answered. "Why are you such a comforting person, I wonder? You don't know how glad I was when you came this afternoon. Let's walk. Or must you go home?"

"No," he said, so proud of this invitation that for once he spoke hastily as though he feared the chance might be snatched from him. "Home? God forbid. . . . Where shall we walk?"

What they spoke of during this walk was afterwards forgotten. George remembered chiefly that, when she took off her hat, the sun, penetrating her hair, laid a mesh of light upon her which, certainly, had fallen upon no other woman at any time, and that, in his company, she was neither bored nor shy. And she remembered of their companionship, its happy, calm reassurance. She was finding her feet; she was moving towards decision; she had wanted their walk to continue until the light had gone out of the trees and the hedgerows were asleep; but the June day was long and, when they returned to the Rectory for George's car, nothing of evening had come but its stillness and a leaden somnolence of the stream under the white bridge.

"How lovely it must be here at night!" she said to Helen. "Do you sit on your lawn after supper? Are there bats and owls?"

"Yes," Helen said. "There are bats and owls."

"I think you have the loveliest house in the world!" Mary exclaimed. "If I had it, I should never want anything else. Do you hear the stream through your bedroom windows at night?"

"Not in my room," Helen said. "In the front of the house, you do. And sometimes the ducks wake up and flap their wings."

Mary, perceiving that she was being laughed at, laughed at herself.

"You musn't laugh at me! I'm serious."

"That you would rather live here than anywhere in the world!" the Rector asked. "I take it as a promise that at least you will come and stay with us. Spring is the time. Or autumn. Shall it be next spring?"

"Yes," she said. "Please! May I come not just for a week-end but long enough to feel that I live here? May I?"

"You shall help me with my sermons," Mr. Hardy said.

"I?"

"Who better? You have only to sit in the room while I write."

She looked at him, wondering, and smiled.

"But won't you be in Italy in the spring—with your husband?" Helen asked.

"I suppose I shall"—and it was said in such a tone that the old man turned from the doorway in which they had been standing and plunged into the house, his shoulders up, his hands knotted behind him.

George and his car were ready.

"I am coming to stay at the Rectory," she said as they drove away. "Your father has just invited me."

"When? Now?"

"In the spring."

"And your husband, of course," George said with courage.

"Do you think Peter would like it as much as I should?"

"I don't know. He ought to. You'd be there."

"I think," she said, "I should like to come alone some day."

He answered gruffly. "Nothing to do, you know. It's very quiet."

"I know. That's why."

But at the outskirts of Chelmouth her tranquillity forsook her and George knew it, for he had become sensitive to her moods.

"Will your Peter be back from cricket?" he asked.

"I expect so."

"Then you'll find him and his letter together."

"His letter?"

"You asked for one from him as we came out," said George, having long persuaded himself that this was so.

"No," she answered, "not from him;" but she seemed not to care for her answer. Perhaps she wasn't listening, George thought, exempting her from a lie—the only alternative possibility that appeared to him; and his desolate feeling that she had shut him out, and must always shut him out, was sharpened by the way in which she said good-bye at the door of the hotel. She looked at him and thanked him; she took his hand and said, in reply to his question, yes, of course she would come to the Rectory again; she made no haste to leave him. But her mind was in haste, there was in her eyes the brilliant abstraction of fever; her impulse had carried her so far from him that he did not know whether she was indeed happy as she seemed outwardly to be. For an instant he thought: If I were to take her in my arms I believe she'd cry her excitement out of her, then be peaceful like a child. But she went in through the revolving door with such spring in her step, such a liveliness of shoulder and uplifted head, that he doubted the pathos he had so comfortably invented for her. She's young enough to look after herself, he thought; the sooner I learn that, the less of a fool I shall be; and he hunched himself into his car, slamming the door.

There were two letters for her. One was from Peter. The handwriting on the other envelope, easy, vigorous, and compact, had, in ink, an appearance so different from the hasty verses on her band programme, that for a moment she was uncertain that it was Sparkenbroke's. She ripped the envelope while still wearing her gloves and looked at the signature. Her fingers tightened over the sheets, for there is in a letter unread a suspense of fate. By what is written the world has, perhaps, been changed;

when it has been read the change will be operative, and, putting Sparkenbroke's letter into her bag, she let her eyes travel over the lounge, stricken by the unreality that her secret cast over the familiar things and people she saw there, and over herself; stricken also, so that her mind fell into a confusion of fiery rain, by the unreality of her secret, for she was still able, while her life shook under her, to see in herself a schoolgirl dazzled by Sparkenbroke's fame and by the sight of his signature on a letter.

Finding herself seated before a little table, glass-topped and rimmed with brass, she drew off her gloves and laid them upon it; then, with cold fingers, took out Sparkenbroke's letter:

"DERRY'S COTTAGE
Wednesday morning—very early

MY DEAR MARY,

Here is Wednesday morning looking in through the curtain chinks at the lamp still burning on my table. Sunday, Monday, Tuesday—all passed since I left you. I wrote an earlier letter, not sent. This, if I know myself, will be no wiser, but whatever comes I have at least given one meal to my waste-paper basket. I believe that when men and writers come to judgment their waste-paper baskets will appear for the defence. Five minutes ago a pile of manuscript—Sunday, Monday, Tuesday—slid over the table's edge. It lies on the floor, a fine pattern of ghosts. Away it went, as I stretched out an arm for it, at the moment when I wanted it to re-read if I was to continue, for I revise everlastingly, every passage, every sentence holding in it the impulse of the next. If for an instant my mind wanders, I must read back before I can go forward—and my mind had wandered to you. Where is she? What is she doing? What is she becoming? Where is her face? Your face was misty. My imagination would evoke but not define its loveliness. Away went my papers, all sheets unnumbered, and I was down on my knees to gather them, to put them together laboriously by fitting the last word of one sheet to the first of the next. Suddenly I couldn't, or wouldn't. I was written out. Now for sleep—

long, greedy sleep to make up for the arrears of Sunday,
Monday, Tuesday. But I was on edge; I am still; no hope
of sleep yet. In half an hour it will come like a blow on the
head. Meanwhile this letter to you, which, unless my
conscientious basket has it after all, shall be left for Bissett
to post early. It will be in Chelmouth by evening.

And now, what am I to say? 'Come and see me again'
or 'stay away?' Does it matter what I say? If I meant
you not to come, it would be very simple—I should not
write to you at all; and if you mean not to come, you will
drop my letter into your own basket at this WORD, which
I underline three times that you may not mistake it. But
already you have read and I have written beyond it.

You have been so brilliantly in my imagination that
now I am light-headed in the thought of you. Though all
my pleasure, my curiosity and eagerness cry out for you
again, I have destroyed a letter bidding you come; but
whether I owe this noble deed of self-sacrifice to some
scruple for you or to fear for myself I do not know. To
both, perhaps; and it is extremely odd that I should be
afflicted by either—as the world has, doubtless, informed
you since you have known who I am. Come, but come if
you can with light heart; by then I may have recovered my
own, and yet have honesty enough to say again what my
verses said to your band programme. How did they go?
I have forgotten the words; and, though I say now that I
will repeat their meaning to you, it is a thousand to one
I shall not when you are here. For when you are with me
I shall be asking myself what it is, within your beauty and
beyond it, that makes you unique. Nothing is more open
and less bound by experience than your face; it is like a
child's; and yet it is what I think the face of Persephone
must have been, mysterious with the anticipations of
destiny. When first you appeared in the wood you were
a stranger who had broken in upon me; you knew nothing
of the art of writing, nothing of my mind's preoccupation;
then, suddenly, you began to speak of my burying-place, my
tree and water. How did you know? You have an intuition
for truths outside your knowledge, and that is a form of

genius. You will smile at that. Very well; I will watch
your smile; it opens heaven to wise fools, who, though
they have the key in their hand, cannot find the lock.
You smile and shake your head. But why did the Mound
and its inscription fire you also? What brought you to my
wood and stream? Who are you? I do not know, but your
beauty has a recognition in it that I can neither seize nor
escape. You are asleep now, your arm curled round your
head. Is that how you sleep? I imagine it clearly, as though
I were looking through your window, and there is a part
of me that would let you sleep on.

Another part, I suppose, sends this tangled letter. His
name is
                                                SPARKENBROKE"

From the signature, a long arrow led her to the upper
margin. Here was added:

"Who is not very proud of himself or his letter. No
one yet has lived or written well in two minds. But perhaps
there is no better excuse for a man's writing—or for man
himself—than that in five minutes his lamp will be out
and he asleep."

The sheets lay on her lap, unreturned to their envelope.
Her elbows crushed them, and over her clasped hands
she stared at the flash and glitter of the revolving door.
After a little while, looking back with cold surprise into
her former life, she opened her other letter and did not
know that she had opened it until she saw Peter's signature,
fat and sprawling, as though it had been written with a
joiner's pencil. Under the signature was a postscript: "I'm
afraid I've missed the post after all and this won't fetch
up much before I do."

She turned back to the beginning:

"MY SWEET,
        I came here quite safely. You mustn't be angry
with me for coming will you. Cricket's so frightfully
important to me and this was a chance really against
these bowlers and I made 73 yesterday. And then I was
run out. So it was a good thing I came and I'll make it

up when I come back. I'm glad really you are so severe. I like girls to be like that. You mustn't think I'm not because of what happened the other night. But I'm human, and dancing with you makes me weak, specially as we have to be engaged such a long time. Why must we? I hate being away. There's no one here nearly as pretty as you. I must stop. We are going out again after the interval. I must find someone to post this for the afternoon post. Cross-country it takes so long. Will you think it over and be kind and perhaps we could be married in the autumn. I wish I could say what I feel but I don't think I'm a poet. Must go. Love.

PETER"

She read this, and the postscript, a second time. They produced at first no response. Once, she would have persuaded herself to discover in this letter an awkward, puppyish charm and have smiled an affectionate pardon of its clumsiness. Now she received it without sensation of any kind, for she knew that it had never been possible that she should marry the writer of it. Her mind underwent no process of rejecting him. While the letter was still in her hands, she perceived, as though she were recalling a severance already deep in time, that he had no part in her life.

He came up behind her, and, when she turned, kissed her cheek. She let him kiss her, accepting the contact with an indifference more conclusive than hatred.

CHAPTER THIRTEEN

Two days later, soon after five o'clock, George showed out his last patient of the afternoon. Having watched him vanish into Regency Crescent with umbrella hoisted, he closed the front door and returned to his room. His work in Chelmouth was over; his car stood at the gate; there was nothing to prevent him from driving home as soon as he had ordered the few papers on his table and locked up. He let his keys slide from one palm to the other, but did not use them. Instead he sat down at his swivel chair, making little dents in its leather arms by the pressure of his finger-nails, and stared at a landscape in photogravure that hung on the opposite wall. Beneath it, on a plated and flexible arm, was an electric lamp with a shade of green glass, the only conspicuously modern fitting in the room, and under the lamp, pressed against the wall, was an old couch, darkly upholstered, perched like an ill-bred dachshund on legs too long for it, and having at one end a sloping support, not high enough to be of use to anyone seated but a fair substitute for bolster and pillow when a patient was stretched out for examination.

George had often wondered whether this couch should be replaced by a piece of furniture less clumsy; but it was of a convenient height; it was not slippery or cold as a leather couch might have been; and he had a distaste for the spick and span paraphernalia of his profession. A woman was better pleased to find that a cup of tea had been brewing while she dressed than to be laid out on a fine contraption that screwed up and down and gleamed like the apparatus of a conjurer. If she was a woman worth

helping, more of her truth came out over the teacup than
hands and eyes had discovered in her body, for, except to
doctors very young and very vain, the body was a secretive
thing that told even less than a face to strangers in a hurry.

The lamp was innovation enough. For a month or two
it had been a little joke at the expense of his conservatism.
You'll be having a new couch soon, doctor, or a dicta-
phone like that young chap Mellish in the New Town.
But he wouldn't have a new couch; he had decided that
long ago; and why should he sit here now, stumbling over
the old decision? Up went his eyes to the landscape again.
A team was ploughing; the horses strained at a gradient;
above them was a pattern of birds. What birds? For years
this picture, which belonged not to him but to his land-
lord, had hung before him, and he had taken the damned
birds for granted. Rooks presumably.

He tried to shake himself into action, to break free of
this slumbrous meditation which was no more than an
avoidance of thought. If he went now he could be at the
Rectory in less than half an hour. Unless he was called out,
an evening of leisure stretched before him—with luck, a
fine evening, for it was soon after he left Mary at her
hotel on Wednesday that the rain had begun to fall. For
two nights and two days rain had continued with a thin,
drizzling persistence now almost spent. If she had lain
awake in her bed, perhaps she also had heard it, and had
driven her cheek into her pillow, had wrapped her arm
more closely over her breast, imagining the heavy night,
the iron, moony sky. Now the rain was over. Across his
patient's umbrella had lain a steel panel of sun; the roofs
and chimney-stacks were lightening and on the window-
panes were thin streaks of gold. He whipped himself to
rejoice, to taste again the familiar pleasure of a countryside
that draws breath of light when rain is done. This evening
the Rectory garden would be sweet of flower and earth.
White pansies would open their eyes, fir-needles sparkle
on crystal threads, mossy paths gleam at the edge of the
thicket. The terra-cotta of the flower-pots, this morning
dark and sodden, would dry to a washed pink, and over

the chubby cabbages would be a sheen of blue. Before the sun went down all the scents of the garden would be afloat; they would come to him while he read if he put his pipe away; and to-night, if he lay awake again, they would drift in through the open window, the very scents of his childhood. He would be glad that the gentle continuity they represented had not been taken from him, and at last, forgetting them, would fall asleep.

So it should have been; so, he tried to persuade himself, it would be; but to one who loves vainly all former pleasure reflects only the vanity of his love; and George, thinking of his garden and the summer night, thought only of her whose youth pierced him, whose loveliness turned all the credit of his experience to sand. He had no wish to go home, for his home's placidity threw into relief the change in himself. There was no part of its routine which did not now, by evocation of a past when these things had been sufficient to his life, lay emphasis upon his present desire; and he sat at his table without moving, wearied by the obsession of love.

Determined to overcome it, he sprang up and went to the bow-window to look out. He had been right; the rain had ceased; already, perhaps, she had left the hotel; and he imagined in her face, as the wind touched it, the joy of being in the open air again. To be beautiful, to be happy, to be young! To be so young that beauty and happiness were in the nature of things, to be lived—not wondered at! In his imagining of her thus transfigured, he was for an instant released from the conditions of love and forgot that he desired her, but the figure of a girl crossing the road towards his house recalled him to tormented remembrance, for in height and suppleness of movement it resembled hers. The head was down and the hands were thrust ungainly into the pockets of a waterproof. How like, he said, and how unlike! When she comes near, the resemblance will vanish suddenly, but he watched, saying: It is she! It is she! In a moment she will look up! but knowing that he deceived himself.

At his gate the girl stopped. She looked at his house,

thrust her hands deeper into her pockets and passed on.
The expression of her face filled him with terror and an
ungovernable hope. He went out hatless and came up with
her.

"Mary!"

She turned but was silent.

"My dear," he said, "what are you doing here? Where
are you going?"

"Nowhere."

"You're tired. Come in and rest. Why did you go by?
You looked up at the house."

"I didn't want to worry you."

She was swaying; she made a little movement as if she
would turn and escape him; but he did not touch her, for
she had the perilous tenseness of one that walks asleep.

"Come and brew some tea," he said. "My job's done
for the day."

Her will was to refuse, to accept no help of him or any
man; but suddenly, with a little sigh, she said: "Yes," and
walked back at his side. In his room, she sat down
in the armchair by the hearth, her hat on, her body rigid,
the waterproof dragged round her.

"Summer," he said. "Would it be ridiculous to light a
fire?"

"I should love that," she answered, and in a moment
sticks were crackling and under his brown kettle the gas-
ring was lighted. Going to a little table at the end of the
room, he came back, glass in hand.

"Now, will you take this—and give me your hat and
coat?"

When she had obeyed him, he laid his fingers on her
wrist. "How long have you been wandering about?"

"Some time."

"Any lunch?"

"No."

"Breakfast?"

"Yes, of course."

"Coffee, I suppose. . . . Any food?"

She shook her head. "But I'm not hungry."

"Sleep last night?"

"Not much."

He looked at her. "Well, that's enough questions. Don't sit there all stiff and hard. That armchair's comfortable. Go slack in it until the kettle boils."

"I can't," she said.

"Very well. Sit on the floor and make toast if the fire lets you. And don't burn it—unless you want to go to sleep. If sleep comes, sleep where you drop."

She did not sleep. When he gave her tea, she wrapped her hands about her cup, warming them.

"What a comfortable cup!" and, as she drank from it, her eyes gazed at him over its edge as if she were still surprised to find herself in this room and in his company.

"Better?" he asked.

She nodded, and put down her cup; then roused herself, determined to give the explanation which, she evidently felt, was due to him.

"Don't talk," he said. "Not yet, anyhow. Not at all unless it does any good. And don't worry your head over me. It's quite enough for me to have you here. I'd been thinking about you, you know."

"When I came?"

"Not then only."

"I oughtn't to be here," she said. "I saw Peter off this morning. I felt I had to do that. I don't want us to be enemies. I thought that if——"

He checked her again.

"While you're here," he said, "you are my patient, and you will keep quiet."

"But I'm not ill."

"You will be. Put your feet up on that stool and go slack. Shut your eyes; be certain that every muscle is relaxed."

She obeyed for a moment, then shifted and said: "I mustn't wait here. I must go to the hotel."

"Not until I say so. There's time enough."

Her eyes opened and she smiled for the first time. "I like being ordered."

"Of course you do. So do we all. That's being free."

"Being free?"

But he would not trouble her now with his cherished theory of discipline and freedom. Instead, he talked to her of concrete things, certainly remote from whatever in her own life might have troubled her; of his garden, of her days at school, of Sparkenbroke House and the walk they had taken together when they had left it. She answered little and he did not care. Perhaps she would fall asleep after all, and he asked nothing better than that. He would, if necessary, send a message to the hotel saying that she had fainted and was in his charge; then would sit beside her until she awoke. But now and then she replied to him, and, in the intervals, the rhythm of her breast told him that she was not asleep. At first he looked at her seldom, preferring to watch the flames curl backward over the chimney-breach and to feel her presence in the room; but he found after a little while that he could without disturbance let his eyes rest upon her while she talked, so profoundly had her evident suffering changed the incidence of his love for her. What in her youth and its freshness had set her apart from him was dissolved, and he could feel in her company now—not, indeed, the complacent affection that had seemed all wisdom before desire burned it away, and not the hunger that had replaced it, but a brilliant, approaching intimacy; and her body thrown back, the rippling surrender of her weariness, the line of cheek averted, the stream of her throat, filled him with that emotion towards beauty which, projecting the beholder into the timeless essence of the beauty seen, creates in desire the illusion of immortality, and is called love. The impulse of the body continues, but in a lulled suspense, as the speed of a ship, though the traveller's awareness of it is suspended, continues in calm water; and George was at peace, his longing for her quieted in a passionate tranquillity. He dropped beside the hearth to tend the fire, and the action, because it was simple and commonplace, gave him a special pleasure in agreement with his own nature, putting the seal of an habitual plainness on his enraptured mood. The coldness of steel under his hand, the sparks that shone among the ashes, the flames' gleam across the bars, seemed to have been created anew and for him only; they were alive with his own life; they presented to him that peculiar crystallization of joy which love discovers even in material things. Forgetful of her externally, she being present in him and diffused in all he felt and saw— an impregnation of his summed experience—he was silent and still, emptied of thought, until her touch recalled him, and he looked up into her face with a new shock of wonder.

"George," she said, "I don't know why I should come to you with this."

"You didn't. I wish you had," he answered ruefully. "In fact, I brought you. . . . Can you tell me now what's happened? I may be some good."

"Peter's gone away."

He clambered up from the floor and took his place again in his swivel chair. "You said so. . . . For always?"

"Oh, I ought to have known!" she exclaimed. "It has been happening a long time. I ought to have known at the very beginning. But I didn't. We weren't to have been married until next year. It seemed such a long way off. I never came close to it, I suppose. And then——"

"When did this happen?" he interrupted.

"Yesterday, Thursday, morning." She spoke very quietly, but with a peculiar, low vehemence, as though she were cross-examining herself. "You remember—it was Wednesday evening you brought me back from—you brought me to the hotel in your car. There was a letter from Peter then, and——"

She checked herself and her expression changed in a way that George could not understand. Her thought, he knew, had turned suddenly away from Peter; her eyes lighted; for a moment her excitement seemed to be the excitement of joy.

"There was a letter from Peter," she repeated, commanding herself. "I sat down to read it. He was in the hotel; I didn't know that; but he came up behind me and——"

"My dear, there's no need to tell me if it hurts."

"He kissed me," she said, compelling her voice. "It wasn't that I—I mean, it wasn't hateful. It was no different from other times. But I was dead. Do you understand? I suppose I always had been—poor Peter! But I hadn't known it before. . . . And that night I knew I couldn't marry him. I never could have. It had always been hopeless. In the morning, I told him."

She has broken off her engagement, George said to himself, and naturally enough it has shocked and disturbed her; but what more is there? That there was more he did not doubt. She was baffled, tired, sick at heart, but never had she been more alive.

"You told him," he said, prompting her silence.

"I don't believe I ever hurt anyone before, not really, not wilfully," she answered with meditative slowness. "I know now, as I shouldn't have known a few days ago, how much I hurt him. It was horrible. We went swimming, before breakfast. It was drizzling, but the sea was warm, and Peter loves it when we swim together. I couldn't spoil that, so I waited. I told him on the way back. At first, he didn't think I was serious; he just couldn't believe; he thought I was going to take it back. That made it worse—to know that by saying half a dozen words I could make him happy again. . . . The night before, it had just seemed impossible to marry him, that was all. I didn't think about him. I was thinking of myself, I suppose. But when he stood there in the rain with his face pink as if I'd struck him, I remembered all we'd said and all I'd meant to be to him—and there he was like a boy going to cry. I felt cruel and helpless, both at once, and I couldn't say anything but the same thing over and over again."

She slid down from her chair on to the hearth-rug. Her neck and the little white segment of her back exposed by her frock's tension were those of a child, and the lobe of her ear, touched by the gleam, was small and soft as a child's. She stretched out her hands, the fingers separated to the warmth, their edges pink and transparent.

"All yesterday," she said, "it rained and rained. Father had to be told. He was so angry, it made him ugly and frightening. I've never seen anyone like that."

George moved his hand and would have laid it on her shoulder, but did not. An intuition warned him that she would shrink from any physical contact. She was scarcely aware of him. Sitting back on her heels, slim and poised, she talked to the slackening fire.

"We argued and argued. There wasn't anything new to say. Father said 'Why? Why?' and Peter was miserable. What had he done? he said, and I couldn't help him. It wasn't his fault. He hadn't *done* anything. I hadn't a reason except that I didn't love him. We sat in the lounge; it was half dark there until they turned the lights on; the windows were streaming; every now and then Father said we must keep our voices low. We went in to meals and sat there, eating. Then in the lounge again. Father went grey and sick-looking, and sent me to my room. He followed me there. He said we were ruined if I didn't marry Peter; he'd spent so much on the holiday and other things. He wouldn't say what other things, but something he said made me guess. He has been borrowing money— at least I think so; from Peter's father, I expect. And then——" She caught her breath and struggled on. "Suddenly he stopped being angry. He put his arm round me and began to plead. Almost cringing. I hated him. It was like a cat rubbing against your legs. I began to shake and feel cold as if I had a fever, but I wouldn't say 'yes.' I couldn't. I couldn't."

George leaned forward, seized her wrist and made her face him. The interruption steadied her. Gently releasing herself, she took his hand between her two hands and held fast to it.

"Then," she continued, "he stopped begging. Perhaps he saw it was no good. He caught hold of my arms, and swayed me to and fro, talking and talking very close to my face. I've never seen anyone's eyes like that—wide open and the lids white, and his mouth white, too, like the silvery glisten on meat. I made it worse, I suppose, by saying nothing. He thought I was being stubborn and refusing to answer his questions or defend myself. It wasn't that. I couldn't speak." She threw back her head as though she were shaking herself free of her father's humiliation. "He went at last," she said. "I sat down on my bed. After a time there was a knock on the door. I said 'Come in?' and Peter stood there, twisting the handle backwards and forwards even when the door was shut. We went over it all again. He couldn't understand what had happened. He thought it had been all right between us when he went away to play cricket. I said it wasn't, it wasn't, it hadn't ever been, but I hadn't known till now. 'But what *made* you know?' he said." She threw a wild, slow look upon George as though he might find the answer for her. At last she added: "There wasn't anything new to say."

Something, some distinct happening, must have made her recognize that she couldn't love the boy, George said to himself. Perhaps Peter's own letter? and his lips moved to question her further. But he checked himself. The thing was done: for whatever reason, she was passionately decided; and she was afraid. Remembering the face he had seen raised up towards his window, he asked:

"Where were you going when I saw you?"

"I don't know."

"Not to the hotel?"

"I suppose so—in the end. Father hasn't spoken to me since last night, except to say that we leave on Monday."

"But you're not afraid of him?"

"Afraid? Not that he'll kill me or hurt me. No. But to live with him now——"

"In time," George began reassuringly, "he——"

"No," she exclaimed, shaking her head. "Never. Not after what happened. He couldn't endure to live with me, nor I with him."

"Perhaps in time you'll forgive him."

"That doesn't mean anything," she answered. "Forgive? Forgiveness doesn't cancel anything. I shall always remember how he looked and what he said. It's as if I had seen him turned into an animal."

"Mary, you don't mean that!"

She smiled a lovely, scornful smile. "You think I'm a child. I'm not any more. But I shall have to live with him as if I were. He thinks that in the end I shall marry Peter to escape from him. 'In time you'll come to your senses,' he said. 'In time you will.' Our own house is let furnished," she went on. "So we're going to an elder sister of his outside Tadworth until we can go back into it. That's why we are waiting here till Monday—for her answer to come."

She spoke now in a tone so even and strictly commanded that it might have been supposed that her agitation was past, but George saw the quiver of her shoulders, the pulse in her throat. He knew that her control would break suddenly if her fear was not expressed, and he said: "Mary, if not of your father, what is it you're afraid of? Can you tell me?"

There was a low, sobbing tremor in her breath; then a long silence.

"Everything that's coming," she said. "Going back to life at home. It's not real any more. Everything will stare at me—most of all, the things I love. . . . Oh, I don't know. I can't tell you. Just as I couldn't tell them."

"Is it," he said, "like—like a dream of being sent back to school after you're grown up?"

She uttered a little cry, almost of laughter, a grateful cry, as sweet a sound as he had ever heard. "Yes," she exclaimed, a child again now, frightened by her own fairy-tale. "Yes, and everyone in the school is dead. But outside, you know, everything's alive. It's spring. It's awake and alive. But the doors are shut and the windows, and inside it's winter. All the loveliness is out of reach. . . . It's lonely at home. I didn't know how lonely until now. I used to think it was peaceful and safe and lasting and good —almost like your Rectory. I thought that Father—— And now that's gone. It *is* like going back into a kind of nightmare that will go on and on."

"But some day," he said, "you'll fall in love."

She shook her head.

"But you will, my dear. It's in the nature of things."

Her eyes met his an instant, but she made no answer, except to repeat: "'In the nature of things'!"

"Meanwhile," he said, "I've a plan. My Rectory. If it makes you feel peaceful, would you come and stay there for a bit? Company for Helen. The old man would be glad; he took to you. No one would worry you there."

"Do you mean," she said slowly, "do you mean—stay in Sparkenbroke Green?"

"Of course. Why not?"

Her cheeks grew pale.

"There's a big spare-room," he said, "at the top of the stairs, looking out over the bridge. It used to be my mother's room. Father doesn't use it—hasn't since she died. You'd hear the stream when you woke."

She was grave and still.

"Come," he said. "I shan't worry you."

"You? . . . Oh, I want to come so much. Too much."

"*Too* much? Why that? It would be peace for a little while—until you decided—what to do."

She jumped up from the ground, and with the earnestness of a vow: "I want it to be just that. . . . Isn't it strange?" she added, moving her hand across her forehead. "Now I want to sleep. I couldn't before. I want to sleep, for hours and hours."

He smiled. "The stream won't wake you. . . . Shall I take you to the hotel now? Then I'll talk to Helen. We'll come down and see your father."

"Perhaps he won't let me go."

George began to slide his papers into their drawers. "I think he will. Leave that to Helen and me." In this, there was for him the boyish pleasure of a conspiracy. Imagining his sister's face when he unfolded his plan to her, he smiled to himself, and looked happily round the room. Mary had seated herself on the old couch. From it she stretched out a hand to him.

"I've been such a fool, George. I won't be. It's a different world since I—since I was out there. Suppose you hadn't seen me and I'd gone by."

He dropped his keys into his pocket and held out her waterproof.

"Streets are drying fast," he said. "I wish you could have been at home this evening to smell the garden."

CHAPTER FOURTEEN

THE labour of nights and days which preceded the
writing of Sparkenbroke's letter to Mary had brought to a
period his story of Tristan's adventure, and for a little
while he could not go beyond it. Renewal of impulse
would come; meanwhile the battle of narrative was suspended and he was happy in his leisure, spending the
greater part of two days at Sparkenbroke House with his
wife and Richard. He swam with the boy in the lake, rode
with him and told him stories—so many stories, old and
new, that Etty, wishing only to show that his work still
occupied her mind, suggested that he should make a book
of them.

Why did she not understand that this suggestion crossed
his mood? Did she not know that he himself turned all
things to art, that everything he heard and saw and
touched was turned to glass for him by his passion to
discover, beyond it, a reality more intense than its own?
From this obsession he had for a few hours escaped.
Swimming, riding, talking, laughing, he had been able to
take life at its face value. Now, since she had spoken, he
would inevitably see, in the stories he had delighted to
tell, the underlying struggle for form. But she had intended
to please him, and he checked the intolerant comment that
sprang to his mind. He said: "Richard had better write it
himself; you might help him, Etty," and was rewarded by
seeing that she smiled with quiet pride, not unhappy.
Afterwards, he and she discussed Richard together; this
was their common ground; and when she told him of her
stewardship at Sparkenbroke, he praised and thanked her,

saying with truth that without her the estate would break up.

"And it does mean something to you?" she said.

"Sparkenbroke? Indeed it does!"

"But more than an inheritance? More than a possession?" she insisted. "Doesn't it? You must have it—to come back to as someone comes back to the place where——he knows——" She glanced at him, choosing her words carefully. "To where he knows there's a spring of water?"

It was long since they had come so near to intimacy of thought. For an instant he remembered in what way he had formerly loved her and, having no words that were not too sad to be spoken, touched her arm with a quick pressure of confidence familiar to them in the past.

"Then, in a way," she said, "I am helping your work still?" The awkward eagerness of this froze in him all emotion but pity. Afraid to see the tears that he knew were in her eyes, he set himself in defence against the past, and the little movement of her hand with which she answered his pressure became for him bleakly importunate.

"Am I?" she repeated.

"Yes, my dear," he answered, and spoke with shame, not because the answer was untrue, but because he could not love her. Not to be cruel! Not to be cruel! he cried within him, and whenever he was not with Richard he spent his time with her, seeking her company, glad of her good sense, her quiet wisdom, her friendship, her intelligence, but feeling always that, though to stay away was cruel, to come and to observe with detachment her joy in his coming was a patronage more contemptible than cruelty. On Saturday morning very early he left his bed in Sparkenbroke House and returned to the cottage.

The dew was heavy on the open grass and in the hollows were pools of night; but the sky was growing pale above the church, and even in Derry's Wood the upper limbs of the trees and long streaks of undergrowth were blanched by morning as by a ghostly frost. Sparkenbroke paused at the cottage door, surprised by the beauty and stillness, surprised, too, that he should be in this place, for he could not recollect the impulse that had driven him from his bed, and he seemed now to have come across terrace and meadow without volition, in an observant dream. Hours must pass before Bissett, finding his bed empty, would follow him, and he was glad, for the wood, in which no breath stirred, was gazing at him, and he knew that, if he waited, it would speak.

He did not enter the cottage, but began to walk to and fro on the path at the stream's edge by which Mary had come. As he walked, his spirit was at first quiet in him. A hush fell upon his being correspondent to the quietness of the world; he was emptied of will, and aware of nothing but the even rhythm of his own footsteps in the general presence of the wood. In this whiteness of mind, he was free of conditions, without purpose directing him to the future or memory binding him to the past.

Turning at last from the stream, he went down into the churchyard, where he had found always not the fear of death but the springs of life, and there, in the lightening dusk beneath the elm, he lay down and slept, awaking to find the bright silver of morning on grass and briar. He looked about him as Prospero may have looked at rumour of Ariel unseen. For a long time he stood listening, with a shiver in his limbs as though he were about to run a race.

It was at such an hour of the morning that, in his imagination, the ship that bore the Holy Face to Lucca approached the Italian coast, and now, with a flash of recognition, he saw the poem that had haunted him before his return to England and had been long put away. Put away, because he had failed in it, and remembrance of failure was intolerable. The pressure of imagination had been withdrawn from him as he wrote; his pen had laboured; the images had ceased to visit him, in Keats's sense, "naturally"; poetry had become a labour not of choice among riches but of struggle with poverty. But the great legend had hung in his mind. The form I chose was wrong, he thought; I hampered myself with a triple rhyme; the measure was too smooth; but his momentary care for

metre was overwhelmed by his delight in the poem itself
which seemed to be in the air about him, inaudible, waiting to be born, formless as yet but only because unseized.
It was as if he were in the presence of one in whom his
being would presently be dissolved.

> *Our breath shall intermix, our bosoms bound,*
> *And our veins beat together; and our lips*
> *With other eloquence than words, eclipse*
> *The soul that burns between them. . . .*

In this lull of ecstatic coldness, he stood blind and enchanted, interpreting Shelley anew. All that morning,
while he thought but fleetingly of the poem or indeed of
the legend itself, they were alive in his experience. When
he took his key from his pocket and admitted himself to
the Mound, he did not seem to be, as others would
have said, entering a tomb; nor, while he remained
there, looking out through the door-frame at the increasing exterior brightness, was he touched by any fear
of mortal decay in his own person. This place was,
and had always been, the cradle of his rest, where the
entanglement of the flesh was lightest upon him, and,
seeing now in his imagination that ship which voyaged
across the Mediterranean without crew or helmsman
and would not suffer capture or be turned aside until
she had brought the image of Jesus, that was her freight,
to the harbour of Luni, he felt himself to be present in her
and without surprise in her progress. The legend appeared
no longer as a legend, to be considered with external eye
and so interpreted, but as present experience, natural in
the nature of miracles; it would have been a reversal of
Nature if the ship had been wrecked or becalmed; and,
thinking not at all of the poem to be written, he was wrapt
in the poem itself, as though it had been written long ago
and was completely known to him, having become an
element of his own truth. Not this legend only, but all he
saw, heard and felt, confessed itself to him, and became,
in its earthly form, transparent, so that through each particular beauty of leaf and light-shaft a universal beauty

shone; in the glory of which he walked at ease through wood and meadow until afternoon, when he returned to the cottage, the assurance of poetry high within him.

The window of his room was open, and, looking in, he saw a girl seated near the fireplace, her back to him, her hands concealed in her lap, and her head inclined towards her right shoulder in such a way that the window-light, falling upon her from behind, threw up against the room's shadow a sculptural line of brow and cheek. That she was Mary, he knew at once, but he did not think of her in terms of his previous association with her. Her presence was neither surprising nor expected; it appeared in his consciousness as fresh beauty may appear in water beneath the shifting influences of light; and he continued to gaze at her, free of that tension which ordinarily visits a watcher who knows himself to be unobserved. How seldom, he reflected, had any woman the pregnant repose of a great picture! To suppose movement to be the essence of life was among humanity's most dangerous errors—an error into which, as the years passed, men fell more and more complacently. Life was less alive than art, for in life vitality was dissipated in a thousand irrelevant and contradictory movements; its essence seldom appeared. Was not that, he asked himself suddenly, the origin of Iseult's power, ascribed by legend to a potion, and, on the same imaginative tide that had borne him to the ship carrying the holy image to Lucca, he was swept on to a fresh understanding of his novel, which, since he wrote his letter to Mary, seemed not to have been in his mind. Tristan, as he came with Iseult to Cornwall from Ireland, must have asked himself continually what it was in her that set her apart from other women, so that her beauty seemed to him different in kind from theirs; and, though he looked at her with wonderful questioning from sunrise to dusk, he could give himself no answer, until one night at sundown, the sea very calm, he saw her in the forepart of the vessel, her back to him, her cheek engraved in light

upon the eastern sky, and knew that what enchanted
him was her power to gather all her spirit into the
lines of her body. So marvellous was this discovery
to Tristan—for he seemed to be looking through the
flesh of Iseult into a life shining within her—that he
also, without thought of himself, fell into a repose of
gazing, and even when she had moved her head and seen
him, they two were still for a long time, so quickened by
their miracle that none of the language of the body could
avail them. Rising at last, she said, like a child holding
up its toy to be praised: Tristan, look at the sea, and
they looked, not at the sea but at each other, not at their
appearances but at their very selves as they were, so that
if at any time a messenger should say: Iseult is dead, or:
Tristan has forsaken Iseult, they might know, remembering this instant, that he lied, though the messenger
were Death himself. In that continuous life, which the
womb and the grave do not divide, they had been solitary
hitherto, and were no longer, but neither word nor touch
could speak their recognition. They were dumb with
love, and Sparkenbroke, standing within them like a
ghost, felt the long, delicious quiver of their flesh which,
promising them all the rapture of appearances, yet
mocked them, so that there were tears in Iseult's eyes.
A puff of wind laid a pennon of hair across her lips when
Tristan would have kissed them, and she laughed, as
though in laughter and tears she might discover a language
that words denied her. But, like poetry and song, they
spoke of nothing but the desire, which is in all men, for
a language of silence; they had not that language itself;
and under Tristan's kisses she sighed, thinking that only
some folly in herself—her newness to love, her inequality
with him—prevented her from pouring her fullness into
these kisses. Was he happy? she asked, and Tristan,
perceiving in what way she loved him and that beauty
itself shone through her loveliness, fell into a tender awe
and dared not kiss her again. Under the ship, the water
clucked and whispered; the deck was washed in that
airy translucence which, on the open sea, shines in calm

weather between dusk and darkness, and Sparkenbroke
had, in that instant, three lives—one of Tristan's ship,
another of the miraculous voyage that brought the holy
image to Italy, a third of his actual experience as he
looked through the window of Derry's Cottage. They
were not, in his consciousness, divided. To imagine was
to live, to live was to imagine. He yielded himself to the
exaltation that possessed him, cleansed by it of his confusions, and endowed with that sense of being absolved
which was, in him, the emblem of aesthetic passion.

He did not know or inquire how long ago Mary had
turned her head and begun to regard him.

Uncertain what arrangement she had made with George
and whether he or she was to speak to her father on the
subject of her going to stay at the Rectory, she had come
up from Chelmouth after luncheon. George had acted
before her; already he and Helen were on their way to
visit Mr. Leward at his hotel; Mary had passed them
unobserved on the road, and the Rectory had been empty
of all but servants when she reached it, even the Rector
being out. Invited by Joanna to wait, she had seated
herself in the parlour, where she could hear the trickle of
the stream and no other sound. Her thought was confused
and restless; even in this quiet house where, perhaps, she
was soon to be a guest, she could not be at ease, and she
decided to wait no longer. To return to Chelmouth on foot
would do her good; but in the road a desire to enter Derry's
Wood came upon her. The cottage also was empty; even
Bissett was not to be found; but the door stood open, and
she sat down in Sparkenbroke's room. The table was clear
of papers; the room had an air of not having been lived in
for several days. Perhaps he has gone away, she said to
herself, and she stayed where she was, wishing to rest.
She sat with folded hands, imagining herself as she would
have been ten years hence if she had married Peter, and
possessed by a desire to dedicate her life, to enrich herself
with purpose—not to drift through casual years. Soon she
would be old; and she laid her hands upon her cheeks,

drawing a frightened breath; then let them fall again. Was she capable of boldness and adventure? Would she, in fact, have made anything of her life, when the time came for her to die? She would like to have lived fearlessly—to *have* lived! She might now run away from her father and somehow establish her independence; but the project, as soon as she considered it, appeared to her theatrical, extravagant, contrary to her nature. If she had courage, it was not courage of that kind; she was without masculine ambition; she had no desire to rule or to become famous or rich; it was in the company of such men as George Hardy, who were themselves free of this ambition, that she was at peace. Then, suddenly, the thought of Sparkenbroke swept over her, filling her not with confidence but with a wild submissiveness to Fate. Feeling his presence in her and about her, she turned her head towards the window and saw him.

Soon afterwards, he left the window. In the interval of time during which he was out of her sight, she braced herself to encounter an intellect and speech so much swifter than her own that they had produced in her, even when she had been happiest in his company, the fascinated pain caused by a light too harsh, brilliant, mobile. She was in stress, flicked by desire to hide herself before he came; she was afraid, and the more afraid because, amid this childish tumult of shyness, she was aware of a tremor of her limbs as though she were naked to a breeze.

When he spoke, he seemed to her different from the man she had known, as though a disguise had fallen from him. "Do you know the story of the Holy Face of Lucca?" he asked with such abrupt eagerness for her audience that she began to laugh; then, perceiving the intense absorption of his mind, she was ashamed, as though she had been laughing at the seriousness of a child. She imagined that she had wounded him; but he said only: "Nearly all laughter is ugly or cruel. My own is cruel, more often than not. But yours was happy. Why are you happy—in that way?"

H

"I was afraid of you," she answered, "but when you asked me about the—the Holy Face at——"

"Lucca."

"—in such a queer, solemn way——"

"Listen," he said. "Sit there. No—sit quietly there, as you were when I came. Your hands were clasped in your lap," and he began to tell her the story of Nicodemus who took Jesus down from the Cross and laid him in the tomb. "All his life Nicodemus had known Jesus, had seen him continually, and now he saw the form of death in his face. I think Nicodemus must have known more than any man has ever known of the beauty of the human face, for he was an artist; that is to say, he saw, beyond the appearances of a thing, the nature of the thing itself; and what we shall never fully understand—whether Jesus was god or man, and in what sense god and in what sense man (for god and man are not divided and separate, but aspects of each other)—this Nicodemus knew. Afterwards he hid himself in the mountains, for he was too great an artist to be safe from the persecution of men, and in his sleep an angel came to him and said——"

He paused with caught breath.

"Are you one of those," he asked, "to whom the word 'angel' is meaningless?"

To her an angel was an angel. "No," she answered, "but I suppose there are no angels nowadays. Just as there are no miracles. Once we had a sermon about them at home. The Vicar said that the world had outgrown the need of them and so God sent them no more."

"The air has been full of angels this morning," he said. "And one said to me, as he said to Nicodemus, 'Arise, ponder no more, take thy tools.' 'Take thy tools,' the angel said to Nicodemus, 'and fashion in wood the likeness of thy Saviour Jesus Christ.' "

"Is this," she asked, "a story that you are writing?"

"It's a poem I began long ago, and couldn't finish. But now I shall finish it, if I can tell it to you." He came near to her and put his hands over hers. "Nicodemus," he said, "wondered what likeness of Jesus he should make, for he had seen so many appearances of Jesus in the flesh that he could not choose among them. For a time he was in doubt, but at last he understood that only in the form of death, which permitted the absolute light to blaze through the carnal veil, was the essence of Jesus, and he began to carve the likeness of him on the Cross; the body, the hands, the feet, the shape of the head, but not yet the face. He could not carve the face. Whenever he approached the features, his tool refused."

"Refused?" Mary said.

"As though a hand were laid on it," he answered, and added that whenever, in the making of a work of art, the tool refuses, there is no remedy but sleep; so Nicodemus slept; and when he awoke his work had been done for him, the face was finished. The joy of that! The knowledge that his work was perfect, having been done by the angels themselves! "By God himself," Sparkenbroke said. "There is a flame of truth in every word of the legend. All perfect art is a likeness of God carved by himself in the sleep of the artist."

He continued the story, telling how Nicodemus was commanded by another angel to hide the Holy Cross in a mountain cave, and how he dwelt with it until he died. Many years later a bishop found it there.

"A bishop?" Mary exclaimed.

"His name was Subalpino," Sparkenbroke said, with a smile, "but his name is of no consequence. With a crowd of people following him, he was led by an angel to the cave. They brought the Holy Cross to the seashore and there built a ship and put the Cross in her and launched her. A little wind carried her seaward. On she went with no helmsman, no crew, an empty ship carrying Nicodemus's masterpiece. All the merchant ships she met tried to capture her with ropes and grappling irons. They came so near that sailors sprang into the water and swam towards her, but always she turned and escaped until at last she appeared off Luni. The people of Luni were no more successful than others had been, but when they were exhausted and the good bishop Giovanni of Lucca came to the beach, the ship swam towards him; he drew her ashore with his own hand. So the Holy Face had come to Lucca."

"And is it there now?" Mary asked.

"Yes, it is there to-day. And if ever you go to Lucca, you will know that the legend is true. The town has the quality of the legend. From its ramparts, walking through a continuous avenue of plane and chestnut and mimosa, you look outward to the country or inward on to the towers of the city. In that sunlight, flowing down over the shoulders of the hills, filling the plain with watery gold, ribbing your path and the grassy bastions with great shadows of trees, you walk in heavenly cloisters, built of sun and air. You feel there is, I think, the rarest of all sensations in the modern world—that imagination and wisdom are identical and that everything observed or felt carries its saving antithesis within it. I mean, that within cruelty is gentleness, within man God, within the new the old, within sin the forgiveness of sin—an antidote for every poison, a perfection for every imperfection. Within every passionate truth is childlike invention, which is the light of these great legends—the light we have lost. Pride in our own reason has lost it to us, but in Lucca it seems possible to see by it again. It was there I used to think of how the Volto Santo came across the sea. Subalpino and his companions, building their ship and hanging little lanterns on it; the absurd, astonished Genoese swimming about in the Mediterranean; the people of Luni furious because the miraculous ship would take no notice of them; the Lucchesi full of local pride and all agog for a triumphant *festa* because the image insisted upon coming to them—all these groups, the whole pageant running over with laughter and wonder and awe, had in Lucca—they had," Sparkenbroke continued, "what your face has had in it while I have been telling you the story."

"What?" she asked.

He shook his head. "I have destroyed it now—in you and for myself. We are separated, as human beings always are when they begin to think of each other. It is only when they are lost in the same imagining that for a little while they are one."

"I shall always be separate from you," she said.

"From me in particular?"

She did not know how to reply. It was in her mind, not only that by intellect, birth, tradition, he was divided from her, but that the circles of their nature did not intersect. For this she had no words. She could say only:

"I never feel at home with you. . . . Until this afternoon," she added swiftly. "That has been different. And even this afternoon, though you haven't been——"

"I'll say it for you: 'though I haven't been arrogant, and cruel and spectacular.' Is that it?"

She nodded. The natural movement of her life was on a plane different from his—yet it was true that for a little while she could be lifted by him outside her own nature. When he was absent, her reason governed her; in his presence, she was entranced; but even in her entrancement a core of natural judgment survived, and she would not say to herself that she loved him. Love, she had always believed, would be, when it came to her, a supreme sanity and reconciliation, a coming into harbour, not this blind, stormy impulse that drove her to him in desperate surrender of her will. Her perplexity was in her face, and he asked whether he had made her unhappy. "No! No!" she heard herself cry, and she sat upright and rigid, her lips trembling, while he looked into her eyes.

"What is it," he said, "that gives you power to receive confession? It is sovereign power over me," and, seeming to fear this power, he moved abruptly away, to return when a minute had passed and stand behind the stool on which she was seated. His hands came down until they were crossed over her breasts. She felt that she was imprisoned by his touch. That the little weight of her breasts was lifted by his fingers' strength was to her neither a soft pleasure of the senses nor a fulfilment of any anticipation of hers, but an agony of new experience by which all her knowledge of herself was blinded and cancelled. He released her, drew her up by her hands, and began to talk to her at once of her own interests. She told him that she was to be a guest at the Rectory, but of Peter she said nothing.

"While you are at the Rectory, come to see me when you can," he said.

"But if you are working?"

"Then you will be sent away again. We must take our chance."

At last, saying good-bye to her at the door of the cottage, he took her by the arms, and for an instant, in imagination, their kisses were upon each other's lips, but when he had let her go without kissing her and she was retracing her path through the wood, her ordinary life began to fold itself about her again. What is it, he had said, that gives you power to receive confession? Though she remembered the words, she did not understand them or struggle for understanding of them. She knew only that she had found a second world in which she might live. She wished to maintain it for a little while against the invasion of criticism, and could not endure to relate it, in motive or consequence, to the world she knew. It had become for her, by the time she reached Chelmouth, a secret to be guarded even against herself.

CHAPTER FIFTEEN

GEORGE's persuasion of Mr. Leward had been easier than he had expected. At the outset he had perceived that, where he might fail, Helen would certainly be successful, and had left the conversation to her, astonished by her feminine adroitness. She spoke of Mary in the tone of a schoolmistress discussing a child with a troubled and conscientious parent—a part that Mr. Leward was evidently willing to play. She explained that sudden wilfulness was in the nature of young girls who saw marriage ahead of them; it was not necessarily to be taken very seriously.

"You think she may come round?" Mr. Leward said.

George waited for his sister's answer. He and she had decided that nothing was less probable than that Mary would "come round"; the breach with Peter was final.

"One can never be sure of that," Helen replied. "The one thing certain is that to press her or scold her or drive her would be fatal. In a girl of your daughter's temperament, quite fatal."

Saying with carefully weighed pathos that he was a widower, Mr. Leward expressed his reliance on Miss Hardy's judgment. "You have, of course, great experience of young girls. . . . You understand that I don't wish to compel her to this marriage. Why should I? It would leave me a very lonely man. I want to do what is right. But I must say she seems to me to have behaved very badly. And I can't make out why. We always used to say when I was young that a girl never let one man go unless she had another within reach."

Helen's expression hardened. This, George knew, was a sentiment of the kind that awakened her most ardent feminism. He awaited a destructive retort, but she repressed it, and led the conversation on until Mr. Leward was able to match his duty with his convenience and to agree, with a sigh of self-sacrifice, that it might be all for the best if Miss Hardy were to take Mary under her wing for a little while.

"When she is in a more reasonable frame of mind," he said, "then she can come home. If our own house isn't free by then—it's let, you know—her aunt will take her in all right."

It was arranged that Mary should come to the Rectory on Monday. When should he make arrangements to have her again? her father asked.

"Shall we decide nothing for the present?" said Helen. "That is, if you can spare her."

"Oh, bless my soul," Mr. Leward replied in an outburst of candour, "in her present mood, she's much better with you to look after her. School would be the best place for her until she comes to her senses."

"Very well, then, that's settled. The longer she stays with us the better I shall be pleased." And Helen added with secret irony: "I'm very fond of her, you know."

As she and George drove out of Chelmouth together, she did not speak.

"Tired?" he said.

"Very."

So seldom did she admit weakness in herself that he turned his head anxiously: "The journey has been too much for you. I oughtn't to have brought you so far."

"It was important, wasn't it—for you?"

"For me?"

"That she should come?"

He did not answer this. "You managed him splendidly. I couldn't have."

"No. But you helped."

"I? I said nothing."

"You held your tongue. That's your genius, George."

He grinned and said no more. As they were approaching Sparkenbroke Green, she spoke again.

"George."

"Yes."

"You're in love with her, aren't you?"

"Yes."

"I see. . . . It's as well to know these things." After a long silence: "Do you mean to marry her?"

It was a question he had not asked of himself—easier to joke about than to answer.

"And do you suppose she'd marry me?"

"Why not?"

"My dear Helen, she's eighteen."

"She's your kind."

"And that means—what?"

"She's *good*, George."

"And again, that means—what?"

"If you don't know what is meant by a good woman, I can't help you. But she's romantic and—passionate too."

"In other words," George said, "she's eighteen and I'm not."

"You think that's final?"

"I try not to think about it too much."

"Then why do you have her here? To torment yourself?"

He was silent. To say that he had invited her because he wished to give her time to be at peace was true, but sounded like hypocrisy.

"You know it's not final," Helen said. "You happen to be the kind of man who could make her happy."

"In spite of our ages?"

"In spite of your ages."

Because he knew that Helen's sharp, matter-of-fact speech was but a concealment of emotion, George was the more affected by her tenderness towards him. How seldom their personal affairs had been directly spoken of between them, but how well they understood each other! George is in love, she was saying to herself, and she faced that embarrassing truth in the same spirit in which she would have faced a discovery that he was ill, or had lost his

money, or found himself in some scrape for which not he
personally but the surprising fatuity of mankind was to be
blamed. For his sake she would make the best of it and
help him to do so. To test her, he said:

"It sounds as if you wanted me to marry."

"I recognize facts, George."

He laughed aloud, at himself and at her. "That's one of
the things I pride myself on, too!" he exclaimed. "We are
very alike, you and I."

"Except that you are a romantic and I'm not."

He smiled. "We both have our blind spots."

"I suppose we have," she conceded. "What are mine?"

"You think of marriage as if it were friendship."

"Well, isn't it—at root?"

"Not when you're eighteen."

"Still," she persisted, "in this case that isn't final. . . .
And you know it."

"Why do you say that?"

"Because you are happy. You weren't. You were miserable. You were in love and thought you hadn't a hope.
But since last Friday, when you came home telling me you
had asked her to stay with us, since then——"

The car had come to a standstill. Helen did not
move.

"You'll have to help me out," she said.

He came to her at once. "You're in pain."

"A bit worse. All right if I can get to my room. I shan't
be fit to look after her, George. You'll have to be hostess
as well as host."

"Never mind about me," he said. "Come, put your arm
over my shoulder. I'll carry you up."

On Monday, his work made it impossible for him to
drive Mary out from Chelmouth. She would make her own
way and arrive in his absence. Since Helen was in bed,
the Rector himself must receive their guest. "I'll come
back as soon as I can," George told him. "Probably before
you've finished giving her tea."

"I shall find something to talk to her about," his father

answered. "Don't you scamp your work on her account—
or mine."

"No," said George. "But don't frighten her."

"Frighten her? Why should I?"

"Your questions. . . . She's not a scholar or a philosopher
or a saint or a poet. Your sudden challenges frighten people,
you know. They're not used to being taken at one bound
into the heart of a subject."

"Better if they were," the Rector answered. "Half of
life is wasted on neutral ground. Why shouldn't I find out
at once what interests the girl and talk to her of it?"

"As long as you remember that she's very young."

"All the more reason," the Rector said, "for not playing
down to her. Nothing annoys young people more."

And when, after his day's work, George returned home,
he found a group of three, pacing the lawn together—his
father in the midst, Mary and Sparkenbroke on either
hand.

"No, no!" his father exclaimed, when Mary, looking up,
moved to welcome George. "Don't break away. This is
good talk. George shall join in it. Now, Piers, go on. We
were saying, George, that the world is full of evil and
suffering; a good part of it seems to think that our present
civilization is so bad it can't be mended, and that the
whole system ought to be overthrown and built afresh.
Writers in Piers's position have a great influence. What he
said of social conditions would be listened to. And yet this
is the moment he has chosen to turn away altogether from
the contemporary scene and to write of Tristan and of the
coming of the Holy Face to Lucca."

The lawn had dried since the rains and they sat under
the sycamore discussing the whole duty of an artist.
Sparkenbroke brilliantly defended his own position, rang-
ing through the history of art for justification of it and
saying that, though a writer was fully entitled to take contemporary circumstance as his subject if he would, he did
so at his peril and was certainly not in conscience bound
to it. "Even if I hate the Bastille, why should I call upon
people to storm it? If they succeed, it will be rebuilt in

another form. Besides, the imprisonment that men suffer within stone walls and iron bars is as nothing to the imprisonment that they impose upon themselves by their fears, their hatreds, their false ambitions, their failures of imagination. The only escape from spiritual imprisonment is—but you shall tell us that, Rector. Is it in Christianity?"

Sparkenbroke had deliberately checked himself. Though his challenge to the Rector was lightly spoken, it was plain in his expression that, on the edge of self-confession, he had been struck dumb and was tormented by his dumbness. Without giving Mr. Hardy time to answer—for the answer, he knew, would have forced him back on to the course from which he had so violently retreated—he began to speak of the difficulty and delight of a legendary subject.

"I wonder you chose Tristan," George said. "So many others have written of it."

"But that's the advantage. The outline is known, the tradition established. There are corresponding advantages in translating. If you translate, you haven't to bother your head about invention of anecdote or structure of narrative; you can concentrate all your forces on language; some of the most beautiful, single-minded prose in English has been written by the great translators. And if you choose to re-write a great legend, two things are certain before you begin—the general form of the tale and the power of the tale continually to re-interpret itself to generation after generation. If it had not this power, it would not have lived, and the knowledge that it has this power, that it is spiritually universal, gives me a security that I can never have when I am inventing a story with a modern setting. I don't mean that I shall always write of the legends. I am not turning from the modern world on any silly plea that, because it is outwardly ugly, it cannot be aesthetically interpreted. Of course it can; there's a special excitement in piercing the hideous disorder of its appearances; but what a relief it is for once to have a great legend as your subject! You can pour your whole self into it, discover in it new aspects of all your truths, recognize your friends, interpret your dreams—it's a new kind of liberty for me to work not wholly suspended in the thin air of invention but with the firm earth of a story beneath my feet. . . . Wouldn't you rather re-write an old story than invent a new one?" he said, turning suddenly to Mary.

"I?" she answered. "I think I should remember all the other versions and be afraid of them."

"They are not rivals," he said, "but collaborators. And the best of it is that, when Tristan's the subject, one of them can be made to collaborate not in words but in music."

There was a long silence. The Rector lifted his head abruptly:

"You were saying, Piers, that 'the only escape from spiritual imprisonment is——'?"

But Sparkenbroke was already on his feet. "How often one begins a sentence!" he exclaimed. "Then someone claps his hand over your mouth and forbids you to end it! Do you think that happens to angels as well as men?" and with this he was gone.

"Did you know who that was?" George asked. "I'll make a long bet that father didn't introduce you."

Mary replied that she had known it was Lord Sparkenbroke.

"Do you remember asking me—the first day we met—what he was like?"

Before she had need to answer, the Rector said: "The lawn settles down again when he's gone. I feel with Piers as I should feel if I saw an angel coming through the gate with a telegram."

"And you spend your life trying to make him decode the message," George answered.

His father's eyes opened wide. "Do I? I suppose that's true. That's where we prosaic men are liable to make fools of ourselves," he added, taking Mary's arm. "You know, my dear, don't you, that a poet's job is to deliver his message, not to explain it?"

But Mary had been alarmed by Sparkenbroke's coming. She had enjoyed sitting at tea with the Rector, gazing at the solid white house and at the chimney-smoke drifting across the summer sky. Her father was on his way to London; the hotel, which had become terrifying to her by association, was far away; the emotional stress through which she had been passing seemed to be ended; the life of this house, continuous from day to day, happily protected by conventions that she understood, would be, she thought, a life of peace and healing. After supper they would talk a little and go to bed early; to-morrow, when George had gone to work and the Rector to his study, she would sit with Helen and perhaps learn from her something of the running of the household. While you're ill, she would say, let me do some of your work for you, and, though Helen might insist at first that she was a guest, not a housekeeper, she would win her point, and before many days were gone she herself would be part of the Rectory's life, with a working routine such as she loved. In the afternoons, she would go for great walks, sometimes with George, who was as reassuring and constant as the house itself, sometimes with her calm, reasonable self. She would not go into Derry's wood again; and she was able to face this decision without an agonized sense of loss, without feeling, as she had felt while she remained in Chelmouth, that to cut Lord Sparkenbroke out of her life was to condemn herself to barrenness and death. But when Sparkenbroke himself had appeared upon the lawn and greeted her as if they were unknown to each other, their secret—not the secret of their meeting but of their unexpressed pledge—had sprung up round her like a wall of flame, and while he remained, while he was visible, within her reach, within her hearing, the world outside the ring that included them and them alone had died. No sooner had he gone than the speed and tension of her being slackened. She could think even: perhaps I don't love him; perhaps what I feel is only some desperate madness when he's near me; and, though she knew that it was with more than her body she worshipped him and that his genius was a window suddenly opened in the normal enclosure of her life, she knew also, and with terror in this failure of her control, that the idea of his physical nearness stripped and prostrated her in imagination, filling her mind with a delight which the more passionately inflamed her because her experience gave to it no precise form. Her impulse submitted absolutely, but her will cried out against her impulse, for to her the act of adultery was a sin equivalent to murder, a cancellation of the soul's tranquillity, in her impossible. Never, even in thought, had she approached it before, and now she sprang away from it, covering the eyes of her mind.

"What a sigh!" George exclaimed as he led her into the house.

Though he pretended to blame his father for neglect, he was delighted when he found that she had not yet been taken to her room. "It used to be my mother's," he reminded her, and, seeing her shadow move on the white panelling and her image cross the mirror, he was filled with so profound a love for her that the instant became suddenly one of those ever memorable instants that are felt, even while they are present, to initiate a new period of life. With the eye of imagination he looked back upon it from the future, thinking: always, always, I shall remember this; everything that is to come will date from it.

She had brought a picture with her. It was leaning against the wall. She picked it up, showed it to him, asked if she might hang it.

Olive-trees; bathers, sunshine—a modern picture. "Of course," he said. "Hanging is easy. There's a picture-rail. But where——"

"The painter lent it to me," she explained. "I have known him all my life. I brought it with me."

"Even to the hotel?"

"Yes," she said. "Father grumbled about so much luggage—but why shouldn't one have a picture, even in a hotel?"

"I suppose there's nothing against it," said George. He wondered whether this picture would always hang in the Rectory, and watched her set it down against the wall. Everything that is to come will date from this! he repeated, and perceiving that this implied, as Helen had said, an inward faith in her marriage with him, he was overwhelmed, the passionate strength of his hope having caught him unawares. If she were his wife, this would be her room and his. She was at the window now, and, the door also being open, a breeze moved in her frock and in the hair that lay back from her temple. Her weight was on one foot, her body curved a little backward from the waist; her head was lowered as she watched the bridge and the stream. As unapproachable, and to him, suddenly, as sacred as childhood!

Asking her with stifled, difficult words if she had all she needed, he said, stretching out his hand: "Look, Mary, there's the bell. The old-fashioned sort. I hope it rings."

She came from the window abruptly, took his arms in her hands, and said how good he was to her.

"You like the room?" he asked.

"It's a lovely room!"

Still she did not release him. In the pause, he felt her body tremble. "Thank you, George," she said at last.

He tried to smile. "For what? It's little I've done."

"For everything. Last Friday when I was miserable. And now—making me safe."

"Safe?"

"I shall be safe here. I trust you more than anyone else in the world. . . . More than I trust myself. More than anyone in the world."

Deeply moved, he stood away from her and, having for a moment gazed as though he might never see her again, crossed the room, unable to speak. His eye observed the bell-rope. "Hope it rings," he said. "Can't have been touched for ages. I'll give it a tug."

A distant jangle came up from the kitchen, and a moment later she saw him, through her open door, leaning over the banisters.

"All right, Joanna. Sorry. Don't come further. I was only trying the bell. It rings all right?"

"Oh yes, Mr. George. It's shakin' still. A proper tug you must have given it, too."

CHAPTER SIXTEEN

How strange it is, he said to himself continually during the following days, that with all our powers of language we human beings are so little able to communicate with each other, for he could not decide whether she was happy, so various were her moods. Often when they walked together or she came out with him on his round, sitting in his car contentedly while he visited patients, he felt that he had known her all his life She was eager to learn from him and he from her; they had the same pleasure in little things, the same dislike of emotional extravagance, the same profoundly English habit of under-statement. So easy and confident was their friendship at these times that the division of age between them was dissolved and he became aware that his company was as pleasant and necessary to her as hers to him.

Once, as they came away from a house where lived together a man and wife seemingly incongruous but deeply in love, she said: "I wonder what it is that holds them to each other," and he began to answer that the woman had been very pretty when she was young and that they had common interests.

"That isn't quite what I mean," she interrupted. "There were other pretty girls and the interests of these two aren't exceptional, are they? I mean: what is it that makes a man love one woman and not a hundred others who have the same——"

"You'd better ask my father that," George said with a smile. "He has a theory about it. What is it that converts *amour physique* or *amour-goût* into *amour-passion*? Being a discreet old man, he may not recommend Stendhal to you, but he'll probably think it a safe bet to ask whether you have read Goethe's *Elective Affinities*."

"He did. He lent me a copy in English. Does his theory come from that?"

"No. But it's part of the material of his theory. His idea is that though love may have a thousand originating impulses, thrown out almost haphazard like a handful of seed, it doesn't take deep root or grow into a consuming love unless the two people have the same intuitive direction of their subconscious minds."

She considered that in silence.

"Correspondent wish-fantasies is the jargon," George prompted.

She turned her head towards the house they had left. "So you think that Mr. Glenn and his wife had the same—but wasn't he twenty years older and an educated man while she——"

"That's the haphazard part of it," George said. "Whether the thing starts at all may depend on things of that kind—looks, age, education, taste, ambition: conscious things. But whether it grows depends on whether the two have the same stars in their subconscious heaven. Anyhow that's the idea."

"Do you agree?"

"More or less. Not rigidly."

"Where did your father get it from—Goethe?"

"He says," George answered, "that he gets it from the confessional—or what corresponds to the confessional in a Protestant parish."

"But if it were true," Mary said, "if it happened at all in that way, then wouldn't the two people always be equally in love?"

George laughed. "I don't think it's mathematical! Besides, all Mr. Glenn's stars may have been in his wife's subconscious heaven, but only some of hers may have been in his. I confess," he added, "that what interests me more than my father's theory—and ought to interest him, seeing he's a priest—is how much of a total individuality is given to love. It seems to vary in the most astonishing way."

"Between men and women?"

He glanced at her. "Oh, you mean: 'Man's love is of man's life a thing apart'—and so on? . . . No: not on the Byronic principle. That's true enough, I dare say, of *amour-goût* or *amour de vanité*. But I didn't mean that."

They drove on without speaking. At length she said: "What are wish-fantasies? How does one know them? They're not the same as wishes, are they?"

"When you were a child," he answered, "did you ever lie awake and tell yourself stories?"

"I do still!"

"With yourself as the chief character?"

"Not by name. . . . And yet, I suppose so. Half and half."

"Well, if you can remember them, they'd give you a line on your wish-fantasies."

"It's not easy," she said, "because, you see, there are two kinds of stories. Quite different. As if there were two of me."

"Perhaps there are," he answered, and often he remembered this confession of hers, for though, during these hours together, so close an intimacy was established between them that his love for her was untroubled and it seemed to him not impossible that she should, in her own way, return it, he felt sometimes, when he had been absent for several hours and came back to the Rectory, that their contact was broken and that she was beyond his reach. She did not avoid him; she appeared, indeed, to be more than ever eager to be with him, as though he had power to quiet and reassure her; but the ease of their companionship was gone. What was the nature of her mood, he did not know; he would have said that she was afraid, if he had not believed that she had nothing to fear; but he measured the change in her by the change in himself. When she was, as he expressed it, "on edge", she exercised upon him a sensual power from which he could not escape; his sense of guardianship over her was weakened; he became aware of her body, its curve and movement, of the colour and

texture of her flesh, of the physical implication of his love
for her, and at the core of his burning was fear that he
might lose her. This possessive hunger seemed to him a
form of madness, a poison in his idea of her, for under its
influence he was tormented by a causeless, undirected
jealousy—a jealousy of what? Perhaps only of time. The
summer was slipping away. Her father would recall her.
She would be gone to the other end of England; he would
not see her again, and the hours they spent together now
would become a fantastic delusion of memory. And the
hours they spent apart? What was she then? What did she
become beyond his sight? He began to imagine that, like
the creatures of fairy-tales whose aspect changed between
night and day, she had a secret life from which, with the
marks of fear and transmutation upon her, she emerged at
his return.

Perhaps she was lonely. He asked her. She said that
she was not, and he decided that what she lacked was
feminine company.

"Why don't you walk over to the House and visit Lady
Sparkenbroke? Do you remember, when we were there
together, she invited you to come again?"

"Yes," Mary answered, "I must go."

"Why not this afternoon? Would you like me to telephone and make sure that she will be in?"

But she had not wished to be committed, and, in the
evening, when he returned from Chelmouth, there was in
her eyes the expression of a child who had run in from a
darkness which fascinated her and to which, she knew, she
must inevitably return. "Did you go to Lady Sparkenbroke's after all?" No, she had been for a walk. Which
way had she gone? Ancaster way.

The mood passed and its effect on George. Late in
the evening, when she came into his dispensary to say
good-night, she sat in a chair opposite his and began to
talk, to his profound astonishment, of chemistry and
physics. With pencil and paper he explained to her the
form of a chemical equation. To amuse her, he said that
it was possible for water to boil and freeze at the same

time, and drew a diagram of the experiment, the jar in which the vacuum was created, the shallow dish of water with ice forming upon it and bubbles rising beneath the ice. Suddenly she said:

"I've often dreamed of this—at least, I think I have."

"Of what?"

"Sitting up very late and talking to you about real things. And learning—as if I were a man."

"Talking," he said, "to me?"

She smiled. "To someone very like you. . . . No, I suppose I didn't dream it really. But it's so different from my own home and so like what my home might have been. In a way, the Rectory's the first home I've ever had."

"Do you wish," he asked, "that you were a man?"

"No."

"You're very unlike one."

"I suppose I am. . . . But I like to be friends with men as though—as though being a woman weren't a gulf between us which might—which might suddenly swallow us both up. If I'd been a young brother of yours," she continued hastily, "you'd have taught me chemistry in just the same way, wouldn't you?"

He nodded. "Perhaps I should."

"I've always longed for a brother," she said. "That's one of the things I've told myself stories about."

Even their silences were without stress. The beauty he saw now was of the face, not of the body, and when at last she stood before him, candle in hand, ready to go to her bed, he could let her go with composure.

"To-morrow," he said, "your prettiest frock."

"But why?"

"The garden party at Sparkenbroke House."

"But I'm not going, am I?"

"Of course."

She said no more, but the wild look of her transmutation awoke in her eyes. She is a stranger to me! he said. In spite of everything, she is lost to me! and, hearing her footstep on the stair, he stood rigid at his table and

remained without movement long after her door upstairs
was softly closed and the house fallen into silence.

She stood beside her bed recalling Sparkenbroke's
words: Not to-morrow. I must be at my wife's garden
party. But the next day—come then.

Her head had moved in assent: Friday.

You promise?

Oh yes . . . I promise.

He had been holding her hands, as he often did when
they said good-bye to each other, and had drawn her
towards him and kissed her. It was not the first time that
his lips had touched hers, but always before there had
been in his kisses a deliberate lightness, a glancing
pretence that they were not kisses at all, which had
enabled her to receive them with a corresponding lightness of heart, telling herself that her blissful association
with him was still innocent, a rapture of friendship, not
finally perilous. Only by this self-deception were her two
lives, her two selves, bound together, and she had sus-
tained it of necessity. While it continued, her visits to
the cottage, which were a compulsion upon her, might
remain free in her imagination of the last, intolerable
burden of sensual guilt.

This afternoon, when he took her in his arms, her
self-deception had ended. She had opened her eyes that
she might see, and forever remember, his face while her
lips lay beneath his. His own eyes had been shut; the
angle of his brow and cheek-bone had stood blurred and
mountainous in her sight; but still with open eyes she had
regarded him, and while his hands had pressed her body
against his own she had driven herself to ever more
active and complete consciousness, until, suddenly, his
eyes opening, she shut vision out and tension broke in
her. When he thrust her head back, she had known that,
in an instant, his lips would be upon her throat. Beneath
such new, intolerable bliss would she not cry out? But
she had not cried out; no more than a sobbing breath had
escaped her, and, suddenly afraid that she was losing him,

she had opened her eyes and put up her hands behind his head and with her own lips discovered his lips again.

The day after to-morrow, he had said.

Yes.

You mean that?

While she was re-living this scene in her memory, she had quietly and without variation of the customary order of her preparations made ready for bed. Now she drew back the curtains that her room might be full of sun when she awoke, opened her windows as widely as possible, and stretched out into the warm air, listening to the stream. The night was starred and gentle, and the bridge, in which she had observed the same change on other nights, appeared to be narrower and more steeply arched than by day. This trick of vision, because it had already become familiar, pleased her as much, and in the same way, as the low ripple of the water, and she turned back into the room with a little sigh of contented gratitude for the good fortune that had brought her to a place she loved so well. It was only when she had blown out the candles on her dressing-table and was carrying a single candlestick to her bedside that she said to herself: it was while I was brushing my hair that I was thinking of how he kissed me, and even when I was at the window, calm and peaceful, I was imagining him. At the same time, she remembered, she had thought of many other things—of the pressure of the low window-sill against her, of how easily one might fall out if one slipped, of the diagram George had drawn for her, of her need to buy new emery boards when next she went into Chelmouth. What Piers said is true, she reflected—that one feels and sees and wonders and remembers, not in turn, but at the same time.

While she was thinking this, she had known, as she had known under his kiss, that he intended to lie with her and that her passionate assent was already given in her imagination. She had known also, as men know that death, certain in others, will not visit them personally, that her assent was impossible. On Friday, the day after to-morrow, she would go to the cottage. The door would be open, and Piers, having heard her step, would be standing when she entered. Not in turn, but at the same time, she saw two contrasted scenes enacted before her and observed each of them in two contrasted moods. In one, with rapture and incredulity, she saw the surrender of herself to him; in the other, at once acknowledging the lie and quietly accepting it as the truth of normal experience, she saw the afternoon spent as others had been, and could even ask herself why she had made a secret of her visits to Piers and why he, when they had encountered on the lawn, had concealed from the Rector their previous knowledge of each other.

On Friday she would go.

You mean it?

Yes.

This evening, in George's company, her pledge had lost its reality of consequence. It had become a pledge given in an exterior world by a being distinct from herself. When he had moved the lamp towards him and begun to draw his diagram, she had thought suddenly, watching his hand and its lumpy shadow on the paper, that in the happiness she gave to him, in her gratitude and affection, was the fulfilment of her life. She would not go secretly to Piers again. She would not kiss him again as she had kissed him to-day. She would put the madness of him out of her life.

In the dispensary, this resolution had seemed not easy but simple and natural. Now, upon her bed, taut in darkness, the whiff of her extinguished candle still upon the air, she lay in deadly confusion of life, having two futures, two selves. If her task had been to choose between them, still she had strength enough to choose, but they did not present themselves to her as alternatives. Each was a part of her destiny already accepted in imagination, for it is the special quality of passion that it creates new life without cancellation of the old. That she would go to the cottage, she knew; and, turning upon her pillow, her cheeks hot and dry, she set herself to believe, against belief, that to her, alone among mankind, the future, held in suspense, would grant exemption from final resolve.

CHAPTER SEVENTEEN

ON the afternoon of the garden party at Sparkenbroke House, it was George's custom to put work away from him, and he followed his father and Mary through the wood with no burden on his mind heavier than his regret that Helen was not with him this year. Usually he drove her up in his car and, on the outskirts of the great oval lawn, found for her a chair that could be easily moved between shade and sunshine; but to-day she had preferred to keep her room. Mary had wished to stay with her.

"But you must go to the Sparkenbrokes' party!" Helen had insisted. "Three counties will be there. And it's worth seeing Piers on his best behaviour! I must say he rises to an occasion. Like a prince—or an actor. There's not a better host in England. You must go, Mary."

"I'd rather stay with you—honestly I would."

"Nonsense, my dear. Father will be as pleased as Punch if he walks across that lawn with you on his arm—and George too."

So here we are, George thought. I'm glad she came; she'll enjoy it; something to remember. It's amusing, too —the mixture of types: the old County, none too rich, stalking round, slow and wary, careful not to catch the wrong eye; the new County, smarter, not yet quite sure of the difference between Sparkenbroke and Ascot; the small landowners, solid, affable, accustomed; the professional sprinkling from Chelmouth and Ancaster, sharply observant; the Cathedral clergy, poking their smooth noses out of the pages of Trollope; the country parsons, the lawyers, the doctors, wandering about in search of old

239

friends as they do between innings at Lord's. Good, said
George to himself, seeing, as they breasted the meadows,
that the sun and Mary's white frock and the green of the
meadow-grass and the streaking glitter of the windows of
Sparkenbroke House were conspiring for his pleasure.
Your prettiest frock! he had said. But I'm not coming, am
I? she had answered. For a moment he remembered her
face as it had been while she stood at the door of his dispensary.

"Mary!" he called.

She turned, smiling, so lovely with her lips sunlit and a
little veil of shadow let down upon the bridge of her nose
that it was hard to find an excuse for having summoned her.

"Look," he said, "here's the grass you were asking me
about."

It was in his hand; he had seen it at the edge of the
churchyard path and plucked it for her. She ran downhill
a few paces to his side. While she examined the grass he
forgot what her expression had been as she parted from
him last night. His father was waiting ahead; they joined
him and went on slowly towards the house.

In the hall, Piers and Etty were receiving their guests,
who passed beyond them in a thin stream, down the
corridor, through the north drawing-room, towards the
lawn.

"I wasn't wrong about the Raeburn!" George heard
Lady Sparkenbroke say to Mary, and, turning his head
to seek again the likeness in the portrait above them, he
felt his father's hand on his arm.

"Come on, George. This is no place for star-gazing.
We're stopping the traffic and we shall lose our lady if
we don't look alive."

They came up with her in the drawing-room, standing
a little apart from the general movement. Outside, dazzled
by the blaze of the lawn, George checked her by a touch
at the top of a broad flight of stone steps. "This is the
place to see it from," he said.

"Look!" she exclaimed. "I wish we could go and swim
in the lake," and there, away to the left, was a slice of the

lake, shining, beyond the yew of the water-garden, like the blade of a scimitar, curved and damascened.

The lawn was equal in length with the house itself. Beyond it to the north, the ground rose through flower-garden and meadow towards Ancaster Ridge, which stood up now in hard outline against a sky so richly blue that it seemed to have on it the gloss of enamel. To the west, on the side of the water-garden, and to the east, the lawn was clipped by two crescent-shaped avenues of elm, which, rising from flowery banks some three feet high, gave to the great expanse of grass, in this angle of the sun, an appearance of slight concavity, as though it were the shallow saucer of a giant in which were walking all the dwarfs in Lilliput. Far away, a little copse broke into the oval as a peninsula thrusts itself into a lake. Here brass instruments and scarlet uniforms gleamed under a dark roof of foliage, but the music was too distant to be heard, except incomprehensibly and at long intervals, through the murmur of the increasing throng.

"Is that the Chelmouth orchestra?" Mary asked. Did you know they had a quartette—a really good one? I wish they weren't so far away."

"That's easily remedied," George answered and led her forward. This scene, with its mingling of brilliance and friendliness, of the familiar and the historical, had smoothed the last of his perplexities away. He was happy, and would have liked to accentuate his happiness by wandering about the lawn with Mary beside him. She was continuously in his thought, and to have her near him eased the stress of imagination by fulfilment of it. And how he would enjoy watching the faces of his friends when they encountered her! Pretty girls were as common as apples, but Mary wasn't "a pretty girl"; she dawned on men's consideration; as they watched her, the power of her beauty increased; they looked at her again with different eyes. George would have been proud to have had her with him, but his old father captured her; with a dry, mischievous smile, he was using her, as a boy uses a mirror, to dazzle the Cathedral. So be it! George

thought. No good being jealous of one's own father!
Later in the afternoon I can steal her away. Meanwhile,
he strolled on across the lawn, talking now and then to
those he met, but happier in his own company than in
theirs.

The people near him turned towards the house.
Following their gaze, he saw Sparkenbroke and his wife
come out together on to the lawn. There they separated;
for the rest of the afternoon they would move singly
among their guests. There's not a better host in England,
Helen had said, and it was true. He was not near enough
to see Piers's face, but he knew how lively was the
expression it wore—an expression of keenness, renewed
and varied by every encounter, which made of his greeting
not a formula but, in each instance, a personal response.
There's something diabolical in the skill of it, George
thought. Piers hates this crowd; he hates all crowds; he
has since he was a boy; they are for him dead men
going through the antics of life; and when he's driven
to approach them at all—in war, in a ballroom, on this
lawn—he plunges into them because he daren't be afraid
of them. Then his pride touches him. Whatever he does
must be done supremely well—even this. Everything?
George remembered having asked.

Everything.

No matter how trivial?

My dear George, Piers had exclaimed with a laugh,
there's not one of 'em at "The Maid's Head" can touch
me at shove-halfpenny!

But why?

If you give your whole mind to a thing while it lasts—
fighting or a woman or a shove-halfpenny board—you
can always win, unless you come up against someone
with the same insanity.

It's not worth it, Piers. Why do you want always to
win—things that you don't care a damn for?

To get out of the crowd.

To escape from life?

My God, Piers had cried, "to escape from life!" That's

the language of fools! They are so persuaded that there is no life out of the sound of their own voices that they would call the Ascension an act of cowardice! To them all the great acts of transcendence are "escape"—the acts of poetry, of contemplation, of death—every act of genius—everything but playing round-games in their own gutter. And all that, he had added with a sudden smile of self-mockery, to justify my passion to be victorious at shove-halfpenny!

As George walked on, remembering this argument and recalling in particular, with a hostile jerk of his mind, Piers's spectacular phrase about the Ascension, he heard behind him two voices, a man's and a woman's, the one smooth and thick and slow, the other a clipped treble.

"Queer fellow, Sparkenbroke. All this . . ."

"Show. . . ."

"I wonder what he sees in it."

"Advertisement, of course."

"I doubt it."

"Do you? Why can't he live like other people, then? At one moment he's lost in Brazil and found in the newspapers. Then he marries an heiress. Keeps a palace and lives in a cottage. All this mystery about not being photographed, the legend about women, the legend about his being bullet-proof in the war——"

"Or not fearing death."

"Nonsense. Everyone fears death."

"May be. . . . You know the story about his being shut in his tomb when he was a boy?"

"You don't believe that?"

After a pause, the thick voice said: "How you hate a man to be different from the rest!"

"I like a decent conformity. Freakishness is a form of vulgarity."

"It wasn't always."

"I hate it," the woman exclaimed. "I hate nothing so much. To me it's the sure sign of a cad."

"Since Dr. Arnold."

"Dr. Arnold—what has he to do with it?"

"He was the grandfather of the Boy Scouts."

The woman hesitated. "But you—you conform!"

"I'm a Jew," he answered. "I shouldn't if I were an English aristocrat. Aristocracy was always vulgar—in your sense, until it lost its imagination and forgot its ancestors."

"Sparkenbroke certainly hasn't forgotten his! He might be one of them—he's spectacular enough. I believe," she continued, "his elder brother was charming. It's odd. Wasn't Sparkenbroke at Eton too?"

"He went there," the man answered. "But so did I!"

When it was certain that they were to say no more on the subject of Sparkenbroke, George remembered that he ought not to have been so long and so deliberately an eavesdropper, and moved on, but not without a glance over his shoulder at the speakers. The woman had those wide, pale eyes, of a melancholy acquired by bloodless and bored self-indulgence, which would have reminded a painter of Sargent's more cruel flatteries but suggested to George dyspepsia; she wore a blue feather boa into which her head was driven like a wedge, and had, in her appearance, that fatal power of charmlessness which provokes an observer to reflect upon the absurdity of human dress and the more tragic absurdity of the human body except in perfection. The man was not physically more beautiful; he had already thickened; jowl, belly and knees had sagged a little as though he were made of wax and had begun to melt; but in his black eyes was an ardour of imagination, cooled by that ironic sadness of the civilized among barbarians which is peculiar to his race. I could get on with that fellow, George thought, and I'd take a long bet that, if Piers comes across him, he'll lead him off into a corner and try him out.

"Why are you neglecting me this afternoon, George?" said Lady Sparkenbroke. "And you make it worse by looking as if you were enjoying yourself!"

"I've just heard a most illuminating conversation," and, suddenly fearing that she would ask him to tell her of it, he added: "Who are the man and woman—the Jew and lady in the feather-boa with janglies round her neck?"

But they were out of sight. By his description she could not identify them, though she puckered her brows and smiled thoughtfully.

"What have you done with your Raeburn?" she asked.

"My father has carried her off," he replied, and when a little group that had been waiting to speak to Lady Sparkenbroke succeeded in taking her attention away, George looked for Mary up and down the lawn. He could not see her, but was content in the thought of her presence there, and in the world. He took off his hat and mopped his forehead. How hot it was! In the shade of the copse, the scarlet uniforms of the bandsmen had deepened in colour; their instruments, now silent, drew, from a background increasingly sombre, an almost silvery gleam; overhead was a soft whispering turbulence of leaves; and George, with a glance to the north, saw above Ancaster Ridge, not defined clouds, but a dark veiling of the sky. Thunder, he said to himself, but not yet, not until evening perhaps, for the women's dresses fluttered no more and among quieted branches birds settled again.

With the branches, his own mood was stilled; the little tremor that the changing light had caused died in him; and, drinking his tea, talking to his acquaintance in the tone of unassuming intelligence that had endeared him to them, he watched shadow and sunlight flow across the lawn, praising in his heart the variety and, beneath variety, the permanence of this English scene. In his tranquil gladness, he praised her also, who, though she was not his and might never be, had made him hers. In a moment she would emerge from the crowd; there would be in her recognition that lightning glance of relief, of confidence, of home-coming with which she had acknowledged, during the past few days, that the years between them were no barrier to an intuitive intimacy, subtler, more various, more permanent than desire.

"There, you see, it's always the same with him!"

He turned his head to listen.

"Oh nonsense," the Jew answered, a rasp of irritation in his voice. "It's one of the merits of the man that he isn't a handshaking machine. If someone's presented to him as if they didn't matter—an awkward boy at his father's coat-tails or a grey old spinster in cotton gloves—he singles them out and leads them off and talks to them as if there was no one more important in all the world. That girl's one of them. She's scarcely out of school."

"Watch her face, then," the woman replied, resetting her boa. "She's an apt pupil."

Knowing, even in the instant before his eyes were raised, that it was of Sparkenbroke and Mary that they were speaking, George looked out eagerly across the lawn. His feet moved; his welcome was already spoken in the forward sway of his body; his lips had parted, when, suddenly, he became fixed, the incredible pang struck him, and, observing together the two beings whom he loved best in the world, he felt himself held, like a strangling ship between walls of ice.

Their faces moved for an instant towards each other. Piers checked the words he was speaking; his breath was dragged in across his lips; his hand moved in that swift, uncompleted gesture, a quiver beneath the impact of vision, which George had long known and loved in him; and Mary, as though upon her had fallen not a silence of words but the silence that is at the heart of a cry, whitened in rapture, and her loveliness was at once exalted, shaken, abased, as white blossom is that a wind tosses and pours out. Piers, the world reminding him, jerked his head away from what he had seen, but the knowledge of it was in his face. At sight of George, he touched her arm, but the recall was too slow; the instant continued in her; even her recognition faltered; her mind did not interpret her eyes' message, and, in the moment before her voice was added to Piers's, George was filled with the terror of exclusion that would have been his if she had stood before him naked and mad. They began to ask him where he had been, what he had been doing; they had looked for him everywhere. He answered dully that he had been having tea; he saw the cup, felt the saucer's rim under his thumb. When he and Mary were left alone, she said: "Rain!"

"Not yet."

"But a drop fell on your spoon."

A shattered drop trailed across the handle like a sweat, and beyond the scoop of silver a dry forest of grass blades was stretched in the ground wind.

CHAPTER EIGHTEEN

THE shower was brief. Thunder became soon an echo from the north. The Rectory, when they returned to it, was full of serene light and the evening so calm that George, standing at the front door before supper, heard over Derry's Wood the thin whirring of the church clock as it made ready to strike the hour. Mary was passing across the hall behind him, and he held his breath, afraid that she also might come to the door. He wished to be alone. The walk from Sparkenbroke House had cost him enough. Each curbed and guarded instant of that return, each driven word and commanded silence, had been so contrasted with the joy of his outward journey by the same path that a thousand times he could have cried out in mockery of himself. So dull, so fond, so complacent, so ridiculously deceived!

Now, in his humiliation, he wished at all costs to be alone. Remembering with how much delight he had looked forward to this supper-time, he dreaded to sit at table with Mary and his father; but when the time came he went in and sat down, not looking into her face, but hearing her voice, in every tone of it a rapture from which he was excluded, and behaving rigidly as it was his custom to behave.

His father was in easy mood, and Mary, asking questions, meeting his challenges, leading him on down the tracks of thought that he loved to follow, was so happy and care-free that George, as he listened, slipped away from his unhappiness as a man does who almost falls asleep in his chair; then, with waking agony, returned to it.

248

"Did you know," his father asked, "that Piers had been translating again? What has happened? Has *Tristan* come to a check?"

"I don't know," George answered; then drove himself to inquire. "What has he been translating?"

"A bit of Catullus. You know: '*Iucundum, mea vita, mihi proponis amorem . . .*' Took me by the arm, dragged me over to the avenue by the water-garden, sat me down and pulled out a scrap of paper from his trouser pocket—like a boy. '*Aeternum hoc sanctae foedus amicitiae*'—what do you make of that?"

"This eternal treaty of holy friendship," George answered.

"*Amicitia?* Friendship? No more? Remember the context."

"It's not love," George replied stubbornly.

"No, but *sancta*, taken with the rest, makes it more than friendship."

"What is the poem?" Mary asked. "Did you write it down?"

"I can remember it." He pushed his plate forward and laid his hands on the white gleam of the table-cloth. Now George looked up. His father, reciting Latin verses to them on summer evenings, was among the profoundest recollections of his childhood. He looked into his own past and saw before him Mary's eager face, so like a child's that his lips quivered. Was it in these eyes he had seen that burning, passionate, confessional glance? She was hushed now; again she was within the range of his life.

> "*Iucundum, mea vita, mihi proponis amorem*
> *hunc nostrum inter nos perpetuumque fore.*
> *di magni, facite ut vere promittere possit,*
> *atque id sincere dicat et ex animo,*
> *ut liceat nobis tota perducere vita*
> *aeternum hoc sanctae foedus amicitiae.*"

Having spoken them once, the Rector began to murmur the verses again, until suddenly, at "*di magni,*" his voice rose and stopped.

" '*di magni* . . .' First, he speaks to the girl herself; then to the gods *about* her. It is intolerably difficult in English. In Latin, the change from '*proponis*' to '*possit*' marks the swift turning away from the woman to the gods, and marks it without breaking the poem's form, but in English— Listen:

> "*You that are my life have promised love*
> *Joyful and deathless. God, let it be true!*
> *Let it be said in knowledge of her heart.*
> *So against Time may yet sufficient prove*
> *This timeless pledge of loving constancy.*

"Well?" he said.

"Is that Lord Sparkenbroke's? Some of it is lovely."

"Some of it?"

" 'Joyful and deathless. God, let it be true!' " Mary said.

"He was proud of that line. But 'loving constancy'? Well, *sancta amicitia* is drier. . . . 'Let it be said in knowledge of her heart'—that's a brilliant compression, but isn't it too cold? What do you say, George?"

"Give me the Latin again."

" '*atque id sincere dicat et ex animo*': 'Let it be said in knowledge of her heart.' "

George did not answer, and his father repeated that the English had not the warmth and depth of "*ex animo*." "But the last two lines," he added, "do preserve the undercurrent of irony, of hope—almost despair, that is Catullus's own. The repetition of 'time' gives it. The chief trouble is '*proponis*.' Piers has made a mess of his first line. Dr. Cornish gives 'promise' for *proponere*, but it's hard to justify. Catullus wasn't the man to use *proponere* in one line and *promittere* in another if he meant them to be read as synonyms."

"But——" George began.

"No, boy, the idea of a promise is hinted at, but the word 'promise' won't do. '*Proponis*' means something by which, in Catullus's sceptical opinion, his lady was far less certainly committed. '*Promittere*' is the contrast;

'*promittere*' (if only the gods will give the lady a firm lead) carries the idea of an effective pledge, which '*proponis*' doesn't. Now, George, what does *proponere* mean?"

"To put before."

"Precisely. Get back to the basic meaning of a word. Then watch it grow. To put before him, to propose to him, to put into his mind the idea of an undying love. . . . Isn't that nearer?"

"I suppose it is," George answered.

"And that's not all. Not by any means. 'You that are my life' is a mouthful for '*mea vita*.' I told him he needed something simpler and shorter—something that would leave him room for '*nostrum inter nos*,' which he'd left clean out. And look at '*facite*.' Surely that's strong enough? And look at '*atque*'—why not *et*?"

"Because it wouldn't scan."

The Rector threw his napkin on to the floor. "Wouldn't scan! Wouldn't scan! There's the Lower Fourth kindly excusing Catullus! For heaven's sake let us assume that Catullus knew his trade! I don't know, George," he continued more mildly, "this may be a pedant's gloss— but, unless I'm greatly mistaken, *et* and *atque* seldom meant the same thing to the poets. '*Atque*,' here, doesn't mean simply 'and.' It means: 'and what is more.' 'And, what's more, make her sincere if you can!' The point is that, as the verses go on, the poet's misgivings increase. 'God, let it be true!' is too mild; and 'Let it be said in knowledge of her heart,' good though it is, is too calmly expectant—not desperate enough. The gods are going to have their work cut out with this lady. If they are to be of any use to Catullus, they'll have to *make* her true to him, not *allow* her to be true." The Rector picked up his napkin again and neatly folded it. "Sorry, George," he said, "and I apologize to you, my dear. Latin verses go to my head. But, you know," he added swiftly, "I gave Piers all that and more! He took it as patiently as a scholarship class. Growled a bit, asked questions, then went off. Later he came back with another piece of paper in his hand. Listen!

"Thou dost propose, beloved, this our love
Joyful and deathless. God, make it come true!
Bring her to swear it, knowing all her heart!
So against Time may yet sufficient prove
This timeless pledge of loving constancy.

"I give him marks for that," the Rector said, looking
round for approval as though the verses had been his
own. " 'Swear' may be too strong for *promittere* and for
dicere, taken separately, but 'to swear it, knowing all her
heart' isn't far off the two, taken together in their context,
with '*ex animo*' and my emphatic '*atque*.' Is it? What do
you say?"

George, for reasons not a Latinist's, preferred "let it be
said in knowledge of her heart," but he did not argue,
and his father continued to discuss the difficulties of
Catullus and the vanity of nearly all attempts to translate
verse into verse.

"Then why——" Mary began.

"Why does he try it? I asked him. 'To amuse myself,'
he said. In fact, it's a form of self-discipline. I know that.
I've known him, my dear, since he was a child, and if all
the fools who call him selfish and rash and irresponsible
knew him as well as I do, they'd talk less nonsense. Whatever his life may be, he's a more rigidly disciplined crafts-
man than any man I've ever known. He is everlastingly
teaching himself—going through his manuscripts, pruning,
balancing, rejecting, testing every word, trying a passage
first with dialogue, then without it, writing version after
version of the same paragraph—he has an inhuman
patience."

"I know," Mary said, and her words, which, this
morning, would have seemed but a plain assent, had for
George now a fresh significance. What did she know of
Sparkenbroke's methods of work? Had they not met this
afternoon for the second time only?—a question that had
long been answered in his mind, though he had not
acknowledged the answer. The look he had intercepted
was itself answer enough; it sprang, not from sudden
impulse, but from an existing intimacy. Again and again,

he said within him, she has gone to the cottage. He looked steadfastly through the shadows for her face, but except in the mirror's paleness the room was dark. As he watched, she rose and seated herself on the window-sill. So they remained, none speaking, until George said:

"I must go and work."

"Not this evening!"

There was no lie in her voice. She wished him to stay.

"Why not this evening?" he answered. "I've had my holiday."

"The moon's rising. Couldn't we go out—all of us?"

The Rector turned in his chair. "We'll wait for the moon. You'll come then, George?"

"Not to-night."

"To-night of all nights!" she exclaimed.

But he could do no more than repeat stubbornly: "I must go and work." His mind was in turmoil. In his thought he had tracked her down with the speed of personal jealousy. Again and again she had gone to the cottage; but he understood now that, as she sat in the open window, she was without consciousness of guilt. She was deceiving herself, not him. And who am I, he said, to have the jealousy of a possessor?

In his dispensary, the door shut, he said: Perhaps it's untrue! Perhaps what I saw was not what I supposed it to be! For a few moments he allowed himself to be persuaded; his pulse quickened; he experienced the wild joy of awaking from an evil dream to find that, after all, the world is unchanged; then fell back dully upon the truth. On his table were his account-books. Near them a newspaper was folded back at the list of stock-exchange prices. It was long before he remembered why they were there. He had been valuing his possessions. What had seemed, when he began it, almost a game appeared to him now in harsh, ridiculous crudity. Beside the names of certain trustee stocks were two faintly pencilled letters: 'M.S.'—marriage settlement.

Through the open window he heard footsteps on the gravel. The moon was up. His father and Mary had set out. He imagined them—the old man in his long, rusty cassock, she in white, their shadows hard on the bright pebbles. When the sound of their feet could be heard no more, he took a pencil and wrote down, as a boy writes an imposition, the price of Old Consols, and began to calculate the market value of his holding. The church clock reminded him that the time had come for Helen to settle for the night. He went to her room and sat near her bed, but beyond the ring of candlelight in which she had been reading.

"Tired of your book?" he said, for it was lying face downwards on the coverlet.

"Thinking."

"Of what?"

"You, George," and she would have spoken to him of Mary, but he turned the conversation away, telling her of the garden party and of those he had met there.

"Well," he said at last, "I think I shall go to bed early."

"Do," she answered. "You look tired."

CHAPTER NINETEEN

NEXT morning, soon after breakfast, Mary went out to
gather flowers and speak to the gardener. She found him
in a greenhouse, balanced on a pair of steps while he
tended a vine. He came down as she entered, his rounded
lips pressed together into a smile. She would have liked to
stay among the hot, earthy smells of the greenhouse,
listening to the potting-earth run through his fingers as he
talked and to the scrape of his boots when he moved on the
slated floor; and so pleased was he to see her, so delighted
by her questions, that he did his utmost to detain her,
finding always, at each sign of her going, a story to begin,
with an air of mystery, in his thick, eager voice. "Can I
have the Etoiles this morning?" she asked. They were his
favourite roses after the Jacqueminots; concession was
hard, but princely when it came. "Who better?" he said.
"You take 'em, miss." Still it was necessary to discuss
what vegetables should be granted to the kitchen. In this
matter, he found her as determined as Miss Helen herself,
and, cheerfully surrendering, set himself to persuade her
on to the step-ladder to inspect the vine. "To-morrow!"
she promised, and made her way into the upper part of
the garden, between lawn and orchard.

To-morrow! she repeated within her, and through her
composure glinted the thought that between this morning
and the next lay her meeting with Sparkenbroke.

From above the lawn she looked back upon the house.
Already it was her home, as her own home had never been,
and it gave her pleasure to observe the familiar evidence
of life within it—Helen's profile as she lay on the couch

beside her bedroom window, and a white gleam from the book which the Rector carried open in his hand as he went to his library across the dark aperture of the garden door. How long will Father let me stay here? she thought, and was glad that, in his stiffly parental letters, he had not spoken of her going home. If I go, certainly I shall come back, and she thought that the place would be even lovelier in early spring when the woods were no more clouded by leaves, and their forms appeared, the birches lifting their brilliant spray skyward, the elms dark and solemn but, beyond their major branches, flecking the pale air with buds; and somewhere perhaps an oak still crisp and brown with autumn's foliage. In Derry's Wood, at the edge of the clearing in which rue had been planted, was a wych elm, and she remembered that Sparkenbroke had promised her that on the first of April it should be heavy with red blossom. If you are here on the first of April you shall have a spray of it, he had said, and as many more as we can reach. I'll lift you on my shoulders and you shall take them for yourself. She had asked if the blossom had a scent. A scent! Yes—of almonds, and imagining the smell of almonds and herself lifted on his shoulders, and the cool April breeze on her cheeks, she found herself among roses. All her imagining of the April woods had been an echo of conversation with him, and this afternoon, she thought, I will take some of these roses to him. Against the whitewash of his work-room the profound red of the Etoiles appeared in her mind with so fierce a glow that she was afraid. Never before had she been afraid while in contact with flowers; they were the tranquillity of her life, to which she now returned, forgetting, or almost forgetting, by what magic these flowers beneath her hand were made lovelier than roses and she herself exalted to their company.

"Look!" she exclaimed, when George was at her side. She held them out to him, feeling that she and they and the summer's morning were included in such a radiance as there had not been in the world—such a radiance, her heart cried, as will never shine again. "They're new," she said. "They've never been like this. Touch them."

"New?" He looked at her searchingly. "Yes, for you—you make them so."

She drew breath, reading in his eyes her own confession.

"Mary, is it so marvellous a dream as that?"

She did not answer, and he said gravely: "My dear, if you feel—if the thing falls on you—" His face began to work and his eyes remained fixed on her. At last, mastering himself, he said: "Tell me something."

"Anything," she answered, stricken by the suffering she saw in him.

"That day in Chelmouth, when I brought you in from the rain—had it begun then?"

"George—what?"

"You and Piers. Had you met him then?"

"Yes."

"And since you have been here—every day?"

"Not every day."

"In the cottage?"

"And in the wood."

"Alone," he said. It was not a question and she made no answer. "What can it lead to—for you? What can it lead to?" he repeated as though he were asking it of his own life. Then, in a tone of harshness: "There's no good in talking. You know all I can tell you. You know what he wants of you."

"No," she said. "You are wrong—all wrong."

"I know him," George cried, "better than you or anyone on earth knows him. I know well enough how great his value is. If ever he loved a woman—if he found in her what he looks for everywhere—and loved her for that, then— Do you believe that he loves you in that way? If not, he will search you and find nothing and throw you away."

While he was speaking, she, knowing that he spoke the truth, was yet incapable of accepting it. Her association with Sparkenbroke was for her timeless. To ask what it would lead to was to ask not an unanswerable question but a question beyond the range and necessity of answer. It seemed to her that George had failed to understand this, and, wishing him to understand so that he might be at peace and she liberated from the torment of tormenting him, she began to tell him of her meetings with Sparkenbroke—how they had met at the book-shop, in the wood, on the sea-front at Chelmouth, and how, until that evening, she had not known his identity. As she told the story, tension was eased; George's face was relaxed by his interest, and when he heard how Sparkenbroke had written verses on her band programme, he smiled and looked into her eyes. "What a child you were!"

"That's what he thought—and thinks still."

George's expression was clouded again by disbelief, but her narrative comforted him, not because he believed that the whole truth was in it, but because it seemed to represent her understanding of the truth. If I have it out with Piers, he said to himself, then, perhaps—and so ardent was his desire for reassurance that he allowed his agonized passion to give way to anxiety, and anxiety to hope. When she had done, he said, looking not at her but at her roses:

"My dear, you've been very patient with me. I was wrong; you won't find it easy to forgive." Then, his fears renewed: "But I saw you together! I believed my own eyes! I can't help it! Your face was—was lighted up, as it was lighted just now when you held out the roses—as if—" But he had no words to express what he had seen. "For God's sake don't lie to me, Mary," he said. "If Piers died, if he vanished to Italy to-morrow——"

"Why should you ask that?"

"Could you let him go?"

"He has his own life," she said. "When he goes— Meanwhile——" she began again and hesitated.

"But don't you see the peril of 'meanwhile'? My dear, you're blinding yourself. You're trusting to an impossible compromise."

She shook her head. It was true, but she shook her head, bidding time be still that the truth might not be proved. Looking from George's face to the roses she had gathered, she knew that among them, visible but undeclared, were those that would soon appear to her against the white wall of the cottage; yet, when he grasped in his own the fingers curled over the handle of her basket, and asked with desperate pleading whether she would give herself time to think, whether she must go on, whether her visits to the cottage must be continued now, her heart went out to his urgency, and she said, with a quick radiance of compassion: "Not if it means so much to you," lying to him as she would have lied for the immediate consolation of a haunted child, but lying also with that spontaneous and intuitive subtlety of women which, when passion is fallen upon them like a hood of light, enables, and indeed compels, them to divide their enchantment from their experience, and to deny the truth of their character that the truth of their instinct may be preserved. Nothing is as it was, is whispered within them. In the change, perilously, they are free, and from the soaring freedom of a single idea they look back upon the world with pity so gentle, with indifference so pitiless, that, though they lie, they are endowed by the beauty of their instant, which none but Leonardo has made permanent, with a privilege of angels to believe themselves and to be believed. But in the instant only. "Not if it means so much to you," Mary said, and no sooner were the words spoken than she would, if she could, have recalled them.

To George they were a reversal of despair. His face changed. Vigour, expectation and eagerness returned to it, gratitude to her, a wondering and reprieved gratitude to the Fates. With painful joy, she saw this joy in him. What had she said? What promised? So little! To him, seemingly, so much! Watching life return to him, she could not strike him down, could not retract the words of which his reading had made a lie now recognized by her. The recognition brought her back to the plane of her affection, and she perceived with George's eyes, and with the eyes of her own character, the peril in which she stood. With knowledge of peril came sharpening of delight, and, for the first time, a conscious pang of her body for surrender. Swung between her dream and her knowledge of herself, she heard George say:

"You know why I had to say this? I hadn't meant to. Coming down from the garden party, and last night, and even coming across the lawn this morning, I'd meant to keep quiet. Then you pushed the roses at me and I saw your face—out it came. I hadn't the right. I know that."

"Yes," she answered, "always."

He came a step nearer to her. "But whether or not I had the right—perhaps there are no rights in these things —anyhow, I'd more need than anyone living to say what I did. Though Piers is my friend—partly because of that— I had to. And I must say more now. Months, years ahead, I thought perhaps—I'd say it—not now. But I must. I must." He stood suddenly away from her, his arms loose at his sides. "I love you, my dearest. I love you with my whole life. You knew that?"

"Oh!" she cried softly—a breath of fear. "Have I hurt you so much? . . . So much!" she repeated and thrust her hand into his.

"But you knew?"

"Yes," she said, remembering. "That first day, when you took me half-way to Sparkenbroke House and wouldn't come farther, I knew then, I think." She could not tell him that, although she had so long ago acknowledged the upspringing of his love, she had been blinded to its implications; and, perceiving again her own cruelty, she perceived also that she had been cruel to a man who had become a part of her habitual life as Peter had never been, as even Sparkenbroke was not.

"You're not angry?"

"Angry!" And as though she were listening to a distant echo, she heard herself continue: "I love you too, in a different way, perhaps. I'm never so peacefully happy as when I'm with you."

The expression of joy and doubt and hope that appeared on his face when she said this moved her as even his suffering had not. Pulling himself out of his dream with the courage of acceptance, he looked about him—at the trees, the flowers, the whole flash of summer—with a swift glance of recognition, a slower gaze of remembrance.

"Well, bless you, I've heard you speak the word once."

"What word?"

He smiled. "If you've forgotten——" He checked himself, unwilling to reprove her. "I must go," he said, then added with a glance into her eyes: "*Sancta amicitia.* I shall have to learn to translate it."

She watched him go. No more a child, she knew that she had deceived him. In all the time they had been speaking together, she had not been emptied of her promise to go that afternoon to the cottage. The relief she had had in telling George of her meetings with Sparkenbroke, the tenderness and admiration she had felt for him, had been threaded with betrayal of him and of herself; and as she carried her flowers into the house she thought: It's simple. I have given my word. I can't go to Derry's Wood to-day, and she sat down at Helen's writing-table in the drawing-room. I will not go to the cottage, she said, and felt the security that would be hers when the letter was written and given to the gardener to send across by his boy. Everything in her life would be clear again; she would lie no more to herself or to others; the speed of experience would slacken; she would be her own possessor.

On the table were roses in a glass bowl. Their scent, because it had once been familiar but came to her now as part of a state of life altogether new, sharpened her exile from her former self. Sensual images had no place in her consciousness; her virginity looked through them, unaware of their presence, as a child looks through glass; but as the glass it looks through nevertheless affects a child's vision, so did her passion colour and penetrate all her ideas. So it had been with her for many days. The words she read or heard spoken had, in her mind, a special significance distinct from their simple meaning. If she took down a book from Mr. Hardy's shelves, she found secret messages, promises or warnings, on every page. This morning, while she was speaking to George, the sparkle of dew on the lawn had seemed to be a discovery, almost a creation of hers, proceeding, as everything now proceeded, with terrifying uniformity of origin, from within; and the scent which came to her across the table was a part of her failure to write this letter; it was no longer an independent delight external to her, but a form of her passion, a part of that emotion which gathered all things into itself.

She dipped her pen and let it stand in the pot.

From the first, and within her knowledge, this letter had been a ghost; she would never write it; but all the morning, as she went about her work in the house, she awakened and reawakened a fire in herself, that ran like an icy bracelet on her wrists, by pretending that the letter had indeed been written and that she would see Sparkenbroke no more. George did not return for luncheon. She and the Rector sat down at the dining-room table together, and she carried up Helen's tray. Afterwards she went to her own bedroom. There was some darning in a basket at the foot of her bed and she did it, looking from time to time at her travelling-clock. When the darning was put away, she rose and, having stripped herself and stung her body with cold water, put on fresh clothing, a white skirt, and a blouse of fine white linen, embroidered with a Hungarian design of rosemary flower, and drawn in, below the hollow of her throat, by a cord of deeper blue. The darkly gleaming face of the oak chest in the hall was for an instant surprised by her whiteness; a convex mirror acknowledged her; a plane of sunlight in the open door threw back her shadow as she advanced, then let her go.

CHAPTER TWENTY

WHEN Sparkenbroke, looking up from a manuscript disordered by cancellations, saw her standing in his doorway, and Bissett behind her, she was to him no more at first than the girl who he had known would come—an expectation fulfilled.

The door was closed. He gave her a bowl in which to put the roses she had brought him. They spoke a little—of what he did not afterwards remember. While they were speaking, his thought receded from her, and suddenly, when he looked at her again, she sprang new-born out of his imagination. He laughed and stared at her. "How you have changed!"

"Changed!" She did not understand. Colour rose in her cheeks. "Better—or worse? Why have I changed? In what way?"

She was frightened, and to calm her he took her hand. "There's a spirit stove," he said. "I'll light it and you can brew tea if you want to."

While he was on his knees holding out a match to the wick, she said: "What is it? How have I changed? Please tell me."

He let the match go out and dropped it. On the floor beside her chair he raised himself up, put his hand over hers that lay upon her knee, and was at once aware in her body of that tenseness which is trembling without movement. What precisely he had meant in saying that she was changed he had not then known, but now he knew, with mingled joy and terror, that if she was silent he could communicate to her what hitherto had been hidden from himself, as though she were a piece of paper which, lying under his pen, would draw from him truth that could not otherwise be given form. The weight of his hand commanded her silence, and he began to tell her that last night at dinner there had been guests at Sparkenbroke House. To them he had played the part that in early manhood he had imposed upon himself, talking with a challenging, reckless energy that was its own incentive. "I hear myself lie, misrepresenting every truth I believe in, and still I lie— or is it lying? I don't know. It's playing a part and, like an old actor, I haven't the courage to abandon a part I have outgrown." His conversation at the dinner-table had run against his thought as wood-fire spreads upwind, phrase lighting phrase. Intellectual positions, which had long ago become indefensible by his faith, he had defended the more eagerly by wit's impetuous attack, pouring his strength into the task of entertaining and vitalizing those who heard him. "Like hitting their faces," he exclaimed, "and watching them smile and laugh and turn the other cheek. And how I loved the sting and excitement of it! How proud I was when I had them there, hushed and taut, like an audience at a play! I was feverish with it all night. This morning, even when I'd got away from them down here, I was slack and dull like a boy after a party. I turned over the manuscript of *Tristan*. Two days ago it was in flood. Now—not a trickle. It wasn't I that had written it. I sat down to it and my pen was dumb. If I wrote at all, I knew, even while I was writing, that what I wrote must be cancelled. Worse: I began to think that the theme was stale because it was familiar. Then I said to myself: Soon she'll be coming. I was glad. Any excuse to be idle serves a powerless artist. No good working! Soon she'll be here! Then you came—with your roses. At first—nothing. Just that you were here. Then, suddenly, the stale bitterness and vanity went out of me. Do you know what it is when you've been in pain and it ceases? You feel as if you'd been given a new body, and no-pain is an extraordinary, childlike joy. When I looked at you again——"

He gazed at her and shook his head. "Autobiography," he said, "the most difficult of the arts!"

"Why—if you tell the truth?"

He smiled. "So easy? . . . I've been trying to. And I've told you nothing—have I?—except that I chattered at a dinner-party?"

"Yes," she answered gravely, a light of happiness appearing in her face. "You've told me that you wanted me. I wasn't sure. I spent the morning trying to write a letter to say I wouldn't come."

"Never?"

She nodded slowly. "That's what it would have meant, I suppose. . . . I was a coward, too. You see, you have two lives, haven't you? And what happens here, in this room, is a kind of—I mean," she said, struggling for her words, "that whatever happens to you, you can say: 'Still I've got my work,' just as if a man had two houses and one was burnt down and he said: 'Still I've got my other house.' I've only one house," she added. "Do you understand now?"

Never before had she made so elaborate an essay in self-analysis, and she looked at him with misgiving, as a child that has spoken out of its childish part looks up in fear that it may have spoken foolishly and be laughed at. Sparkenbroke was stirred by her look to a delighted compassion and curiosity.

"Go on," he said. "I'm beginning to understand. Go on."

"I say it so stupidly."

"Autobiography," he exclaimed, echoing himself, "the most difficult of the arts. . . . Do you admit that now?"

"I suppose it is." Her gaze was lifted from his face and moved slowly across the room. "How lovely it is to be here! I wonder whether you and I see the same thing in the same way. I expect you're so used to the trees outside your window that you scarcely notice them, but it's wonderful to me to feel that I'm in a house in a wood. The leaves are rustling now and the branches are creaking. I suppose it will rain before evening as it did yesterday. But I've

noticed: when it's quite still, you can just hear the stream
moving. Do you sleep in this room?"

"Work, eat, sleep. I hate moving from room to room
when I'm working."

"Is that where you sleep—that thing like a couch? . . .
When you lie there, do you hear the stream? From my
own window at the Rectory I can hear the water flowing
under their bridge. I've never slept within sound of running water before. There's none at home. To me it's almost
a new sound." After a pause, she said: "It goes with your
name."

"Sparkenbroke?"

He did not wish to interrupt her and was silent, for he
knew that, though she had broken off from her "autobiography" to speak of the wood and the stream, nothing
she said was irrelevant; her innermost being, schooled in
reticence, was expressing itself in its own way, was learning
to speak. Rapt and patient, possessed by the absolute and
timeless patience of his art, he listened to her as he was
accustomed to listen only to the creatures of his imagination, to Nicodemus, to Iseult herself, when they began,
with the extraordinary subtlety and the seeming irrelevance
of spirits, to whisper of themselves within him. How she
is changed! How she is changing! he thought, and to arouse
her from the dreaming stillness into which she had fallen,
he said: "The sound of water will be new for me when I
hear it again."

"Is that true? Is that really true?" she said. She spoke
with profound eagerness as if his admission of her share in
his imaginative life were an absolution of her soul, and
Sparkenbroke, perceiving in what way her spirit was
moved, pitied her, and rose suddenly and kneeled upon
her chair, stooping over her, and said: "Listen. Listen to
me. I—" But she could not listen to him. With the movement of a child growing that instant into woman, she
raised her body towards him and cast up her head, so that
she was gathered into his arms and her head laid against him.

"My dear," he said, "you mustn't believe that you love
me. I'm nothing to love. Not with your heart."

And instantly, as though she were speaking from within her own fated legend, she answered, "If you were nothing to love, should I love you as I do?"

Long after she had said this, he heard the saying continue, for there had been in it, as she spoke it, that certainty transcending judgment which is the signature of love; and he was silent as once he had been when to him, a young man, spring cried through winter. The pulse of that experience, until now incomparable, beat in him again; the scent of that instant was in her hair, the warmth of earth in her body; and he kissed her lips, not in the age of desire, but with a rapture through which all time was flowing.

When he spoke her name, there rose from her a low consent of the breath lovelier than the naming of names. Her lips were a little parted, her hands came up to enfold his head, and suddenly her adoration mocked him; her entrancement was a mirror in which he saw only his self-deception, and starting back he broke the clasp of her hands so that they fell and lay where they fell until she, having looked into his face, covered her own.

"You must go," he said. "We shall entangle our lives."

"They are entangled."

"No."

"Always. Always. Mine with yours."

To kill the assent in his own heart, he dragged her hands away and caught her up, compelling her body to his own until her identity was for him submerged in physical contacts and no consciousness remained to him but of a back's muscles under his hand, a prim fragrance of lavender, a loosening and surrender of limbs.

There is, in the anonymity of lust and the ludicrous sameness of its manifestations, a drug against imagination of all but carnal forms. To this influence now deliberately submitted, he thrust back her head, covering her eyes that he should not see them. The boundaries of his existence were contracted to the area of golden flesh that was her throat, to the sudden whiteness, near and dazzling, of the breast from which her frock, its cord undone, was sliding away, and she was no more Iseult for him nor the

confessional of his secret life. Already he could mock his own
delusion—that he so nearly should have fallen again into
the trap of love!—and his light, sensual resolve to take her
and be done returned to him. Soon she would be lying,
used and naked, across his couch. He would cover her, and
she, kissing him again with tired lips, would speak—of
what? He would not care. Having taken her without hope
of love, he could take her again, as it pleased him, with no
false expectation of ecstasy, or let her go with no renouncement but of the pleasures of the flesh. So, compelling himself, he compelled her, drawing her across the
room as he would, but suddenly his sensual concentration
lifted like a shadow from his brain and, remembering her
in the woman, he searched her face with unpitying
curiosity, asking himself what was the nature of this beauty
that had for an instant given him youth again and enthralled his extreme hope. As he watched, his thought
flowed back from the idea of sensual appeasement in her
body, a whiteness intervened upon his desire, and she
sprang out again from his imagination, as from darkness a
form, blindly touched, springs into knowledge.

Her eyes were shut. When he spoke her name, she did
not answer. She drew breath as though she were awaking,
and her fingers, separately cold, tightened upon his wrist.
Her eyes opened, her lips moved, she began to release
herself from him with an absolute will, a submission to
character and destiny, which sprang neither from fear nor
reason; and he let her go. She walked across the room,
her shadow curling upon his papers. When she reached
the fireplace, she would turn and face him.

With a detachment from personal circumstance that
was almost hatred of himself, he wondered, when she
broke this silence, what words she would speak.

CHAPTER TWENTY-ONE

GEORGE entered Derry's Wood by way of the stile from the Ancaster road and the bridge over Derry's stream. A light at the back of the cottage told him only that Bissett was in; if the front was in darkness, Piers would have gone up to the House, and I shall go home, George said, I shall go straight home; I can't follow him there on this business. But from the window of Piers's writing-room a patch of whiteness fell across the path and for a few brilliant inches climbed the opposite foliage. From this illumination rain seemed to spring upward into the darkness. George halted and gazed at it, swinging his lamp.

He went forward and knocked on the door with his own double knock—the prelude to how many good evenings of talk before this misery came.

Bissett welcomed him.

"Working?" George said.

"No, we've done for the day, sir. His lordship'll be glad to see you." The door in the passage opened; a head came out; then all of Piers in an eager stride.

"You. Good. Come in." He took George's arm and led him into the room. "Damn you, you're wet," and, while George blew out the lamp he had been carrying and took off his overcoat, Piers began to brush the wetness from his own sleeve. "Bissett, take the doctor's lamp away. It stinks. And we might have a fire to look at. Are the logs dry?"

A fire was made and lighted, a decanter set on the table. Piers crouched on the hearth, stretching out his hands to the blaze, talking with swift gaiety over his shoulder. He's had a good day, George thought, staring at a little sheaf of papers clipped together that lay, face downward, beyond his wine-glass, and, though he had come with a fixed determination not to be led aside from what he had to say, hoping almost that Piers by a fit of ill-humour would make hard words easier, he could not resist the warmth of this companionship, could not but feel in himself response to a delight so brilliantly communicated.

"Done much to-day?" he said, knowing well that it was his duty to say nothing of the kind.

To his surprise, Piers answered: "Nothing worth speaking of, nor yesterday."

"You're in uncommonly good humour, then."

"Yes," Piers answered and was silent. After a pause, he said: "It was going like smoke until the garden-party broke in. That budget's the last day's work. Count it."

"Ten to the line?"

"Thereabouts. Rather less, perhaps. It went easily. My writing spreads a bit then."

George counted; it was a task that yielded him the pleasures of avarice. "More than three hundred lines."

"The Lord be praised. And as much the day before. It will stand more or less or I'm mistaken. I shall never get out of the habit of wild calculation. One day: three thousand words. Two days: six thousand. Fifty days: a hundred and fifty thousand. Seven weeks and the story done—all in one mood, seen whole like a picture! To-night it seems possible. It always does when I work it out in that way. In fact, I've been fourteen months at this book and it will take me as long again to finish the first draft. Still, just for to-night, pretend it's true. To-morrow morning up I get; half-way through breakfast my pen walks into the inkpot; about twelve I'm written out—shaving-water, bath—and suddenly, in my bath, I'm hungry to write again. And so on all through the day: the blur of a story hanging round you like a fog while you shave or bath or eat, and blowing into clear weather when you get down to paper. At the end of the day, your pen stops but the story is waiting, ready to flow again—like the ink in the pot. And you feel like death; and at the same time you feel as if you'd scaled two mountains and drunk two bottles of wine; alive as fire, deep and sleepy and good like the sea. There's only one trouble. No one to talk to, no one to tell—except Bissett, and Bissett thinks writing is half witchcraft and half wild eccentricity, not a job for an officer and a gentleman—except me. When I've been writing, he looks at me with a kind of jealous, protective awe as if he were a plebeian hen and I some chicken of superior breed that had been standing on its head all day. . . ." He lay down full length on the hearth, his hands clasped under his head: "O George, it's good to have you here. You have the virtues of a father confessor who has shared one's sins."

"Shared them?" said George.

"Not all, George. The ones I confess to you. When I boast, you boast with me. When I can't write, you pretend that pecking at a paragraph for ten days is my special virtue and you argue like hell about a relative clause. When I can write, you count the words like an old nurse counting the money in my money-box, and you turn up in the middle of the night and drink my madeira and purr. Look at you. . . ."

"Do you want to read your piece?" George said.

Sparkenbroke rolled up on to his knees. "Of course I do." His eyes were shining with eagerness and laughter.

George did his utmost to harden his heart. "Well," he said, "get on with it. Afterwards I've got something to say. That's what I came for."

"Bad?"

"I don't know. As you take it."

"That sounds very bad. Medical?"

"No."

"Moral? I'd rather it were medical. But in fact, George, I've had a long spell now without an attack. I'm beginning to imagine that I'm exempt. Tell me: is it true that people have recovered from angina?"

"Yes."

"Why? Any particular reason?"

George moved his shoulder. "We know little about the cause—less about the cure."

"In that case," Sparkenbroke said with a smile, "let's talk of art and women."

"O Piers, for God's sake. . . . Why aren't you in one of your damnable yellow moods to-night? You say you've done no work worth speaking of for two days. Why the devil are you so cock-a-hoop?"

Piers smiled. "Because what I didn't do to-day, I shall do to-morrow. Because the curtain's going up. Because an audience has been delivered into my hands. . . . A hundred reasons, George—all different."

"Read your piece, then, and stop rocking about on your haunches like a boy. You'll fall into the fire."

When Piers began to read aloud what he had written two days earlier, George yielded his mind to it. He knew the story so well and had discussed every aspect of it so often that a few preliminary words were enough to give him his bearings on this fragment, and the scene sprang to life before his eyes, he heard the voices of the speakers and felt exercised upon him the peculiar influence of that style, dry, quiet, deceptively ingenuous, with which Piers would imply the frailties of characters he loved. The method was a perilous one, but at its best it brought great rewards, casting over the scene that unifying light of personality by which alone a new world, or a new aspect of the known world, may be revealed.

"That's what you want," George said, when Piers stood by the table and laid his papers on it.

"No stumbles?"

"There's one bit of talk worries me," and across the corner of the table they leaned towards each other under the lamp. "I know well enough," George said, pointing to a piece of dialogue, "that the question is not whether she would in fact have spoken these words; she relates to your world, not to my memory of how people turn a phrase; but still——"

"The question is as clear as day," Piers interrupted. "Did she, when she said that, jerk you back out of your illusion?"

"Yes."

"Any particular word? Or the whole speech?"

"I can't tell you, Piers. That's where I'm useless to you. When you began to read, I let the story take me in its drift. Then there was a jolt. I can tell you where—not why."

Piers took up a pencil. "Probably it twists further back," and he bent to the search.

"I may be wrong."

"No."

George dropped down to the fireplace to resettle a fallen log. "It's odd you don't hate me," he said. "I seem to have spent half my life sending genius back to correct its exercises."

There was no answer. The sheets of paper turned; the pencil hovered. Half an hour went by.

"No good," Piers said at last. "It's too big. I shall have to tackle it in the morning." He spoke with the rising, confident tone of one who, having encountered a minor difficulty, brushes it aside as a thing that need trouble none but himself—a tone that George distrusted in him. It was used, he knew, to conceal a disappointment greater than Piers would admit.

"Why turn back," he said, "if you're in the swing? Can't you leave one sentence to be disentangled some other day?"

Sparkenbroke leaned his elbows on the mantelpiece. "It's more than one sentence, George. It's everything that leads up to it. What the girl says is right; the rest is wrong. I must go back."

"You say it like a peasant who has come ten yards down the wrong lane. It's two days' work. I seem to have torn it up for you."

"I started at the wrong point," Piers said, disregarding him, "too near the crisis. Everything depends on the lull before the crisis. And it must be a genuine lull. You must almost forget that there's a storm coming. The lull must be an integral part of the illusion. And like a fool I have been continually jogging the narrative—'look, here's the

storm coming!'—'listen, there's the rumble of it!'—and to
say that is to say: 'this lull is all make-believe.' It won't do.
I must go right back."

George, contrasting with Piers's impatience in all else
the steadiness of his approach to his art, said, with a hand
still on the manuscript:

"Is this what you care for most in life? What do you
want out of it—fame?"

"To do it," Piers said.

"But why? It must go beyond that?"

"If it does, it goes beyond my reach." He looked at
George with the smile of a very old man. "You're making
your everlasting mistake," he said. "You are failing to
distinguish between wants and necessities. A boat is on a
river above a great waterfall. She wants to go down river;
she wants to go over the waterfall at a particular place that
seems wisest and safest, she wants to steer, and does steer
—perhaps with courage and skill, perhaps ignorantly and
in fear—particular courses within the main current that
carries her on. These are her wants; they take her in the
same direction as her necessity; but the waterfall is her
necessity. I may want fame from my writing; or money, or
women. Would you go on listening to my work, George,"
he threw in, "if you guessed that a successful book is the
best pandar in the world?"

George shifted in his chair.

"That shock you? It's true."

"I happen to know it's true. Go on."

"What I want from writing is a side issue," Piers continued, "but to write is my necessity. You say I have a
fanatical patience when I write. I remember your saying
once that in other things I was selfish, arrogant—all the
vices—but in this one thing a saint. . . . Behold the
patience and single-mindedness of the little boat which
nothing can prevent from going over the waterfall!"

"So to-morrow," George said, "you start where you
started four days ago?"

Piers crossed to the window and jerked back the curtains
on their rings.

"Still raining. Look—the window-light on the rain."

But George did not turn his head. He must say what he had come to say. If he waited until he had filled his pipe, it would be time enough to begin. From the special density of the silence, he knew that Piers, standing behind him, hand on window-curtain, watching the rain, was far away, beyond the rain and the logs' crackle and the reckoning of three thousand words. His power to fall, from any present mood or stress, clean out of time, suddenly, as if there were no time, no pressure of actuality with strength to retain him, was, for George, the keenest edge of his delight in Piers's company. To watch him "take wing" was like watching a child go to sleep; it was like watching a man die, as many died, their faces visited by that expression, of which he had spoken to Piers and to Etty, not precisely of joy, not even of release or oblivion, but of cancellation, as though after all there had never been an earth; and George, having filled his pipe but not lighted it, rose with bitter reluctance and turned about to face the room. His plans of approach failed him.

"You know," he said, "that Mary has broken her engagement?"

"I heard that the youth had gone home."

"And her father. She's in the devil's own mess."

Piers seated himself on the edge of the table and threw up his head.

"Is this what you came to see me about?"

"Yes."

"Well, don't. It's off your beat. It doesn't fall within the category of sins that I confess to you."

"In a way," said George steadily, "it is on my beat. We brought her here. She's our guest at the Rectory now. She was Helen's pupil. What's more, we're fond of her, and she—she's in a very deep confusion."

"Is she? George, you're making a very great fool of yourself. You'd better come away from the fireplace—standing there, warming your moral coat-tails, doesn't become you."

George tried to smile. "Very well. . . . Very well," he

said awkwardly, swerving before ridicule. Then he went
on: "She's been here often?"

"You know that?"

"Yes—in fact—I do. She told me."

"Then you needn't have asked."

"Does Etty know it too?"

"I'm sure she does. She has an intuition in that. Her
only one."

"Piers, you say damnable things! They're not the truth
of you."

"Then why in God's name invite me to say them?
What are you? The Mother Superior of this girl's convent?
Or my wife's confessor?"

Even his voice had changed. Hitherto they had spoken
with rigid quietness. If I stick to it, he'll see reason, George
had said to himself. If I keep my temper and don't let my
personal feeling drive me wild, this may all come through.
Now by the choke of anger that had sounded in Piers's
words, he was baffled and confused as by some harsh shrill-
ness in his ears. His hand moved upward from his side; it
would have gone to his forehead, for he was already tired
—it's been a long day, he said inwardly; but he brought it
down again and thrust it deep into his pocket. There were
his keys; he turned them over; there's the latchkey, there's
the key to the bureau.

"You can say what you like," he said. "I'm no match for
you. Probably after this you won't want to see me again.
That may be over. I knew that, when I came. Still—I
don't ordinarily interfere between you and your women."
The foolish bitterness of that phrase shamed him as he
spoke it.

Piers was quick to his advantage. "So many? All under
your protection?"

George was determined to recover himself. "Let that
go," he said. "Mary is different. She's terribly young.
She's thrown away all her supports. The young man's
gone. Not that—anyhow it's an illusion broken. That hits
you when you're young. She's made her home unlivable.
Her whole life, as she saw it a few weeks ago, has crashed."

"Does she mind?" said Piers slowly.

"What do you mean?"

"I mean that you're trumping up a tragedy. You must let people live their own lives. I gather that neither the young man nor the father is much loss."

"But Piers, what will become of her?"

"She'll marry and have three children and a secret romance." Suddenly Piers smiled; his anger was gone. "George, you have the extraordinary delusion that all women, as long as the dew is on them, are by nature nuns. If you wrote a novel, you would say that your heroine 'gave herself'. A bed isn't a martyr's stake unless it's the wrong one. All women——"

"Nothing's true of all women," George said. "And you know it or you couldn't write. Anyhow, Mary is different."

"In what way?"

The turbulence of his emotion left George without words. In a moment, he knew, he might flounder into vague, ecstatic generalization and shameful entreaty—I love her. I can't bear to lose her. Why must you take her?— in a moment, if he didn't keep hold of himself, he'd be pouring out his heart like a boy. The sight of Piers, swinging his leg and waiting, steadied him.

"She's a virgin," he said.

"Is she? I thought that was what you came here to find out," Piers answered, rising suddenly to his great height. "If she is, can't you rest in peace?"

It was said in such a way—slantingly, with open meaning—that, though George knew he was falling into a trap, he asked: "Is she?"

"If you reckon by the physical act."

"What do you mean?"

"Surely you know your gospel, George. 'Whosoever looketh on a woman to lust after her hath committed adultery with her already, in his heart.' Are you so romantic that you exempt women even from the words of Jesus?"

"Then she hasn't yielded?"

"Yielded! You talk as if she were a fortress. She comes here of her own will."

"Not uninvited."

"By chance in the first instance. Then by choice."

"She will never come here again," George said. "Never. I'll see to that. . . . If she went away—would you care?"

"She would come back. They do in the end. Before marriage or after it. But they come back."

"And you take them, and don't care."

"You may put it that way if it amuses you. And if you believe it," Piers added, swinging round and striding across the little room. "Do you believe it?"

"I don't know what to believe. You talk as if you were mean and shallow and corrupt. As if you had no feeling and no insight deeper than the naked skin. As if you had no imagination. There's no link, in this mood, between you and what you write. If you don't want her, for God's sake leave her alone."

"I do want her," Piers said, taunting him.

"And is she," George cried, not caring now what he said if he could but hurt by his mockery, "is she also part of your necessity—a drop in your waterfall, like your art and——"

"Go on," Piers said.

"And your tomb."

When he had said this, George gazed helplessly before him. He saw nothing of the room. Dizzy and sickened by the impact of rage, he felt nothing but an aching of all his limbs, a profound weariness in his throat and eyes. With a slow movement of his head, he looked for Piers. The blood had gone from the face he saw; the skin was tightened on the bones.

He sat down, heavily, in the chair beside the hearth. A log began to whistle a thin tune.

"You said that because you love her."

"I?" George looked up. "You are her god. You are her god. Don't you know that?"

The log foundered. Piers drew the curtains across the windows with a soft clack of their rings. "But unless I'm mistaken, you are the man after her own heart—the man in accordance with her nature." After a long silence: "We do no good," he said. "Better go."

"I'll go."

In the passage, George fumbled for matches with which to light his lamp. There was nothing in his pocket but his keys—the latch-key, the key of the bureau. He remembered Piers's voice: Take the doctor's lamp. It stinks. The door of the sitting-room stood open. "Bissett's turned in," he said, and let himself out into the dark.

Far away, beyond the darkness of the wood, a cock crew. No good, George was saying to himself. No good. "No good," he said aloud, and, hearing his own voice, "Oh, my God, my God!" She came through this wood. And when she comes again, he will be hard and bitter to her perhaps, because I've driven him to it; it's not his nature to speak or think as he did. Or is it his nature? Have I been a fool all my life? He doesn't know himself. That's it: he doesn't know. He believes his own words. And if he doesn't know, how can she? He began to pity her, to feel that in his selfishness he had made everything harder for her and disaster more certain. I've no rights over her, he said, none. It's true. None.

Sparkenbroke stood long without moving. His body swayed a little, his eyelids fell, the panels of the door shook before his eyes. Can't sleep like a horse; and he threw off his coat; when his shoes were off he'd lie and sleep. Sleep would rush over him like the wind of a dive, a fall into darkness. In the morning, Bissett——

"Bissett!"

In the morning, he'd sleep on. Then work. Back. He must go back. But if he woke fresh to it——

"Biss-ett!"

Bissett's turned in, George had said. And your tomb, George had said. Suddenly rigid, awake, Sparkenbroke thought: To-morrow she'll come; to-morrow she'll stand naked here, her clothes about her feet, her hands at her sides, her eyes open in the daring of intense shame. Nothing in a naked girl is as naked as her arms, and the

K

curve of her sides under the straightness of her arms. To-morrow she will come, and all external consciousness this side of the grave will for an instant be blinded in consciousness of her. And afterwards the world will return, shutting her out. She will lie still, her face hidden, a body with hands over its eyes.

He walked into Bissett's room, shouting his name.

"What? Who's there?"

Sparkenbroke struck a match and held it out. Bissett was reared up on his pillow, his eyelids crumpled, his hand groping. From another match a candle drew its flame and Bissett's fingers went to his hair.

"What is it? What's those lights?"

"Wake up, Bissett, turn out."

"You, m'lord?"

"We are starting for Italy."

"Very good, m'lord."

"But now—now—turn out and pack."

Bissett thrust a foot over the edge of the bed.

"Now, m'lord?"

"London by morning—or half-way."

Bissett rose in his night-shirt.

"Very good, m'lord. And will there be breakfast?"

"On the way. You can drive the car. I shall be asleep. Come. Now."

BOOK III

THE RECTORY

CHAPTER ONE

NEXT morning it was decided that Helen was well enough to leave her bedroom. Mary helped her to dress and carried out books and cushions on to the lawn. As she stood beside the chair, looking at the dried and patient face of the woman extended upon it, she was filled with so brilliant a sense of her own vitality, of youth shining within her, that her body shook, and, turning away into the sunshine, she tautened her muscles, and lifted up her arms, and drew breath as if she were indeed awaking from the sleep of her former life to a new morning of experience. Though even now, on the edge of her consciousness, was a remembrance that she had refused what Sparkenbroke had asked, this refusal presented itself to her without moral colour; she neither regretted nor approved it; for there are conditions of the human mind—and love is one of these—which, though they do not create an oblivion to external facts or change the light of character in which these facts are seen, nevertheless give to them, for the time being, transparency; and she looked through her refusal into an imagined acceptance, a predestined fulfilment, already in spirit accomplished, whereby her self was made new in another self that comprehended him also, or her image of him.

"The gods offer their own nature to all of us, but only a god knows how to accept." It was a saying of Sparkenbroke's own, and it appeared now in her memory as though he were at her side on the lawn, reading her thought, aware of the exaltation of her spirit, observing and pitying her. She let her arms fall, relaxed the tension of her limbs, and saw Helen's eyes curiously regarding her.

"You were like a kitten—stretching there in the sun!"

Through the delight of the mood that possessed her, arose again the memory of her refusal and of the profound intuition that had commanded it. That transparency of conflicting ideas, which is singleness of mind, was taken from her, and she drew back, rigidly self-protective, from the rapture of love because the idea of unchastity had broken into it. As she turned towards the house, where the Rector was standing at his open window, she knew that this conflict would continue in her always: a battle between the known safety and the desired peril, between earth and air, between character and aspiration, the thing reasoned and the same thing imagined.

She lifted the window. "Do you remember where Lord Sparkenbroke wrote this?" she asked, and quoted his words.

The Rector waited as though he expected her to say more. It was in his mind to exclaim: Was it of that you were thinking out there on the lawn! but he had, in a different application, his son's gift of silences, and he twisted round into the room, saying only: "One of the essays, I think. I'll find the reference. Come in while I track it."

She climbed through the window and sat down.

"There!" He laid an opened volume on her knee. While she read the passage and read it a second time, he did not interrupt her.

"You see," he said at last, answering her unspoken question, "I'm always half afraid of contradicting myself. Piers isn't. He's a poet, not a theologian, and he has the power—which distinguishes a poet from a poetaster—of crystallizing not only his own intuitions but the intuitions of others who are made differently from himself. When he says that the gods offer their own nature to all of us, he's writing what most people will deny. They deny the offer because they can't bear to remember their refusal of it; but I think it's true that the offer is made. I know it was made to me. There was a moment in my life when I was capable of changing my nature, perhaps of becoming a saint. It was partly my curiosity for mankind, and partly —by an odd paradox—my love of it, that prevented me, and instead of a saint made new I became what you see— a scholar, something of a pedant; a parish priest, a little puffed up by the simplicity of my life; not a failure, not unhappy, but not what Piers calls 'a god.' 'Only a god,' " Mr. Hardy repeated, " 'knows how to accept.' It's a hard saying, and harder for Piers than for the rest of us; he knows how to accept but cannot. The offer was made to him when he was a child. It is made to him continually, it is always open to him—that's the meaning of genius. But because his genius and his life are incomplete he can't fully accept."

"But everyone?" she said. "He—yes. And you. But everyone?"

"Isn't it true?"

She looked at him, almost with entreaty against inquisition. "That we have a chance—once at least—to change our natures?"

He said instantly: "I think so. To me it's one of the Christian evidences, though Piers wouldn't see it as such. Everyone—usually when very young—goes through a kind of spiritual crisis. It varies greatly in intensity and it varies in form with the temper of the age, but in its essence the thing doesn't change. Sick of a world seemingly stuck fast in the mud of human nature, the young man believes, in certain instants, that he alone has wings. In those instants, he does indeed possess them. He has power to tread the air as St. Peter the water. He cries out, like St. Paul, 'Who shall deliver me from the body of this death?' and for answer, the gods, as Piers says, offer their nature to him. No one knew this better than Paul himself, but even he couldn't accept fully, even his great genius was incomplete. And the rest of us? In the very impulse of flight the young man remembers the earth and fears it and desires what he fears. For a little while, he thinks it is circumstance or the folly of others that ties him down. He

goes through the green revolutionary phase familiar to
his father and grandfather. At last, he finds that it is his
own character that binds him, his nature terrestrial, his
being man—not god or genius. That, not the Church, is
what makes him a scholar and a parish priest. But he had
his chance to be a saint. The heavens lay open. Perhaps
they open again at last."

"But if St. Paul himself could not completely accept,
who——?"

"For me there is but one perfect answer," the Rector
answered. "I mean Jesus. The idea of Jesus as a supreme
genius capable of the divine nature—in Piers's sense, as
well as in the Christian sense, a god—that idea means
much to me. It suggests that towards myself and others
those flashes of divine lightning, which seem to mock us
because they leave us in darkness and disillusionment and
self-distrust, are not cruel, as they seem to be, but manifestations of Jesus himself. I don't insist that you use his
name. You may speak of 'the gods,' as Piers does, if you
want to. What is important is to understand that the chief
suffering of youth—this coming and going of the divine
light, seemingly obscured because we haven't the genius
to be permeated by it—is evidence of that light, and that
here at any rate is a part of the explanation of suffering
itself. Suffering, in this aspect, is our own refusal of bliss,
our incapacity to accept it. We see his face, we turn from
it back to earth, and we suffer, not because his face is
changed or his grace absent, but because we have turned
away. We turn away because we have not yet power to
cast off our own natures and are, as it were, stagnant,
standing apart from that principle of energy, of movement, of perpetual becoming which, as Heraclitus con-
ceived of it, is an essential principle of the universe:

> Man is a king in exile. All his greatness
> Consists in knowledge of that Kingdom lost
> Which, in degree of quickness, is his fate
> And character on earth.

We are in exile. We have lost our power to 'become'

because we haven't the genius to die and be reborn—that is Piers's idea. If the genius of death fail us while we live; if —as he puts it—we can't die of ourselves; if we're so weak that we can't seize any of the opportunities of transcendence, then death itself will accomplish what we cannot, endowing us with the resurrection." He paused and began to move up and down the room with short, even strides, like a seaman on the quarter-deck. "Has it ever struck you," he asked, halting abruptly at her side, "how often metaphysical doctrine, particularly of the kind that has a double root in reason and in mystical experience, may be expressed in terms of more than one religious system? I have expressed my thought—and my experience—in terms of the personality of Jesus, yet it is rooted in the teaching of Heraclitus; and it corresponds very closely to Piers's thought and experience, though he—if one must seek a label—is rather Platonist than Christian. It is the universality of a truth that establishes its truth. I have never been able to understand those who think to discredit the gospels by the discovery of parallel 'myths' or 'legends' in the history of earlier religions. It's true that the doctrine of renaissance and the symbol of the resurrection don't belong to Christianity alone; if they did, I should value them not more but less. As it is, they have, in their support, not only the statements of the evangelists but the traditional imagination of mankind. They are true for man because they are necessary to man. If their truth didn't exist, it would be necessary to invent it."

And, pursuing the line of his own thought, he began to speak to her of Voltaire and of the value of scepticism in driving faith back upon its sources. It was long before he perceived how far he had wandered from the special perplexity that she had brought to him, and he reproved himself for pride and lack of charity; he had allowed his own interests, his love of dialectic, to divert him from a nearer duty. Where had her thoughts been while he spoke? At first she had followed his argument; afterwards—he did not know, for he had forgotten her; and he watched her face, saying within him that beauty such as hers was as rare as

genius and that the philosophers had given too little attention to the nature and purpose of human loveliness. The
face before him seemed, in its perfection of form and
colour, to be exempt from carnal estimate and to have now
a meditative transparency through which there shone towards him a light not hers; yet she was a girl, as others
were in all but the degree of beauty, without genius, without
even—one would have said—exceptional qualities of spirit
or intellect. A girl?—she was little more than a child. But
suddenly he asked himself: has she not perhaps understood better than I? did she not already know within her
all that I have laboured to explain? and he perceived, in a
stress of humility, that she had been passing through the
experience he had described. Then she is in love, he added,
and, his mind turning to seek the object of her love, he
was stricken with fear. There was but one that could have
evoked this quality of love in her. While the name stood in
his thought he remembered having been told by the
gardener that Piers had gone during the night.

"Why do you look like that?"

She rose, alarmed, seeming already to know the truth,
and laid her hands on him. "What is it?" she cried. "Why
do you look like that? Is someone dead?"

He was bound to say at last that Piers was gone. She did
not flinch. Her eyes were filled for an instant with suffering
confusion; then they became set and her limbs rigid. At
last the stony fingers on his arm slackened their grip and
fell away; a heavy flush rose in her face, and she said: "To
Italy?"

During the days that followed she was like a child that
had seen a ghost and would not confess it; she was like a
woman who had for the first time looked into her own old
age; and the Rector watched her strangled silences as he
might have watched the suffering of a beautiful animal. I
can do nothing, he thought, and George can do nothing.
Perhaps Helen does more than either of us; she can at
least talk of Piers in the girl's presence.

"It's just his taste for the theatrical made him go off like that," Helen said, and Mary answered: "I suppose so," with a docility at once gentle and terrible.

At last, at tea one afternoon, she said, with a glance from face to face, that she had decided to return home. "I think I must," she repeated, "I'm sure, quite sure." Helen alone urged her to stay; George and his father, separately aware of necessity within her decision, accepted it without words.

That evening, soon after supper, she went upstairs to pack. She kneeled on the floor beside a trunk half filled, folding and smoothing with intelligent economy of space; but at last she became still, her wrists plunged in tissue paper, her back taut, her head raised as though she were listening, and tears began to run down her cheeks.

After an unreckoned interval of time, feeling that there was darkness in the room, she rose, lighted two candles and set them on chairs, one at each side of the trunk. The tissue paper surprised her by its whiteness and the fierceness of its hiss. It was by an act of self-discipline that she finished her packing and went to bed. The journey that she was about to make seemed to her meaningless; it would do nothing to protect her from the feeling, which had become each day more acute and persistent within her, that she was losing, as it were, the senses of her individuality— those senses which, as the senses of taste and smell and touch define the body's place in the physical world, are the individuality's means of self-definition, its evidence that it exists. To lose these senses, this assurance of I, is the precise meaning of despair, for hatred is not despair, nor terror, nor suffering in any degree; only self-loss in confusion is despair, as self-loss in a more intense reality is alone bliss; and to lie down at night, when young, without fear of the morrow or desire for it, without any sense of participation in the years to come, even memory being sterilized as though the past itself were the possession of another, is to be near to that death from which, though the body continue in its hungers, there is no resurrection. So she lay that night, without ownership in her tears.

CHAPTER TWO

"COME back again," the Rector said as he walked with her to George's car. "Perhaps you'll feel like talking some day; then come, child," and the unexpected word thrilled her body and quickened her.

She and George drove away in silence. The morning was yet early; Helen had not come downstairs; but she had crossed from the back of the house to the front and was at the window of Mary's bedroom. Her lips were moving but what she said could not be heard.

"You'll try to explain to her, George, won't you?"

"Explain?"

"Why I'm going—like this—suddenly."

"I'll try."

The Rectory vanished; the village slid away. At the point of the road from which, she knew, Sparkenbroke House was visible, Mary did not look back, but in Chelmouth itself the gilt lettering of the Grand Hotel Sparkenbroke confronted her as they swung westward by the sea; then the bandstand, the bastion near by, the morning bathers going down to swim, the blind man at the edge of the esplanade with his tinkling musical box, his retriever, his metal cup—the same blind man, she had thought when she and Peter passed him together, that had grunted his thanks long ago for the pennies of her childhood. Suddenly they were at the station. George was busy with her luggage, then climbed into the compartment beside her. Comforted by his presence, afraid of the time when he must go and she be left alone, she looked at her watch. Taking her wrist, he turned the watch towards him.

"I've dragged you down here too early," he said. "I'm sorry. I'm always too early for trains. But, as a matter of fact," he continued, "I meant to be this time."

The confession, at once so clumsy and so gentle, brought a smile to her lips, but before she could ask why he had come early he went on: "There was something I wanted to tell you. I haven't been able to during the last week. We haven't seemed able to speak of what we've been thinking about, have we?"

She nodded her head and clasped her gloved hands, erect in her corner.

"Did you know—that night—I went to see him?"

"That night?"

"After the morning when you were gathering roses." Then he said, looking at her: "Perhaps it was my fault he went."

"No," she answered.

"I wanted you to know."

"He—he didn't belong to my life," she said. "That's all. I think—I think, in a way, I invented a life for him to belong to." She looked up with a swift, shy, startled glance. "If that means anything."

A newspaper boy halted outside the open window, shouting the names of magazines. When the noise was gone, George took a letter from his pocket and, leaning forward, laid it on her knee.

"And this," he said. "You'd better read it. Then you'll know all there is. Not that he says much, but he speaks of you."

She did not touch the letter. "From Italy?"

"No. Savoy. You know, he's moving house in Italy. I forget where. The place isn't ready yet."

"Savoy," she repeated and turned the letter over. "That's not his writing."

"Bissett's. It's his job to write addresses."

Her fingers tightened. "I can't read it now."

"I didn't mean you to." He felt in his pocket again. "Look, I've brought an envelope—stamped, addressed to me. You can return it that way unless—unless you'd like to keep it."

She shook her head. For the first time since her self had seemed to die within her, she became aware of her own suffering and of George's response to it. She could have laughed at the envelope, carefully addressed in his handwriting, and have cried for the tenderness that had prepared it. It was as though a dog had brought her his bone.

At the sound of slamming doors, she said dully, out of her loneliness: "George, I wish I weren't going. I don't know why."

To her astonishment, his caution, his fixed loyalty to plan, left him.

"Then don't go!"

"Don't go?"

"Get out now."

"But my luggage is in."

"Never mind. Now. There's still time." He stood up as though to lift her suit-case from the rack, but she did not move, and he, surprised by his own rashness, pretended, with his slow, rueful smile, that it had been a joke.

"Good-bye, then. I must get out."

"Good-bye."

"Good-bye. . . . Bless you." He took her hand, dropped it, stooped without haste, and kissed her cheek. Within her was no feeling for him but of a wondering, remote gratitude, and she let him go. When the train had drawn out of the station, she took Sparkenbroke's letter from its envelope and gazed at it.

"My dear George."

She read these words again and moved the paper between her fingers; then thrust it back and enclosed it in the envelope which George had addressed to himself. At the next station she would hand it out to be posted.

After a week in her aunt's house, she went to her own home in Warlingham. Her father had ceased to be angry with her, having fallen into a lethargy from which nothing

aroused him. Chelmouth was not spoken of. For him the
incident was closed.

A letter came from Sparkenbroke, still in Savoy. In
its brief references to the past, it was affectionate but
colourless, giving no indication that he had wished to be
her lover or of his knowledge that at their next encounter
she would have yielded. Sometimes, as she turned the
pages, it seemed to her that a kind of conventional
chivalry, an unwillingness to insist upon his power over
her, had dictated this letter's avoidances, and they were
for her more cruel than cruelty would have been. For
him and in him, she had created a new life for herself,
growing, as she had believed, towards his stature; now,
in his absence, the life she had been willing to abandon—
her own life, bred of her childhood and character—was
dead; he had drawn her out of her nature, and she, in her
own home, among things long familiar, could recognize
neither them nor herself among them. But I suppose, she
said, he thought he had broken away in time. I suppose he
pitied me and let me go, and he has written, not because
he wished to write, but because to be silent seemed to
him a kind of brutality. Now he has written and for him
it is ended. She replied in his own tone, saying that no
one at the Rectory had been greatly surprised by his
going (weren't his movements always sudden?) and
hurrying on to tell him her news—how she had come
home, that she had been very busy getting the house into
working order again, and what she had been reading. She
asked of his own work—had he done more to *Tristan and
Iseult?*—but her question was put in such a way that it
required no answer. When the letter was done she posted
it at once; then set out for a long walk through the summer
rain. No reply came and she looked for none.

Once a week the postman brought her a letter from
George:

"Sunday morning again. I expect you will be tired of
getting letters from me and you will laugh, I know,
because I always write them at the same time. But I like
doing things in that way. It gives me something to look

forward to all the week. Besides, on Sunday mornings
the others go to Church, so this is the quietest time.
August will soon be over, but September is a lovely
month here and so is October if you don't mind rain.
Yesterday, when I had finished work, Father and I went
into Chelmouth to watch the cricket. His sermon for to-
day was done and he was like a boy. We didn't go to the
seats but found a place under the trees on the other side
of the ground. He said he had heard from you and that
you wrote a very good letter, but it wasn't like having you
here. . . ."

To answer her letters from the Rectory was her chief
pleasure, for she had become shy of encounters with
the people she knew in Warlingham, and lived more and
more within herself. One day Peter came over in his car,
but her father took no interest in him. So surprising was
this to her that while, after luncheon, Peter was preparing
his car to take her for a drive, she said:

"What's wrong, Father? You're not ill?"

He answered with a weary sarcasm that was almost a
sneer. "Ill? Not at all. Don't you worry yourself about
me," and when she returned from her drive he was still
in his armchair in the shadows by the empty fire-place.
She touched his hand; it was cold, but he would not
allow her to light a fire.

"In August? Nonsense."

At the outset, her meeting with Peter had been unexpectedly easy. "Of course," he said, "I was pretty hard hit
at the time," and his eagerness to show how easily he could
talk of the past and that it was the past for him accorded
with her own mood. That she might have been his wife
appeared to her as fantasy. When she recollected that, a
few weeks ago, she had lain in bed at Chelmouth hoping
she might learn to love fully this youth before her, and
saw again his flushed face and swimming eyes while she
broke off her engagement to him, her memory seemed to
lie, and she was glad that he also recognized the lie. But
during the afternoon his mood changed. He stopped the
car and suggested that they should walk a little. Suddenly,

in the open expanse of a field, he halted and began to scuffle the footpath with the side of his boot. Then, jerking up his head, he exclaimed with hungry timidity: "You know—you know, Mary—sounds stupid, doesn't it?—but I shall never find anyone as shatteringly beautiful as you."

She opened her eyes wide and could not choose her answer—so alien to her present knowledge of herself was the desire she saw in him. "I suppose," he said, "you wouldn't think it over?"

"But, Peter," she answered, "why do you begin that again? You haven't really been thinking or caring about me."

"At first I did, horribly. At night, you know, I used to—and now! And now!" he repeated, his hands coming out to her. Because she turned abruptly, one of his hands touched her breast, and through her body there flowed suddenly a tide, not of revulsion from him, but of remembrance so sweet and fierce that he was blotted out. She became alive again with the agony of a limb that has long been frozen, and she uttered a low cry in a voice that seemed not to be her own.

"Did I hurt you?" he cried, for her cheeks were bloodless and he feared that by some mischance he had struck her. Confused, frightened, chilled, he fell back; but she said: "No, but let's go home."

What he took to be the violence of his repulse had tamed him. At tea, her father speaking scarcely at all, awkward silences fell. She was glad when Peter was gone. With a hardness of sentiment unaccustomed in her, she said: Perhaps I shall never see him again, and no sooner had her thought spoken this phrase than a new meaning appeared in it. Perhaps, she said to herself for the first time since the news of Sparkenbroke's going had been brought to her, I shall never see him again, and, kneeling on the carpet in the morning room, she pulled down from the shelves book after book and turned the leaves without attention.

Her father had fallen asleep in a wicker armchair which creaked when he stirred. "I'm cold," he said, waking abruptly. His grey head, tousled and limp on its neck,

rolled towards the plaited edge of the chair and his eye
regarded her. Since he would have no fire, she brought a
rug and wrapped it about his legs. She had expected him
to reject it petulantly; instead, he nodded and dragged it
across his stomach.

"Would you mind if I went to stay again at the Rectory
for a little while? Would you mind, Father?"

"No. . . . Do you need money, though?"

"I have enough for the journey."

"Of your own?"

"Out of my allowance."

"You save then?"

"A bit."

"That's as well. There's just my pension. Little else.
You know that?"

She did not know what was passing through his mind.
She saw the litter of opened books on the floor and the
bleakness of his hair, which, where it lay close to his ears,
was matted with a light sweat, and she remembered that
this was he who, with the awkwardness of a self-conscious
man unaccustomed to children, had yet played with her
when she was a child. Now she despised him, and in the
thought was a new desolation.

"Father," she said, "you look so wretchedly uncomfortable there. If you're cold, why not have a fire? Or go to
bed? I'll bring your supper up."

"I'm well enough," he answered.

"You were so silent at tea."

"I don't like that young man."

"Don't like him? But——"

"I know. I know." And he added, in a low voice, with
suspicion incomprehensible to her: "But to-day, you
know, he came here to watch the siege." His eyes closed,
then opened and stared at her. After a little while he
sighed, his jaw dropped, a trickle of saliva overflowed his
lip. When she took his arm, at first gently, then with the
grasp of fear, the chair creaked, but not beneath movement
of his, and the eyes rolled upward a little in their sockets.

CHAPTER THREE

AT five o'clock next day the dead man's sister, Mrs. Lindt, reached the house. Partly of her own nature, partly because she had been married to a Swiss watchmaker, she was persuaded that the rest of the world was irregular and incompetent, but she had none of the martial airs of a managing woman. Her weapons were quietness and unswerving certainty. "You will always find, my dear, that if one has *knowledge*, there is no need to raise the voice." Against uncommonly stubborn resistance, such as the undertaker's, she threw in her only rhetoric. "Allow me," she said, "to know best." "Undertakers," she observed afterwards, "are always very wilful men, spoiled by the laxity of their clients."

Mary had written to Helen, telling of her father's death and asking that she might come to stay at the Rectory when she was free to leave Warlingham. On the morning of the funeral, she received a telegram: "Arriving this evening about 8.30, GEORGE."

She ordered a room to be prepared for him and, after the funeral, showed the telegram to her aunt.

"What concern is it of his?"

"Just a friend's. To help."

"He knew I should be here?"

"Of course. If not, he couldn't stay in the house."

"I see. But you say he is the local doctor? How can he leave his practice?"

"Oh, Aunt Emily, I don't know. I don't know. I suppose he's made some arrangements. Does it matter so much?"

"Now, my dear, control yourself. Understand, I have
no objection to the young man. None whatever. But I had
proposed to stay a few days myself—for your father's sake
and yours—to help you put things in order. And to have
a stranger here at such a time——"

"He's not a stranger!" Mary exclaimed. "I trust him
more than anyone in the world." The phrase echoed to her
from the past, but it was a little while before she remembered that it was to George himself she had spoken it. He
had been showing her her bedroom in the Rectory for the
first time, and she, aching and happy, feeling that in some
miraculous way she was made safe, had said this to him
in a sweep of gratitude, not weighing her words. Now,
watching her aunt, and, behind her aunt's head, the little
cherubs carved in the white marble of the drawing-room
mantelpiece, she saw, in ghostly recollection, George's face,
and said within her: Thank God he's coming. To be with
anyone else is to be more alone. "You see," she added in
an even voice, "he isn't a very young man, Aunt Emily.
He's one of those quiet, solid people you can rely on. He's
two or three years older than——"

"Than yourself? Even that is not very old, my dear,"
said Mrs. Lindt with an amiable smile.

"No," Mary answered, stumbling, "not than *me*—that
isn't what I meant. Than——"

"Than whom, then?"

"Than Sparkenbroke," Mary said. There was an
unspeakable relief in the word, the end of so long a
silence, and in speaking it she forgot all but the pang of
life that it awakened in her, forgot its relevance and the
conversation that had preceded it. When her aunt repeated
it—"Sparkenbroke?"—she wondered how that name had
sprung from the lips of the little woman with a tight black
bodice and a brooch of plaited hair.

"Ah!" said Mrs. Lindt. "Lord Sparkenbroke, the
writer? He lives there, I suppose." She smoothed out the
telegram, reading from it: "'Sparkenbroke Green.' . . . But
he must be a man of almost middle age. And this Dr.
Hardy, you say, is older?"

It was beside the marble cherubs, after supper, that they sat again to await George's arrival. He came as the half-hour chimed on the porcelain clock. Mary went into the hall to welcome him. From the open door of the morning-room came the lingering smell of lilies, challenged by the wet smell of his tweeds.

"Raining," he said; then, drawing her by her hands until she stood beneath the gas-bracket, with its shade of red glass held in the claws of gilded dragons, he searched her face: "You haven't a fever?"

She smiled, shaking her head.

"Just a rosy complexion, then? Good."

"I'm excited." Then, very quietly: "George, I am glad you've come. I didn't even think of it. And now you're here."

He was taken into the drawing-room. Soon Mary heard her aunt saying:

"Yes. It was a shock to her, poor child, happening as it did. Of course I had known for two or three years that my brother might be taken at any time. But we had no wish to frighten my niece. . . . Unfortunately," she added, "the life had become uninsurable. But we will speak of that another time, Dr. Hardy. You will wish to see your room now. Or have you had no supper? . . . Very well. . . . No, Mary, I will show Dr. Hardy to his room myself. Then perhaps, when he comes down, we can have a little chat. My niece tells me," Mrs. Lindt continued as she moved towards the door, "that you are a friend whom she trusts. I am glad. There is much to talk of. I can see for myself that you are not a young fly-by-night."

"Was that what you expected, Aunt Emily?"

"I distrust telegrams, my dear, and hasty journeys. They are generally a mark of character. It is very seldom that a letter won't serve the purpose. Isn't that true, Dr. Hardy?"

"I promise you," he said, "telegrams aren't a habit of mine," and from the door he looked back, his eyes twinkling.

Mrs. Lindt's confidence in him steadily increased, and

it was in his presence that she told Mary what there was to tell. The pension was ended, the house, in part, mortgaged; there were debts. "My poor brother went very fully into his affairs while he was staying with me—a few short weeks ago." If Mary kept the house, she would be too poor to live in it; if she disposed of it, she would have, free of tax, something less than £150 a year. "Of course," Mrs Lindt added, "when you were engaged to be married, that was another pair of shoes. When the engagement was broken off, your poor father was naturally alarmed. He came to see me, and we talked over your future. Now, I'm not rich, as you know. Indeed it isn't easy for me to live even in my own quiet way. If you came, with your little contribution, it would make things easier. Easier for both of us, I think. It will mean certain changes. I don't like changes. I am old, you are young; we should have to adapt ourselves, I suppose. But I see no alternative."

"I could work," Mary said, but she was unqualified except for the work of a house, which she understood and liked, and her aunt's plan appeared to her as neither wise nor unwise, pleasant nor unpleasant, but as a decision already made; for she had none of that vanity of independence which is a form of self-pity. She would have accepted if George had not intervened.

"That needs a bit of thinking over," he said.

"Certainly; but I see no other way," her aunt replied.

"Mary could come to stay with us for a little while."

"But that would scarcely solve the problem of a permanent arrangement."

"No," said George, embarrassed for an answer, "but the arrangement you suggest couldn't last for ever, Mrs. Lindt."

"You mean, I shall die some day? Mary would have what I leave."

"No. I wasn't thinking of that. I wasn't looking as far ahead."

Mrs Lindt raised her eyebrows.

"Some day," George continued, "she may wish to marry."

Mary said without smiling, without looking at him, "That won't happen," speaking with quiet assurance, as though of an accepted past. This certainty of tone deeply affected him; what she said was probably true; if true, his future was lost in it; and he was struck by a desperate impulse to forbid, however vainly, such finality in her. But to protest against a woman's decision was to emphasize it; she would forget at her own convenience or not at all; and George shut his mouth firmly. To delay her going to Mrs. Lindt's was his immediate purpose, and this he seemed to have attained.

"Still," he said, taking his first fence and stubbornly ignoring those that lay ahead, "there's no reason to decide about your aunt's proposal at once. I'm sure Mrs. Lindt agrees," and, in the time that remained to him at Warlingham, he was content to persuade Mary that, at Sparkenbroke Green, she might decide her future in peace.

CHAPTER FOUR

I⊤ was a condition of life at the Rectory, giving to it a special quality of peace and order, that Mr. Hardy and George, though they had respect for each other's reticences, were closely bound in sympathy; and while, after Mary's return, summer passed into autumn, the Rector, himself impatient in many things, understood and valued his son's active patience—perceived that it was indeed active, with strength and wisdom in it, not a dulled acquiescence. And if he succeeds? the Rector said to himself. If, in the end, she married him—what then? He knows as well as I do that, though she may give him her loyalty, her love even after a fashion, she will marry with a ghost in her bed. But George, who has such a tenderness in him that all the worldly-wise would call him a sentimentalist, is, in his own odd way, nearer to reality than any of us. He knows what her character is as a seaman knows a ship that he loves. He is prepared to let life work itself out on the basis of character—and abide the consequences. Meanwhile, what to other men would be a wounding humiliation is to him a test of faith. Time and character exorcize ghosts.

But even the Rector did not fully understand the peculiar intimacy that existed between Mary and his son or in what degree they were already bound to each other by that most English of bonds—a capacity to communicate feeling without parade of words. Each was suffering, each knew it of the other, but it seemed to them simple and inevitable, not dramatic, that this should be so. Once, when by chance their bodies touched and the delight of contact filled his eyes with pain, she said:

"George, I believe I oughtn't to be here at all."

"Yes," he answered, "you ought."

"I've wondered. . . . Like this? Week after week? Does that make you happy?"

"That's for the moment," he said. "That's not the point."

And another day, when he had missed her during the afternoon, she said, with deliberate firmness: "I was out for a walk. I met Lady Sparkenbroke. She took me home to tea." And, answering his silence, she added: "I'm glad. It made everything seem easier—because it was easier with her."

"Has it been hard with her?"

"We haven't met often—but yes, in a way, it has been. To-day it was easier—much easier for me, *in myself*. We talked about him. She's going out to Italy. Something to do with money. She's taking Richard."

"For long?"

She shook her head. "Just a visit, I think."

He knew that deep in her mind, while she was listening to Etty Sparkenbroke, had been the thought: She is going to Italy! She will see him again! but he felt no humiliation, only that he was in the presence of a mystery which, though her being was now wrapt in it, was no more a reason for jealousy in him than an enchantment would have been. Often in the past, when Piers was at the cottage, she had come into the Rectory with the air of one returning slowly from some alien amazement to the reality of her own world. It had puzzled him then. He had not understood why, on certain evenings, she had been so silent and watchful of familiar things, like a traveller come home after a fantastic voyage; but he had never doubted, and still did not doubt, that here and here only, in the Rectory and in its ordered existence, was her reality; all else was, in his eyes, a dream, contrary to her nature as he understood it, from which she would certainly awake. From which, he thought, looking into her eyes with a curiosity at once expectant, indomitable and loving, she is beginning to awake. To-day it was easier, she had said, much easier for me, *in myself*. Was it not this she had been trying to tell him—not that she was forgetting Piers but that the dream which included him was becoming for her more and more evidently a dream?

Which doesn't mean, George told himself, that she'll ever love me—only that she'll see the world squarely again; and with that he ruled himself to be content, careful, when he was with her, not to importune her with love, and working harder than ever because there was in his work a cool sanity and moderation that had become the necessary ballast of his personal life. Even when he was alone, he drove down the hope that her loving-kindness gave him. 'Loving-kindness' was his father's word for this distinguishing quality in her—a piety of the emotions and a natural simplicity of conduct through which shone continuously a praise of life itself—and George, loving the word for her sake, clung to it because, while answering his love, it made no promise to his desire. He loved her in such a way that he could, without sense of belittlement, identify her with even the lesser delights of his mind. The sound of a distant train, of church bells, of a clock, the weighted stillness of cattle in the fields—these and a thousand other things, seemingly commonplace, but endowed for him with a significance that was, perhaps, salvage from childhood, he gave in his mind to her, because he had loved them. All that had been confused in his world was promised in her its atonement. In her was the pardon of his follies, the compassion of all his years, the secret, impossible understanding of his joys and miseries, his stubborn prides. There was nothing in his thought to be hid from her. Even those little shames and failures, which had not the dignity of sin, might fall asleep in her arms, silently confessed.

In the first days of December an epidemic of influenza appeared in the village of Sparkenbroke Green and in the country round about. George was at work day and night;

and, on certain afternoons, when the lamp was carried into the parlour through a daylight already netted by dusk and was set upon the table ready to be lit, strokes of the church-bell came from the wood, telling that the Rector also was about his business.

George was no longer the slow, easy, genial man whom Mary had known. When he came in, he was weary with a desperate, active, mechanical weariness beyond her experience. He would eat from the side-board; demand wine; sleep like a dog, suddenly; and, after twenty minutes, stand up from his chair and go out. If she urged him to rest, at any rate until he was sent for. "Sent for?" he said, and took her hand from his arm.

Once he came to her room in the night and rattled the handle of her door. A night-light on the landing table showed him to her—woollen gloves, and an old service waterproof buttoned to his chin.

"Mary, I'm sorry. Do something for me."

"Yes. What time is it?"

"Three. I'm promised at Sarrem's Cross about six. I ought to be there now, but I'm all in. I must get my clothes off and sleep for three hours. Whoever rings or calls, keep them out—say what you like, say I'm dead. Get me up by six. But if there's telephoning, I want the messages. I'm expecting some. Go and wait by it." He sat down abruptly on a hard chair by the table on the landing. "About time I had a break. Trouble is, I'm not safe driving the damned car."

She brought her bedroom candle and, dropping on her knees, unlaced his boots.

"Kick them off."

"What?"

"Your boots."

He looked down at them in surprise and said words she did not hear; then, shambling off to his room, turned and asked her:

"What time is it you are to call me?"

"Six."

"Not later."

She went to the kitchen and put kettles to boil.
On the table was a smudged exercise-book, lying
open, with an indelible pencil on it. Joanna's private
accounts:

Bus (return)	1s. 6d.
Stamps	9d.
Hair-net	4¾d.
Tram (Chel.)	2d.
Tea	1s. 1d.
Pictures	9d.
Chocbar	2d.
Cold-cure	11¾d.
Fortune-teller (slot)	1d.
Try-your-weight	1d.
Poor boy	1½d.
	6s. 1d.
Have left	3s. 11d.

She had read the list before she understood that she was
reading. It was true, then, as Piers had said, that you could
think of two things at the same time. She had been able,
in imagination, to follow Joanna's afternoon in Chelmouth,
her shopping, her tea, her visit to the films, and, at the
same time, to watch George sag into the hard chair and
his body sway and jerk in the candlelight as his boots
were unlaced. Where was he now? The house was still.
There was a film of coal dust on the milk in the cat's
saucer; the pendulum of the kitchen clock, shining in its
glass case, was unnaturally alive. Had he undressed and
gone to bed? Suddenly she knew that he had not, and
went upstairs.

His bedroom was dark, its door wide open. He had
curled himself into an armchair, his legs thrown over its
arm. One boot gaped on the carpet; the other he wore still,
its laces hanging loose. It seemed a cruelty to disturb him,
so heavy was his sleep, but in his clothes he would not
rest, he would awake stiff and bitterly cold, and she began
to draw the boot from his foot. Nothing disturbed him,
not even the wrench of his collar at the stud. Now and then
he opened his eyes and by movements of his arms and

shoulders helped her in the undressing, but he seemed
unaware of her.

When he was stripped to the waist and his feet were
bare, she covered him and, going to the kitchen again,
brought the kettle and washed his feet and compelled him
to get into his bed where she gave him hot soup to drink.
"Drink some of it. Then you can sleep."

At six she came back to his bedside. He was lying on
his face, his head turned, his left hand thrust under his
pillow, his hair starting up from the back of his head in a
short, stiff plume. Mightn't she leave him for another
hour? Her breasts ached in her tenderness for him; her
hands moved, and she jerked up her head. Suddenly she
was filled with an admiration as fierce as her tenderness
had been gentle. He had trusted and commanded her.
There was pride and love in the cruelty of awaking him.
But he won't be easy to wake, she thought, and remembered his having said that, like a seaman, he awoke to the
sound of his name. She touched his shoulder. "George,
six o'clock," and he sat up instantly.

"Six," he repeated.

"Sarrem's Cross."

"Right."

She would have left him.

"Wait till I'm up. . . . Now. Good." He walked across
the room, pulled open a drawer and took out a clean shirt.

"All right now, Mary. Bless you. I can trust myself not
to climb into that bed again."

She hesitated: "Could I do any good at Sarrem's
Cross?"

"You could."

"I'll come then."

"With me?"

While he dressed, she brought food and drink into the
hall where, before setting out, they shared it.

"What exactly happened last night? I'm afraid I gave
you orders."

"You can," she said.

"What I remember is making you repeat them—to

make sure. What time? 'Six o'clock,' you said. That's
odd. . . . What's the time now?"

"Twenty past."

"We must go. . . . It's still black dark outside. . . .
Listen, Mary, ought you to come? What about to-morrow?
You've had no sleep to speak of."

"I like doing jobs with you." She put down her cup and
looked at him, knowing suddenly what was to come and
glad that, in so clear a knowledge, she was alive. Not
to-day, not to-morrow; when this is over, I'll tell him. . . .
This is my home, then, she thought, and it was here, in
this moment, that I decided. The candle-light shone on
the blue and white bowl on the hall table and on the
crockery in their tray. There was a knife-blade on the edge
of the tray: S. G. Whipple & Co., Sheffield.

"Now," he said, "if you're ready."

George's work made it impossible that he and Mary
should be away from Sparkenbroke Green for more than a
few days after their marriage, and they were content that
this should be so, there being in the place a quality of
peace which was valuable to them at that time. To him the
continuity of his daily routine was an anchor; it was, too,
an enhancement of his delight, for in the Rectory every
room and passage, every instant of the day and of the long,
tranquil evenings, was full of memories of the time in
which he had been divided from her, and he was made
doubly alive to his happiness by the recurrent shocks of
contrast. To her he appeared, in this setting, as the man
she had grown to love, an element in her own healing, an
essential part of spiritual balance regained. In him, in this
place, were her love's reason and assurance; elsewhere she
knew and understood him less well, and there had been
moments, during the first days of their marriage, in which
she had seen him as a friendly stranger, with whom, as if
in a dream, she was entered into an incredible intimacy.
Seeing him asleep at her side, she had looked at him with
curiosity, as though he were a changeling, and it was not
until they had returned to Sparkenbroke Green that her

marriage became real for her and happy in its reality. There, even the act of love ceased to trouble her, and though it seemed surprising that for this pleasure the world should so often have been accounted well lost, she was glad in his gladness, and received this new experience into her perspective. The day was full of familiar work and pleasure; the strain of George's unsatisfied longing was ended; life had lost its perilous transparency. The parts of it were solid and consistent, within the grasp of her character; she could build with them; and when he asked her again, as he had before their marriage, whether she was content to live in his father's house, she said:

"But why not?"

"Most brides want a home of their own."

"This is my home. . . . Or do you want to go, George?"

"No," he answered. "It wouldn't be the same anywhere else."

She put her arm in his. "Not in your heart of hearts?"

"No."

"I mean," she said, determined that there should be neither fear nor misunderstanding between them, "I mean—because Sparkenbroke House is here. Piers will come back. If that makes you unhappy——"

"That's one of the reasons I want to stay," he said. "It's no good running away from ghosts. There's only one thing to do—walk through them. We can do that together?"

"Yes. . . . Oh, my dear, why did you begin to talk of that?"

"I didn't," he answered. She smiled, interlacing her fingers with his, and he added quickly: "But in the spring or the summer we'll have a holiday together. I haven't had a real holiday for five years. To have it now with you! . . . It's like being very young again. It will be like a new miracle every day—waking up and not believing it, and then coming to believe it all over again."

"Which means?" she said, loving and teasing him.

"Means?" His face puckered. "That I love you, and there aren't enough intelligible ways of saying it."

They had entered the path above the lawn in which he had found her with her basket of roses. Not wishing to go this way, she hesitated and would have turned back; but her hand was held, he was thinking of the future not the past, and she went forward, ashamed of her own whim and looking beyond him at the naked trees and the scoured wintry sky. "Where shall we go?" he said, "for our holiday, I mean," and she answered: a voyage, not a cruise but a real voyage in a ship doing her ordinary business.

When he was gone on his round and her morning's work was done, she went into the Rector's study for his big atlas.

"The Greek islands," he said in answer to her question, but, though she had asked where she should go, she did not listen to his reply. The atlas would tell her, and she carried it up to Helen's room that Helen might share her adventure.

"But that is the Pacific," Helen said, looking down from her chair upon the great book that Mary had spread open on the floor.

"I know. Why not?"

"It would be too far for George. He hasn't the time or the money."

Mary reasonably abandoned the Pacific.

"You can tell me!" she exclaimed, looking up. "If I ask him, he won't say; he'll want me to choose; but I'm sure there's some place where George has always longed to go—isn't there?—some special place, like your Florence?"

"Sicily," Helen said. "I should like that too. It is very rich in remains," and Mary, her chin propped on her hand, began to trace across a fire-lit Mediterranean her course to Palermo.

CHAPTER FIVE

THEY set out neither in the spring nor in the summer, but on the last day of September, for it had been decided that, if the extreme heats were avoided, Helen might travel with them. They would go by ship to Sicily and stay there until it was necessary for George to return. That Helen should be tired as little as possible by train journeys, she and Mary would take his ship as far as Genoa. There he would go north by train and they south to Florence and afterwards to Rome.

To Mary, luxury was little known; her closest experience of it had been in the Sparkenbroke Hotel and it was associated in her mind with loneliness and confusion and the barren arrogance of men in gold lace. But in their outward liner she was happy. Pacing the deck, standing in the light headwind beneath the bridge, basking in the sun at the edge of the swimming pool, dancing at night in the open air, she was delighted by what seemed to her an almost magical variety of impression. George had never been a younger or more rewarding companion. When dancing was over, he and she would walk up and down the boat-deck together, reviewing the past day — she swerving suddenly to the Sicilian history she was reading, or asking when they were going down to look at the turbines, and he, who loved continuity and was ordinarily inclined to pursue an argument paragraph by paragraph, alive and responsive to her mood, remembering his own youth not with sadness but in the joy of recapture.

"I wish there'd be a storm!" she said, but the Atlantic and the Mediterranean were asleep; even in the Gulf of

Lyons, where Helen dreamed of Nelson, there was no movement but of the bow-wave; and soon Mary forgot her desire for rough weather. She was sorry to reach Sicily, envious of the passengers who waved farewell from the ship's side, but, once ashore, was glad. She was awed by Sicily, so very old did it seem to her. She saw in it, not a part of modern or of medieval Italy, but, as though the intervening centuries were transparent to her, a colony of Greece; and so powerful was the impact of this imagining that for long she kept it secret, confessing it at last to George almost in fear that he would laugh at her. And when he did not laugh, she felt that there was, in this place, something miraculous in the quickness of their sympathy.

He understood even that when, at supper one night, Helen began to speak of Sparkenbroke, there was no need to check her or to turn the conversation away. Mary could join in it with a heart at peace and ask calmly where he was.

"Probably at Lucca," Helen said.

"At Lucca? His poem was about Lucca."

"Now he has a palazzo there."

"Where is Lucca?" Mary asked. "I did look at the map once—long ago; but I've forgotten."

Helen helped herself to salad. "This oil probably came from there. . . . Sleepy little place, I believe, with nothing much to show. Interesting enough, I dare say, as most Italian towns are; but you have to select. It's right off our track."

While Lucca was being spoken of, Mary imagined it as a town of many pinnacles standing on a little hill, the slopes of which were covered with olive-trees, but because she had no knowledge of olive-trees it was a beech wood she saw; and, tripped in her imagining by olive and beech, she allowed the thought of Lucca to slide away from her. Later in the evening, as she walked with George along the narrow sea-path that had become theirs by usage each night before they turned in to sleep, she wondered for an instant whether the calmness with which she had heard

Piers spoken of was not a proof that something had died within her, and, in that instant, was sad. As though aware of her mood, if not of her thought, George laid his arm across her shoulders, giving her his presence to which she might hold fast.

They stood still, hearing only the sea below them.

"Let's climb down and go out in a boat," he said. "The moon's rising and the water's like oil."

It had been her own wish; he had spoken it; and it was this that gave an almost ritual delight to their escapade— the return to the hotel for more tobacco, the long descent, the night-sound of their oars whose pine creaked and talked as never by day, the liquid silence when they lay at rest. Already, when they came back, morning was at the sea's edge; the scrub was glazed with daylight and from all the rims of earth and tree the needles of day sprang up. The little staircase of the hotel drifted under their sleepy eyes. They undressed with few whispers and, in the eye of morning, were fast asleep.

When the time came for them to pack, Mary was possessed by sudden fear of their parting at Genoa and begged that she also might go home.

"But, my dear, what about poor Helen? She can't go to Florence by herself and she has longed for it all her life."

"I know. But still . . . Couldn't she go another time?"

"There may not be another time for her. Bringing her with us at all was a risk. I hadn't the heart to leave her. If I'd been her doctor only, not her brother——"

"I know," Mary repeated. "I love her, too, George. Not only for your sake but for herself. She's brave and she has hold of herself and she doesn't borrow from other people. I'd do anything for her. I don't want to be selfish and cruel. But, this once, isn't there some other way? I mean, suppose I was ill, then I should have to go home with you, shouldn't I?"

She was sitting up in her bed, very straight, her arms straight beside her, the stuff of her nightdress white and taut; and George, who had been wandering to and fro

through the open door by which their rooms communicated, came to a halt, shoes in hand, at first smilingly
astonished by her vehemence, then, seeing her face, serious.

"My dear, what do you mean? I don't understand.
You're not ill, are you?"

"Ill? No. . . . But, George, I'm not ordinarily unreasonable, am I? I do what I say I'll do?"

"You do, my dearest." He put down his shoes, seated
himself on the edge of her bed and waited.

"But you see," she said, her lip trembling, "no one's
reasonable always. Perhaps it's this place. I don't know.
Sometimes, after you've loved me and I'm in your arms
still and you asleep, I look out over your humped shoulder
into this little hotel room, and there's the gleam on the
white jug and the plain walls, and the window with the
night set in it like—like a panel with painted stars, and
below is the sea. I imagine it all slack and glinting. Then
a dog howls and another dog answers it, and I hear you
breathing, alive and close. And I move my fingers on
your loose arm. There you are, firm and alive and warm.
I'm so grateful I don't dare to breathe. But here, in a way,
it's unreal. I want to cling to it and cling to it until we
get home, just in this—this state of mind that we're in
now, and make it real there for always and always. *Us*, I
mean, as we are now. Happy. Quite sure. Quite, quite
sure. Do you understand that?" . . .

"As if," he said slowly, "you'd been given a cheque,
rather a miracle of a cheque, and wanted to pay it in at
the bank?"——

She nodded.

"But isn't the cheque good?" he said. "Won't it keep?"

"In reason, it will. . . . Oh, of course, of course it will!
. . . But I'm happier now—happier and safer than I've
ever been, and it's bad to cross happiness."

"Superstition?"

"I suppose so. . . . But it's real, George. At least, to
me it is. I can't explain any more."

She kneeled up suddenly in the bed. If she had thrown
herself into his arms and pleaded and wept, he would

have resisted her whim and soothed her and put her to sleep. He had fully intended to resist her, believing that the mood would pass. But she knelt there, stiff and expectant, dry-eyed, in the special helplessness of a certainty that no reason will support, and he said to himself: This is one of the moments in which to be sensible is to be a fool.

"Very well," he said, "I'll tell Helen in the morning."

She did not answer, but looked at him for a moment incredulously, then with such love as he had never hoped to see in her eyes. The tension went from her body. She sat back on her heels, drawing the sheet up before her, and he saw, like a memory, her hair threaded with candle-light against the whitewashed wall and her shadow climbing above her.

"Now, sleep," he said, "there are no dogs howling—and if they do howl, don't you listen to 'em."

She lay down and, when he had spread the sheet over her, raised her head from the pillow and kissed him, and, seizing his hand, pressed her lips to it and her warm cheek.

But, in the morning, she would not let him speak to Helen of any change in their plan.

"I was foolish last night. Now, I'm a reasonable woman."

He did not overrule her. Next day they returned to Palermo, and on the following afternoon joined their ship.

BOOK IV

LUCCA

BOOK IV

LUCCA

CHAPTER ONE

On a morning early in November Sparkenbroke drove his car from Lucca into Pisa, having heard that an old woman, who sold books and prints in the Via d'Arancio, had a drawing, claimed to be by Andrea del Sarto, of Nicodemus at work on the Lucca crucifix. The drawing was not by Andrea nor, though Nicodemus was certainly its subject, had it any interest for Sparkenbroke; there was even less in it for him than in Cosimo Rosselli's fresco; and he came down disappointed to the river's bank, striking it above the Solferino bridge. Small repairs were necessary to his car, which would not be ready for an hour or more; and he leaned against the parapet, gazing at the swift crescent of the Arno and at the pretty, lace-like elaboration of Santa Maria della Spina, a toy of black and white marble on the opposite bank—much praised but by him little loved, so conscious was it of its own decoration, like a woman with no mind but for her own daintiness. But in Pisa was another church, San Pierino, which he had long thought of as being, in a special sense, his own. A year ago, when Etty and Richard had visited him, he had taken the boy to it with the pleasure there is always in admitting one deeply loved to a private enchantment. Long silent, Richard had said at last: "Isn't it a special church? It's friendly," and the quickness of his response to San Pierino had almost persuaded Sparkenbroke to do what his wife asked—return to England, settle in Sparkenbroke House and re-make their life together.

He had been living at that time among the hills outside

319

Lucca, in a villa near Vipore. His quarters in the Palazzo Ascani, which he now occupied, were being prepared for him, and the builders delayed. Still there had been time to change his plan, and this morning, as he walked along the river's bank with San Pierino and Richard's visit to it in his mind, he remembered an afternoon on which he and Etty had driven out from Lucca together and, before reaching the villa, had left the car and sat on the wall flanking the road at Vipore. Below them the ground fell sharply away. The red, crinkled roofs of a few houses tucked into the hillside looked up out of the softness of olive branches, and far down the hill the olives continued, yielding green to silver as their distance increased, until at last the distinct form of trees was lost and the eye rested on Lucca itself, set in the autumnal plain.

Do you understand now, Etty, why I want to live there?

While you are writing of the Volto Santo—yes; but afterwards, when that poem's done——

That isn't the reason.

Tell me, she had said, and, when he was silent: I want to understand. Tell me.

Instead, he had told her how he had taken Richard into San Pierino in Pisa, and how that, more than all the persuasions of reason, had bidden him not isolate himself in Italy.

Do you mean, she had asked, that you want him to live with you out here? She was gathering courage to make even this concession, and he had been filled with shame, not so much by her generosity, her willingness to let go for his sake the only recompense of her marriage that remained to her, but by the deadness of his own heart to all but pity for the love she offered him. In that instant, his hands gripping the warm brick of the wall, his mind tormented by recollection of the tenderness he had once had for her and of the vows they had made together, more binding, because more secret and voluntary, than the vows of marriage itself, he had seen the relationship between them from her point of view only, had felt, in imagination,

the glow of joy, the abounding hope and determination
with which she would have welcomed his consent to return to England with her, and had almost consented. To
refuse and not to explain his refusal, though she so gently
asked to understand him, was not to be forgiven. If there
had been fault in her, if even—however unjustly—he had
hated her, then he might have explained, but she was
blameless, and, as he looked into her upraised face, the
grave, calm face of the woman who had once been his
refuge, he had been pierced by his own cruelty.

No, he said, Richard must have roots in his own country.

She had accepted that silently, and afterwards had said:
Piers, is it—is the reason, quite simply, that you find it
intolerable to live with me? Is that why you stay in Italy
and why, when you do come to England, all your life—your
real life, your work—is in Derry's Cottage?

While he delayed his answer, a cart, with a waggoner
half asleep over slack reins, had creaked past them uphill,
and they had followed it with their eyes; the hot smell of
horse and leather had come to them across the air and the
tugging jangle of the harness.

My dear, he had said at last, you do everything on God's
earth that woman can do.

I may *do* everything, but *am* I everything?

Her own eyes had miserably answered before his could
answer her.

Listen, he had said, I'll try to tell you the truth. It's no
good. But I'll try now.

Why is it no good? Because I shan't understand? I
think I shall, Piers. Even now, why is it no good?

Because, he had replied, it's one of the things that can't
be said without figures of speech, metaphors, vague things
that leave gaps in understanding. It can't be said, Etty—
only felt. Is it worth the wound of trying to say it?

Silence is a deeper wound, she had said quietly, and
with the futile agony of words he had struggled to tell
her that because, for him, love, in his imagining, and
poetry, in his experience, were aspects of the same transcendence, his own failure in love excluded him from her.

I understand, she said, and, driven now by vain longing
to expose the truth to himself and to exorcise it with
words, he had told her that, in her company, he was
bitterly conscious not of her failure but of his own, as
though he were being compelled to read again and again a
poem in which he had failed. He tried to explain to her
that love was for him not affection only, however profound, nor passion only, nor a sum of these two as she
believed, but an ecstasy, a dying to be reborn. This he had
longed for but not found. Such was the compassion in her
eyes that for a moment he had believed that, in truth, she
understood, but she had felt his suffering without com-
prehending the nature of it; and he had replied: You say
you understand, Etty, but no one can fully understand
except myself. I am as capable as the world is of seeing
it as insane egoism or, worse, as a twist of language to
explain—and exalt—and falsify—a mere slackening of
appetite. You are even-minded and gentle; you won't
believe evil of me. But inside you, you don't understand.

No, she said, not fully. But I love you. Isn't that enough?

In the impatience of despair, he had stood beside her in
the road and begged her, for her own sake, to make an end.

Divorce you? Not unless you need that more than anything else in the world. I mean—not unless you have
found with someone else the love you need?

He had answered: no.

Afterwards, when they were returned to the villa, she had
said: Piers, when I said "no" to divorce, I wasn't being
just tolerant or patient. I was thinking of myself too. You
understand that? It's hard to speak of, because the money's
mine—at least, my trustees'—but with a divorce, the
whole estate would break up. My life's in that.

It would still be there for Richard if you held.

But not for you, my dear. I shouldn't hold for him only.
It's not just property. Anyway, the world he'll grow up
into won't be that kind of world. I want to hold it for you,
because you need it, don't you, Piers? Now more than ever
if there's no other love.

Like a man, he had answered, recalling the words

she herself had once spoken, who comes back to where, he knows, there's a stream of water.

Glad of his recognition that, at least in part, she understood the connexion of his life with the Sparkenbroke Mound, she had stooped down suddenly to his chair and kissed him.

Oh, my darling, I wish you could find your love. I wish it existed in women for you to find. Not only in your work and in the grave.

Across the year that had passed since they were spoken, her words returned to him as he made his way by the Lung' Arno Regio towards San Pierino, and, remembering that he had deliberately not taken Etty to this church but Richard only, he could not now enter it, but turned back to the river, unquiet in all his being. In the little Piazza del Ponte, three cabs were standing. Their drivers, as he watched, awoke to a sudden activity of hand and whip; a foreign tourist was approaching them. She entered one of the cabs and was driven across the road towards the Ponte di Mezzo at the entrance to which Sparkenbroke stood. His eye was drawn by the girl's beauty, the poise of her body graceful and erect, her bare head against the dark background of the folded hood, her hands clasped before her—her air of being engaged in some breathless and frightened errand.

"My God!" he exclaimed. "*Ferma! Ferma!*"

The driver drew up his horse, and Mary, in swift protest against delay, turned towards the pavement. Before she could speak, Sparkenbroke was in the carriage beside her.

"*Avanti!*" The cab moved forward. "What is it?" he said. "My dear, you're frightened. . . . Not of me?"

"No," she breathed. "Not of you. I'm going for another doctor. They say he speaks better English. At least I think that's what they meant. The one we have doesn't really understand. And I can't understand him."

She spoke fast and unsteadily.

"Tell me," he said. "Who is ill?"

"Helen—terribly. In the train coming here. That's why

we got out at Pisa. Last night she was better. And now she's worse and——"

"Where?"

She turned, pointing behind her towards the side of the river from which she was come.

"In our hotel."

"Is the doctor there now?"

"Yes, but——"

"I'll make him understand. Can we go back?"

"If you think that's right."

He stopped the cab, turned it.

"It was in the train she became so much worse. She went all stiff. She could scarcely speak at all and then each syllable slowly and separately. In the hotel she seemed to be asleep and not in pain. We tried to get a doctor but couldn't until this morning. . . . She ought to have a real nurse. And I don't know— The hotel people get so excited. She must be moved, they say. They don't want a death. . . . They don't want a death. . . . But where to?"

"Could she be moved?"

"I don't know. I think so. But where——"

"My dear," he said. "I know this place. And the language. Everything that can be done, shall be. You're not alone any more."

"No," she answered, and leaned back on the hard cushions, looking at him steadfastly, as though to assure herself that this was he.

CHAPTER TWO

THE Italian doctor, Francesco Celli, had never been in
doubt of his patient's condition. When Mary asked his
advice, he had found it hard, without an abruptness from
which he shrank, to tell her the truth. She was asking of
the future—of obtaining an English nurse from Florence
and of making the journey to England. To this there was
no answer except the plain one, which he was reluctant to
give to this girl so pitiably young and startled, that for his
patient there was no future. "Wait a little while," he had
said in his own language and, trying to comfort her in-
action, had unwittingly led her to believe that he did not
understand her.

Fortunately, when she left the hotel, her quest of another
doctor had been unknown to him, and he received her
with encouragement, for Helen was holding her own. At
Lord Sparkenbroke's name, his eyes widened in curiosity,
observant of adventure, perhaps of romance; and, stepping
back from Helen's bedside as a painter from his easel, he
said he was not doctor only but reader also and that this
meeting would remain always in his mind.

"And your name, too, doctor is very familiar to
me."

"Mine?"

"Was it not a namesake of yours, Celli, who was an
authority on malaria?"

"Yes. Yes. And your lordship?"

"I have, or rather, I had, the worst of reasons for being
an authority," Sparkenbroke replied. "What's wrong with
me now isn't malaria but a cleaner and swifter disease.

325

There's nothing you or anyone can do about it." And
Celli, like a terrier on the scent, explaining rapidly that
angina was a disease that profoundly interested him and
of which he had indeed some special knowledge, began
to pour out a stream of questions—had Sparkenbroke an
accurate record of his attacks, of the timing and length of
his paroxysms? had he observed whether——?

"But I am not yet your patient," Sparkenbroke answered
with a laugh, and Celli, with a fencer's acknowledgment
of a touch, returned to the bed. But soon, as he stood at the
window of Mary's room, which communicated with his
patient's, his face, shadowy with stubble, curled into black
smiles, his teeth glistened, and his eyes, shrewd and deeply
brown as a lively dog's, threw up their whites as his hands
rose in gesticulation. Sparkenbroke's fluency delighted
him. Here was an English wit who jested drily in Italian—
an Italian the more amusing because it had an absurd, in-
advertent flavour of Dante, as incongruous as a *trecento*
feather in a twentieth-century hat.

"Is there nothing we ought to be doing?" Sparkenbroke asked.

"At the moment, nothing," said the little man. "I gather
that a kind of paralysis developed in the train. How the
young lady got her out at Pisa and into this hotel, I don't
know. She must be brave. What has happened is plain
enough. A new patch of sclerosis has developed near the vital
centres of the brain. The actual paralysis may pass away.
Indeed I think it is already passing, but—" He drew down
his brows, his eyes opened wide to a wrapt, concentrated
gaze, and he returned to Helen's bedside with the quick step
and stiffened body of Italian efficiency. He stayed in the
hotel for two hours, an earnest, keen doctor, anxious not
only for his patient but, in the presence of the Englishman,
for the credit of his country.

"Pisa," he said, when again they stood together at the
window, "has other great associations with English
literature."

Sparkenbroke smiled. "Yes," he answered, "in the past,
English exiles had good taste."

The doctor smiled also, bending his head a moment to acknowledge a compliment gracefully returned.

"Now," he said, "I must go. I will come back in an hour. Meanwhile she will do—to my surprise, I confess. She has great endurance, an English trait."

Sparkenbroke asked if it might not soon be possible to move Miss Hardy to Lucca. "If she were in my own house I could see that she was looked after."

"If all goes well, nothing could be better. Nothing. If it were not," the doctor added, "that I should no longer have the honour of attending her or of your lordship's company."

"But is there any reason that you shouldn't attend her and I have your company? If you have special knowledge of angina, I assure you I shall be glad of it."

"The attacks are frequent?"

"The last was in early spring."

"Your doctor was from Lucca?"

The scruples of etiquette were quieted by Sparkenbroke's assurance that he had summoned no doctor. "I am my own, I and—this." He took from his pocket a tube containing nitrite of amyl and turned it over in his palm. "My servant is my nurse. He knows as much of the thing as is good for any man. But your special research——"

Dr. Celli admitted with his eyebrows that he was persuaded.

"Then it is understood," Sparkenbroke said, "that if your patient moves to Lucca, you will continue in the case?"

Dr. Celli bowed again and would have gone with dignity, backwards, to the door, but a thought, flashing in his quick brain, disturbed him.

"Listen," he said softly, a forefinger laid to the side of his nose. "We must have care for the young *signora*—we must care for her too. She did not sleep last night I am sure. She is very tired." He looked at Sparkenbroke now with a new interest. The tight pink mounds of his cheeks came up under eyes that sparkled with curiosity. "Ah! but I know you are not the man to forget so beautiful a lady. *È proprio uno splendore!*"

The first letter written by George, after he had heard of Helen's illness and Sparkenbroke's intervention, betrayed his anxiety in trying to conceal it. Mary knew that his impulse had been to start for Italy and that his loyalty to her had withheld him.

"It was a godsend for you that Piers turned up when he did. I'm glad. I mean that, my dearest. I'm really glad, not only because his help was valuable to you and Helen, but because, in a way, it wasn't good that, through the accident of his being at the other end of Europe, there should be a kind of permanent gap in your knowledge of yourself—in our knowledge of ourselves too. I don't express it well, but you know in what way I love you and will understand what I mean. I'm glad this meeting has happened. It had to happen some day. Best now, and get it over."

His letter had deliberately swerved at this point into detailed instructions for the nursing of Helen.

"Show the Italian doctor this:

Pot. iod.	.	.	.	.	gr. v—x
Aq. menth. pip.	.	.	.		ad. ℥ ss
		t.d.s.			

Tell him, with tact, I've found it useful for a few weeks. He can convert into grammes and choose his own strength between five grains and ten."

At the foot of the sheet, under the date, was written: "4 P.M." Mary imagined George stooped over his writing-table under winter's early lamp, his lips set in determination to be calm and without jealousy. Her own reason responded to his, but her reason only. The past is dead, she thought; Piers himself has made no attempt to revive it; not to accept his help would be melo-dramatic and foolish. She was grateful that George did not doubt her, for she did not doubt herself; and yet, she said, if George were here now or on his way —and she wondered at her own unreason that would have made her glad, suddenly glad and secure, if he had come.

She sent a cable:

"Helen better Piers arranging nurses invites us stay
with him Lucca   HELEN MARY"

He replied:

"If necessary glad come out if not accept Lucca use
own judgment   GEORGE"

She showed this to Helen, who said: "But it may be
weeks before I can travel to England. It's no good
bringing poor George out."

"You will go to Lucca, then?"

Helen, who was always doubtful of her liking for
Sparkenbroke, did not answer at once. "He–has–been–
good–o–ver–this." Her syllables were divided; she spoke
laboriously—a slow, monotonous staccato. "I should
think that he's never given as much time from his writing
to anyone before, unless for his own pleasure. I don't
like being under an obligation to people——"

"But if they wish it, Helen, if they are generous? If
everyone refuses, no one can give."

Helen looked up from her pillow. "I know that point
of view. I dare say you are right, my dear. The young
generally are. . . . Let us accept then. Really, I see no
alternative except some foreign nursing-home." She smiled
slowly. "I expect the palazzo will be better than that."

Mary went into the lounge of the hotel to find Piers.

"Well, is it decided?" Seeing her hesitate, he said, with
an edged impatience: "But why not? It's insane. If she
goes into a nursing-home and you into some *pension*, it
will cost you a little fortune. She'll be alone, too. And,
though she thinks she speaks it, her Italian's cruel. Don't
you see that——"

"But it is decided!" she told him.

"That you're coming?"

Though she was smiling when she spoke, there followed
a wordless tension between them.

"To-morrow then?" he said at last.

"Yes."

Silence continued. The balance of decision was still swaying in her mind. She moved towards him; her hand touched his arm.

"Piers. . . ."

He waited. "Well?"

But she shook her head. There was nothing she could say until, having looked through the glass door of the hotel, she returned to him and said:

"Will you come out with me to send a telegram?"

"You can send it here."

"I'd rather go out."

As they walked, he began to tell her of Lucca, and how Marius, too, had come there from Pisa on his way to Rome.

"Marius?"

"Pater's Marius."

She made no answer but walked, silently, where he led. In the post office she wrote:

"HARDY
        Sparkenbroke Green
                Inghilterra
Address Palazzo Ascani Lucca   HARDY"

"Now," she said. "I'm sorry. Tell me again about Marius. Which Marius?"

"The Epicurean." He looked down at her, smiling. "Have you come to life again?"

"And tell me about Lucca. Do you live there all alone?"

"Bissett and Italian servants."

"Is there a garden?"

"Between the house and the city ramparts. But it isn't exciting in November. The ramparts themselves will be your garden. I told you of them once, but you have forgotten. A great avenue, raised up, surrounding the whole town, with the roofs and the towers inside the circle, and, outside, the country and the hills. But they may be dead for you."

"It's odd," she said. "I had imagined Lucca as a hill-town. Is it in a valley after all?"

"In a plain," he answered, and began to tell her how, five years ago, he had gone to Lucca for the first time, driving over from Pisa by chance, for Lucca, having few treasures, was a place little visited except by those who had business there. He had gone again and again.

"But what was it," she asked, "that made you love it?"

If it had been a liking, an admiration or interest, that she had asked him to explain, he might have answered easily, but the word she had chosen was the right one, and to explain a love so personal and intuitive—it was the "feel" of the place, he replied, its ancient smallness, the green enclosure of its trees, its grave, unchanging, cloistered welcome. It was *il riso santo* of Lucca, he exclaimed, like the smile of Dante's Beatrice; an evidence that, within these walls, it was possible to be at once thoughtful and happy.

"But to-morrow," he added, "you will be there. I shall tell you no more of Lucca. You mustn't go there expecting marvels. I have known people—not fools either—say it was disappointing: there was nothing much to see—a dull little provincial town without a great school of art of its own, even in the Renaissance. But for me it's a place where life isn't an enemy."

"An enemy?"

"You hate my saying that? I wonder why. You are not my mother. She might have hated my saying it."

"Anyone who loved you would hate it."

"What am I to do then?" he replied, beginning to mock her seriousness because he at once loved and feared it. "Am I to count my benefits, as you taught me once? Do you still count yours?"

"Yes."

"And say your prayers? Do you pray for me? I need it."

She turned her head sharply away. "For your work," she said. "That is praying for you."

This quiet answer fell upon him, in his raillery, like the touch of a hand.

"Look at me," he said, halting at the riverside, and she obeyed him. "Is it true? You pray for my work?" And, after a silence: "You know that I was making fun of you?"

"I know."

"Then——"

"Piers, don't suffer like that. And don't ask to be forgiven. You are forgiven, always. It was only the foolish part of you that——"

"You forgive me," he said, "as if I were a child."

"Well?"

Watching her eyes, he said: "*Il riso santo!*" but she did not hear him and continued, as though he had not spoken: "Why is life an enemy?"

"It is I," he answered, "who am an enemy of myself."

CHAPTER THREE

THE Palazzo Ascani, set between the walls of Lucca and
the square of Santa Maria Forisportam, faced upon a
street so narrow that the ambulance in which Helen lay
could have entered it only with difficulty, and Sparkenbroke checked the driver in the Via delle Rose. "It will be
better to carry her," he said. "Stay with her, Mary, while
I fetch Bissett."

From the corner of the street, Mary looked up at the
dark front of the palace. As dark as a prison, she thought,
seeing the heavily moulded architraves of the barred
window-openings and the curling, pitted shadows of their
ornament. When Bissett and an Italian servant had taken
the stretcher from the ambulance, she followed them along
the uneven street, surprised that Piers should have chosen
to live under so narrow a ribbon of sky, but as soon as
they had passed through the entrance-gates she saw a
stone courtyard, open at the farther end, and beyond it a
garden, and beyond the garden a grassy rampart with an
avenue of trees upon it, and, between the branches, the
sky's gleam. The courtyard, in its centre, was full of light,
for it was unroofed, the house being built round it in the
shape of a rectangular "U" that rested on the street; only
at its outskirts, on three sides, was it heavily shadowed—
by two flights of stairs, attached to the walls, and by a
landing which joined them. This landing, above the
entrance, spanned the courtyard.

"Is all this yours?" she asked.

"The first floor and the second and a set of attics to
house a battalion," Sparkenbroke answered. "The rooms

on the ground floor are let as offices. . . . You look out over
the ramparts from the top windows—south; you get the
sun—too much in summer."

The Pisan nurse had been left behind. An English-
woman, Nurse Craven, whom Sparkenbroke had summoned from Rome, came down the staircase to meet her
patient, and, as soon as Helen was settled in her room,
Sparkenbroke took Mary to her own, in the same wing as
Helen's and above it; so large a room that she hesitated in
the doorway, gazing at the distant windows and the long
path of light that ran over stone pavement and rug between
her and them. The bed was a little canopied island; the
rare furniture stood up from long shadows into the slanting dust of the sun; the painted ceiling was dim above her
head; but in an open grate a fire of logs was burning and
she went to it at once, stretching out her hands.

"My workmen are rewarded," Sparkenbroke said.

"Your workmen?"

"There wasn't a fireplace in the building. They are all
—what the old architect might have designed if he had
been interested in fireplaces. At least, I hope they are.
They took months to put in." Then: "Can you be happy
here?"

"Very happy."

"But you are cold! You're trembling!" He took her
hand. "Like ice."

"I'm not really. This fire will soon——"

"Are you beginning to wish you hadn't come?"

Her lips were still. She took her hand from him and
kneeled on a low stool, bending towards the fire.

"With us here, and a nurse, and a doctor coming to and
fro—won't you hate us soon, Piers?"

"That may be."

"Ought you to have let us come?"

"God knows. . . . I take no credit as a generous host.
I'm not disinterested."

She looked across her shoulder. "You told me long ago,"
she said, "that when I met Sparkenbroke he would blackguard himself."

"Yes," he answered with a slow smile, "I suppose even that is a form of vanity." He swung away abruptly towards the door. "I'll send women to you. There's tea downstairs."

The generosities that most pleased him in others Sparkenbroke distrusted in himself. All his giving—of time, money, hospitality, even of friendship—he wrote off in his mind as at best an obligation of his breeding, at worst, self-flattery. He had confidence and vanity, knowing that he did well everything to which he set his hand; but, except as a writer, he was without that faith in the purity of his motive which is to self-confidence what genius is to talent. To write was indeed an act of faith, and selfless, for there was no answer of this world to the question: why did he write? Fame was a pleasure, it ministered to his pride, but fame was no answer. Nor was it enough to say that art was of value to mankind; its root was not and could not be in social conscience, in service to one's neighbour; to rest in this belief, though it had an appearance of humility, would be in effect hypocritical; for the service of men seemed to him to occupy, in the motive of art, a corresponding place, not contemptible but not of the act's essence, with the need to shelter a congregation in the building of a cathedral. He wrote in the hunger for perfection; in the desire to feel and to acknowledge a pulse, not his, alive within him; and the word "creation," applied to art, appeared to him misleading, an artist being, in his view, not an origin but a contact.

This was his only absolute faith; all else in his life lay open to sardonic and destructive criticism; and when he reflected that, contrary to his most determined usage, he had admitted Mary and Helen to his house while he needed solitude to write, he discountenanced every reason for his action that might, by the world's judgment, have been put to his credit. He chose to accept as sufficient truth that he had brought Mary to Lucca in desire of her body. Memory of the different emotion he had experienced when he had left Derry's Cottage at night and of the impulse to adoration that had swept him when he and she had stood beside

the Arno in Pisa, he stifled as romantic excuse invalidated
by experience. She will be, he compelled himself to say, as
other women have been. To use of her the word love, which
had for him an identical finality with poetry and death,
would have been to throw in all the reserves of his life.

As the days passed he observed, nevertheless, with the
detachment of self-criticism which was his mind's satirical
habit, that he was using towards her none of his customary
methods of approach. He did not speak of the emotion that
had existed between them in the past; he made no use of
the powerlessness of women to resist a retelling of their
own story; he allowed to stand unattacked the barrier of
cool discretion which she imagined was preserved between
them and which, he supposed, might be instantly overthrown. In brief, though she was within his reach, he did
not touch her, but complied with her avoidances, saying to
himself that what withheld him was neither awe nor love
nor any expectation beyond the flesh, but the pleasure of
watching and living with her still unpossessed, the imaginative delight of accumulating hour by hour, as she
moved about this once empty house, new aspects of her
sensual presence and of allowing the tension between them
to increase.

In the evenings they had supper together. Sometimes,
during the day, when Mary was not taking duty in Helen's
room, they walked together in the city or on the ramparts.
Their conversation was seemingly at ease, but in both
their minds, while conversation continued, another language was being spoken silently.

On the fourth day, unable to work, he drove his car
into Pisa to fetch Dr. Celli, who, after his visit to Helen,
stayed to supper. He was evidently as surprised as he was
pleased by Sparkenbroke's invitation; he sat down to his
meal with the air of a conspirator in a play, for it seemed
to him impossible that his two companions were not lovers
and he could not understand why he had been admitted to
their privacy. If this Englishman were French, he thought,
I should suppose that what he desired was an audience;
perhaps the cultivated English also have come to under-

stand that another's envy is a salt of love. The smiling thought of *amour de vanité* gave him a subject of conversation and he began to speak of Stendhal and of Parma, finding in them excuse for a discourse on romantic love which produced, in the young *signora's* face, changes of expression so enchanting and, he thought, so sad, that he fell in love with her himself and could not bear to continue. It is as if I were a street-boy with a chipped mirror, flashing the sun in her eyes, he said to himself, and he turned the conversation to England, of which she spoke eagerly.

How eagerly she spoke of its woods and streams, of the sea in November, of Lord Sparkenbroke's estate and her own home near by, and into what silence she fell when Lord Sparkenbroke also, in English which the doctor could understand less easily than hers, spoke of these things! As if the memory of them had come upon her unawares! As if she had been touched on the shoulder! "Alas, alas," he exclaimed to Lord Sparkenbroke, "when you speak English, I understand—but how much I do not understand! I see in the *signora's* eyes that I am missing a new world!"

They had forgotten him. At the sound of his voice they recognized him anew, and he thought with Latin pride in a pretty fancy: *Nel bosco d'amore!* They are in the wood of love; at the sound of a voice they look out, startled, through the trees!

He observed that his host was excited and pale. As though he were being pursued and dared not look over his shoulder, Celli said to himself; and, leaning back in his chair after supper with his fingers interlaced over his watch-chain, he was content to talk very little, an amused spectator.

Sometimes the Englishman talked with such decorations of wit, such a swagger of intellect, that one might have supposed the girl to be the centre of a great *salon* and all the world to be listening. Sometimes it was as if she were for him a child and he alone with her, so tenderly did he drop his pose and give her the explanations for which she

asked. Sometimes—and this made the doctor open his
eyes and jig the medallion on his watch-chain—he would
speak of his own work as though the girl were to him—
what? not a critic, not an adviser, but in some mysterious
sense a talisman.

"Did you know, Dr. Celli," she said, "that Lord
Sparkenbroke was writing about Lucca—about the
coming of the Volto Santo to Lucca?" and Sparkenbroke
said at once: "I've put it aside."

"But I thought it was almost finished? When we were
in Pisa I asked and you said——"

"It is finished. The end is written," he exclaimed. "But
there's a gap in it," and with the simplicity of a young
man explaining his difficulties he began to tell her the
nature of this gap and the cause of it, looking at her while
he spoke with such a mingling of enthusiasm and shyness
as contradicted all else that Celli had seen in him. "The
trouble," he said, "is this. Nicodemus is commanded
by angels to carve a figure of Jesus. I have told that.
Then comes the gap. Then you see him at work on the
carving, and so on to the end."

The girl did not answer and Celli himself, to break
the silence, asked: "But is there need of anything between
the command of the angels and the beginning of the
work?"

"Need? Yes. The angels didn't tell him what form the
sculpture was to take. The command was indefinite, as
most inspiration is. The idea that came into Nicodemus's
head was the idea of making *an* image of Jesus—not a
particular image. It is always best that it should be so.
When the idea of a work of art springs up in the mind
complete and, as it were, ready-made, it is to be distrusted.
The work that results from it is in danger of being too
closely and narrowly representative. The valuable impulse is the impulse of subject—Jesus: just that; not
Jesus as he sat at a table with his cheek on his hand,
not Jesus standing or Jesus walking or Jesus teaching or
Jesus at a carpenter's bench; but Jesus—the whole man.
Then the artist draws down the general into the particular.

First, he has to choose his aspect; then to pour all aspects of the subject into the single physical aspect he has chosen. It is analogous to the process of love. No one loves a woman for her own sake only—because she is she; he may desire her for that reason or be her friend for that reason, but if he says that he loves her for that reason he is no lover or is without understanding. He loves her only when he has poured into her a thousand aspirations and imaginings which have not their origin in her personally, and has, so to speak, re-created his whole being in her. What he loves is his idea, which crystallizes in her person. That is why, if she betrays him, though he can pardon her and perhaps desire her again and be her friend again, he cannot, in the same way, love her again. She has destroyed an idea and ideas have no resurrection. So an artist must not give himself precipitately to a single aspect of his subject; to do that is to mistake infatuation for love itself. He must not believe that, in representing a particular form of his subject, he has made a work of art; he must not begin to work until certainty comes to him that all aspects of the subject that lie within range of his perception are crystallized in the selected form."

"But how can he be certain"? the doctor cried. "That is the question: how can he be certain?"

Sparkenbroke turned on him. "Are you a Catholic, doctor?"

The hands went out from the waistcoat. "Yes."

"A devout Catholic?"

"I am a man of science."

"I see. But you had faith once? As a child? As a young man? . . . Then your memory will answer your own question."

Dr. Celli smiled. The man is a fanatic, he thought, but a lovable one, and, without moving his head, he let his eyes come round to the girl. She had not stirred. Her feet were drawn up under her on to the sofa; one hand clasped her knees; the fingers of the other touched her throat; her body was erect, her head raised; her lips were closed

but so lightly that she seemed to be on the brink of
speech. Sparkenbroke turned back to her, and it seemed
to the doctor that, when their eyes met again, her beauty
increased.

"You mean," she said, "that Nicodemus had to wait
until—absolute faith came to him?"

"How could he rush from his idea to his workshop?
First, it was necessary for him to re-live all his knowledge
of Jesus, and I think he must have been long in doubt what
form to choose. He would have come slowly to his decision
to show Jesus on the Cross, though, when once the decision
was reached, he would have felt that it had been inevitable
from the beginning. 'But all of Jesus is in that and in that
only!' he would cry. 'How slow I have been! What a fool!'
But he would know in his heart that his long meditation
had not been a waste of time. He would know because now
he would be certain that his selected form was the right
form. He would have that assurance of finality which is
the essence of art, the essence of love—the essence of all
religion, doctor. To grasp finality," Sparkenbroke added
slowly, "to transcend the flux, is the only absolute good.
Or so I believe," and he looked from one to the other of
his two listeners in momentary bewilderment. "But, you
see, Mary," he said, "why there is a gap? Nicodemus must
re-live in his mind all his knowledge of Jesus. That meditation is the heart of the poem. It beats through the whole
narrative; without it the story is an empty fairy-tale. And
yet, when the angels have spoken to Nicodemus, some
action is necessary. He must not sit in idleness and think.
The impulse was passionately strong; he didn't hesitate;
he sprang up from the company of angels in the bliss of a
single purpose. At that point, action is necessary. While he
thinks, he must act. What action is possible that isn't
irrelevant? The time for him to begin to carve has not
come, but what else can he do that will not break the whole
continuity and tension between the coming of the idea and
the first movement of his chisel? I have left a blank space
in the poem. I have begun to wonder whether it can ever
be filled."

She answered quietly: "It will come."

He smiled: "Can you make even that come true?"

Her eyes moved; there was a recognition between them that Celli did not understand; and in a moment Sparkenbroke was asking him what he knew of the history of San Pierino. The conversation flashed from subject to subject, in English and Italian, in French, for Celli found it amusing now and then to pretend that the *signora's* English was incomprehensible to him, for then she would struggle to remember the Italian which, she said, her father had taught her, or, failing in this, stumble into French. Then she would laugh; her laughter whipped a new colour into her cheeks and she threw back her head in a little gesture of despair.

"Piers, you know what I am trying to say!" and Sparkenbroke interpreted her in Italian, giving such a fantastic embroidery to her words that in a moment they were all laughing without well knowing what they were laughing at. The gust ended abruptly.

"It's hot in this room," Sparkenbroke exclaimed. "I want air."

A window was opened. Once on his feet, the doctor saw the clock and began to excuse himself for having stayed so late. He stooped over the girl's hand and kissed it, feeling as he did so that she was scarcely aware of his presence.

"Come with us, Mary," Sparkenbroke said. "The drive to Pisa and back will be good to-night."

She shook her head. "I'd rather stay."

"Come, then, doctor."

They drove in silence until they were beyond the outskirts of Lucca.

"How long will this go on?" Sparkenbroke demanded suddenly. "Your patient—when will she be fit to travel?"

"To England?"

"Where else?"

"It is impossible to say."

Sparkenbroke shrugged at the answer.

"Never mind," he said. "Let it go!"

"To have the ladies in the house must be an interruption of your work," Celli remarked affably; then with a deliberately provocative thrust: "I had always understood that artists were very ruthless in that matter—your Shelley for example."

"Shelley! Shelley was a saint. The gentlest being God ever made. The ruthless bandits who break crockery over their wives' heads are for the most part charlatans. That is the theatrical formula for an artist—used by people who imagine that art is an affair of bulging eyeballs and disordered hair. It is not a madness in that sense. It is a divine sanity. Shelley—good God! When the donkey could no longer carry him, or his baggage, Shelley carried the donkey." The roadside was illuminated by the headlights of an approaching car. Sparkenbroke drew in for the curve.

Celli allowed the silence to rest. His attempt to lead his companion into conversation about the women at the Palazzo Ascani had failed.

"Of course," he said at last, "one is often forced in an emergency to do things that turn out awkwardly later."

"For example?"

"I was thinking of the two ladies—your guests."

"Ah!"

"The young lady's husband is a great friend of yours?"

"I've known the family all my life."

"Then I suppose you were bound to take them in. Still —if I may say so—you are imposing a great strain on yourself."

"A strain?"

"I speak as a doctor. I have watched you all the evening."

"I was aware of that. . . . Well?"

"To be thwarted in your work in this way——"

"My work!"

"Is it not that?"

"There is nothing to prevent me from working. You don't know how careful Mrs. Hardy is not to interrupt me."

"Still, you do not work—and you do not sleep?"

"I can do without."

"No one can do that for long."

"I shall sleep!" Sparkenbroke exclaimed. "I shall sleep! With all this air in my lungs, I shall sleep like a log!"

Celli could get no more from him. At the beginning of the evening, he had assumed that the girl was Sparkenbroke's mistress; now he knew that she was not. *Nel bosco d'amore!* he repeated to himself, and yet they are divided from each other. Why? What scruples? Friendship? Fidelity? In her, perhaps; not in him.

He looked at Sparkenbroke, venturing to say with a sigh:

"Lightness of heart! Everything depends on that. When I was young I wanted a reason for everything. I wanted to be sure that I was right. Now I trouble myself less. I take what I want, if I can get it——and I sleep well."

"And if what you think you can take in lightness of heart becomes—suddenly—not that but— Something is offered you. Wine, good to taste—say that. You take it up. You are about to drink it; light-heartedly, as you say. Then an idea enters your head. It isn't wine. It's enchanted with power. It offers you all the kingdom of the spirit; it is absolute and final. Then another idea: that all this is a lie; that you're deceiving yourself; the wine is wine—no more."

"For my part," said Celli, "I should drink it and see."

The speed of the car had risen. Now, as though he had wrenched himself violently from an abstraction of mind, Sparkenbroke changed his touch on the wheel and let up the accelerator.

"I was almost asleep, I think. What did you say?"

"I said I should drink it and see."

Sparkenbroke made no answer. It was evident that he did not know what was being spoken of. They were at the outskirts of Pisa. He drove carefully, breaking the silence only to say that the woman who kept the shop in the Via d'Arancio believed that she had a drawing by Andrea del Sarto.

M

CHAPTER FOUR

SPARKENBROKE drove out of Pisa at high speed. As he approached Lucca, rain began to fall. The streets were black and empty, the walls asweat.

When he had put the car away, he walked the four hundred yards that separated him from the Palazzo Ascani. A bell above the gates wheezed without ringing, for its tongue was taken out each day at sundown that Helen might not be disturbed. A night porter, shuffling out from his lodge, swung back the gates and Sparkenbroke went in.

In the courtyard, he thought: She is asleep in this house, and remembered how in the past he had come home at night thinking only of the story of Tristan. Now Tristan was divided from him by a wall of glass. She is in the house, he repeated, she is in all the breath of my thought. How easily, when he decided to bring her to Lucca, the idea of her presence had flowed in his mind! He had been content that circumstances should lead him, perhaps to the pleasures of her body, perhaps only to a renewal of the delight he had formerly had in her company. His meeting her had seemed to him a chance of which the event might be watched, as Celli had said, light-heartedly, without commitment.

Not wishing yet to go indoors he stood on the open landing, propped against a stone pillar. From the darkness of the garden came the soft patter of invisible rain and the earthy night-smell of plants. It was not a new thing to be thrown out of the stride of work by the nearness of a woman. Such disturbance had its remedy, and he asked himself with scorn what it was that withheld him from

344

it. Scruple on George's account?—he was no respecter of
human property. Love for the girl herself? An immortal
and solemn passion that ringed her with a fictitious
holiness or, at any rate, made casual adultery not enough?
If that is to be the tune of the lie, he said, let us examine
these romantic intentions! Do I mean to tell Etty that here
is the love she spoke of, and, inviting divorce, hand over
the estates to the Kaid trustees? In the midst of his self-
taunting, his face changed. The idea of himself exiled
from Sparkenbroke—an idea which he had raised up as no
more than an ironic pointer to folly and self-deception—
appeared to him for a moment as a thing that might be;
in the next, with a twist of mockery that distorted his
features, he repelled it.

For how many years had he believed that in love was an
ecstasy comparable with the ecstasies of poetry and death!
How often the belief had duped him! He repudiated it
now with the violence that men bring always to repudia-
tion of beliefs that are part of their natures. It is false and
vain, he cried within him. It is a trick of desire! And yet,
he added, if it is false, why am I writing of Tristan? and
the structure of his book seemed to founder under
him. While she is near me, he thought, I shall not write
again. All else I can put out of my mind, but her I cannot.
He felt himself to be hemmed in by the beat and
counter-beat of a double thought: that she was in this
house, near him but asleep, and that in the garden black
rain was falling on the vine.

Staring into the darkness whence came the muffled
hiss of leaves, he saw that close to the wall of the house
a glittering line was traced across the rain. From a
window of the room in which they had been sitting a
vertical beam was projected outward between drawn
curtains. At the thought that she was awake, his energy
sprang to expectation. He moved at once into the house.
In the same instant he was filled with dread that the
room might be empty, though the lights still burned in
it. With his fingers on the door-handle, he listened to
the silence within, then entered.

She had drawn her sofa across the corner of the hearth. A book lay open in her lap, but her hands were folded across it.

"Didn't you come in long ago? I heard the gates."

"I've been watching the rain."

"Raining?" she said, and her eyes looked out into the shadows of the room, but her thought, with his, preserved a separate tension unrelated to their words, and when she saw that he also was looking at her, as she at him—not at appearance, visually, but at imagining within appearance —she felt that she had begun to exist anew and for a new reason, and said within her: are these my hands and my feet? is it I who am alive with this life? for she was awakened to a second perception of herself as though she were music that had moved into another key. When he kneeled suddenly at her side and held her, she was at first conscious only of the naturalness of their being in each other's arms. There was no external world of pledge and responsibility to threaten her love, nor sensual pang to deride it. Her happiness was without form in experience; it sprang from a life that had origin and completion in this instant, and she kissed him, without guilt or fear, in singleness of heart.

"I love you," she said. He did not answer, but took her hands and pressed them across his eyes and held them. Then, withdrawn by a little distance from her, he said at last:

"So it's true—that everything might be lost and found in you?"

She moved her head, not understanding him, and could repeat only her knowledge of herself, that she loved him. Because the excluding instant was past and he separated from her, she began to be retrospectively aware, in terms of her existence ordinarily recognized, of what she had enjoyed and permitted. The singleness of her rapture, which had been unsensual because single, was disintegrated; she felt again, in its absence, the pressure of his lips on hers, of his arms upon her body, and, lying still, thought of the rain beyond the curtains, the attendant darkness of the countryside; she saw the sweep of Europe, like a map, between her and all that she had known hitherto, and heard, in her mind, the sea. A tremor of fear passed through her, that delight of fear which is the contrasted bliss within pleasure's heat, the breeze of passion; and the words that he, stooped over her, was speaking, near and low, were not words but sounds, not sounds distinctly apprehended but images floating in her mind, until, slowly, their meaning emerged from her sensation of them and she perceived in his face an expression that had not before appeared in it, not of desire or of pride or of intellectual splendour, not even of that smiling gentleness which was his, but of serene confidence and light, and she thought: I have never seen happiness until now. Knowing that the rapture she saw in him was drawn from within herself, she was filled with love, beyond passion of the body, of the maker for the thing made, and she understood him now when he told her that, restrained from her presence, he had been tormented by the divisions in himself, but, in her presence, was inwardly reconciled, "as I was long ago," he said, "when my brother, Stephen, shut me into the Mound and into an unspeakable liberty." He pressed his eyes again into the darkness of her hands; then, with a movement of profound calm, hid them in the darkness of her breast. "It is the same, it is the same," he repeated, then, raising his head, would have kissed her, but dared not, and drew back, whispering "Is it the same?" for though, in her arms, there had been such a purgation of spirit that the ecstasy of his boyhood had indeed stirred within him, though the two experiences were, in this sense, of the same nature, they were not of the same intensity, and to kiss her again, in a struggle for intensification, had appeared to him as a kind of vanity or hypocrisy from which his intuitions withheld him. Suddenly he asked her: "Do you remember, once I knelt and drank from your hands?"

"I remember."

Later he said: "My dearest, there's nothing we can say to each other to-night except in silences."

"It was silent so long," she answered, "until you came. The gates clanged and you didn't come; yet you were in the room, invisible; and then you became visible."

"What were you thinking of?" he asked, kneeling beside her. "While I was driving that car into Pisa and back, what were you thinking of?"

"Of Nicodemus," she said.

"Of Nicodemus?"

"And his angels. How does a man see an angel? How have you described it, Piers? I don't think the angel came suddenly to Nicodemus. I mean, it was not—just an empty room—then, like a flash, an angel. The angel was always there but Nicodemus didn't see him; then, just as easily and naturally as if he had looked up from his table and seen someone waiting at his elbow, Nicodemus raised his eyes and saw him. Is that right? . . . And when the angel left him," she continued, her eyes bright with her story, "then Nicodemus sprang up; he walked out into the air; his face was happy with the kind of happiness that your face had in it now."

He waited in silence, recalling that he had entered this room in tormented belief that each accent of his persuading, and each response in her, must be staled in the little vocabulary of lust. So it must always be, he had said, but afterwards, when it is done, I shall write, imagination will flow, the clot be gone. Now it seemed to him that from her, unpossessed, new language was arising. He felt, closing in upon him, those urgent and encircling wings which, driving the energy of genius in upon itself, compel it to withdraw from the vagueness of external experience and to gather, instant by instant, like an army that retreats on interior lines, strength for the spring.

She moved. He feared that she was going. "No, stay," he said. "I want you here. Lie by the fire a little while."

She lay upon the sofa, her fingers on the spine of Conrad's *Nostromo*, gathering in her life to this instant and watching, as though it were the fulfilment of a prophecy, the movement of Sparkenbroke's shadow on the wall.

Behind her were double doors, deeply panelled, that led to the room in which he slept and worked. Once, she thought that he had passed through them and that she was alone, so long had he been still, but his shadow reappeared again, and she asked herself whether, if to-night or at any time Piers and she had known each other in the flesh, her perception of the essential unity of all experience beneath the surface of sensation would have opened yet another perception, deeper and more precise than itself, from which she was now excluded. This she would never know. Against the bodily act of love with Piers she had given binding pledges; her remembrance of George confirmed them; the rule of her life, all her understanding of herself, made them absolute; and the sudden thought that they were not absolute but subject to her will shook her as the discovery in her own heart of a desire to murder would have shaken her. By irresistible imagining, the barrier of her vows was pierced; what had been impossible appeared to her as a necessity of her being, and when, by a violence of will, she put it from her, she ached, not only in a starvation of the senses, but in a denial of life itself. For the assault was not primarily sensual, smoothly insinuating; it had the force of revolution, subverting her conscience until her evil became her good. She could hold fast only to a remembrance of herself as she had been, to a rule emptied now of intuition, and she thought: To-morrow I shall be sane; it is only because he is near me that I am mad! and, to drive out the imagining of his lips upon hers, she began to repeat to herself the little rhyming prayers that she had learnt in her childhood and to count with her finger-nail the silver ridges on the cigarette-box at her side. Slowly she was quieted. She thought of Helen, asleep in her room; of the journey by sea to Genoa; she heard the groan and clangour of George's train as it drew out on its way to Paris, and followed it a little way through the tunnel of the night. Sometimes she heard Piers's footstep at the end of the room nearer the garden; once his forearm, reaching out from a black sleeve, barred the area of her sight and a plume of sparks from a new log curled itself across the sooty wall; but after a little while she ceased to be conscious of him as a distinct, physical presence. Her thought began to weave for her a story of how, in the Rectory parlour, she took down a volume of Sparkenbroke's poems and, turning the familiar pages, came upon a poem, not familiar, in which the name of Lucca appeared. The page was clear in her sight, the texture of the paper and of her hand upon it. The name of Lucca was a summons to her; it was repeated as the verses continued until at last she had power to obey it, and she was no longer in the Rectory parlour but in a ship, alone. The coast of Italy appeared, and many people on the shore, among whom was one whose hands and wrists and arms stretched out over the water to drag in the ship; the pluming bow-wave curled towards the stern, and at once, over the heads of the people, the walls of Lucca, crested by plane-trees, rose out of the countryside. With no journey she entered the city under a narrow ribbon of sky and recognized it as a place in which she had formerly lived; yet she was reading a book; the page she was about to turn lay across her finger, the weight of the volume pressed her lap, and she knew that, if she lowered her eyes from the gigantic head and shoulders cast in shadow on the opposite wall, the poem of the Holy Face would be in print before her—the transitional passage that Piers had been unable to write—and she said:

"Piers!" He came to her at once; his shadow vanished from the wall; it lay over the back of the sofa and over her knees like a cloth. "Piers," she said. "I know what Nicodemus did. He took an axe and went out into the forest and cut down a cedar-tree. It was while he was hewing that he decided what image of Jesus he would make; he saw the form of his statue inside the cedar-tree. He was alone among the trees, and at each sound of his axe——"

"The sound of his axe!" Piers cried. "That is what I have been listening for all these months! The stroke of his axe! How did you hear it?"

He stooped and took her head between his hands and
kissed her eyes. Within her eyes' darkness she felt his
touch withdrawn, and her two lives of fantasy and experience ran on together indistinguishably. Lying still,
she heard the sound of water and of leaves moving overhead. So clear was the rustle of branches that the plane-
trees on the ramparts appeared in her mind. The wind
is rising, she said.

But the night was quiet, and the leaves she had heard
were of the ash in Derry's Wood. How long ago in the
past! She remembered the morning on which the Rector
had told her that Piers was gone to Italy. She felt again
the pang of knowledge that a part of herself, which existed
only in him, had died. Never again the spring of power
within her! Never again that experience of personal
magic, a burning core, at the heart of being alive! Never
again! she had said; yet now these things were restored to
her, who was near him, a part of the same silence. Her
imagination rested among its miracles. In all her limbs
and in her spirit she was still.

The towers of Lucca rang the hour. Logs fell in among
their ash; chime followed chime; below, in the courtyard,
were voices, then silence, and the final thud of bolts. There
was no sound in the room nor any presence, and when she
turned on the sofa she saw the panelled doors wide open
and, through them, Piers twisted away from the table, a
pad on his knee and a pencil in his hand. She would have
gone without disturbing him, but he looked up and said:
"Good-night!" then added, as though he had already forgotten his words, "Good-night." His pencil was moving,
and, without answer, she left him.

CHAPTER FIVE

THAT night he wrote until his hand sagged on the paper; then, with curtains undrawn, slept far into daylight.

When his bell rang, coffee was brought, and Bissett, with the air of a man who performs a meaningless duty, told him the time. He did not answer, but, sitting at his table, drank slowly, his hands curled round the hot cup, and seeing, over the cup's brim, the pencilled sheets of last night, began to read them as they lay, first with detachment, then with awakening curiosity. Across a corner of one of them appeared in slow, heavy script: "*N.*—the sound of his axe," and now, balancing the cup in his left hand, he scrawled, below the letter N, the rest of the name—"*icodemus.*" He underlined it idly with those graded lines that decorate the coast in old maps; the note for Nicodemus was made, but art seldom responds at once to its stimulus, and it was of Tristan, not of Nicodemus, that he had been writing. The cup was set down, his hand went out to the papers, his pen to revision, and soon, drawing fresh sheets towards him, he passed without check, from old to new, and continued until more than two hours had passed, when the narrative broke.

This was not a flagging dullness to be fought against and overcome. No burden of the unexpressed still lay upon him. What had been in him to write was written. A happy day it would be, with a stretch of work accomplished, for the desire to write resembles the desire of the body— until appeased it is a tension that drags the life out of all other experience, but its appeasement is a renewal of

352

external life, the cords are slackened from the head, the breath of thought comes easily. In time the desire to write would return. Meanwhile he was at peace; his pen clinked in its tray and he rose from his chair in the freedom of a mind poured out, delighted by the knowledge that day, not sleep, was before him.

When he was bathed and dressed, it was already afternoon. The room where they had supped, which he called the Long Room, was empty, the leavings of a mid-day meal on the table. He visited Helen but did not stay with her. The night had brought more pain than sleep; the nurse had used morphia and wished her to be alone. Mary was not to be found. He went out on to the landing that bridged the courtyard and, for a little while, walked to and fro there, angry that she did not come. To-morrow, to-night perhaps, I shall be at my desk again, but if she came now—and he thought that she would come out of the doorway on his right and stand beside him, her hands bent sharply back at the wrists as she leaned on the balustrade. I have done my work for to-day, he would tell her; she would ask him what point in the narrative he had reached and, as they walked down the steps, he would describe to her the tournament in which Tristan was about to take part—a scene that he dreaded, for a tournament was so full of technical difficulties, of rules, customs and etiquette, that he had made an elaborate study of the subject; his notebook and his mind were burdened with knowledge of it; and always, when he had looked ahead to the tournament, this knowledge had blocked his imagination. It isn't assimilated, he thought; I shall work in scraps from my notebook and lose Tristan in the skill of an armourer's craft; I shall be entangled in detail; a week or a month may pass before I have cleared the entanglement away; but if she were here now we should go out on to the ramparts, and while we were together, forgetting Tristan, the scene, being forgotten, would be simplified. It would simplify itself, and to-morrow morning, over the edge of my coffee-cup, I should see the first draft of it lying on the table.

But she did not come and he set out alone. Two abrupt
turnings brought him into the open space dominated by
the façade of Santa Maria Forisportam. As he crossed the
piazza to north and east, emerging from its shadowy
corner, his own shadow ran out before him and, at the
sun's touch, he straightened himself and trod more
lightly, glad of the swift, patterned changes, the sudden
angles of darkness and brilliance that marked this city in
which he had chosen to live. Day after day he had come
by this circuitous way to the ramparts, preferring it to a
shorter route that led directly thither, and every yard of it,
every house in the Via Santa Croce, was knit in his mind
with work he had done. Here for the first time he had
become aware that all his transcriptions of Iseult's thought
must be revised, there being in thought, as well as in
conversation, a distinguishing, personal rhythm that was
a part of character; and here, on many a day, he had come
in the blackness of disappointment, his patience almost
exhausted, saying to himself that his story was receding,
that its people were divided from him by an enmity that
could not be overcome. But it had been overcome—and
always, in the end, how simply!

Under a stony gateway, ribbed with arching shadows,
he passed beyond the ancient boundary of the city, and
walked southward by the stream of the moat, the Via del
Fosso, towards the ramparts. He was full of that joy which,
having ceased to be consciously related to its cause, is
above the happiness of reason. In the end, how simply! he
repeated, without troubling to recollect from what thought
the words had sprung; but he had not advanced fifty yards
when an aching of his left arm and shoulder, which was in
him a warning of attack, stayed him, and he sat down on a
low wall overlooking the stream, gasping, and thrusting
in his pocket for his ampoules of nitrite. That's what
comes of a night's work, and of excitement—and of
happiness! he thought. But the expected pain did not
follow; soon he would be able to move again. He gazed at
the passers-by to test his recovery by the steadiness of their
appearance to him, and, when he judged by this that he

was fit to move, stood up. No more than a touch! he said, and went forward, but at the foot of the slope leading to the ramparts a curtain of darkness fell like blood over his eyes and he halted, his fingers clutched against pain and his feet arched in his shoes. The pain gripped his chest like contracting rings of a barrel. While it lasted he sat on a stone bench at the foot of the slope, and, though one woman gazed as she passed, she did not interfere with him. He was left alone, as he wished. Soon the pain ebbed, and having, in relief from it, an exquisite pleasure, he was warmed by that physical gratitude, a thanksgiving not of the mind but of the body, which they that are without pain cannot know. From a window above his head came the sound of a schoolgirl practising her scales, and, as he drew breath and felt the sun on his hands, now relaxed, that had lately gripped his knees in agony, there seemed to be as much joy in this regular, tinkling sound as in the song of birds in Derry's Wood, and joy of the same quality. His heart went out to the unseen schoolgirl because she was young and not in pain, because at that moment all her mind was bent upon her foolish scales, the world shut out. The piano faltered, struggled, stopped. Soon it began again, perhaps because a schoolmistress commanded it, perhaps because the player herself was an artist, inwardly commanded to an undying, invincible persistence. Her "foolish" scales, he had said, and, even in rebuking himself for that gently scornful word, he smiled at the solemnity of his own rebuke; but, artist or not, he added, she's thinking now only of how to play the next scale better than the last, and that is the grammar, if not the art, of living.

The piano ceased and he looked up, thinking that at one of the open windows the girl might appear, but they continued to gape between their green shutters. He stayed long on the stone bench, desiring movement but too exhausted to move. The light had changed when at last he went forward up the slope.

The carriage road at the summit of the ramparts stretched out on either hand in the arc of a circle. Ahead

was the bastion of San Regolo, wooded with cork oak and
plane-trees, where three Italians, one bearded, all wearing
braces and the cloth caps worn in England by those who
attend association football, were playing cricket with a
large rubber ball and, as their wicket, a statue of Mazzini.
In the outer curve of this bastion Sparkenbroke was
accustomed to sit, but the flood of returning life was in
him, and he moved westward into the great avenue within
whose raised circuit the city lay.

There were few people abroad. The place had an air of
dignity and leisure. A nursemaid was at her sewing on a
bench; she looked up as Sparkenbroke approached and
followed him with slow, brown eyes, like a cow's; the boy
in her charge, dressed in a jacket that was a shock of red
against the grassy bank, stood beside his hoop and stared
and smiled. Sparkenbroke waved to him, an old friend.

He came soon to that part of the ramparts from which
the Palazzo Ascani and its garden were overlooked. The
courtyard was sharply divided between light and darkness
by the mounting, diagonal shadow of the wing that lay
across the sun. To the east, the wall, the staircase that
clung to it, and a part of the balustraded landing lay in a
glow of honey-coloured light. The house, with some of its
windows shuttered, some barred, and all so deeply se that
no curtains affected their stony outline, had that air of
desertion which, even more than the architecture itself,
gives to Italian cities their appearance of great age. A hush
seems to have fallen upon them; no one stirs; they are
given over to lizards and white dust; and when, beneath
their walls, in a crowded street, the flood of Italian life
sweeps by, these austere but decorated palaces seem to
harden their stones and darken their windows, remembering the past and to all the hubbub of to-day blind and
deaf. Here there was no street visible; no movement of any
kind; only the formal garden now disordered and the stone
figures staring down into the fountain's empty pool.

Gazing at these, Sparkenbroke heard again the axe of
Nicodemus ring in the wood. She heard the axe with
my hearing; she inhabits my mind; and yet, he cried

within him, how weak imagination is on the plane of
external experience, for now I starve for her company and
cannot summon her. I need her voice's sound, the fiery
impulse of the nearness of her body, and cannot rest upon
an inward knowledge of her; yet, if she were at my side,
should I be nearer to her than I am now? Not nearer, but,
by proximity, the more divided. How close we were when
she heard the sound of the axe! How far separated when
my lips upon hers were thrusting for an impossible union!
For her hearing of the axe was a miracle; it was like a cry
in a silent house that awakens suddenly all the corridors of
imagination. A streak of fire touched the muscles of his
back; words, with the excitement of wings, stirred in his
mind:

> How like a movement in a still house beauty is,
> Stirring in him that hears it a dark tremor of fear and
>   wonder,
> As in Adam that heard God's voice and cried: "I am here.
> Return me into thyself, O God, who, creating, forsook me.
> Let me be in thee whence I came. Here I am alone.
> The Woman is strange to me; and none may be alone but
>   God."

He began to say the verses aloud, fearful that eagerness
might cheat his memory of them, and it seemed to him
that, if imagination had power indeed, she would appear
in the sunlit part of the landing, at the stairhead, but the
house gazed at the courtyard, the stone figures in the
garden reached out towards their shadows, and she did not
come.

An impossible unity? he thought, turning again to the
rampart. The fusing of two lovers in the act of love was
impossible only if it were thought of as a distinct thing,
attached to the idea of individual pleasure. So was death,
in its creative meaning, impossible, as long as it was
attached to the ideas of cessation and fear; and poetry
impossible while it was attached to the idea of effect. But
as it was in the power of one dying to abrogate the idea of
this body's decay and, being detached from the fleshly
circumstance of death, to advance into perception, so

might it not be within the power of love to annul, even in
the act of pleasure, that consciousness of carnal separat-
ism in which pleasure consists, and, passing beyond I
and Thou, to enter into an indivisible reality? For only
appearance is divided, he thought; only men have names,
as witness to confusion here; in reality are neither divisions
nor aspects; all art has the same subject, all love is for the
same being, all deaths are the same birth.

All love is for the same being, he repeated, the words
seeming to have been spoken to him, and he was so filled
with assurance of a springing virtue and reason in creation,
that the visible earth became newly visible, as though it
had been asleep and were now opening its eyes to his own.
There was no shock, but the supreme chime of an expectation revealed by its fulfilment, in his seeing, across the grid
of sunlight that paved the avenue, the sway of Mary's
approaching figure, and he caught his breath in joy not of
her only but of experience perfected in her; for above her
the chestnuts, mingling their high gold with the rusty
green of the plane-trees, seemed now to have flame and
texture that had not been in the world. The air was silken
beneath their canopy, and from their leafy intervals were
cast down to earth such glassy sprays of light that shadow
itself was splintered with fine gold; and he saw that on the
outer bank of the rampart mimosa was turning its feathery
greenness upon the air.

In these natural miracles, the scene became for him
evidence of things unseen; and, waiting until Mary should
raise her eyes and encounter him, he knew in his heart,
with the delight and terror of one to whom final opportunity is given at last, that in her was the confluence of his
energies. It seemed to him, when they had spoken and she
was turned to walk at his side, that if he looked at her
again there would be found within her beauty another
beauty of Nature and, within this, a beauty recognizably
of his own essence, as though his own angel were his
companion. But when he looked at her, the dazzle of her
appearance threw vision back. He saw only the texture
of her cheek, the sharp, deep shadow beneath her ear, the

boyish grace of her shoulders' movement, and he commanded her to stand still, and she stood, wondering.

"But why?"

It had been to command her, to taste her actuality in her obedience, but he laughed and said: "To give an edge to the delight of your being here!"

Colour rose in her cheeks and she answered: "I came out to find you. Bissett told me you would be here. I wanted to talk."

"About?"

"Last night."

"Are you going to tell me——"

"Piers," she said, "what does this mean—between you and me?"

They were halted behind the bastion of San Colombano, and she, looking down into the city, added swiftly, as though she dared not await his answer: "There it is now, the Duomo, honey-coloured, with little black lines; I'm seeing it now and I shall always remember it, and the great square tower with its tiers of arched windows, and the flag on the top, and the feel of the ground under my shoes and this frock I'm wearing—and you. There they all are, and I'm happy, and yet what we are going to say in the next minute or two will put it all into the past, and this evening, at supper, it will belong to the past. I shall have begun to remember—and to forget it. But now it's here," she said. She took his hand, held it an instant, trembling, then tossed up her head. "O Piers," she said, "my darling, you must help. I can't say it alone."

"That I am not to be your lover?"

She could not answer.

"But do you want to go away?"

"Not if it's said."

"My dear, lovely one, have you been shut away from me all day, fighting that battle?"

"And you?" she asked.

Deliberately, to snap the tension that held her, he said: "I wrote half the night, slept into the morning, and wrote again. Then, as I came out here, there was a little girl practising scales in a high window and the scales fell out of the sky."

She smiled at him. "And now?"

"The world's enchanted. And there are tears in your eyes. And still the world's enchanted. And there's the Duomo still. My dear," he added, "if it were not to be as you say it must be, would you be nearer to me than you have been this morning or than you were last night when you heard the axe?"

"I don't know—only that I love you—and that for you to lose yourself in me would be, would be— O Piers, I love you. When you are near me, everything else I've known and believed and loved slides away, and only you are left. It's like being the sun on the other side of a cloud. I can't say it. It's like being——"

"If to-night," he said, struggling to recall his former mood and to persuade and quiet himself, "if to-night we were naked in each other's arms, should we be nearer to each other?"

She looked into his eyes and said: "Why do you say that? To comfort me? Do you believe that we shouldn't be nearer? I don't believe it. Nor you, in your heart?"

"Nor I," he said, "now. . . . Now, even to kiss you——"

"Kiss me then."

She dropped her arms to her sides and, as her body came to his and her head fell back, she sighed and shivered and his fire was in her breasts. The cool final air was on her breasts when he was separated from her, and she said: "To hold you—to let you go—it was as if my own life were dying in my arms."

It was in his mind to prevail then, urging her shaken resolve, and saying, in whatever words should come, that the act lay in the instant, without consequence except in peace of the body; but the familiar persuasions, ridden for him by many echoes, could not be spoken to her, and he was silent until, turning abruptly, he said:

"There's your Duomo still. Come down and look at it."

She gazed at the tower for an instant and followed him. As they came down from the ramparts, Sparkenbroke was visited by the peculiar lightness of heart that springs from decision and endures until the weight of decision is felt. Seeing in her face a serenity that had not been in it while her struggle continued, he had an impulse to ask if she was happy, for the joy of hearing her say that she was; but he hesitated, not knowing how to give form to a question that might wound her, against his intention.

He began: "Mary, now it's said——"

"Yes," she answered, quick in understanding, "I'm glad now; I'm glad we know certainly." And she added with the same timidity of opinion that he had seen in her when she was little more than a schoolgirl: "Piers, do you despise me for it?"

"Despise?"

"Think it little of me and narrow and cowardly. From the point of view of women different from me, it would be, I know; and I thought, perhaps, from yours."

"It depends on what one believes to be true of the act of love," he answered. "Either it's a pleasure and a stimulus like the drinking of wine; if it's that, to hoard it and bargain for it and hedge it round with vows and taboos is stupidity and meanness. But if it is the spring of life itself, and to poison it is to poison the imagination——"

"Which is it?" she said.

"It is both. It is what you imagine it to be."

"But to you, Piers?"

"My dear, you know my life. People haven't been slow to tell you."

"But you have not told me."

"Yes," he said, "I have told you, though not in words. You have your answer or you would not have the mercy and wisdom to love and to refuse me. Twice you have refused me—first your virginity, now the virginity of your marriage—and fools who think that chastity is a negative virtue would say that you have been bound by a narrow, prudish rule. The damnable women who speak of 'giving' themselves to men would say that; the world is full of canting, lascivious generosities. But your rule has been a rule of your intuition. If you had loved me less and yourself

more, you would have broken the rule 'courageously'
enough. Isn't that true? And perhaps," he added, "if I
loved you more, if I loved you absolutely——"

She repeated the word: "Absolutely?"

"All my life," he said, "I have longed for that—to love
one human being with an absolute love, equivalent to
faith, which transcends the reason it sprang from and
exists of itself."

They were now at the foot of the ramparts' inner slope.
Here stood a seat, withdrawn a little way from the descend-
ing path. In front of it were two small lions in marble, fragments of a dismantled staircase, having on their flanks and
the ridges of their manes a deep, ivory gloss, and Sparkenbroke watched the crinkled lights on their manes, thinking
that inanimate things are mirrors of the spectator's life;
they are for ever changing as he changes; at each encounter
they are new or, if they are not new, it is he that is stagnant.
These toy lions are changed because she is here, he
thought, never before have they had individuality for me,
now they will never cease to have it; they are listening
companions, awakened by her companionship, who know
that some day I shall pass by this place and say: Here she
and I sat together.

"You know," she said, "I think sometimes we spoil the
present by thinking too much of the past."

"Of the past and of the future!" he answered, and told
her that what she sought was absolutism in the present.

"I?" she exclaimed. Her lashes were raised suddenly,
her eyes shone.

"Now," he said, answering in his tone her astonished
smile, "you yourself have told me what I meant by an
absolute love," and, because she had come to the edge of
laughter, he felt that there was a natural and intuitive
understanding between them; she put even the struggle of
his words at ease, and he was able to say that the desire
for absolutism did not depend upon some obscure metaphysical theory or twist of the individual mind; it was a
universal desire. "All men are possessed by it," he said,
"though in different men it takes different forms and

they call it by different names. The desire to be single-minded in the present, is one form, which most people express vaguely by saying that they want happiness. The religious impulse to enter into God is another form, for, whatever view we take of God, we are certain that, if a divine being or essence exists, it exists of itself; it is an originating and inclusive essence; it does not depend on cause or effect outside itself, for it includes all cause and effect. Longing to be received into this everlasting present, is, in men who have the will to death, the strength of that will, and many are content to wait; they believe that absolutism cannot enter into this world; life to them is an impenetrable smudge of appearance by which, until it is wiped away at last, reality is shut out. But they have mis-read their Shelley. The radiance shines through the stain. Since my childhood, I have known that to be true; it shines through the contemplation of death; and there is a corresponding ecstasy to be found elsewhere on earth than in the idea of death. In art certainly; in love, I think, for there seem to have been men and women who have entered into absolute love which has not been related to themselves as they formerly were or affected by any act of their separated selves—not by betrayal, not even by forget-fulness. Tristan and Iseult are the symbol of such lovers, and the legend of the potion is the parable of an absolute love between man and woman. When the potion is taken, the boundary between absolutism and temporal reason is passed, the act of love becomes not a delight of the senses but an ecstasy in which separate being is consumed. For lovers who find it, death has its alternative here and poetry its equivalent. That is what I understand by the story of Tristan. Tristan is, in appearance, the antithesis of Don Juan; they do not recognize each other; but they are com-panions in the same journey—the same journey, I think, with the poets and the saints."

While he spoke, she, leaning forward a little over her hands clasped tightly together, had watched him with the compassion of a child for a complexity of suffering remote from its own experience. How gently she listens to me, he thought, patient of my stumbling, as though I were a child pouring out my heart at her knee. She does not blame or judge.

"You see," she said, "it's all different for me. My mind works very slowly when I set it to work, though sometimes faster by a kind of chance. Helen says I have no philosophy of life; that may be true. I think out practical things for myself. I remember thinking out what Father meant when he said that one must never use capital as income, and, after I'd thought it out, it seemed to be right, and it has become a rule ever since. And other things that I can't really think out—I mean about what is right or wrong to believe and do—they have rules too, what you call rules of intuition, I suppose."

"You mean the rules by which you govern your own life?"

"Or try to," she answered.

"What are they, Mary?"

She looked at him with grave shyness. "The Ten Commandments and the other two. And one more," she added, "of my own. It's part of the others, really."

"What is the one more?"

"Simply, to keep my word."

"You mean that nothing can release you from your word once given. Even the Pope grants dispensations."

"I know," she said, "that seems to me the one flaw in the Catholic rule."

"My dear," he said, "you are an absolutist too!"

"I know," she answered. "It's my form of single-mindedness and peace. For other people it's different; they can make up their lives as they go along; I know I can't. Does that seem hard and rigid and selfish? I'm not hard and rigid towards other people. It's just how I personally am made. I love you not less but more because you are made differently." She rose and said: "Now the lions have heard both our confessions. How many they must have heard!"

They went on, through an entanglement of alley-ways, into the Via delle Rose, content to be silent. Sparkenbroke understood now in what way he loved her and watched her shadow curl and ripple over the rounded stones on which they were walking, gathering in her presence against the time when Lucca should be empty of her. In the rare temper of a mind not armoured against the world by knowledge but endowed by a special grace with immunity from its corruptions, she had for him a quality of redemption and release; a quality, he thought, to be found in certain priests who, being themselves but peasants, can yet in confession lighten the burden of minds subtle beyond their range—a penetrative simplicity, a creative power to liberate by acceptance. And he had lifted his eyes from her shadow to seek her face when she turned aside.

"Are these the roses?" she asked, looking at the carvings on the little church that leaned, like a marvellous shed, against the wall of the Archbishop's Palace, and when Sparkenbroke showed her the Virgin and Child under their canopy of stone she stood still, not so much to admire them as to feel their presence and record in her heart the instant of her encounter with them; for, she said within her, though I can revisit them, I shall not see them again for the first time, and at this hour, in this light. She was so happy that she could feel the waters of perpetual life running through her fingers and turned her head swiftly towards her companion as though there were help in him. A glance to take the breath away, all child, all woman in it! The awe of being still young is fallen upon her! he thought. Time has his wings about her. Suddenly she is armed with power, for now in her imagination she raises the dead, who are absolved in her by no act of absolution; and he watched her silently, until her eyes, coming again to his, returned to their natural acknowledgments and she walked on at his side into the Cathedral square.

"Just now," she said, "when we were looking at the Madonna—do you know how changed you were?"

"Changed. In what way?"

"Not so proud—not so desperate." And she added slowly: "Not so frightening. As if—as if——"

None but fools cry out: What did you see? What did
you see? to one who has seen the invisible, and, saying
nothing, he led her on beside the northern front of the
Cathedral. She gazed across the piazza at the wall of
the Micheletti garden and its crown of leafy branches,
the loveliest wall in Italy.

"You were looking," she said, " as if your life had been
forgiven you," and the words which, on other lips, would
have been corrupted by fallible judgment, were, on hers,
without judgment. They told what she had seen, and so
great was their light within him that he moved his hand
towards hers but could not take it, and stood before her,
unable to speak.

"What have I said?" she asked.

"You have absolved me."

"I?"

"Not you," he said, "but the imagination in you."

His saying this was to remain in her memory when
much else of her experience in Lucca was dulled by time,
for she perceived then that he did in his heart attribute
to her a power over his destiny beyond her knowledge
of herself. He drew her on with a touch of his hand. For
him, the tension between them was released, but not for
her. It was part of the joy of being in his company that
no heaviness of thought accumulated upon him; he threw
off a mood as a swimmer shakes the water from his eyes
before plunging anew; and now, as they walked across the
Piazza Napoleone and into the market-place of San Michele,
he seemed to have not a care in the world and to discover
new gaiety and loveliness in all he saw. But she, though
she was happy with a barbed and penetrative happiness,
felt that she was living in an imposture from which she
could not escape. Even he did not know her for what she
was; he was loving her for qualities outside her nature; all
she saw and experienced—the glint of a ferrule on a
walking-stick as it swung by, the shape of light on a
paving-stone as her foot touched and changed it, the wild
tingling of her wrists and the soft, tapping coldness of
a pendant between her breasts—this was experience

imposed upon her by some agonized change of identity. The change was complete; she was as powerless to escape from it as an actress from her part; she accepted it as one accepts a dream, but remained aware of it; and the word "Pisa" on a time-table attached to the wall of a railway-office sent her mind back to the girl who had come there with Helen, and had set out next morning from the hotel, and taken a cab and felt the cab stop suddenly and seen him and heard his voice, the voice that now was speaking to her in a life beyond the looking-glass. Lucca was upon her now, very close, its scent in her nostrils, its air between her lips, the gusty bleakness of November air, not cold; and knowing herself to be beyond the mirror, she threw up her head and looked at all she saw as if it must vanish or she from the midst of it.

CHAPTER SIX

BY narrow streets, bulging with the stalls of grocers and ironmongers, they came into the Via Fillungo, itself winding and overshadowed, but crowded with leisurely strollers —young men, hatless, with proud, curling tufts and the padded shoulders of Italian dandies; women with large bags of American cloth who had come out for the evening's shopping; old fellows with trim white beards and beringed fingers whose dignity and animation gave them the air of ambassadors in a musical comedy, and children innumerable, darting from side-streets, trailing at their mothers' hand, twisting in and out among the knees of passers-by.

"Where are we going?" she asked.

"To a *caffè*. . . . Tea."

But before they reached the *caffè*, Sparkenbroke, encountering a goldsmith of his acquaintance, paused in the doorway of his shop to talk to him of the news of Europe. If all hair were of the colour of the young *signora's*, the goldsmith said, his trade would cease, and, patting her on the shoulder as if she were a schoolgirl, he drew them to his counter, where, for the bubbling delight of conversation, he showed them his latest stock; and Sparkenbroke sat there, as eager as a boy in an engine-room, demanding of him the detail of his craft, chattering with his clients as they came and went, showing an old lady whose parcel fell loose how to secure it with a reef knot. "In the end," he whispered, "we shall be invited inside," and Mary did not understand his eagerness, his persistence. She understood only that they were an eagerness and persistence separated from her. He was exempt from the stress of her mind, for he inhabited his own world and could at will visit any part of it, but she was an alien, observing it, and herself, with a stranger's eyes.

"Piers," she said, "do you want to go in?"

"Into the workshop," he whispered, with the glance of a conspirator, and, looking across the counter at the panel of light that slid in from the half-open door of the workshop, she thought: soon we shall be in there, and tried to imagine the room they would find, but could not; there was no reality within her compass but the pricking gleam thrown upon her flesh by a chain of topaz that Piers had wound suddenly across her wrists, and when the chain was gone the cold pressure of the stones remained and the movement of his fingers under them. She thought: it is resolved, we shall never be lovers, and for a moment the resolve comforted her; it restored her knowledge of herself; but the word "never" cried out, her flesh grew old and withered, there was neither sun nor air, and all the weight of her body pressed up through her elbows and forearms that rested upon the plate-glass of the counter. She remembered the tower of the Duomo and the ramparts' earthy freshness; his kiss upon her and her arms' uplifting, the falling blackness of leaves and branches that slid over the ice of the sky; her breath and its ending; the end of sight also; and the sudden leap of sight's return, the still, light blaze of the Duomo's honey-coloured tower. Through the goldsmith's shop came the sound of a chime from the inner room; and soon, when they had passed beyond the counter into the workshop, she saw the clock on a bracket with the name Vacheron et Constantin inscribed on its face.

"What a lovely clock!" she said.

"And the inside is as good as the outside," the goldsmith told them, lifting the clock from its bracket with the tenderness and the smile that he would have given to the lifting down of a child, "and that is more than one can say of all clocks. It was my father's. He went to Geneva for his wedding journey and my mother fell in love with the chime; it would always tell her again of those young days, she said; and my father brought it home with him. You understand clocks? Look, I will show the inside to the lady. . . . It is a pretty movement. When we were children, my brothers and I were allowed to look at it on holidays in the evening. It kept us very quiet; we were told that we must not breathe into a clock."

Piers observed at once that the escapement was exceptional in its period. "But you know clocks!" the goldsmith exclaimed. "You should have known my father. He dreamed always of writing a history of clocks," and he himself would have given them the history of clocks, but he had reached only the fabulous days of Pope Silvester II when Piers diverted him to his own trade in the working of precious metals. They examined his tools and used them; they were shown the history of his firm in its ledgers and instructed in the price and fineness of gold; and Mary knew that she was forgotten.

In the street at last, Piers remembered that they had been on their way to a *caffè*. He condemned himself for a loiterer and put his arm under hers with so much tenderness, so genuine and simple a remorse, that in a return of confidence she laughed with a sparkle in her eyes that made him catch his breath.

"You see," he said, "the inside of an Italian goldsmith's isn't to be met with every day. That odd tool with an egg-shaped handle—I know the feel of it now."

"But, Piers, you're not writing about a goldsmith?"

"No, but I hate vague knowledge. That little shop was a new world to me; I had to go inside. I shall go again and again. It may lead to nothing; I don't know; but I love the feel of things, and people doing their job. Did you know before what the smell of a goldsmith's workroom was like —a dry, cedary smell, half-way between metal and pencil-shavings? No one can imagine that. You have to know it."

She looked at him. "Do you ever stop writing—in your mind?"

"God knows!" he answered slowly. "Do you ever stop breathing?"

"Yes," she said.

"What do you mean?"

"Sometimes I stop breathing."

"When?"

"O Piers!" Her hand clung to his and she jerked her head away.

His perception, awakened and challenged by the tremor that passed through her, leapt to her meaning.

"Just now?" he said. "On the ramparts? When I kissed you? Then you stopped breathing. And you mean——"

"No, Piers, I wasn't questioning you. You are as you are. It's that I love. I wasn't——"

"But it's a good question to ask myself: did I stop writing then? There's no answer that isn't half a lie. In five years——"

"But I know the answer, Piers."

"Tell me."

"Isn't it all the love there is between us and the division too?"

"The division?"

"The world I came from: the world you make."

"My dear, such foreboding!"

"Certainty."

"Of what?"

"That I shall go back. Here, with you, there's no other happiness; no other life. But it's not my life, Piers, is it? You know that. Do you remember me as you found me?"

"But you are changed."

"Only for you. In you. Not in myself."

They were stopped at the entrance to the *caffè*, and there, looking into his face steadfastly, she said: "Will you tell me something I'm not sure of? That night, in Derry's Cottage, why did you start for Italy?"

"Wasn't it best?"

"For my sake?"

"Better assume that what I do is done for no one's sake but my own."

"But you knew that if you had stayed, another day perhaps——"

"Yes, I knew that."

"Then?"

"Mary, is it of any use to ask 'why' of the past? I can tell you why not. It wasn't scruple for you—nor George's tantrum. It was"—he spoke very slowly, struggling for the truth in himself—"I think it was fear that I might imagine I loved you. When first I saw you, you were the loveliest animal in the world. Then, in Derry's Wood, by the stream, there was more. Always more at each meeting until—my dear, I can't analyse it. I told you once you were miracle-minded. Isn't it true?"

"For you," she said, "perhaps; I don't know. . . . But in the end, if I were to break your work, you would hate me."

He smiled. "That would be a way out!"

"But it's true?"

"Not 'hate.'"

"Shut out. Forget. It is true. You have that power. . . . And if I went away, then——"

"That would end my work!" He said it lightly; then regarded what he had said and added: "The odd thing is—that may be true. I don't know. That, precisely, is what I don't know."

He drew her into the *caffè* between the two high counters with their glittering urns. While the waiter brought their tea, he was silent, then continued:

"Living alone here, as I have for months, one returns to one's origins. When I'm going about the world, gambling, going to parties, making love, talking for the sake of talking, anyhow meeting people continually, I feel myself to be very much what they think I am. I live my pose. But no one can live his pose for very long when he's alone. He begins by dressing his soul for dinner every evening, but soon he gives it up. That's why most people are afraid of solitude—they like their pose; the wind cuts their nakedness if they put off their social reach-me-downs; but I hate my party suit, though I do my best to wear it like a dandy when I have to wear it at all. I have a great sympathy with Donne who stood in his winding-sheet while Nicholas Stone carved a statue of him. There is no freer dress."

"But life itself, Piers. You are not indifferent to it?"

He threw towards her an amused, questioning glance. "It isn't a dungeon," he said, with a smile. Then, speaking straightly, he continued: "Why do people imagine that a will to death implies a hatred of life? It's not true. It was true of certain extreme ascetics, but it wasn't true of Socrates or of Jesus, and, in both of them, the will to death, which is a will to transcendence, was all-powerful. The modern school of optimistic materialism holds, against them, an opinion of death never before held in the world. The fear of death isn't new; and there'd be nothing new in believing that it is annihilation; but men have never before treated it as they treat it now—with a coward's fear hooded in a fool's blindness. What is new and terrible is the idea that physical existence in the body is an end in itself and that death is, as it were, an unwarrantable interference with our human right to do as we please. You can believe that bodily existence is an end in itself if you believe in annihilation by death; but city-bred materialists don't fully accept that; they cling to a vague hope of survival, not with faith, but as they cling to a hope that they may win a prize in this week's newspaper competition. They are so obsessed by what they call 'social consciousness,' which is at best a desire to increase the amenities of their lodging-house, that they can think of transcendence only as 'escape.' They think that a man with the will to death is gloomy and neurotic, blind to the splendours of life which they proclaim. It is not so. He is the more sensitive to life in the senses because, like Shelley, he is aware of ecstasies beyond the senses. The world isn't a dungeon; there is light and pleasure and hope and reward in it; but the walls go up unscalable, and all energy —life itself—consists in making them transparent and, ultimately, in passing through them."

"Can they be transparent?"

"If not," he said, "poetry is meaningless—poetry, music, mathematics, all the supreme exercises of human perception, are meaningless; not only that, but they are fraudulent, for they announce a transcendence—they claim to be, in themselves, a transcendence that doesn't exist. Are you going to believe that? The poets are not liars."

"But in your own experience," she repeated. "Your personal experience, apart from poetry?"

He turned his head away. "Seeing visions as well as dreaming dreams?" But he did not answer her, for an Italian whom he knew had come up to speak with him, and others followed. Soon they were seated about him, straddled across chairs, listening to his talk in Italian and in English, their eyes flashing, their hands coming out in broad gestures of argument or assent, their lips eagerly parted in readiness for speech or laughter. Others, entering the *caffè*, joined them, and the waiters, in the intervals of their business, stood within earshot. He was arguing that the value of any polity was ultimately to be judged by the art and philosophy it produced or enabled, and that so Fascism would be judged by history, and she listened to him in a dream, marvelling at the many-sidedness of his life and at his power to throw his energy, his intellect, his whole self into each encounter—into the goldsmith's workshop and now into argument with these men.

"Tired?" he said as they went out together into the street.

"And you, Piers?"

"I? No."

"You never save yourself."

"Why should I?"

"Not even for your writing?"

"I shan't write to-night."

"Because you're tired?"

"No!" he exclaimed. "Because I'm too close. The tide's up. I write on the ebb. . . . What shall we do to-night? Read? Talk? Shall we drive out to the Bagni di Lucca—it will be cold but it's a clear night. You shall choose. . . . I want to-night to last. I don't want to-morrow to come."

She repeated with the emphasis of her own fear: "I don't want to-morrow to come," and silence fell.

They were passing through the piazza of the Duomo.

There was enough light from the sky to throw across the open space before them a glassy film which, shining in the intervals of their combined shadow, fell away into a distance of mist and darkness, as though they were at the edge of a gleaming lake, horizoned in cloud; and from the lake arose, near at hand, the flowing steps, the three black arches of the cathedral's atrium, and above them the ghostly ripple of the many-arched tiers of the façade. A cathedral, she thought, that one would love with all one's heart if one were a child in Lucca, for it was without the majesty of Gothic. Huddled against the neighbouring wall so that its design was crushed out of symmetry, it had the appearance of a toy that some child had left behind in a careless hour; only the deep shadows of the porch held it down, the shadows of its higher decoration seeming to be without weight, as though, if a gust should come, they and the little twisted columns between them would, like lace, be puckered and blown away.

But Piers said: "You shall choose, then," and, as they went over the glassy pavement, her longing to establish unity between her world and his led her to ask with plead- ing, as though she feared that he would laugh her sugges- tion away, that after supper he would come up to Helen's room and read.

"To her?"

"And me."

"What am I to read?"

"Ages ago you were reading Shelley's *Prometheus* to the Rector, and Helen came into the room and heard you and stopped to listen."

"I remember," he said. "What made her tell you of that? It's the only time she has ever really liked me."

"She has always remembered it. She used to say no man could be really bad who could read Shelley like that."

Sparkenbroke laughed aloud. "There's a passport at Peter's Gate! But it's odd—I should never have guessed that Shelley was her poet. . . . But she doesn't like me, Mary. I go to her room now and then to make sure that she has what she wants, but not for long. Wouldn't it irritate and distress her: my being there—with you?"

"No, Piers; not now. She has changed."

"Towards me?"

"Towards everyone. Towards herself even. Her old prejudices have become less important, in some way. I don't mean that, because she's ill, she is tired or indifferent. It's more than that. It's a kind of—of——"

"Repose?" he asked sharply.

"Yes, I think so."

"But, Mary, doesn't it trouble her—I mean, for George's sake—that you and I should be together as we are?"

"No. She says: 'Go out and enjoy yourself. Don't stay with me or think I'm lonely. I'm not. Every day in Lucca you will learn something.'"

"An educationist still!"

Mary answered his smile: "This time I think she didn't mean it in that way."

It is true, Sparkenbroke thought as he sat in Helen's room that evening, she is a schoolmistress no more. He had paused in his reading; Shelley's book was closed upon his finger.

"I won–der why I like that man," Helen said. "I sup–pose I should be one of those who disapprove of him if he were alive. Now, even in bit–ter moments when one despises the race of men, Shel–ley is ex–empt. And yet, he must have been hard to live with."

She had now the utmost physical difficulty in speaking, but persisted, slowly and indomitably. She asked to be raised up and lowered again in her bed, for her legs had stiffened so that she could not bend them and it gave her relief if her body was turned a little to one side or the other. When this had been done, she remembered Shelley.

"I think," she added, "he was with–out malice. That's more than to have char–i–ty. . . . Here, we are so far away from Eng–land. It frightens me sometimes to think of the long journ–ey and the rattling trains. . . . It is kind of you to read, Piers. Did you dislike me when you were a small boy?"

"Never. I always knew where I was with you."

"Yes," she answered, "that's true. I've always want–ed people to feel that a–bout me. Now it seems less im–portant. It is a pride that repels love. No one knew where they were with Shelley."

Surprised by this sudden reversion to Shelley, Sparken-broke looked closely into her face and saw that she was smiling, but not at him; her smile was for herself, as her talk had been; the lucidity of her separated phrases had consequence in her own thought; there was a childlike swiftness in her with which he could not keep pace. It was this that caused him to think suddenly: is she near to death? Is this the speed and precision of release? and he looked from her face to Mary's, set back from the candle-ring, as though he might find in it an echo or a denial of his intuition. But Helen said:

"Now I have some–thing I must tell you both. While you were out a let–ter came from George. I would have told you of it sooner, but I thought that first we might have Shelley in peace. Fa–ther is very ill."

"Ill?" Mary said. "How ill?"

"He seems to have had a stroke," and she told them that, even though no other stroke followed, the Rector would be a cripple all his life; his mind was unaffected and his speech; but a part of his left side was paralyzed. "He will sit in his room or in the gar–den. If I am there, you will have two invalids in the house. The letter is on the table at Piers's side—on the shelf under the table. You had better read it, Mary."

"Oughtn't I to go home?"

"Read it, my dear."

Mary took the sheets from their envelope and held them towards the candle. "Poor George!" she said. "Why didn't he tell us? Why didn't he cable?"

"And what would have been the use of that?" Helen put in with a return to her old severity of manner. "There's nothing we could do. George isn't one to send tel–e-grams without purpose. . . . One always knows where one is with George, too," she added, throwing towards Sparkenbroke, without moving her head, a keen, questioning glance; and she repeated: "It is a pride that re–pels love. That is what has bound us together, brother and sister. And yet he has other qual–i–ties. He is lovable."

Mary, when she had read the letter, folded it, and leaned back in her chair. They talked a little of England, hoping that after all the Rector might be able to continue a part of his work. "It will come hard to him," Sparkenbroke said, "to give it all up."

Mary replied: "As long as he can read, he won't be un-happy. At heart, he's more scholar than parson," and there was silence between them; their thoughts were in this room, not with the old man in his chair. Already, Sparken-broke thought, Helen is away upon her own voyages, and to me the Rector is a ghost; old friend though he is, my imagination will not seize him or his suffering; nothing burns for me except that Mary is within reach of my hand, that our knowledge of each other runs between us like a luminous rope.

"Mary," Helen said, "why are you cry–ing? You mustn't cry."

"I'm not. Not crying. It's just that the tears come."

"But he's not suffering. George says so. And he won't be unhappy. You were quite right."

"It wasn't for that I was crying. Not for him."

"Then why?"

Mary did not answer and, at Helen's request, Sparken-broke opened his Shelley again.

CHAPTER SEVEN

As part of a regular system of relief given to the nurse, Mary spent the morning with Helen; then wrote to George, a long, troubled letter which she was reluctant to end, for while it lay under her hand and she might imagine it in his she was secure in her old security; yet she could not open her heart to him, and the simplest description of Lucca seemed to her an avoidance and false. Even her anxiety for the Rector and her news of Helen came to paper as if they were lies, stiffly and slowly, for her mind swerved continually from them to Piers and to a thousand remembrances of yesterday. If I do not see him, she said, I shall starve, and she looked over her shoulder towards the window of her bedroom from which, she knew, the windows of his own room were visible. Before her letter was done she went down into the Long Room, thinking that his door might open; but it was shut; she turned from it in cold shame and remounted the staircase by which she had come.

The letter done at last, she visited Helen again and found her lying as she had lain all day, on her back as though she were sleeping, but with open eyes.

"I've been writing to George. Is there anything you want me to put in?"

"I wish he were here."

"Shall I say that?"

"No. Don't say it; he would come. He has troubles enough."

"Then there's nothing?"

"Give him my love. Tell him I have been think–ing of

379

him to-day—of how we did Latin vers–es to–geth–er and made our garden."

Mary sat down at the bedside table. The nurse gave her a pen and moved the bottle of urotropine out of her way. When the postscript was written and had been read aloud—"That is all," Helen said. "Have you been out to-day?"

"No."

"You must go for a walk. You can post your let–ter."

Mary went from the room with a feeling of desolation. From the bed had come a murmur of Latin verses that she had not understood:—

> *saevis Liburnis scilicet invidens*
> *privata deduci superbo*
> *non humilis mulier triumpho—*

and by her failure in understanding she was exiled. Dreading the streets, solitary now because thronged with close remembrance, fearing yet more the ramparts whose healing melancholy had been broken by so fierce a joy, she knew not where to go and turned from the courtyard idly into the garden. Here was little colour except a tangled greenness from which emerged an isolated clump of flowers, red but with the shape of bluebells, and, beyond the fountain, a heavier red of cardinali, curling like sculptured plumes. But the garden's history looked through its present; she saw the overgrown paths and the surrounding pergola bright with former inhabitants of this place, whose home had been Lucca, and, knowing herself alien among them, she went out into the street. At the church of Santa Maria delle Rose, she increased her pace and soon was in the piazza of the Duomo, where she stopped. Where am I going? she said, where can I go? A door on the north side of the cathedral was open; people were coming out; soon it would be shut, for dusk was falling; but she entered and, having gone forward a few paces, halted, and stared without sight. If he were here! If he were here! Only for a few hours had she been separated from him and already she was crying: if he were here!

The light of this thought was so bleak upon the future that she strove to muffle it, saying: I ought not to have come to Lucca; I was wrong to see him again; but that had been an accident, and she wondered why it had been permitted—perhaps to tempt her. It was hard to believe there was evil in it, so great had been the increase of life that it had brought, but she knew that in this way evil might disguise itself and so tempt her the more. In her confusion, she knelt down, seeking help and stillness, but had no words in which to pray, for one cannot pray against love. She desired the quiet of her former life, which was in accordance with her nature, and that fiery percipience by which, in Sparkenbroke, her nature was lighted and magnified; above all a harmony of these two, that she might have peace; but to reconcile them was beyond her strength, to choose between them beyond her courage, and she began to feel the hardness of the stone under her, to hear the slack clop of loose slippers in the distant nave; she observed, near to her, the sliced rectangle of a young priest's face as he moved, with weary step, towards the door by which she had entered, and knew by the silence that he had halted not far away. She covered her eyes, but there was nothing in her heart to pray for except that Piers should come, and she said: "O God, let him come! O God, let him come!" repeating it many times until she thought that he was behind her. He would stoop and lift her up; his hands would be upon her, his fingers upon the sides of her breasts. Her body awakened to him; with choking bliss in her throat she stood up and turned. Only the priest was there, who wheeled from his gazing. The padded door by which he went out settled into its frame with a hiss of air.

Before her, in the north transept where she stood, arose a sarcophagus, which at her coming had been dead in her sight, but now lay up from the shadows, suddenly. On its side were three naked boys, in relief, with a flowery cordon festooned between them, and at each corner another—five little boys with round heads chuckled in curls, and flesh creased in the marble's gleam. Their burden of fruit and flowers, slung from shoulder to shoulder and clutched here and there by a tiny, listless hand, was wound in so deep a coil that, while each loop hung, in its lower curve, at the level of their knees, its higher edge drooped but little from wing to wing; and the wings' own curves met steeply at its centre, marvellously answering it, and preserving, in upper and lower ripple, a peerless rhythm of design. The arrowy and failing light obeyed the artist's will in throwing no hard shadow that might have frozen his sculpture, which, in its stillness, was alive, not with the life of nature arrested and by arrest made false, but with an ethereal, imagined quickness, as if these children, at once careless and sullen, who took up their garlands and spread their wings five centuries ago, had even then fallen into some childlike meditation from which they were for ever on the point of being aroused. Or perhaps it was the flight of a bird that raised the head of one or a stirring in the grass that lowered the eyes of another while above their heads a frail sky let in the spring. To the head of one child there clung a shadow deeper than the rest, curled in ellipse between cheek and shoulder by the wing that included it—a chance of shade so lovely in its fall and in the tender emphasis it laid on the relation of wing to head that Mary smiled at what she saw, as one smiles at the discovery of a secret. There was, in this infant and his playfellows, harnessed with garlands, a gaiety that had not yet become a defiance of sadness, but was in perfect reconciliation with it—a serene light within the idea of melancholy that the world has lost; and there shone in them also a sculptural intimacy that made of the sarcophagus neither prison nor monument, but a dwelling-place.

Upon it was the figure of a young woman, a girl, her gentle face calm with included vision, her eyes but lately closed. Over her limbs and feet, at which a dog rested, her drapery lay in austere folds. Her hands were simply crossed, not at her breast or in any symbol, but as they might have been when she slept; and Mary, gazing at her, underwent that process of simplification sometimes experienced in dreams, beneath whose shadow the boundaries of contrary things fade until there is no more conflict in any difference, speech and silence, time and no-time, life and death appearing to be, though separate in form, identical in quality. What was the nature of this miracle, she did not inquire, for it did not then impress her as miraculous; but she received the joy of it as parched earth receives the rain. It presented itself to her as love for the girl lying there, and not for her only but for the principle of life in her tranquillity; she felt that she loved her, not objectively, but from within, and that, in doing this, she had become a part of the divine energy which, loving all creatures from within themselves, was their essence, the perpetual agent of their renewal. Her sense of being thus entered into the work of art, lifted from her all weariness, even of the body, and she stood a little apart from the monument, her hands crossed as they fell, until she became aware of a figure that interrupted the garlands, and thought: this is a part of what he has known since he was a boy in the tomb. She watched silently, as he did. When he left the cathedral, she followed him and touched his arm. It was now dark, but they went on to the ramparts together and walked there under the trees, telling of their experiences and looking now and then into each other's faces as though it were morning and they could see.

That evening, after supper, Piers said: "If we grow old, and know each other then, we shall remember to-day. You will make a romance of it and I a satire; and both will be false." He advanced from the bookcase by which he was standing, knelt beside her on the couch and, taking her in his arms, kissed her and let her go. "You have been nearer to me to-day than anyone has ever been; I am richer than I shall be again; and yet," he added with a little jerk of his voice, "I shan't have the wit to sell out! To-morrow will come and I shall be alive, and you, my dear, will be the Rector's daughter-in-law. What shall you write in your Journal to-night?"

She looked at him, startled and trembling. "How did you know about my Journal?"

"Helen told me. She gave it to you, didn't she—'to keep a record of your tour'? She told me to remind you. Well, I have reminded you now. And I'll tell you what to write in it. 'Went into the Duomo and found the tomb of Ilaria. It was made by Jacopo della Quercia in'—I don't know—'very early in the fifteenth century. She is very beautiful. At her feet is a dog. Underneath there are a lot of fat little boys. Piers came and—' Does the Journal call me 'Piers' or 'Sparkenbroke'?"

She answered with her face turned away: "Lord Sparkenbroke."

" 'Lord Sparkenbroke came,' " he continued gravely, " 'and we went out on to the ramparts together. It was almost dark, but over the country to the south there was a—a kind of residue of daylight, like a thin sheet of ice with tinfoil under it, and the reflection of it ran up the tree-trunks like a spine. I saw it on our hands sometimes as if they had been dipped in—' In what?"

She was silent.

" 'And I told Lord Sparkenbroke without knowing it, that I was two people—the girl by the bandstand and the girl by Derry's Stream; the girl writing this Journal for Helen and the girl who heard Nicodemus's axe among the cedars——' "

"No," she whispered. "I didn't say that. Piers, why now? Why do you laugh at me now?"

"But didn't you tell me that the two girls met and, for an instant, became one beside the tomb of Ilaria? Isn't that what you told me? It was what I understood. . . . With me," he said, answering her confusion with sudden tenderness, "you have never been at peace before. This evening on the ramparts you were. Isn't that true? Weren't you at peace?"

"Such peace!"

The words were said in the hush of so passionate a memory that they were almost soundless; it was her eyes that spoke. He sprang away from her, breaking the mood.

" 'And Lord Sparkenbroke,' " he cried, " 'told me what for the life of him he has never been able to tell to any other human being, what he has been trying to tell in every word he has written and every hour he has lived, and it was I who made it possible for him to tell it.' And now," he added, "it has been told and will never be told again. It will not be written, even in your Journal."

"I wonder," she said, "whether I understood. While you were telling me, I seemed to. You told me what happened when you were a boy in the Sparkenbroke Mound, and, while you told it, I seemed to be there too, and to see and hear and feel everything that you did. Out on the ramparts there were no questions to ask. But now," she added slowly, "I've half forgotten it as though it were too hard for me to remember. It's you, telling it, I remember —not what you told. Or perhaps I do remember what you told, but not the meaning of it—now. For you, in some way, that experience goes on always, doesn't it, Piers? I mean: it's going on now, in this room while we sit here?"

"The expectation of it."

"That's what I don't understand."

"Once," he said, "I knew a philosopher who understood no better than you. He was a historian of philosophy, a scholar, not a mystic; he didn't know—and couldn't know, because he was without direct experience—that interior discipline is only a preparing of the ground, and that what makes the ground fruitful comes, like seed and rain and sun, from outside oneself. Philosophy is the female aspect of the contemplative act. Visitation is necessary, and whoever has been made aware of the possibility of it waits for it always; his life has no other continuous meaning or purpose. . . . Look," he said, with new eagerness. "I can tell you a little of what I mean. Do you see the windows of this room?" She looked towards them. "The curtains are back. What do you see?"

"Nothing, it's dark outside."

"But outside are the garden and the ramparts and, above the ramparts and between the trees, the whole sky lighted up. There's nothing between us and them but glass, and glass is transparent. Now, tell me again what you see."

She turned from the window towards him. "Only the glitter of lamps and candles on the pane."

"They are this world. While they are shining in our eyes, we can see nothing beyond them. Put them out, and suddenly the night and its constellations rush in; all its distances are within reach. That is what happened in the Mound, and why I am drawn back to it. And there are ways," he said, "while we live, if not of putting the candle out, at least of hiding it a little while, in love or poetry; every man has his own way, according to his nature and powers; they are imperfect, but they are all we have while we are shut into the lighted room. In death, I think, the walls go down, the lights blow out; that is all, for death is not a change of state but a change of lodging; it is an incident in a continuous immortality."

When they had been a long time quiet, she said: "Couldn't you write that to-night—as you have told it to me? Mightn't you, Piers? Isn't that possible—when I've gone, and you're alone here?"

"To-night, when I'm 'alone here'—who knows? Perhaps I shall write a poem; perhaps die; perhaps I shall start for Sparkenbroke and, in the morning, when you wake—" and he was silent, for words had begun to look up from his meditation. He felt his way towards them with the sick uncertainty of one schooled by failure.

> *Be in suspense, inquiring, glassy mind*
> *And like a window flung let in the air.*
> *To-night . . .*

His hand stretched across the table at the end of Mary's couch for a small tablet of paper and a pencil that lay there.

> *Be in suspense, inquiring, glassy mind*
> *And like a window flung admit the air.*
> *To-night my spirit waits*
> *Tip-toe . . .*

The idea itself was waiting, unborn, and Mary saw the
pencil-case slide down his fingers until the miniature
galleon carved at its end lay on the paper, throwing there
the tiny shadow of its sails. His eyes rested on her face,
but whether he saw her and, if so, in what aspect, she
could not tell.

When he was alone, Sparkenbroke went to his bedroom and sat down before the manuscript of *Tristan*, but
the poem struggling for life was between him and his
story, and in the stress of a profound confusion he began
to move uneasily about the room, his mind advancing
sometimes towards that whiteness or abstraction, that
lull of conscious intellect which was, in him, a prelude to
creative impact. But the impact itself was withheld, the
whiteness grew scarred and thin, until, like a man that
demands sleep but cannot find it, he became aware of
himself, of his futile wandering to and fro, of the ache of
his limbs, the desires of his body, his exile from peace, of
Tristan unwritten; and to quiet himself in action he
changed for the night and put on the dressing-gown in
which it was his habit to work. He returned then to the
fire in the Long Room. The window-curtains were still
undrawn and he crossed the room towards them, but his
hand dropped from their folds. Across the courtyard
and above him, a light was extinguished behind Mary's
shutters, and his imagination sprang to her, presenting
her to him in many aspects—now in the goldsmith's
shop, now on the ramparts, now in such a sensual blaze
as outshone her identity. He imagined then neither her
face nor her body nor any pleasure in them, but a later
condition of appeasement, itself a death. Not to enjoy
but to have enjoyed her was the compulsion upon him;
to be rid of desire, that he and she, as they really were,
might emerge from its obscurity; and it seemed to him
that he was lying at her side, neither seeing nor touching
her but aware of her presence, and that, in release from
the senses by penetration of them, he was possessed of
an assured expectancy, in common with her, that trans-

cended their former love in the flesh. "Transcended"—
a fine-sounding word! And he turned on himself with
savage contempt, saying that his mind was diseased, not
in its desire for her body, but in its refusal to recognize
appetite for what it was. He had believed that he loved
her; his thought had used the word, which now mocked and
failed him, and mocked his scruples above all else. Take
and forget—or be rid of her! She was as other women
were; why was he not as he had been in his approach to
them? And, his mind swinging full-circle, he knew that
in his approach to no woman had he been the sensualist
of his affectation; he had been seeking always what he
had discovered in her—and he remembered anew her
power to absolve him and his assurance that from her
might spring the miracles of his necessity. His love for
her became single and happy; he was able to yield
himself to it, seeing her now in that aspect of finality,
exempt from the senses, in which she had appeared when
first his poem had arisen in his mind. Mightn't you,
Piers? he heard her say. Isn't it possible when I've gone,
and you're alone here? The desire to write and the
knowledge of what was to be written awoke in him. As
he turned from the window, his opening verses reappeared,
and he stretched himself out beside the hearth, pencil
in hand.

> *Be in suspense, inquiring, glassy mind,*
> *And like a window flung let in the air.*
> *To-night my spirit waits*
> *Tip-toe and would be gone*
> *To light original, not of the moon*
> *Or sun, but more familiar, that once*
> *Dissolved the petty barrier of this eye,*
> *And down the rings of being*
> *Its endless glow outspread.*
>
> *Starred as the night beyond my dazzled pane—*
> *Which, for a candle, shuts Orion out—*
> *My expectation flows:*
> *Now leaps, now quickens to a final rhythm*

And throb of stillness at the core of fever
Where I from what I am
Is not to be distinguished,
Nor anything from love.

If time should break, then must Orion enter
And this candle, in death, go out . . .

CHAPTER EIGHT

On her way to bed she visited Helen. "Did you post your letter?" Helen asked, and, being answered, closed her eyes and said no more. When Mary kissed her, there was no response. "Is she asleep?" But the nurse shook her head; and Mary continued on her way up the straight staircase that led from Helen's door to her own.

There, in conformity with her habit not to loiter over anything, she began at once to undress, but, in the midst of her undressing, hesitated, thought having stayed her hands. The thread of memory snapped and she found herself barefoot and isolated, staring at the fan of shadow above the fireplace. Why am I standing here? and to provide herself with reason she took wood from the chest and put it on a dying fire. The day is over, she thought; I ought not to have made up the fire. It will flame and crackle when I try to sleep and its light flow under my canopy. She might have thrust the new log aside, for it was not kindled, but instead she scraped the charred fragments beneath it with a dry olive twig until a beading of sparks appeared among the ash, and on this she blew until narrow, green tongues darted, like lizards, from the crevices. The warmth on her cheeks reminded her that she was quickening a fire for which there was no use, and, jerking back her head in impatience of her own folly, she rose and went to the table on which her mirror stood. There, when she had lighted the candles, she began with sharp, vigorous movement to brush out her hair.

The steady rhythm and its familiarity comforted her;

there was nothing strange in them. Her plain ebony-backed
brushes had a silver monogram, M.L.; they belonged to
her girlhood and Helen had advised her to travel with
them, leaving her silver in tissue-paper at home. Beside the
mirror was a little heap of books: the poems of Browning,
a Bible, a Guide to Pisa, *Piccolo Mondo Antico* of Fogazzaro
and the Italian dictionary that was its laborious companion,
a map—*Pianta di Lucca*, and a neat blue volume lettered
in gold: *Journal*. She had neglected *Piccolo Mondo Antico;*
it had been bought in Genoa and she was to have read at
least five pages a day that her Italian might benefit; in all,
four pages only had been read; and, glad of so innocent a
reason for self-reproof, she drew it from the pile. But its
words were not only without meaning, they were without
sound in her mind. To gaze at the print, reading the same
group of syllables over and over again, was to be reminded
of the obsession that had lain behind all her actions since
she entered the room and against which these actions, even
the making of sparks with an olive twig, had been a form
of protection. Now, lowering the book, she determined to
run away no more but to face what she had to face, and she
tried to express her mood in terms she understood. It is as
though this were a last day, she thought, the last day of
something—I don't know what; the day in late October
when one says: here's the winter, how little I've done with
the year! the day that the Rector says comes to everyone,
when you wake up one morning and say for the first time:
I'm an old man! I'm an old woman! and look back. It is as
though someone were dying, she thought.

Fogazzaro was returned to the pile. She stared at the
Journal and, though in imagination she heard Piers's mocking voice dictating it, she was determined that she must
have the self-control to write.

"In the morning some shopping, letters. Nothing much.
Wrote to George. I believe Helen is desperately ill. She
was almost unconscious when I went in to-night. She
asked—had I posted my letter, but that was all. I said:
was she asleep? Nurse said no, not asleep. In the afternoon
went into the cathedral late; it was almost shutting.

Ilaria's tomb. I am glad I went. *Always remember when you read this book.*"

She dropped her head on to her arms, thrown suddenly across the inky page.

"O Piers, my darling, my darling, I wish the day wasn't over! I wish it were all beginning again! And I wish——"

She looked up into her mirror, but could find no wickedness in her face. Her Journal was smudged and she left it open. Suddenly tears flooded her eyes, her lower lip twitched upon her teeth, and a thick, soft cry came from her throat. She extinguished the table-candle, ran across the stone floor, flung herself on to the bed and lay there, panting and trembling, until her body was gripped by cold. Then she crept into the bed, to lie with the sheet overlapping her mouth and one candle burning. The new log she had added to the fire took flame, but its gleam, when her candle was blown out, slumbered and became fixed. Perhaps she had fallen asleep and awakened again. She was warm now, and when her mind said to her: always remember when you read this book, she did not know what it was she must remember. You have been nearer to me to-day, she said, than you have ever been; and it seemed that he answered her in her own words. In this there was a significance, clearly understood between them, which lifted the guilt from their loving each other, and she sighed in release, she smiled at the simplicity of an act that had seemed hitherto darkly confused, and, stretching out her arms across the pillow, yielded herself to him. But though she had supposed that she was lying in her bed, it was not its canopy she saw nor the fire's gleam, but an avenue of trees spined with streaky light, the sky above them, and the form of his head between her and the sky.

The avenue was dissolved, the canopy and the taut creases in it reappeared. Nothing is true, then! Nothing is true, she thought; but was it true after all? and between sleeping and waking she became certain that she was not alone; the mattress sloped away from her, borne down by a weight not hers; and she perceived that she could not now be dreaming, for the texture of the linen sheet was under her finger nail. A figure lay apart from her in the darkness; she listened for the sound of breathing and heard none; she whispered his name and spoke it, but dared not move her own body or her hand to touch·him, for his skin would be glossy as parchment, her fingers would slip from it, no murmur of breath coming from the darkness and he being dead at her side.

She sprang up, awake, her eyes shut, but awake, and threw her arms across the vacancy of the bed where he had seemed to be lying. It was a dream, she said; it was a dream, then; and a great desolation fell upon her, outcast from her dream, as though a world had shrivelled and she were abandoned in the dust of it. Morning was far away; her pillow beneath her hands was mountainous, so that she dared not lie upon it. Her nightgown had fallen open; when she kneeled up, the cold was furry on her breasts; and around her on every side the darkness mounted in sliding icy planes, like sheets of black glass that advanced and receded, passing through one another. Therefore, she clung to her dream and would have returned to it as a hunted beast to its earth, but could not; and out of the struggle of her mind there leapt upon her, like a white animal from the darkness, an understanding of what she had dreamed, for had not George said long ago: He might die at any time? Had not Piers himself said—and seeing, in the penumbra of her dream, him dead in the room where she had left him, she lighted her candle and went out, flame and nightgown streaming in the gust of the stair. A straw of yellow light stretched from Helen's door across her path, the keyhole shone. She observed them because they touched her—a streak on her naked instep, a thin ripple on her fluttered sleeve—but, without questioning their cause, fled on over the stones of the open landing and the alternation of darker and paler darkness which marked on them the rounded forms of the balustrade. A night-wind struck in from the garden, bearing with it, on a slant of rain, the toss and hiss and scatter of distant leaves. Her nightgown swirled taut on breast and thigh, licked to her flesh by the raindrops, but she pressed on from column to column, head bent and hair adrift, the candlestick, in which the candle was now extinguished, loose on her finger as she rocked and ran. The courtyard bridged, she found shelter. An opaque, windless gulf between her and the Long Room was sliced by the watery sheen of china in glazed cabinets. For an instant the trick of light baffled her; then, swept by a new inrush of her dream, she advanced with sagging haste and opened the door.

Piers gazed at her from the hearth, his tablet of paper drooped in his hand. She swayed and, in imagination, smiled, but there was no strength in the muscles of her face. There was no feeling in any part of her except for the nap of a rug within her feet's curling grip. The candlestick slid from a finger limply straightened. Though she listened and continued to listen, she could not hear it fall.

To Sparkenbroke she had not entered, but appeared. He had been aware of no swing of the door, no footstep, no reason to look up from his page, and looking up had found her. The stroke of encounter had pierced him with a tremor the more deep because her being there had, in the first intuitive instant, rung through his mind as a natural fulfilment of his own thought. His poem had continuance in her; for a moment she was a part of it; and when he became alive to her physical presence and her need, he made no exclamation or abrupt movement, for he supposed, from her being uncovered and barefoot, that she was walking in her sleep. When he reached her, she was already falling. She stumbled forward and her weight was in his arms.

He laid her down on the hearth that she might have near heat from the fire, for her side was bitterly cold against his wrist and palm. Kneeling on one knee, he supported her with the other.

"I was dreaming."

"My dear—of what?"

"That you were dead."

"You're deathly cold yourself. Can you lie here while I get something to wrap you in?" and he began to reach behind him for cushions from the sofa, with which to prop her head.

"No," she said, "don't go. Don't go. I'm not ill. The fire's warm. O Piers, don't go."

She made a nestling movement towards him and slackened in his arms. When he kissed her, her lips parted, her eyes looked up at him and closed. His mouth withdrawn, she reached for it again, and after a long time fell away, her head thrown back, her lashes spread upon her cheek, her lips, full and soft as a child's, loose with the breath of surrender. Looking down at her, he tried to tell himself, for his own flattery and reassurance, that her dream was a feminine device to explain her coming to him, but he knew this to be a lie; her dream visibly lingered in the joy of recognition with which, whenever her lids were raised, she saw him. She began to whisper of her dream like a child relating an adventure, but before it was told dropped into silence and hid her face against him, and he, knowing by the assurance of her blood that she was yielded up, observed her, whom the firelight and her frail lawn exposed, in that deliberate suspense of pleasure which was, for him, pleasure itself, and, having watched her, shut out sight in her hair, confirming with touch the pliant firmness of her shoulders, the deep, falling curve of her back, re-discovering in her body the springing fawn-like gentleness which was her character, to be as clearly distinguished here as in her face.

"Lie still," he said; and now, when he released her, she obeyed, and lay stretched upon the rug while he brought a wrap to cover her; and when, returning, he had extinguished the lights in the room and had lifted her in his arms, she did not speak until they had crossed the landing and were at the foot of her own stair. Then she said: "Why did you stop?"

"There's a light under Helen's door," but his answer seemed not to reach her. He carried her into the darkness of her own room and, having laid her in her bed, locked the door, lighted a candle, brought it from the dressing-table and held it at shoulder-level that he might see her. She was sitting up, her arms a little behind her, her weight supported by her hands bent back. An unexpectedness in her appearance puzzled him; his untiring mind, searching for the significant detail, discovered that her sleeves were long and full, fastened by plain, narrow wrist-bands; and he began to smile.

"Why are you smiling?"

He could not tell her that she had seemed a little girl sitting up primly to say good-night; or add that she had asked: Why are you smiling? with the same intonation of mingled surprise and confidence that such a child might have used; and he replied from another stream of thought that he had been watching through her sleeves the shape of her arms.

Such was the tension in her and so great her weariness that she gave her head a small, quick shake in her attempt to rouse herself, to follow the changed direction of his thought, to seize upon what she supposed to be the commonplace.

"The shape of my arms?" she repeated, struggling to keep pace with him. "You mean—bent like this? with a backward kink in them? I suppose it is a funny shape." She twisted her head in an attempt to see them, and so lovely were the outer tautness of her throat and her chin's deeply shadowed inclination that his compassion for her struck at his desire and would have purged it. To save his desire he ran her hair away from her brow with threaded fingers and pressed back that faultless head and kissed her, her lips and the first golden springing of hair at the temple. Desire of the flesh is its own spur; it must drive itself or swerve in a different imagination and, having swerved, return, tormented and denied; and Sparkenbroke shut his mind against the flow of panic in her passionate breath, the entreaty in the pressing of her hands, and, seated on the side of her bed, gathered her to him and soothed her into a panting quietness, that the shadows might be still and she finally passive, her burden on his arm.

"Was your dream this?"

"Yes," she whispered.

But she opened her eyes and said: "All this time, they
—" Her weight increased upon him. She's worn out, he
thought, she's near the end of the tether. But she continued: "All this time, they've been swirling in my mind,
and even now I can't remember." She puckered her brows
and added slowly: "But they were about my dream. They
were about your—your dream too, Piers. More yours than
mine, I think. But about everything that anyone has waited
for."

He did not wish her to speak, but his curiosity was
strong.

"What, Mary? What are you talking about?"

"You remember," she said. "I've known it always, but
you showed me it again. News came—do you remember?
News from a foreign country——"

He said:

> *"News from a foreign country came*
> *As if my treasure and my wealth——"*

"I remember now," she answered. "May I say it? I
should like to say it to you now." And in a low, even voice,
tense with the wonder of personal secrets, she said:

> *"News from a foreign country came*
> *As if my treasure and my wealth lay there;*
> *So much it did my heart inflame,*
> *'Twas wont to call my Soul into mine ear;*
> *Which thither went to meet*
> *The approaching sweet,*
> *And on the threshold stood*
> *To entertain—to entertain the—"*

She said no more. Her breathing was smooth. He dared
not wake her; he would not let her go; and she slept on his
arm. Was she dreaming now—and of him? Seeing himself through her imagination, he laughed inwardly at his
splendours and gallantries that had endowed him with no
splendour an equivalent of this nor so humbled him. She
stirred and shaded her eyes and touched him with her hand.
He blew the candle out. The hours passed. Wasn't there a
saint in whose hands the birds nested and who would not

move until their young were fledged? St. Kevin, he thought, shall be my patron and shall bless me in the morning when I tell myself I've been a fool. Once, in the darkness, he stooped and kissed her; her lips moved under his own; and presently to his accustomed eyes the whiteness of her pillow, then her face itself, became visible, and on the air beside her shutters the first bars of morning appeared.

He himself had fallen into a dreaming lightness of mind when he was startled to full awakening by a knock on the door which was urgently repeated. Let them knock! but the handle was being tried, Mary was stirring, and he knew that when she awoke her first word might be his name. In the darkness she would be confused and frightened; she must have time to gather her wits; and he made haste to relight the candle. But his arm that had supported her was dead; he had to press the box on the table with the weight of a benumbed wrist before he could strike a match; and as the flame drew up, she raised herself in the bed, glanced at the door and at him, and opened her lips. He put his hand across them. When she was in a state to understand, he signalled caution and released her. The knocking continued.

"What is it?"

"It's Nurse—Nurse Craven—will you let me in, please?"

Sparkenbroke crossed the room that he might not be seen, and Mary, opening the door, looked out.

"I'm sorry, Nurse. Is anything wrong? The door was locked. I don't know—What time is it? It isn't morning yet?"

At any rate, Sparkenbroke thought, she has sense enough not to let the woman in, and he heard the nurse saying that Helen was dead. Even a professional nurse can't say that someone is dead without sounding as if she were speaking through a wad of flannel! and his impulse was to appear and watch the grave Scotswoman lose countenance. But impulses of this sort were among those to which he did not yield, and he remained hidden until Mary had followed the nurse downstairs and the sound of the opening and closing of Helen's door told him that he might reach his own room without being seen.

When she had taken Mary into Helen's room, the nurse waited there a little while, observing the two silent figures, the living and the dead, until she was satisfied that the girl had control of herself; then went out.

On her return, she found Mary standing where she had left her, rigid, her fingers interlaced; and, taking from a cupboard a fur of Helen's, wrapped her in it.

"You'll be cold. There's no warmth in what you're wearing."

Mary gathered the fur and said: "Have you sent for the doctor?"

"Just now. There was no chance before."

"Poor Nurse! you were all alone."

"It's no help, Mrs. Hardy, rousing Italian servants. I've roused them now, and if you were to open that door you'd hear them bleating. That's all there is to it. . . . And what there was to be done, I could do."

"But the doctor will be coming soon?"

The nurse lifted her shoulders. "They are trying his telephone," she said. "And now, Mrs. Hardy, you'd better be getting back to your room. It was a pity to disturb you, really, but as you belong to her I thought you'd expect that."

Mary asked how Helen had died, in pain or peacefully, and what she had said.

"That will wait till the morning," the nurse answered, opening the door. "You go up to your own room now. This kind of thing is a shock to some—more than you know at the time. In fact, she didn't say anything—nothing except 'George.'"

"George?"

"That would be her brother?"

"Her brother, yes."

"She said his name over and over, but nothing else I could hear."

Mary's eyes returned to the head on the pillow. Unlike in feature, it was yet George's head. She went back to her bedroom. A candle was still burning at the bedside, but it belonged to her dressing-table and she returned it to its place. The other candlestick—long ago it had slid from her finger, but she had not heard it fall; and slowly, through her seeing of Helen's face and George's face, memories of the night flooded up to her, as water rises through sand. In the morning she would send a cable, George would come out; whether there would be a funeral here she did not know; in a Catholic country there might be difficulties about cremation; and when she perceived the word cremation in front of her she wondered how her mind had reached it, for what she had been thinking of was Piers, and the love she had had for him in her dream, and how, when she awoke, his hand covered her lips. But between the dream and that awaking there had been an interval which her memory struggled to supply; and now all the night appeared before her as it had been. It was only in my dream, she said, that he was my lover, and she did not know what meaning there was for her in this distinction. She felt as she had felt sometimes when her father had related an anecdote of her own childhood, describing a scene with which, though she remembered having had a share in it, her self, now present in her, seemed to have no connexion; and to escape, in this chill hour, from a burning recollection that dazed her by its alien heat, she compelled herself to say that, if she had been Piers's lover in the flesh and not in a dream only, the guilt would have poisoned her life. I should have been an adulteress; but the word was neutral in her mind, no emotion sprang from it, and she began to wonder whether Helen, being dead, was watching her now and whether George, disturbed by Helen's communication, was shaken in his sleep. In the kitchen at the Rectory, were the maids already brewing their morning tea? The Rector was awake in his bed, staring up at the dark ceiling, perhaps unable to move.

What do you do if you wake so early?

I say verses to myself. The early morning, until the sun is up, is not a good time in which to let the mind wander.

But do you say them aloud?

Under the blanket, he had answered. I learnt the trick when I was a boy at school, and Mary imagined him with the bedclothes drawn up and his tall, narrow head lifted by the pillow, tranquilly repeating verses into their folds. The narrowness of the skull was his own, but in other things it was George's head, it was Helen's also. George would continue to sleep until his can of hot water was clattered against his door, and Mary was by now so deeply re-entered into her home that she heard the thud of the hot-water can and the maid's retreating footfall in the passage as though she herself were in George's room. She saw his face coming up from the pillow and heard him say, as he always did: That the call? It must be half-past seven. His hand was under his pillow, feeling for his watch. She looked at the back of his head, remarking the way in which the trim edges of his hair sprang away from his ears in two steep curves that gave to the neck an appearance of interrogation which they had laughed over together a dozen times. It's the back of your neck that asks questions and looks surprised! And she began to think how strange it was that she should know so far in advance what the day contained for him. Some time to-day, she said, the telegraph-boy will come up from the village and you will hear that Helen is dead, but he didn't answer her; for him Helen was still alive; for him, none of the events of that night had yet any being.

She pushed back the shutters from her window that overlooked the garden. The sky was growing pale behind the trees on the rampart. Night was draining away, but morning had not come. George was still asleep and the Rector mumbling his verses; even the kitchen was not yet astir. She drew her fur more closely about her. Helen had bought it for the journey. She had worn it in the ship and on the railway station at Genoa. It was an extravagance, she had said, but George was quite right: the Mediterranean can be very treacherous. Hearing the words, Mary understood, with an understanding hitherto benumbed in her, that Helen's life was over, her ambition annulled, her flame of kindness put out. This was the journey through Italy that she had so long desired and waited for with so excellent a patience. For me, Lucca has been an enchanted place, Mary thought, and I have thought of nothing but my own enchantment; even when I was sitting with her I was living in my secret. She remembered that Helen had asked her to read aloud the guide-book to Florence. If we had a second copy, Helen had said, I could look at the pictures and follow the maps while you were reading. It would be like walking through the streets together, and when we go there—Until now, Mary had not given another thought to the second guide-book. O Helen, you were so good to me when I was little, and afterwards when I was unhappy! but she dared not cry, for she knew that Helen would despise her for weeping over the past unless she had courage to be done with it. She heard herself telling Piers that they must see each other no more, and it seemed strange to her that, though she should say this, the winter days would go by at Sparkenbroke Green; at Christmas-time she would decorate the pulpit and the lectern; spring would come and other springs follow it.

CHAPTER NINE

"IF we dine early and drive into Pisa afterwards we shall
have time enough to meet him," Sparkenbroke said.

"At what time dinner?"

"Say, at seven."

Mary repeated "At seven" and would have gone out,
but he checked her:

"What shall you do until then?"

She answered, in the curbed, impersonal tone to which
he had become accustomed in her since Helen's death,
that she would read for a little while. "Unless," she
added, looking away from him towards the nurse, "you
would like a walk."

What the nurse replied he forgot as soon as she and
Mary were gone out of the Long Room together. Soon
from his window he saw the woman, with her cloak drawn
together by her folded arms, pacing the garden—round
the pergola clockwise, across the diagonal path into the
full afternoon light, which, shining over the trees,
dappled her starched linen and long, sheep-like face
with irrelevant flecks of gold, then round the pergola
anti-clockwise, across the other diagonal—on and on,
perhaps counting her circuits like a colonel's lady on
the deck of a liner, perhaps composing one of the letters
she was eternally writing to her relations in Carnoustie:
There are one or two letters I must write to Carnoustie.
He had supposed Carnoustie to be a person until he
discovered that it was a town, near Dundee, in which
Nurse Craven had been born. Though she had lived in
Italy nine years, Carnoustie was "hame"; she had the

gift of speaking of it as though it followed her about and were always within range of her bicycle. Round and round the garden; nose up, arms folded, a loyal citizen of Carnoustie; Sparkenbroke turned abruptly from the window. Three women: one dead, one married, one a Scot—all chaste.

One of them had, in effect, thanked him for having allowed her chastity to continue; and he remembered, with a shadowy smile at his own expense—for who before had been thanked for such restraint and lived?—how, on the morning of Helen's death, Mary had come to him, and with the tense, white lips of a novice taking her final vows, had said that she was grateful to him and that now her mind was made up; one couldn't lead two lives, not two lives of two different kinds as if one were two different people, could one? and she had decided; after she went from Lucca, they must not see each other again.

Then you will be leaving the Rectory? he had said.

Leaving it?

Or am I to sell Sparkenbroke House? You haven't forgotten that our homes are in the same village?

Because his voice was angry, she had flushed and dropped into silence.

What did you expect? he had cried. A pious renunciation? Am I to be a monk because it suits you to turn nun? You must remember that I haven't Abélard's advantages.

Little, paltry sneers, the meaner because she, knowing nothing of Abélard's story, dared not answer, and had stood, uncomprehending, beneath the lash of his tongue—she who had come to him in a passion of renouncement. And he had let her go, having icily repaid, in humiliating her, the humiliation that he himself had, in retrospect, experienced. "Lines to a Lady who thanked him for not having lain with her. . . ." His contempt for himself had flared up again, and since that morning he had allowed Mary to go her own way. His escape from the confusions of his life was always in his writing—if he could write—and since Helen's death he had found it easy to tell of how Nicodemus cut down the cedar-tree and prepared it that he might begin to carve when the wood was ready, and how, while busy with axe and knife, he held Jesus in his mind and looked for him continually within the forms of the wood. The poem was done; Sparkenbroke longed to tell Mary that it was done at last, but had not spoken of it to her; and now the story of Tristan was stirring again in him. But there is nothing I can do to-day, he thought; this evening George will be here; there's nothing to be done until they are all out of the house. In two days, in three days at most, the palazzo will be empty again. I shall come in from the ramparts and find myself at my table, a page written; for the blessed fog will come down on me, shutting out all things; and in a few months I shall go to bed one night—"*Tristan* is done!" and wake next morning to remember that *Tristan* is done. Meanwhile——

He turned over the leaves of his manuscript, rose and went again to the window of the Long Room. The garden was empty. Nurse Craven was writing her letters to Carnoustie. But Mary? He crossed the landing, climbed the stairs, knocked at her door.

She rose as he entered, a book sliding to the floor from her lap.

"Come out," he said.

"Where?"

"Pisa—the country—somewhere."

"Why now?"

"I want you to."

"I thought you were angry with me?"

"Whenever I seem to be angry with you, you can take it that I'm angry with myself."

"Why should you be? That's what I didn't understand."

"Let's not try to understand. There's this afternoon, our last together. Come out and live it." And he added, coming near to her. "Is it our last?"

She trembled, almost in his arms. "Piers, you know it must be."

"Why?"

Echoing him, she said: "Let's not try to understand—now."

"Then, come out. I want that. And you?"

"You know I do," she said. "When you are near me, I want what you want. That's *why*, Piers—why I said what I did."

"That I must be a monk and you a nun?" He smiled. "Leave it to the gods. They'll decide anyway."

"But we have our wills, Piers."

"That may be," he answered. "At any rate we have this afternoon. I have written your Nicodemus passage."

"When?"

"The last two days—since Helen died."

"Read it to me!"

He shook his head. "It will wait. Daylight won't."

Her determination was fixed—now the more firmly because, by his presence, by every breath of the autumn air, by each warm scent of leaf and flower, she was tempted to reverse it and to play with the future, saying: Next April, next May, when spring is in Derry's Wood, then— It would have been easy to pretend that she might keep a part of her love for him and by will set bounds to it. He had laughed at her solemn renunciation. Never, never, never—monk and nun—perhaps it was to be laughed at! It was to be laughed at if you believed that even to be lovers in the body—if it came to that—was a pleasure without significance or pledge. But she did not believe it. Nor did he. She knew him well enough, and loved him well enough, to be aware that, whatever sensual mask he might wear, pleasure was not for him an end. By the act of love between them all her former life would be cancelled. She had chosen, and must stand by her choice.

This was their last afternoon together, and, as they left the city by the road that passes through Diecimo and Bettone on its way to Bagni di Lucca, she wished Piers also to recognize the finality of their parting so that, until they parted, they might be at peace: not to mock at her renunciation and refuse to believe in it, but to give it strength by his acceptance of it. Though it was inevitable that they should meet in the company of others when he visited Sparkenbroke, she wished him to promise that he would never seek her out, never write to her, never use his power over her.

The road, lined with silver birch, by which they had been travelling was left behind. A small town, Ponte a Moriano, appeared ahead. Before we enter the town, she thought, I will ask for his pledge, but at the outskirts a little stream shone at the roadside and Piers said:

"Look. I love streams that flow close to a road. Perhaps because I used to play in the stream at the bottom of the churchyard at home."

He drove on, through the town, past the bridge spanning the Serchio, and she had not said what she intended to say. She lay back, treasuring the instants and thinking that now, whenever she crossed from the Rectory to the church, she would be reminded of the stream at Ponte a Moriano. Is that true? When I'm old and Piers, it may be, is dead, shall I remember, day by day, this stream at Ponte a Moriano? Is this the past? and she looked around desperately to seize it, to catch sight of the stream once again, but it was gone. I shall never forget those flaming things hung out on the walls. "What are they—those red-gold pillars?" He said they were maize, set out to dry.

The town died away into a straggle of white cottages and soon they were in open country again, the broad Serchio on their left and, on their right, pine-clad hills, a heavy green, cut by blocks of gold. The river bent sharply, and on either hand were steep mountains that carried the eye upwards to a still, empty sky; the Serchio vanished, a great avenue of planes shut out the sky until suddenly the valley opened on a mass of silver birch. Soon the square tower of Diecimo stood up to their left and ahead of them was another village, Bettone, which seemed asleep and the more asleep because in one of its higher windows was a piece of red material, perhaps a petticoat, which hung, limp and dead, on the sunlit wall as though it had been forgotten.

Mary did not speak. If she was silent, Piers would drive
on and on, and the Serchio for ever curl and vanish and
return. Formerly dark and sad beneath mountainous
shadows, the river took on now a milky olive green,
which, as the water flowed shallow across its stones,
whitened into patches that had the texture of silk, and
round these patches appeared a thousand tiny crests, a
tracery of white at once so alive, so rigid, so frail that
Mary could not let it pass. She touched Piers's arm.

"May we stop?"

He stopped and shut off his engine. Then she could hear
the water.

I wonder: shall I come to Italy again? and after a little
while she silently consented that he should drive on.

That she should be fallen into so long a meditation
pleased him. Nothing in her was lovelier than this repose,
and he did not disturb her, knowing that soon enough
she would awake from it. Her eyes would glance at him
with shy recognition, then be raised fully to his as though
she were saying: where have I been?

At Borgo a Mozzano, she turned her head towards the
Devil's Bridge but did not speak of it; perhaps the fantasy
of its wild sweep skyward and of its irregular arches,
its air of having been raised up by a stroke of magic,
flowed with her imagining; she let it pass, and not until
the first village of the Bagni was gone by and they were
climbing through the chestnut woods did she say: "Tell
me about this, Piers. Why didn't we come here before?
She was looking about her now, and when he stopped the
car she sprang out and would have all the history of the
Bagni from him, so eager was she to people the villages
with their former inhabitants—with Montaigne and Heine
and the Grand Dukes of Tuscany. They went to the Casa
Buonvisi, but it was shut.

"Do you want to have it opened?"

"No," she said. "Let's remember it as it is. Look—
there's Shelley at the window!"

He wheeled swiftly, entrapped and startled, but this she
did not observe, having laid no trap, and they turned away

from the house's blank, austere face to pursue a wooded path until a branch of it led them again into the sunlit quietness of the village.

To him it seemed that he was discovering her anew. She was young as she had been before her marriage, asking him questions that appeared to spring from ignorance but were full of miraculous, intuitive chances; she was gay and quiet, like the torrent of the Lima which they saw now and then, through the trees, in the valley below. When she put a branch aside and held it that it might not strike him, when she rubbed a leaf between her hands and held her hand to his face that he might have the scent of it, when she sat beside him at a *caffè* and asked suddenly if he could repeat now the lines he had written of Nicodemus, he was enthralled by her. He had not known the lines; now he could speak them as though his handwriting lay before him; and he searched her face, thinking: I cannot lose her; I dare not. The thought, which at first had been no more than an undefined impulse to maintain her in his sight moment by moment, startled him by taking the form of these words: I cannot lose her; I dare not; for thought that crystallizes in words becomes an incantation, it seems no longer to issue from within the mind or be subject to the amendments of reason, it assumes the power of an external command; and Sparkenbroke, wishing by speech to thrust this compulsion from him, said:

"You shall tell me. In what way are you different from other women?"

Even while he was asking this question, he knew that the same compulsion had forced him to ask it. How lightly it had been spoken—as if it were the small talk of flattery! And how unanswerable it was! A question to provoke, in another woman, a smile, a glance, a pretty avoidance: but he knew that she would answer it.

"Perhaps," she said, "I seem different for you be-cause—" At that she broke off and looked at him with grave doubt as though she were afraid of saying something foolish. "Do you remember telling me once that men were like the seeds of plants? They need a place in which to lie hidden during the winter so that in the spring—" While she spoke, wishing only to say what she had to say before the memory of it was broken or her voice broken by knowledge that she was speaking to him now, intimately, for the last time, she looked at the edge of the table and the scratches on its paint, and the still, matted head of a dog that stared up from the road, recording them. For an instant she shut her eyes that these things might be gone, as soon they would be gone for ever, and she have the joy of rediscovering them, still present in her sight. She touched the table with her bare hand; then continued: "But plants, you said, have the earth; man has only his imagination, and he uses it always for one purpose."

"'For one purpose'?" he repeated.

"I was trying to remember what you said. 'He uses it to create the darkness from which he may come again to his light.' I think that was what you said. It was one day in Derry's Cottage. You had been talking of Tristan."

"I have forgotten it," he answered, "all of it—even the circumstance."

"You were telling me why, for Tristan, Iseult was different from all other women. She was his earth."

He remembered neither the words themselves nor the thought behind them; they were as new to him as if they had originated in her.

"And Iseult?" he asked.

"You said that, for her, Tristan was different from all other men for the same reason. But I didn't think that could be true," she added. "I don't believe that women renew themselves in the same way. They go back into the race. I never think of myself—myself separately—as going on after I am dead. It seems not to matter. Only that I should have children who don't die until they have had children in their turn. I don't know why. But I do know, deep, deep down in me, that that is what love would mean to me in the end."

The sun had moved away from their table; a low wind was turning the chestnut leaves; the dog stood in the road and stared.

"That's why I can't lead two lives," she said, throwing towards him a glance that besought him to understand what she herself as yet so little understood. "Only one life with all of me."

Though she knew within her that the end of her association with Piers was come, she yet felt that a miracle must deliver her, and, without guessing at its means, imagined its accomplishment, allowing herself to think: after all we need not part, all that is delusion; and yielding herself to the joy of awaking from nightmare. We are together always; his children are mine, my life is his— and she looked up at him as if this were indeed true. But his face was turned away and words began to stumble from her. She heard herself trying to tell him that it was something inside herself, instinct, character —something that—but she was crushed by the futility of words and, in the end, could only repeat "with all of me, with all of me" as if, in this phrase, were contained the whole nature of the love that was being wasted before her eyes.

He knew that if now he were to ask for her life, she would yield it. A movement of his hand, a word spoken, and he would see in her eyes that blind cancellation of judgment with which she would cast herself upon her in-tuition. I cannot lose her, I dare not, he had said, but the words were now an echo; he knew that the moment of opportunity was passing, and let it pass.

As though she had been within his mind, she said: "This is good-bye, Piers."

"Now? Here?"

"I would rather it here—on this little pavement—in the street almost. I couldn't kiss you, or touch you, and say good-bye. But first promise me. Promise me one thing first. Let me go. Never find me again. Without you, I can become again what I was."

"Then we will go to Pisa," he said, "and meet the train."

"But first—let me go. Give me your word."

He could smile now. "What am I to swear?"

"Never to come near me. Never to call me."

"Such faith in my word? What am I to swear by?"

"By your work. That all you write may be corrupt and false if——"

His face hardened.

"Do you mean that? It is final."

"I know."

"So be it." And, having said this, he added: "We are dead to each other. You wished it."

She nodded, very pale. "I saw no other way to live."

"Then we start for Pisa." He held out his hand to her and she took it.

"When I'm gone," she said, "you will write your own work as though I didn't exist?"

"I suppose so. That's part of the oath. The reason of it."

They drove to Pisa at speed and in a light rapidly decreasing. In the Bagni di Lucca there had been, under the chestnuts, an illusion of an English afternoon late in summer; beside the Arno was a mild winter's night.

They were in doubt whether they should dine before meeting the train. George would probably have eaten nothing, and they decided to wait and dine with him before returning to Lucca.

"What on earth shall we talk to him about?" Sparkenbroke said. "Poor devil, he's coming in on the last act without knowing it."

"He will ask about Helen," Mary said, remembering her for the first time in many hours. "He will ask if we were with her when she died, and when we have said, no, the nurse didn't call anyone until she was dead, he will say: 'Never mind. These things can't be helped.' But he will be thinking that she was abroad and alone."

"And you will be thinking that you were asleep in my arms!"

"Why do you say that so bitterly?"

"Because these remorseful retrospects drive me mad. Let's put the car up and then——"

"Then?"

"What is there to do except wander round the town like a pair of tourists, until it's time for the train?"

Turning away from the riverside, they went up the Via Solferino. Mary knew that if she spoke he would reply now in mocking anger, wounding himself by his own unreason, but if she was silent the mood of violence would pass; he would speak suddenly of some new subject, and with a special, petitioning grace. She longed for this, that their last hour together might not be darkened by his evil mood, and often, as they went through the empty street, she looked up at him in the extreme anguish of love that cannot hate even cruelty itself. But his bitterness was in him yet and, when they came to the great open space of the Piazza del Duomo, he took her by the arm and said:

"Can you hear the truth or are you afraid of it?"

"I'm not afraid."

"I thought I loved you," he said. "I flattered myself with that. Because I left you untouched that night, I flattered myself with it. To-day at that table there was one instant when I might have had you. I said nothing and did nothing. I might have had all of you. You would have come blindly."

"Not blindly," she answered. "I should have come."

"I said nothing and did nothing—deliberately," he repeated. "It was a careful, mean, cowardly choice. Not for your sake. Not for George's—I didn't think of him. I thought of being shut out from Sparkenbroke. I weighed up everything, like a grocer with his scales: my son, my position, my independence, the continuity of my present life—yes, my wife's money too: that on one side. On the other, you—and what I saw then was not you, but your body; I could sleep with her in Florence to-night; and I saw the morning, and exile and poverty—a half-poverty— and the discovery that, after all, you were just a naked body to be covered up and left. And at the same time—that all this was lies; my final truth was in you if I could discover it; but I couldn't—it was like something visible under the surface of water; I couldn't lay hold of it. I said nothing and did nothing, deliberately."

She wished to cry out that if what he said were true

he could not have spoken it, but she was beyond the
choice of language; disconnected words fell from her,
and he, breaking in upon her, replied:

"It is true. There was a dog standing in the road. My
eyes were fixed on it because I dared not look at you.
All that calculation was in my mind."

"O Piers," she cried. "Why must you remember only
what seems hateful in yourself? It's a kind of suffering
personal to you—a kind of penance. Such agony to watch
—and love you! Like watching you cut and cut yourself
with knives!" Swaying to and fro, her hands gripping
her own shoulders: "To watch and love you! Now. Now.
To-night. . . . O Piers, I'm cold. . . . My darling, I have
loved you. And I've failed."

"Not you, but I," he said with sudden calm. "You
would have re-created yourself for me; there is no greater
genius than that. I have worshipped and desired you—
and that is all; it is I who have failed. I think I am
without the power to love. In the end," he added, "all
failures are one. There is no failure except failure of the
imagination."

A clock began to strike.

"Now it is time," he said.

She followed him silently. They walked through narrow,
arcaded streets until they came to the place where the car
had been left and drove across the river towards the station.

"This was the bridge," she said abruptly.

"The bridge?"

"You stopped my cab."

He glanced at her. "For good or evil?"

On the platform they learned that the train was late.
Standing at Sparkenbroke's side, Mary said:

"Do you remember that letter of yours, from Aix—to
George—the first after you went?"

"Yes."

"It was in a train George gave it to me."

Passengers for Rome were struggling up the platform
with hand-luggage and pillows. A general movement of
their heads announced the train. Looking for George in

the windows of the corridor, Mary saw a figure that she
supposed to be his.

"I saw him. He's in the second coach.'

They began to walk up the train together. He was leaning from the window, swinging a small bag at the full
length of his arm, and calling "*porteur, porteur!*" as though
he were in France.

Piers took the bag.

"Here you are, George. You've forgotten the Alps."

George's eyes looked swiftly across Piers's shoulder.
Finding her, they changed; their weariness vanished; she
saw his lips move, they were speaking her name. Across
the little distance she waved to him.

George handed his luggage down. "Only three pieces.
One, two, three."

He disappeared among the throng in the corridor. She
stood beside his luggage and waited.

CHAPTER TEN

THE time will pass, Sparkenbroke said within him, the time will pass. The phrase ran like a jingle in his head; he could not exclude it; and when George, comparing his watch with the clock on the mantelshelf, said, in the quiet, deliberate voice he had used since his coming to Lucca, that time passed very slowly at this hour of the night, there was a temptation to laugh, not at him but at the insane, clashing appositeness of his words. But Sparkenbroke dared not laugh, for George would have asked what he was laughing at.

Mary looked up from the stool on which she was sitting by the fire. "It's having nothing to do," she replied. "With a train in two hours, it seems useless even to read."

"Two hours and twenty minutes," George answered, giving a turn to the winding-knob of his watch as if he were going to bed. "I suppose there's no doubt of your time-table, Piers? It looked an old one."

"None. I've confirmed the train. Pisa, one forty-three."

"Good." The watch was slipped away and George brought out his wallet. "You're quite right. The time's on the sleeper-ticket," and he talked with Mary of their journey to England, she asking the questions he expected of her and he answering them.

They were calm, affectionate, commonplace—not a tremor between them. That Helen's body had been lying in the house had commanded them, since George's coming, to a gentle and grave convention—a reliance upon each other, an understanding of each other—foreign to Sparkenbroke. To him death was an ecstasy or nothing; upon

them, seemingly, it had a ceremonial power, the force of
a solemn ritual to command their behaviour. George
wound his watch more quietly because Helen had died;
Mary closed doors more gently. Their conversation had
the formal unworldliness of conversation on the Rectory
lawn before church on Good Friday. George would not
talk of stocks and shares because Helen was dead. But the
body is gone now! Sparkenbroke would have cried out.
Can't you come to life again? Don't you know that within
Mary's black frock—the ridiculous stockinette she bought
in the Via Fillungo—is her living body? Look, there are
the forms of it! She is leaning back; the black stuff is
stretched and pale across her breasts. Don't you see the
nipples pressing upward, the deep fold of her thighs, the
swinging line of shoulder and throat and head—Rembrandt's line?

"What are you smiling at?" George asked.

"That it's possible to see so much and feel so little."

Mary's face came up from the dull glow of the fire.

"Who?" George said, his thoughts elsewhere. "Who is
—what did you say?—seeing much and feeling little?"

"You, George—and I too. And I too," Sparkenbroke
repeated. "That's odd. You have the effect of numbing
me. Do you know that?"

"Numbing you? Well, often I wonder whether you're
not too much alive. A little sedative's no bad thing. What
do you say, Mary?" But she had ceased to listen and made
no answer. "Poor Helen used to say that of you, Piers.
She had a very shrewd eye for human nature. 'It isn't that
Piers feels more than we do,' she said, 'but that he has
never learnt that some feelings are best ignored.'"

"Ignored?" Sparkenbroke echoed. "Can they be?"

"I think they can. At school for instance. In the end
they become numb. That's what courage is—the numbing
of fear. Generally it's action that does the trick. A man's afraid
before he goes over the top—not afterwards!"

"Isn't he?"

Mary turned abruptly.

"Were you ever afraid, Piers? In the war, I mean?"

"I was generally drunk."

"Drunk!"

"Not with alcohol. The kind of intoxication that knows it won't be hit."

"I've heard of men who felt like that," George said, and added solemnly: "Specially protected."

"Specially protected! It wasn't that," Sparkenbroke exclaimed. "I felt as the people must have felt in the fairy-tales when they put on a cloak of darkness—invisible, intangible too, as if in some extraordinary way I had ceased to exist. I wanted to exist. In action, I couldn't. I couldn't fear or have courage or suffer; I couldn't even pity while action lasted."

George's eyes were fixed upon him. "What does that mean if you come down to brass tacks—that you weren't afraid of death or that you wanted it?"

Sparkenbroke smiled and stretched himself. "I expect it means that I wanted to write. Everything means that in the end."

"Except death."

"On the contrary: death above all else." With the im-pulse of one who throws a stone into a pool, he added: "Death and the act of love," but George shook his head. He had taken a pencil from his waistcoat pocket and was making notes for his journey. He announced the time at which they would reach Sparkenbroke Green. "Father will be glad to see you again, my dear."

"It will be lovely to see him."

"I think we had better not talk to him about poor Helen more than we can help."

"Why?" Sparkenbroke put in.

"Why? Oh, because it was he, in a way, who persuaded me to let her make this journey at all. 'If she doesn't go now, she never will,' he said. I told him the risk, but he's a gambler, though he is such an old man. 'Well,' he said, 'there are worse things than dying in Italy if Italy is what you've longed for all your life.' Now this has happened, he may feel, in part, responsible."

"You don't believe that, George—at any rate, you

wouldn't have believed it a week ago. The Rector won't mope over the dead."

"'Mope over the dead'!" Indignation had raised George's voice, but he quieted it; he would not permit himself to be angry. He stood up by the fire and looked again at his watch. "There are one or two last little things I want to put into my bag," and he went out.

Mary was leaning forward, a poker in her hand, and she did not turn round when he was gone.

"Mary." She turned now. "What has happened to you?"

"Happened?"

"You have gone away. Are you dead too?" To test her and himself he added: "In a few minutes George will come back. He will sit here looking at his watch and talking of Helen until it's time to start for Pisa. You and I may never be alone again."

She shifted her body; her eyes closed and opened; the weight of the poker carried her hand back from the wrist; but she did not answer. How far they had become separated since George's coming! George had wanted to talk of Helen only—of her last days, every detail of them, what she had said, what books she had been reading; above all, of her early years at Sparkenbroke Green. The effect of his intense absorption in his own and Helen's childhood had been to shut Mary out, and she had acquiesced without resentment or surprise. George, living imaginatively in a world that preceded his marriage, had been fully alive to her only when she spoke of the days in which she had been a schoolgirl and Helen her teacher. Then he had listened eagerly, his face kindled by her memories of Helen, but nothing else in her had roused him, not even her beauty. She had seemed to understand this and expect it, that part of her convention which had established her values as a child and ruled her as a wife quietly reasserting itself in her husband's presence. She had assumed—as she might have assumed that one didn't play cards on Sundays —that he would not wish to share her bed on this funereal visit, and she had been right. George and she, Sparken-

broke thought, have in common sentiments and taboos
that leave me beat.

"Mary, tell me. How did you know that, because Helen
was dead, George would behave as if he were everlastingly
in his Sunday clothes and treat you as—a younger sister."

"I think it's natural," she answered.

"Natural? At any rate it has prevented his being
suspicious of us."

"But, Piers, why should he be suspicious?"

"Knowing me. Knowing the past. And you in my house.
Didn't you expect him to be, perhaps, a little anxious?"
She shook her head. "But you did, Mary, when we went
to the station to meet him that evening. You did until he
came. And then——"

"But, Piers," she exclaimed, "there's nothing to suspect."

"Is there nothing? Kiss me, then."

Her lips trembled, but she smiled a smile almost of in-
dulgence as though she were recognizing that his request
had not been seriously intended. Sparkenbroke's eyes
flickered. Again she was right. He also was numb, not
now desiring her. If she had obeyed and kissed him, their
kiss would have had no impulse warmer than the
curiosity of leave-taking. He was glad she had refused,
and astonished by his gladness as a man is who touches
one of his limbs to discover no feeling in it. "George
sits there between us," he said, "as unaware as a child
that physical desire might exist in the same room with
him. It's like going about with a blind man—of all con-
straints his blind eyes are the most deadening and powerful. Even when he's not here they have power over you—
and over me." He perceived that he was using words as
a release from embarrassment, and by that perception
was silenced.

"When one's very near the end of anything," she said,
"it's strange, isn't it?—there's nothing to say. Like good-
byes on a railway station—there's nothing more to say."

He did not reply; then, suddenly, wishing to provoke
her and spurred by a profound curiosity for the effect of
his words on her and himself, he said: "It was there, by

that hearth, you lay half-frozen in my arms. Your night-gown was patched with rain. Your hair was flecked with it. Your cheeks were wet—rain or tears—I didn't know. And you lay there—in effect, naked. Do you remember?"

"Your face," she said, "I remember that; and a shadow, slantwise, across your cheek-bone, and a patch on the ceiling darker than the rest, and——"

"Go on."

"The feel of your hands."

He held them out. "Aren't they the same hands? . . . It isn't the same world!"

"Yes, Piers, it is."

"You mean——?"

"I love you just the same. I shall always." She took his hands and for an instant hid her face in them. Then, returning to her place by the fire, she said: "I shall remember them against my forehead. Don't touch me again. Even if you drive us to Pisa and say good-bye to us on the platform, don't touch me."

He watched the shoulder muscles under her tautened dress, and, in imagination, felt still the warmth of her face upon his hands. She is alive again, he said, observing her, and to compel response in himself he let his mind run forward. In less than half an hour she would be gone out of this room, never to re-enter it. Not long afterwards he would return from Pisa and cross the hearth on his way to his bedroom. In the morning, when he awoke, he would remember that the house was empty—but even the idea of her absence struck no fire in him. In the morning, he said, I shall write *Tristan*; but the story did not stir in him, and he was touched by fear for his writing. He would have liked to go at once to the manuscript, to read it, to test it, but I must wait until I return from Pisa and she is gone, he thought. When she is gone, will desire for her return? Will the desire to write return? It seemed to him that the two questions were one, and that he was waiting for the pulse of life itself to stir in him again.

CHAPTER ELEVEN

A LITTLE before noon on a morning of late January, Sparkenbroke came from his bedroom where for seven hours he had been working on *Tristan*. The setting of his eyes had now an appearance of extreme depth, and his hands, browned by long exposure in summer and to the rains and winds since summer had passed, were ridged by their smaller bones. The determination of a natural and defiant pride carried his body at an aching stretch.

The Long Room, when he entered it, was filled by that parchment-coloured light which, during a Tuscan winter, marks a sudden fall of temperature and gives to certain rainless days an atmosphere of age, almost of finality, as though everything visible had been painted by a master long ago and was matured beyond possibility of change.

The tablecloth, on which Bissett had set out cheese and olives and wine, had the sculptural gleam of ivory. Sparkenbroke, when he saw that two places had been laid, paused beside the table and turned his head sharply as though to demand the reason of them; but the room was empty, and he remembered that Bissett had driven the car into Pisa to fetch the young painter, Philip Madden, whom he had met at Christmas-time in Rome. Why on earth did I say he might come? Sparkenbroke asked himself. To Madden's request he had replied by telegram, and the impulse which had prompted the telegram was spent.

He plunged his hands into his side-pockets and advanced slowly to the nearest window. It had the same outlook as the window of his bedroom, and this sameness, which had formerly been an element in the joy of his solitudes

in Lucca and a cause, he had supposed, of their fruit-
fulness, was now a pressure on the nerves of his imagination. For a moment he shut his eyes against it, his face
contracted by weariness and disappointment. A thousand
times, since he had been alone, he had stood at one of
these windows, looking out upon this scene and knowing
that behind him lay the sheets of *Tristan*, a story from
which he was separated, and the wintry garden, the
rampart, the bleak, straining trees, had become associated
in his mind with continuous and reasonless failure. But
in art there is always a reason for failure; the first necessity
is to find it—in ourselves, not in our circumstances; only
the fool defeated by his craft blames his circumstances, his
friends, his living-place, his distractions—as well blame
his pen; and I am not defeated by my craft, he said, the
word obeys me. I can write; I have still, in all my impatience, the infinite patience to write, and the sway and
pressure, the supreme secret communication, like the
touch of lovers, between one sentence and the next.

When, after George's going, he had taken up the
chapters already done, he had found himself listening to
the story of a writer whose understanding of Tristan and
Iseult subtly differed from his own. He had, therefore,
re-examined these chapters with elaborate care, at first
for structural error, asking himself whether, in describing
Tristan's boyhood, he had delayed too long his coming to
Cornwall and so, by postponing his journey to Ireland,
unwarrantably excluded Iseult. He had attempted a
revision that began the tale in Ireland, but after three
days had put it aside. The fault was not in his having
described Tristan's boyhood and youth; the architecture
of his narrative was spacious, and Tristan's upbringing
was a just prelude to his meeting with Iseult. It was not
in the choice of opening that the fault lay, and Sparkenbroke had begun again his examination of the text, not
in reluctance to find error in it but in fear lest he should
find none. He would have undertaken, with no sense of
waste or defeat, a rewriting of the whole book, but all
his criticism had failed to discover such a flaw in his

previous structure, or in what he had lately added, as
might enable him to define and reconcile the difference
between them. Each lived, but with a life stubbornly
independent. Whatever he wrote was in profound but
indefinable opposition to what he had written; and, with
a mind dazzled by ineffectual labour, he had gone to
Rome in the week before Christmas, knowing that, if he
could forget *Tristan* for a little while, he might see it
more clearly after his return.

In Rome, during an evening party, Madden had been
introduced. After a little while, he had overcome a shyness
which, in him, took the form of defensive arrogance, and
exchanged it for an abrupt, penetrating honesty that drew
Sparkenbroke to him. The young man had asked if he
might call upon him at his hotel, and he had answered
with genuine regret that he was returning to Lucca in
the morning.

But you will come back?

No, I shall never be in Rome again.

The words had been spoken as though they had been
put into his mouth. It was in the painter's unquestioning
acceptance of them, that Sparkenbroke first perceived their
truth.

Madden had drawn breath and deeply searched his
face. Then I shan't see you again, was all he said. But I
shall remember this.

The expression of his face while he spoke returned to
Sparkenbroke's mind as he stood at the window of the
Long Room, for soon Madden would come, they would
sit opposite each other at the table, and would say—what?
The mood of that evening in Rome was passed. The
young painter that came to Lucca would be a stranger,
and Sparkenbroke blamed himself for having allowed him
to come. I shall be as strange to him, he thought, as I am
to myself. I have nothing to give him.

To ease their re-encounter—for his visitor was jerkily
embarrassed—Sparkenbroke talked of the friends they
had in common at Rome, until Madden, looking up with

a sudden flash under heavy eyebrows accentuated by their being conspicuously darker than his hair, exclaimed: "You're good to me. I know I'm behaving like a fool."

Sparkenbroke laughed aloud in swift, delighted good-humour. "Then tell me why you're 'behaving like a fool' and it will be plain sailing."

"It sounds foolish and sycophantic—but it's not. It seems a kind of miracle to me to be here. Wouldn't it have been to you, if you were—at the beginning?"

"Modesty wasn't ever my gift."

"But it's not modesty!" Madden cried. "That's just it. If I didn't know inside me what I was, you'd be just another celebrity—and I should half hate you; I should be envious. What I like is that you are sure enough of yourself not to hate *me*."

"I wonder," Sparkenbroke replied, "whether I should have had the guts to say that when I was very young."

There was a long silence.

"So you can paint?" Sparkenbroke said.

"No, I can't. Not for ten years. Fifteen perhaps. But I shall then. . . . In fifteen years, I shall be older than you are now."

"Then you'd better see your studio at once," and Sparkenbroke led his guest across the open landing to Helen's room, which he had ordered to be prepared. No preparations had been made there and, leaning over the balustrade, he shouted into the courtyard for servants. Not that room! they cried. Not that room—the one above! The one above Signor Bissett had ordered! Bissett came out and swore at them—a literal translation from the sergeants' mess.

"The orders were clear enough, m'lord. But they don't listen. They talk so, they can't listen—that's my belief," and he began to drive them up from the courtyard as one shoos poultry.

"No. No. Let it be!" Sparkenbroke cried. "Go back and sleep, all of you."

It was Mary's room they had prepared. Since her going, he had not entered it. The bed had been rolled into a corner and the canopy stripped from it. Its posts and the frame of the canopy, standing naked, combined with the great area of empty floor to give the place a special air of desolation.

"This is where you work. Apparently they don't intend you to sleep here."

"I've already been taken to the room where I sleep."

"Well, work," Sparkenbroke said, "and blessings on you. I wish I could. . . . Those are your canvases? Have they brought up all your gear?"

Madden looked slowly about him. "Everything. But I shall want models unless you will sit."

"I shan't sit," Sparkenbroke answered. "I told you so in my telegram."

"Why did you let me come at all?"

"An intuition."

"Of what?"

"I let you come because once you said something that no one else would have said. It was odd. You've forgotten it. Do you remember my saying that I should never be in Rome again? Anyone else would have questioned that. You didn't. There are very few people in this world who know that an imagination is sometimes the equivalent of a fact and can accept it as if it were an accomplished thing, seen with their own eyes. That's why I asked you here. You seemed to be of value to me—in what way I don't yet know."

On his knees among the heap of painting gear that the servants had piled against the eastern wall, Madden looked up at his host. On entering this room, Sparkenbroke had changed. His conversation, except when he spoke for a moment of their encounter in Rome, was quicker and more superficial than it had been, and he seemed unwilling either to go out or to be still in one place. Twice he put his hand on the door, then reversed his plain intention; and, as if his haunted mood were a thing to be warded off by ridicule, he talked incessantly, seeming not to care for reply.

Madden, wandering to and fro in the room while he

ordered his possessions, watched with curiosity the un-
masked, peering expectancy of the face before him. His
hand, sliding along the fireplace ledge on which he had
laid his brushes, encountered some obstacle over which
his fingers closed. It was a book; he took it down and let
its pages run through his fingers until its fly-leaf lay
before him; and, Sparkenbroke's voice being then silent,
read aloud: "Mary Leward on her Confirmation, Easter,
Nineteen hundred and——"

"Is that her book? Give it——" Sparkenbroke was close,
his hand stretched out.

"It's her Bible," Madden answered.

"Why do you say 'it's *her* Bible'—as if you knew her?"

"I have known her all my life—until she married."

"You have known her all her life? Do you mean that you
were a child with her?"

Sparkenbroke sat down on the edge of a table that stood
isolated in the middle of the floor. "Go on," he said, "get
out your easels and things. Shift the furniture to your
liking." A long time afterwards, he added: "She died here
—in this room."

"She died! What do you mean—she isn't dead?"

"It was Helen who died," Sparkenbroke answered. "In
the room under this. . . . *She* slept in this room." He rose
abruptly, an arm impatiently held out to urge Madden
forward. "Come, let's go into the air for an hour before
dark. Come."

On the staircase, he continued: "Your childhood, you
said. Do you mean that you remember no part of your life
so early that she didn't share it?"

"Yes, I suppose that's true."

"Can you describe her? Had she then——"

"What?"

"A potentiality which—awoke—and went to sleep again
as if it had never been?"

Madden said: "Yes. At least I thought she had—with
me. With no one else—with me. But I dare say that was a
boy's vanity. I had the idea in my head that by being with
her I got—or my work got—nourishment. Not from her—

she didn't care the first thing about drawing except whether it was 'like'—not *from* her, but through her."

They were in the courtyard now, waiting until Bissett should bring out their overcoats. Madden was trembling in the confusion of having said too much and of having said it, against his will, falsely, so that Sparkenbroke would suppose—but the voice at his side answered with assurance: "But, in fact, you were not in love with her?"

"No, no," Madden cried, surprised by so much perception and grateful for it. "That's just it. I said it all clumsily, but I wasn't in love with her at all. I'd grown so used to her, you see, day by day as a child—blackberrying and hay parties and charades and church—that, even to the very end, I generally forgot that she was beautiful—except to draw. I must have drawn her a thousand times before she went to——" He hesitated. "Wasn't the place called Sparkenbroke Green?"

"You didn't associate it?"

"I didn't remember it," Madden replied, bringing round his head with the jolt that was his gesture of negation. "I knew she'd married some doctor outside Chelmouth— that's all. I had lent her a picture of mine. She asked if she might take it with her when she went to stay there before her marriage. Then I gave it her for her wedding."

"A picture?"

"Olive-trees. Bathers picnicking under them."

Sparkenbroke recognized the picture suddenly. "That's what I remembered your name by! I've seen it only once. In her bedroom at the Rectory. One of the figures was a portrait of her? But she was never among olive-trees?"

"Oh, that makes no odds!" Madden replied with a laugh. "I could paint her in any setting. I believe I could paint her as she will be when she's eighty." Observing Sparkenbroke's eye and sobered by it, he added: "I told you, didn't I, I must have drawn her a thousand times?"

"And so are in possession?" Sparkenbroke retorted. "You have acquired a long lease on her soul! . . . I dare say you have. There was another painter once, a mild old boy, who had been doing a landscape in my own grounds. I said something—how it arose I don't know—which implied that the oak-tree in his foreground belonged to me. Suddenly he flared up and said: 'Belongs to you? It doesn't. You have no power over it except to kill it, but I have painted it and can paint it again. It's I who possess it if anybody does.' . . . And it's true enough. You have drawn her a thousand times and could draw her again. I can do nothing except kill her."

"Kill her?"

"Not even that, it seems."

Madden's puzzled eyes cleared and brightened. "You mean that you wish me not to talk of her?"

"I mean that an hour ago I believed it possible not to think of her," Sparkenbroke replied, speaking now with slow, tentative eagerness, a submission of his pride, as though to be understood by this boy were necessary to his self-understanding. "The key to living has always appeared to me to be a power to exclude from the mind whatever has become irrelevant to the future. I thought myself master of it. It is for that—that callousness—that I am hated. Do you remember the advice of Theocritus to Nicias? 'There is no other remedy against love, but only the Muses; and this is a gentle medicine . . . but hard to find.' Until now, I have never failed to find it, and, even an hour ago, I thought I had succeeded again. I had 'excluded what was irrelevant to the future'! But there's a catch in that formula as in every other: the gods don't tell us what is relevant and what is not. Nor do they tell us, in each particular instance, what love is—a part of life, a malady to be cured, or the whole of life including the remedy. You take up your pen; you call in the Muses; your mind submits to their discipline; the remedy works, seemingly, as it has always worked; memory shrivels, even desire ceases. 'Now I am free! Now I can write!' you say. But this time, it's only your pen that writes; no, your mind also; and what you write may even be good—but it's anonymous, it isn't yours, you are not there! You don't know why. You aren't tormented by memory or desire. Then, in comes a young man from Rome and pulls down a Bible off a mantelshelf. 'I've known her since she was a child,' he says. 'I've painted her a thousand times. . . . Do you mean,' he says, 'that you wished me not to talk of her?' And you understand that, though memory can be stifled, there is an apprehension, deeper than memory, which continues; and, when he speaks of her, suddenly it is not he but she who is at your side. Look," Sparkenbroke said, "that is the path up to the ramparts. I will come with you another day," and he went back alone.

One safeguard, he thought, has never failed me; and he turned to *Tristan* again. Each day his work was done; a page, two pages, and once fourteen pages were written, always with the knowledge that they were but exercises; they would not stand. At night, before he slept, he read them over, and again in the morning when he awoke; there was no fault but no cry in them; they were like the prayers of a man that looks through the pallor of his faith; the submission of a woman that aches, through the darkness of her lover's body, for another of whom she knows only that this is not he. But each day the work was done, and when, after a fortnight had passed, Madden said to him: "You haven't been to my studio," he was surprised that this was true and answered: "To-morrow, I'll come," but on the stair he turned back and went to his writing-table and all the morning was bound to it.

At midday and in the evening, he and his guest encountered; sometimes, in the early afternoon, they walked or drove together—once to the Bagni di Lucca, often to Pisa; and they neither spoke intimately, nor deliberately avoided speech, of her; she was an acquaintance they had in common of whom, on occasion, it was natural to speak —and pass on; but Sparkenbroke was unable to suppress in himself the shock of her name. It came to him always with a fresh impact, a significance not of memory but of new observation, as her face would have done if she had been present; and he began to know what clothes she was wearing and saw the glint upon the heel of her shoe and the flattening of her wrist as she drew off her glove. It seemed strange to him that Madden could speak of her, when he spoke of her at all, as if her name were, like other names, a means of reference without a special power of evocation—a name only, not a voice, a rhythm of movement, a texture of flesh, a pulse in the air.

One morning—it was the first of March—he went out alone. Snow had fallen in the night, and lay, but not thickly, on the ramparts, which at that hour were almost empty. The countryside was mottled with snow; trees stood up from it with the appearance of black glass; and, within the city, powdered roofs and naked walls were assembled in so complex a pattern of abrupt sparkle and coiled relief that the eye was at once confused and fascinated, as by a canvas, on which pigment has been thickly laid, when it is a little too closely regarded. The world had an air of artificiality and brilliance, as though it were decked for some mysterious festival. He felt suddenly and without reason that a period of desolation was over, that he had been imprisoned and was about to be released, and, looking above him to the fiery steel of the morning sky, drawing in the cold air and tasting it in his mouth, he heard her say, as though she were the interlocutor of his thought: But, Piers, isn't it possible that the question is not so much of there being a *flaw* in the story as of your writing the wrong kind of story? The wrong kind? he replied. There can be only one kind of story when Tristan and Iseult are the subject of it. What else can the legend of Tristan be but a love-story? It is a love-story, she said, but it is a death-story too, and he remembered that he had known this in the beginning. For this reason he had chosen the story of Tristan and Iseult, and now, its origin recalled, it became his own story again. Quickening his pace, he perceived anew the significance of the potion, and of the two sails that might be hoisted—the red sail or the white —to tell Tristan, while the ship was yet far off, whether Iseult was come. She was in the ship, but the wrong sail was hoisted and Tristan deceived; he turned his face away and died; and now Sparkenbroke was within the head of this dying man, and felt the pillow under his cheek, and knew

that his death was not of despair but of ecstasy, a necessary
correspondence with the act of love. They were identical
and alternative, each a transcendence of the temporal exile,
the death as voluntary and as inevitable as the love and the
songs had been. While Tristan loved and sang, while Iseult
loved and heard him, it was this death they had been seeking, and Sparkenbroke, burning in the recapture of his
theme, stood still, and let his eyes, unseeing, fix upon the
city below, until at last he saw the tower of the cathedral
and heard her voice say again: To hold you—to let you go
—it was as if my own life were dying in my arms. Was it
to her that he owed the recovery of his theme? She had led
Nicodemus to the forest and put the axe in his hand; was
it she that must lead Tristan to his death? He hardened his
heart against a superstition so formless. She cares nothing
for painting, Madden had said, except whether it is "like,"
and her critical judgment of literature was no more to be
trusted than her judgment of painting; but had a critical
judgment of literature been necessary to her hearing of the
axe among the cedars? If she were here, he said, she could
not advise me, for she has not the knowledge to give
advice; but, in telling the story to her, I should advise myself, as, in speaking of my life to her, I illumine it. She has
the quality of absolution and renewal, which is the miracle
within the apparent nature of love. Suddenly the word
would be given me, the word of foreseeing or of recovery
which is all that imagination can borrow from outside
itself, and all it needs, for a narrative is like life, solitary,
incapable of being shared. Collaboration is impossible. No
one, of himself, can help or guide an artist; but confession
is not impossible, it is the means by which a man is made
aware of the form of his life and so of his betrayals of that
form, which are sin, and the means by which a narrator is
reminded of the form of his narrative. In life and in art
the completion of a form is not all, but it is necessary to all,
for which reason a man must not kill himself in hatred of
what has been or in impatience for what is to come, but
must be content to die when the form of his life has been
completed. And he must be content, like Aquinas, to lay

aside even his pen if to write should ever cease to be
necessary to the completion of the form of his life. Nothing
is to be clung to for its own sake; nothing attains its final
value until it is abandoned. There is no such thing as loss
of things past: either they were complete and therefore
not to be mourned or they were incomplete and by Nature
rejected. Only the future may be lost, he heard Iseult say,
and, coming down from the ramparts, he knew that the
word had been given him and by whom.

In his room he turned back his manuscript to a scene
in which Tristan had urged upon Iseult that they should
preserve their love against the world by dying together
in the act of love. He had shown her a jewel, carved with
two heads, into which poison might be dropped; let her
wear it upon her breast; it would pierce them in the clip
of love. By the date scribbled on the first of these pages
Sparkenbroke saw that they had been written in the early
days of Mary's absence from Lucca, and now, with shame,
recognized the falseness of them and how in jealousy of
the past, in fear of losing it, in panic-stricken impatience
to seal it with death, Tristan had betrayed the form of his
love. Iseult's refusal, attributed in the manuscript to her
fear of death, had been as false. The shape of the narrative
had been broken; all the succeeding pages had been
written in vain, and Sparkenbroke thrust them aside,
seeing a new way open before him. Tristan held the
jewel in his hand, not proposing its use but telling Iseult
of its power that he might hear her answer. Only the
future may be lost, she said—a reply which, when Tristan
heard it, seemed to have been spoken in his own mind.

Sparkenbroke wrote down her words and, drawing
new paper towards him, set himself to compose the
sentences of which they were the key; but there's time
enough, he exclaimed—now, thank God, there's time
enough; I know what I have to write, it cannot escape
me unless my craft fail, and he had no fear for his
craft. The book lay before him like a valley he must
cross. He needed to be in no haste to begin his journey.

To-day I will write nothing, he said, and rose from the
table in such a lightness of heart as he had not known
for many weeks, the assurance of his purpose alive in
him again. He went up the staircase to Madden's room
without tremor or hesitation, for it seemed that her
presence had declared itself here, and in all the house,
and within him.

After this Sparkenbroke frequently visited the im-
provised studio, staying in the room sometimes for no
more than two or three minutes, sometimes for an hour,
and going out always not abruptly but with a recognizable
finality of decision, as though the purpose of his coming
had been achieved. Apart from these sudden and, for
the most part, silent visits, Madden saw little of his host,
for his own habit was to sleep early and Sparkenbroke's
to work through the night. They met at an evening meal
and after it separated. Sparkenbroke's visits were nevertheless made in the mornings, generally before ten o'clock.
When he slept Madden did not know. Searching his face
for evidences of extreme mental stress, he found only a
certain sharpening of the features, a tightening of the skin
and an abnormal clearness of eye. That, while they
worked, they could thus live together in a privacy within
companionship, created between them a profoundly intimate web of mutual recognitions. There were passages
in his work that Madden wished to paint in solitude. He found that Sparkenbroke never stayed in his
room, and seldom entered it, while he was engaged in
them.

Why he came to the room at all puzzled Madden at
first. The answer that sprang to his mind had failed to
satisfy him. She had slept here; the room was associated
with her; probably she had been his lover—a mood of
romantic or of sensual reminiscence was explicable enough;
but he learned as time passed that Sparkenbroke did not
come in quest of what had been, but of what, for him,
presently existed, of what actually he felt and heard and
saw in the room, and wished to apprehend.

Snow vanished on the day after its fall. The temperature rose sharply and soon there was no fire in the Long Room until the evening.

One night after dinner Sparkenbroke did not return to his writing-table but lingered beside the hearth.

"A night off?" Madden asked.

"For the moment I'm written out."

"A hitch?"

"No. There'll never be a hitch again in this book. A long sleep, that's all."

"You've been making progress?"

Sparkenbroke smiled. "Bissett counted the pages just now. He tells me I've written thirty thousand words in eleven days. It's a miracle if I average more than five thousand a month. . . . Tell me," he said, turning his back on Madden and pushing the logs with the toe of his shoe, "how did you come to choose that pose for your model—on the bed, leaning back, her weight on her arms?"

Madden was at first astonished by the question; then became aware of its relevance to a passionate watchfulness that he had lately observed in Sparkenbroke during his visits to the studio. Once, looking up from his canvas, he had found his host gazing not at the model but through her, his hands wrapped about the edges of the chair-seat, their knuckles whitened by his grip. The harsher evidences of his appearance had been those of fear—as though he had seen a ghost, one would have said—but within his expression of terror had been another that suffused it, an expression of—of what? Madden had lowered his brush and gazed. Of delight? Of discovery? . . . Rather of attainment, as though at the core of fear, of stricken wonder at some new thing revealed to him, there lay—but Madden had not been able further to define what he saw; he was not concerned with words, but with visible forms; in paint, his definition, already startlingly present in his consciousness, might have been expressed, and he had watched the thread of light within the rim of Sparkenbroke's upper lid, and the filament of it mirrored across the iris, which had given to the eye its openness and distinguished from empty staring the intense activity of its vision.

"Did you choose the pose—or did she?" Sparkenbroke repeated now.

"I did."

"In what way? By chance? . . . By the light, I should have expected you to put her anywhere except in that corner."

"I remember," Madden answered slowly. "On the day I finished the picture of her in her working-dress I tried to pose her for the figure. Nothing was right and I sent her away. I'd had a composition in my mind but in that room I couldn't get it. I remember standing up by the fire, wondering what the devil was wrong and in some odd way deeply troubled. It was absurd, I suppose. A kind of despair, as if there were something in the room itself which stood between me and my work. And then"—he hesitated and shifted in his chair—"I felt, suddenly, the—the reach —the reaching out from a distance—of a new idea. It was like——"

"I'll tell you what it was like," Sparkenbroke interrupted. "It was like the sound of feet—but soundless; the knowledge of footsteps. Or closer—the knowledge that there's someone behind you, in the room, who has been there all the time—someone, or something, that in an instant you'll see—see and touch and be lost in."

Madden waited; then drew breath. "I saw what I had to paint," he said with a little gasping sigh. "Everything— the muscles of the side, the dome of the forward shoulder thrust up, the pattern made by the weighted arms . . ." With his forefinger he was drawing in the air the two dominating lines when his hand paused and dropped. "For you," he began, "that pose had——"

"A special force—yes."

"I remember your face, when you saw it. Were you——"

"Why should we ask each other questions that can't be answered?" Sparkenbroke cried: "Concealing, elaborating, perhaps forgetting, we shall begin to lie. The pose came to you with special vividness and strength. It was familiar to me. Those are the facts—facts precisely of the kind that hoodwink fools; in themselves they may have no significance. At best they are illustrations to a book which we shall understand, perhaps, when we have read all of it. They are not part of the text itself."

He had wished by the tones of reason to steady his mind, but his was an imagination little submissive to reason, and there appeared before him again that instant of the day spent at the Bagni di Lucca on which her life, if he had claimed it, would have been yielded to him. It was a recollection that he had come to hate as one hates the eyes of a man one has betrayed, but he could not escape from it. Only the future can be lost, he heard Iseult say, and he knew that he had lost the future then, at the small, sunlit table, while the dog sat in the road and stared at them.

His work remained and Madden's companionship. Soon *Tristan* would be finished, and the day on which Madden must return to Rome was spoken of one afternoon as they set out together for the ramparts by way of Santa Maria Forisportam. "Very well," Sparkenbroke said, "you must go when you please."

As they reached the carriageway of the ramparts he turned abruptly into one of the bastions, crossed the little copse planted there, and sat on a wooden bench overlooking the country.

"Will you tell me something," he asked, "that has puzzled me ever since you came here? You said that you had known Mary all her life—and yet, when I met her, she seemed to have met no one—no one, I mean, who didn't think on the same lines as her father. What she knew, she knew from books. She wasn't awake. How, in heaven's name, if she had spent her early years with you, hearing your talk and watching you draw, could she have promised to marry the cricketer she was engaged to?"

Madden smiled. "There'd be no mystery about it," he said, "if you knew the place we lived in. It was a small tight circle. I broke away pretty early. It was only when

we were more or less children that she and I were together
at all continuously—and then with our elders about. After
that I saw her on and off. I was a bit older. I was working
in London. When I did go home, as often as not she was
away at school, and when she wasn't—well, once I did try
to ask her very much what you once asked me; what was
she going to do with herself? what was she becoming? But
it was no good. Perhaps it was too early. Anyhow, the
essence of her was that she hadn't really begun to think
about herself. I don't mean simply that she was 'unselfish,' though in fact she was almost frighteningly
unselfish. But the point is that she didn't see the world, as
everyone else does, in its relation to herself. It wasn't a
field for her ambition or her happiness. It was a place
where you heard and saw things—and waited."

"For what?" said Sparkenbroke. "If I knew that, I
should know what she was becoming. As it is——"

"In her," Madden interrupted, "it wasn't passivity or
indifference; it was a kind of—absolute patience, as though
there were some instinct which assured her that one day,
if she waited, she would be told what she was waiting for.
That's why I could leave no mark on her. Sometimes, in
those days, she infuriated me. I was very young and fighting a battle with my own people, and to see her accepting
and accepting drove me mad. Her beauty seemed to me a
power; I wanted her to use it, but she wouldn't. Because
she wouldn't rebel—didn't seem even to know what re-
bellion was—I wanted to drive her. Now I can look back
on it. She was making her own life in her own way and at
her own pace. It would have been wrong to drag her out
of it, and useless, too, in the end. She'd always go back."

"I dragged her out," Sparkenbroke said. "She was beginning to lead a new kind of life—to be a different person.
At least, I believed that."

" 'Believed'? Do you believe it still?"

"If I believed it to the extent of faith, I shouldn't be
here explaining my belief," Sparkenbroke said. "Everything would go down before it. But perhaps what was true
of you is true of me also. I may have changed her very

little; I don't know—probably I never shall. . . . If I had been her lover I should have known," he added after a pause.

They left the copse and continued their walk in silence. Sparkenbroke's own words repeated themselves in his mind: if I had been her lover, I should have known. For many hours they underlay all his thought, and that night, when he dropped his pen, he fell into that emptiness of spirit which follows prolonged imaginative labour—an emptiness so receptive, so little bound by the order of fact and memory, that it resembles the whiteness of a screen upon which shadows, falling from diverse angles, whether from before or behind, are patterned upon a single plane. The sense of time weakens; nothing is impossible; and he started up from his table, stirred by a sound; but it was no sound; it was an imagining of her movement that dragged the icy brush of loneliness across his flesh.

> *I am turned to dust by her and blown in the wind,*
> *As a mote that rises in sunlight and vanishes utterly. . . .*

Even the power to compose was wasted in him. The lines beckoned but he could not follow, and, suddenly exhausted, he sank down upon his bed, very cold, aware of nothing but the frozen stillness of the house:

> *I am turned to dust by her and blown in the wind,*
> *As a mote that rises in sunlight and vanishes utterly.*
>
> *In that annihilation, where is the mote, that little world?*
> *She that was once darkness beyond the beam*
> *Is become the head of radiance, earth's climax and essence;*
> *And I, prince of her earth, her plough,*
> *Her seed and rain, her sky's dome,*
> *I, her master of attitude, the weight upon her breasts, her*
>   *prison,*
> *Dagger of her pain, rhythm and plume of her ecstasy,*
> *What am I but dust, light in the palm of her hand?*
> *She retains me, she pours me out.*
> *With curve of her body, she encompasses and exalts me,*
> *Then sleeps, like a child, like an animal, like God,*
> *And I am dust, floated upon her breath.*

P

Because by passion I am made her child
Whom, till she love beyond passion, she bears not,
I must subdue her as though she were a slave.
Always there is part of her free of love.
Thus invincible, she smiles and sleeps.
Having submitted her body, she is withdrawn from me.
She is intact, an unbroken darkness,
And I am dust, fiery upon her breath.

It appeared to him as one of those poems that are written in dreams; they are without discipline and there is no truth without discipline. He stretched his arms into the air and let them fall outwards across his pillows. In the morning it will be forgotten, he thought, and did not stir to write it down. In the morning it would be valueless, and he turned upon his shoulder, and sighed, and was asleep.

CHAPTER TWELVE

NOT until April had passed did the day come on which he could say, "*Tristan* is finished." There was no one he could tell but Bissett, for Madden was gone, and he tore off from his block the last sheet of manuscript and took up his pen again. "My dear Etty," he wrote, and stared at the words:

"MY DEAR ETTY,

The book is done at last and there seems to be nothing left. Always it is my emptiness I bring to you. Seeming to offer you my triumphs, I bring you only the desolation within them, asking to be taken for a little while out of the dangers of my own pride into the safety of your understanding. You have spent your life in supplying wisdom to my folly. You are sane when I am mad, faithful when I betray you—the more profoundly faithful because undeceived. I have lived in such a way that to say I love you has the colour of fraud and insult; yet it is true, and will remain true in whatever injuries I do you. No one else will be persuaded of this. If you keep this letter and it is read long after we are dead by someone who has know-ledge of both our lives, he will see in it only hypocrisy. 'Look,' he will say, 'there is Sparkenbroke, in the midst of a letter to his wife, trying to catch the eye of posterity!' It is true and untrue. The biographer will not be per-suaded—and you will not need persuasion. Your love is an alchemy that makes truth even of my lies—oh, my dear, as I write that—which is brilliantly and precisely accurate, a flawless description of the relationship between us—I know that the phrase is too neatly turned to carry the accent of sincerity.

Can you understand even this—that it is the nature of my love for you which makes me aloof, withdrawn, stiff in your presence, and gives to my letters a kind of formality and elaboration that I can't break down. I dare not break them down; I should be plunged into intolerable and useless confusion. I know that between you and me there is more of the sympathy and pity of love than is commonly given to men and women, but one thing—I do not mean passion, for we have known passion—one thing, ecstasy, is lacking. I am seeking it always, but you do not know the thing I seek; you are looking for a different element in love—what shall I call it? a supreme romanticism? You would have understood the love of the troubadours and the Courts of Love where the bodily act was chiefly valuable neither as a pleasure nor as a means to an ecstasy beyond itself, but as a symbol of an absolute loyalty and devotion—a seal upon a pledge. In your sense, I am not a romantic; in my sense, you are not an ecstatic; and when I speak of love to you I cannot speak simply, for, though we use the same language of understanding and affectionate tolerance, we speak it with a different accent of the imagination."

At the head of a new sheet he wrote:

"You can give me comfort and consolation, even for a little while peace; but you cannot absolve me. You give me strength to continue my life, but not the power to lose it. And I . . ."

He laid down his pen, destroyed the paper on which these last sentences were written; then, suddenly, tore up his letter and began afresh:

"Lucca, May 3
My dear Etty,

The book is done at last. Your pleasure has always been my pleasure in the finishing of a piece of work, and, remembering how much we have shared in the past, I am

empty without you. Always, when what I wish to bring
is love, it is my emptiness I bring to you.

I shall read the manuscript again before it is typed,
but it won't delay me long; it has already been very
elaborately revised, section by section, and great parts of
it re-written. What remains can be done in the typescript
and proofs. Tell your trustees that it will be published
in time for the Christmas market. The English and
American advances will pay off more than £6000.

I am glad you are going to London for the Season and
glad, too, that our tenants can let you have our own place
for a few weeks. You are right to give a ball. Don't
be economical. Be damned to your trustees. Probably
no one in our family will ever live in Chelmouth House
again. Let it be splendid and let Richard remember it
so. Couldn't Richard stay up late enough to see the ball
opened? We have given none in Chelmouth House since
King Edward's reign.

But, my dear, I can't come to the ball myself, though
it is you who ask me. This morning I have no plans—no
future of any kind. I have finished my book—at wild
expense Bissett will give me Clicquot for luncheon, it's
his way of marking an occasion—then I shall sit in the
sun on the ramparts and fall asleep for the joy of waking
up and feeling the thought break upon me afresh: 'I have
finished the book!' Beyond that, I can't look. I know
that I am making you unhappy, but I am not ready to
come to Sparkenbroke yet—still less to face London. I
am alone here and wish to be alone. Tell your trustees
it has entered my mind that I shall write no more stories—
perhaps verse—perhaps nothing—I have no projects,
and when I say to myself 'Next year' there's no answer.
Tell your trustees. It may not be true but it will alarm
them. 'Not write any more!' they will say. 'But he must
write!' Perhaps they know best. I am a writer; it has been
my life; as long as I live, I must write—unless I can
outgrow this need or discover another satisfaction of the
need at the core of it.

Good-bye, my dear, and forgive this letter. I drew a

line under the last word of *Tristan* less than half an hour ago. Soon I shall begin to know what I must do and become. My love to you, and my gratitude for your patience.   PIERS"

In her letter she had written: "I am sending out invitations to a ball there. I've defied my Trustees who say we can't afford it. Was that right? Really, the ball is being given because—well, isn't it the kind of foolishness that would please you: a ball in Chelmouth House again—your music and your ghosts? Come to it if you can and if your work frees you and for my sake."

Putting her letter down, he drew his own towards him and wrote beneath his signature:

"I can't resist your ball. My re-reading will take a month, perhaps. I could be home in early or middle June. Tell me your exact date. By tradition it ought to be on the evening of the Oaks. Or have you, who remember everything, remembered that?"

He wrote to George also, saying that the book was done, and wondering, as he wrote, whether only this fact would be communicated to Mary or the letter itself shown to her. Why should George withhold the letter from her—the paper and ink? He could have no reason for doing so; nothing could be more natural in him than to put it beside her coffee-cup—a letter from Piers; he has finished *Tristan*. But, observing the scene in imagination, Sparkenbroke saw that the letter might slide into the discreet darkness of a pocket, for George, the least secretive of men, had yet an intuition of what to leave undone, and, above all, unsaid.

George is safe enough, he thought with a smile. With him she is what she was born to be; with me, what I can create in her; and it is our first imagining of ourselves that rules us at last, unless we have the genius of Saul of Tarsus. He remembered his pledge, not to seek her out or write to her, and the sanction she had imposed upon it.

What am I to swear by?

By your work. That all you write may be corrupt and false if——

How pale and set her face had been! He understood now the courage in her that had exacted this pledge from him and the depth of intuition in which she had known that he would be bound by it. It's final, he heard his own voice saying—but then *Tristan* had been unfinished; now the last page was on his desk. In its corner he wrote the date, and the word: "Lucca." Am I a writer no more? he said. Is that done also?

He began to think that perhaps art was not, after all, an end in itself, as to a religious the acts of devotion were not in themselves an end, but that it was possible to pass, as from an outer to an inner room, from story-telling to the story, from imagination expressed to imagination sufficient to itself, and, in all things, even in art, from the experiment of action to the certitude of being. It was an idea in essence long familiar to him, but the impact of it upon his imagining of himself as a writer was new. No more than in the past did he question the supreme value of art among human activities, but he saw that, with them, it might be outgrown.

There's an ingenious consolation for a man who has written himself out! he thought, rising from his chair and stretching his arms above his head. To-morrow, next week, next month—who knows?—I shall be story-telling again! In a drawer of his desk was a scribbled exercise-book containing notes of tales that from time to time it had entered his mind to write. When Bissett summoned him to his meal, he carried the book with him into the Long Room, and, at table, while the effervescence died in his wine-glass, slowly turned the shabby pages, brooding on the themes they recalled. But they belonged to the past; he was interested in them as he might have been in notes made during his boyhood; and what struck fire in him was not the imagining of any story to be written but the perception of a state of freedom and maturity in which even the pride of narrative might be put away.

Such a state appeared to him at first as a kind of death,

and, while the idea of it was unfamiliar to him, he feared
it as men who are still in the childhood of the spirit fear
death itself. I am tired, he said, that is all. In time, the
impulse to write will come back to me. I have just finished
one book. Why should I be troubling myself so soon for
another? But his power to write had always been for him
the home of his being upon earth—the single permanent
and incorruptible thing to which he might return—and
his means of communication with a reality beyond all
accidents and failures. To lose it would be to lose everything, and his intuition that this loss had become necessary
and a thing to be achieved, not resisted, appeared to him
as, perhaps, no more than an excuse for a collapse of his
powers. It was as if one were to fail before a woman, and
claim the virtue of chastity.

His days were spent in revision of *Tristan*, and, as the
end of this task and of the month approached, he watched
with curiosity Bissett's preparations for their return to
England.

"When do you expect to be in Lucca again?" he asked.

"I'm sure I can't say, m'lord."

"But everyone has a feeling for the future, Bissett. Do
you imagine yourself unpacking again in the autumn or in
the spring?"

"That will depend on when you get to your writing
again, m'lord," Bissett replied, and that afternoon, as
Sparkenbroke walked through Lucca, the streets were
quick with the moods and imaginings and passions of
which they had been witness. It was one of the tricks of
his memory that a conversation long forgotten or a particular passage of his own thought would be re-created by his
return to the scene of it; a crack in a paving-stone at which
he had been gazing when certain words were spoken would
recall those words, and the dialogue that followed them,
with startling precision; and to-day the planes of his life
in Lucca moved over one another continually, as though,
he thought, I were drowning and experience were singing
in my ears.

All the morning the sun had shone in a blue sky. When

he mounted the ramparts at about three o'clock a saffron
gauze seemed to have been drawn over the blue, and puffs
of cloud, stiff and rounded, hung in the air. A fierce gust
lashed the trees now and then; when it had passed, the
leaves drooped as though they were made of clay; the heat
increased and stooped upon the earth; the birds were
silent and the dust between the tree-roots was scored by
past eddies of wind.

A desire to be in his own place came upon him—a
desire for his roots that ached in him and stung his eyes
and throat like a fear. In Derry's Wood, he might have
watched the English summer shine among the branches
and throw down its spears on the leafy ripple of the
stream; or have wandered down the broadening path
towards the churchyard, and, in the clearing, leaned
against the elm-tree, a tremor of bliss astir in his mind,
the same that he had experienced at his window when first
his father had summoned him to the Mass, and again
when Stephen had put the key in his hand, and again and
again throughout his life whenever, in whatever form, the
premonition of self-loss had quickened in him.

But he saw only the stormy glaze upon the Apennines
and, near him, her face. Since *Tristan* was done and for
more than a month the book's power of exclusion had been
taken from him, it was into her face that all his thought had
looked up. Desire for her fell upon him suddenly, the
stroke of an invisible arm across his eyes. The air beneath
his hands conformed to the shapes of her body, the air
upon his lips was her breath, and when he shut his eyes,
pressing the lids together until their darkness was shot
with chalky gleams, this darkness also was of her flesh and
struck his reason down. All imagination, even of Derry's
Wood, was consumed in her. He could not look beyond
her, even to his death.

Thunder did not come, and that night, in his bedroom,
there was sweat upon the walls. He lay beneath a sheet,
the fever of his own body striking up at him in heat from
the bed. He saw continually her lashes spread by the closing

of her eyes; then the opening of her eyes under him and
rapture in them and the dew of pain beaded on her forehead; and, hearing her cry his name, he would awake
from this waking dream to a consciousness so acute
that, starting up from the pillow, he would look everywhere for her eyes and for her pain, that had form and
colour, and for her cry that was shaped like an ascending, frozen wave. I must decide, he said, and repeated
the words aloud, but he could not distinguish the prongs
of decision; he did not know what the question was
that he must answer. The prison in which he was confined had neither windows nor doors; it was without
shape. But nothing is without shape! he cried, and struck
a match and held it until the illumined sheet appeared
about his knees like a sea of white oil. The candle-flame
drew up. He heard his breathing, and his voice say:
"Nothing is without shape," but why and in what circumstances of terror he had spoken these words he could not
remember.

> *Now in the despair of love, that windowless prison,*
> *I bend all night to my sleep and my sleep denies me.*
> *Rigid, naked, faceless, my sleep stares up at me*
> *And cries: "O fool of love! Be still. Desire not.*
> *Thou art in the trap of love; thine own cry awakens thee,*
> *And shall awaken thee until thou goest down to the tomb."*

The pencil slid from his fingers, and without question
or answer he saw himself decided, the decision presenting
itself to him as an imagining, not of any acceptance in
himself, but of Etty's peace of mind when she knew that
his life had reached its settlement and that he was come
home. Living at Sparkenbroke, he would meet Mary continually, but his settlement would be in accordance with
hers, and the knowledge of what might have been would
gradually cease to be active and persistent. It would go
out of their bodies when they were near, and out of their
eyes, though the encounter were sudden and unguarded.
For many years, perhaps, it would leave in their consciousness of each other a residue of pride in passion overcome;

but at last, as they grew older, even this pride would give place to a shared humility before a life not without recompense for what was lost. It is necessary, he thought, to believe in life's power to transmute our needs as it transmutes ourselves, and above all in its power so to transmute the appearance of things—even the nature of things in their relationship to us—that what, in prospect, seems beautiful (and is beautiful) as an achievement, a possession, a seizable joy, becomes in retrospect beautiful because it has not been achieved or enjoyed. This is one of the mercies on which the world depends, and what is called the rapture, the agony, the fighting melancholy of youth consists in becoming aware of it and aware that without it life could not be lived, so terrible are its losses. For in youth, and the passionate recurrences of youth, it seems always that what is lost is perjured and cast away, that each loss is a betrayal of life; therefore we seize what we can, and cry out bitterly for what we miss, and are scornful of those who say we must sacrifice ourselves or that the loss is not a loss or that there are other women in the world and other enchantments. And rightly scornful. These are lies. The loss is absolute. There is no other woman but the woman loved. There is no other enchantment. Life is not to be lived by forgetting or by substitution, but by remembrance and transmutation. To forget is to do murder; to remember is to re-create; and the art of life is the art of accordance with its changes, so that loss, though loss indeed, is not a corrupting body buried in the earth or tied to the prisoner but a continuing spirit that informs the freed man.

Freedom, in this sense, springs, he thought, from singleness of mind, and singleness of mind from irrevocable decision. The mood of renouncement must be locked by action, else none has courage to sustain it. The action required of him was not to fall upon his knees and call upon God to witness a conversion, or to sustain himself in the pride of final vows, but the simple action of returning to his own wife and living in his own place until the loss of the woman he desired was transmuted

by rule and suffering from an end to a beginning.
There was something in the plainness of this resolve that
at once amused and impressed him. To return to one's
wife—it is as commonplace, he thought, as to wash in
Jordan! The story came back to him as he dressed—even
its phrases: "Abana and Pharpar, rivers of Damascus. . . ."
It had so dwelt in his imagination that, with the eyes of
childhood, he could see the prophet's servant, Gehazi,
running after the departing guest, and the dust in little
clouds at his feet, his eyes strained and bright, his hand in
air to compel attention. Yet none of these things were
spoken of. "So Gehazi followed after Naaman. And when
Naaman saw him running after him——" That was all, but
to so plain a narrative, because it was faultless, imagination
added a thousand riches of detail, and preserved them,
so that the scene of Naaman's lighting down from his
chariot came back undimmed from boyhood and brought
the years with it. But why am I thinking of Naaman and
Gehazi? he asked, and could not retrace his thought.

Morning had been in the window while he dressed, its
white bars falling through the shutters on to the writing-
table and the deep carving of the bed, but the courtyard,
when he reached it, was still heavy with night; the dog at
the porter's lodge did not stir; and outside, in the narrow
street, the paving-stones were as yet scarcely agleam. So
I shall remember Lucca, he thought—this cool beginning
of day after a night of fever. Soon the heat will come again
and the stones burn, but now, for a little while—and he
threw up his head the better to feel the air on his forehead,
and draw in the scent of foliage that came down from the
ramparts, and see, between the house-tops, a crystal sky
watered with green and threaded with primrose fires. If
she were here, his thought said, she also would look up,
and he knew, in the sudden encounter of their eyes, that
to perceive in each other recognition of beauty was to
rediscover beauty itself. It was true, then, that he loved
her, and with his whole being, for was it not the patent
of love, whether of a woman or of God, that whatever

is seen or heard or imagined stands annulled in its former existence and is newly revealed in the person loved? He remembered that the Rector had said to him of natural chastity, as distinct from the chastity of discipline, that it was an attitude of mind; he was naturally chaste who felt his individuality invaded by the carnal act, and unchaste who saw himself as the invader. But in love there is neither invading nor being invaded, the Rector had continued, taking nor giving, chastity nor unchastity, for the lovers are surrendered not to each other but to God, in whom surrender is victory, and blindness the very light of perception. If a man is not aware of this or does not understand it, the reason is that he has desired but not loved, the old man had added. Desire is not evil, for it is natural, but the distinction between desire and love is that between verse and poetry; love exceeds the purposes of the lover; like poetry it overflows upon the universe and re-impregnates it; and the sign of this is in little things as well as in great, above all in the annihilation of certain distinctions formerly believed to be natural and permanent—the distinction, for example, between what is gay and what is solemn. To a lover, as to a saint, the gay and the solemn are identical; within laughter and mourning he hears always the same silence; and as the saints know one another without tokens, so between the eyes of lovers there shines a mutual light by which they recognize each other and see all that is, the sky, the hills, the bread they eat, not as external watchers or users of these things, but inwardly, with the creative eye.

While he remembered this conversation, it had seemed to Sparkenbroke that Mary was at his side. She had accompanied him through the Via delle Rose, and when the Cathedral square stretched out before him, white and almost shadowless between darkness and light, the impact of its beauty was a consequence of her seeing as well as of his own. There was, he felt, "a mutual light between them by which they recognized each other."

Though it was yet so early, the door of the Cathedral was open. A sound of mallet and chisel came from within, and Sparkenbroke, entering, found masons high on their scaffold, a lamp beside them yellow in the increasing daylight. Perhaps, he thought, I shall not see Ilaria again, for his resolution to live in Sparkenbroke House and effect a settlement of his outward life was firm within him; abandonment of Lucca was a test of its firmness; and the effigy of Ilaria del Carretto seemed not only to represent the city he must leave and the encirclement he had found there and lost, but, by miraculous transition, to foretell also the new life to which he was going—a life of negation, he would have said a few months ago, a life, as he now perceived, vitally expectant within the pressure of its denials. As he stood beside the tomb, which was wrapped in a slumbrous gleam, he asked himself, the last of many times, in what the genius of this figure consisted. As a work of the chisel, it had no claim to supremacy, nor was a giant's mind to be apprehended in it; yet none could approach it without a sense of personal discovery, necessary and ordained. To each newcomer, Ilaria appeared to have been awaiting him; and he bore with him afterwards a remembrance, not of having admired this among other works of art, but of private communication, as though, while he stood gazing, her silence had whispered in his ear. Jacopo della Quercia, Sparkenbroke reflected, had created here a quality that transcended his design, even his capacity — the same quality that distinguished poetry from verse, love from desire, and death itself from the physical act of dying; a quality not of the mind, for thought was an interpretation not an origin, but of the seed that falls upon certain minds gifted to receive it. The figure of this girl was neither alive with the life of the body nor dead with the death of the body, but held in the breathless quiet of one who, having seen reality through blinded eyes and touched it beyond the senses, had the genius to wait in the singleness of her expectation; and he watched the light grow upon her pillow, marvelling at her constancy, which seemed to pity and absolve him.

BOOK V

LONDON

CHAPTER ONE

OUTSIDE the portico of Chelmouth House, on the lowest
step, the butler watched the car drive up the sloping yard
and halt beside the mounting-block.

"Her ladyship in?"

"Yes, m'lord."

"Alone?"

"Yes, m'lord."

As Sparkenbroke advanced up the steps, the door at
their head opened to receive him.

"Bissett is following with the luggage. He may be some
time at the Customs. I told him to report when he arrived.
Tell him I don't want to be interrupted. He is to put out
my things for dinner and wait. Her ladyship is at home to
no one. Nor am I."

"There's a dinner-party arranged for to-night, m'lord."

"To-night? . . . Very well."

As he crossed the marble pavement on his way to the
stairs, he thought: It's like a club. Some day it will be a
club—a stone's-throw from Pall Mall—some day, *there*
(and his eye fixed on a bust of his grandfather, yellow in
the roof-light) there'll be a long hat-stand with rows of
bowler hats and felt hats, and little men, with their bellies
thrust out, looking at the tape. Upstairs will be the dining-
room, and outside it a cashier flicking out notes with a
finger hygienically damped on a sponge.

At the end of the first flight, the staircase divided into
two branches, then doubled back. The walls, glossy enough
to take, even in daylight, the reflection of the chandeliers,
stretched upward to the level of the second floor, which,

above the staircase, had the form of a flattened dome, pierced at the centre by a lozenge-shaped skylight. A bleak yellow gleam shone down, as from the glass roof of a railway station. We shall cling to this house as long as Etty's money can cling to it. When her father dies, she'll buy back the lease for me. She'll give it to me as a birthday present or on our wedding day. And I want that, Sparkenbroke thought. I've been bred to want it. I do want it. God knows why.

To the telegram announcing the time of his arrival, he had added: "Meet me at home." She would have come to Dover and he had a dislike of being met at Dover. Now he wished that she had come to Victoria. A miracle would have happened; she—and he—would have been changed; they would have been at ease, certain at once that there was nothing they could not say to each other; and what he had to say would have been said at once, on the flood of impulse. Now, at this instant, with the drawing-room door in front of them, she would have touched his arm— perhaps, even, have taken his hand—and he would have been assured within him that he wasn't mocking himself with this resolution to begin life with her afresh. He would have spoken it by now, have been committed and brilliantly excited by his commitment. Anything's easy if it's drastic enough and sudden enough—like the plunge of a needle into the flesh.

Disciplined to his whims, she hadn't come to Victoria— not even to the hall. How could she? The drawing-room windows didn't look out on the yard; she didn't know yet that he was in the house. She was waiting for him in the drawing-room, perhaps sewing, or with a book, and he thought that if, when he entered, she flung her arms about his neck and kissed him, if she cried, if with a sudden failure of her reserve she welcomed or upbraided him, if by the grace of God she were unreasonable, passionate, extravagant, wilful—in a moment of salvation, gloriously ill-bred—then—then he could tell her. They could dramatize their doubts away. They could play-act their reconciliation until it became real. But why should she?

That was his way, not hers. Anyhow, he'd come home from Italy before and gone again. Why should she go off her head to suit his unknown mood?

The door opened from within and she stood looking at him, her back to the stronger light. She was surprised, and her hand went to her throat—the mark of emotion in her. She was, he knew, in that instant on the point of running to him, and he stood, his hands moving towards her, awaiting the impossible miracle. She smiled—the doubting smile that forbade her impulses; they went forward to greet each other and, with guarded affection, kissed.

"Piers," she said, walking with him into the room, "do you mind? There's a party to-night. I'd asked them before I knew when you were coming. I couldn't put them off, so I've asked another girl to make fourteen."

This was not what had been in her heart to say. For that reason she said it, stifling her own saving truth, and he remembered that, even in the first days of their marriage, her sense of moderation, of decorum, of duty had weighed her down. Not to be theatrical! Not to spill emotion! So many people, she had said, express more feeling than they have in them. That always frightens me. It's a kind of lie. But sometimes, he had replied, they discover feeling in themselves because they have first expressed it. The lie becomes true. The Rector says that the remedy for not being able to pray is to pray. Probably that applies to other things.

Now he answered, taking her arm in his, "My dear Etty, you know I like parties—some parties. I haven't had one for months."

She looked at him gratefully. Had she in truth feared his anger? "You say so, but you didn't want a party to-night, I know—after your journey." Then she added—and to say even this needed courage—"I didn't want one either, when I knew you were coming."

"Then why not put them off?"

"I couldn't, Piers! It was arranged long ago. Some of them are old." She began to tell him who was coming but he cut her short.

"Well?" he said. "What of it? Here's a June night—and no war. It's worth a judge and a brace of bishops. There's still the telephone."

She raised her eyes and gazed at him; then laughed, as an elder child laughs at the suggestion of an escapade that its responsibility will not allow it to share—a laugh of enchantment cut off. And, like an elder child, her brow shaded by disappointment, she pretended not to believe in his mood.

"If I'd said 'Yes, put them off,' and the telephone were going now," she asked, "what should we have done with the evening? The opera?"

"Is there an opera? Let's imagine an opera anyhow." He looked at the clock. "Too late for *Tristan*!"

A footman brought in a Rockingham tea-pot, and stood with his tray while the silver pot already used was lifted from the table. The butler relighted the spirit-lamp that Etty herself might make fresh tea.

"I know you hate tea made in silver," she said. He wanted no tea, but they sat down.

"Tell me everything," she said. "Your *Tristan* is finished?"

"Yes. It's done."

"Good?"

He nodded. "It's not that I want to talk about, Etty. I——"

She was leaning across the tea-table, her attention on the spirit-lamp. "Yes?" she said.

The conversation adrift in his mind was: Etty, do you remember that day at Vipore? At Vipore? she'd say. In the country outside Lucca. Oh yes, I remember. Do you remember, too, what we talked about? About my coming home to England and settling there and—— But she was heating the tea-pot and testing it with her hand before dropping in the tea-leaves. To tell her now was impossible. Looking down the cool, discreet drawing-room, observing its pale, mirrored length, the sleeping porcelain, the Canaletto opposite him, obscured by distance, but presenting to his memory its everlasting detail—the unmoving ripple of its water, the fixed triangle of sunshine slanting in across its *campanile*—he was glad that he had not spoken. The faded permanence of the room threatened him.

"Yes?" she repeated.

"Only about Richard," he answered. "Where is he?"

"In his bath I expect. He wanted to stay up until you came, but the timing of boats is so uncertain I thought— He needs a lot of sleep. He has been looking tired lately. I'm not sure that London suits him."

"Let's go up to him now. He'd love to be visited in his bath."

Sparkenbroke was up from his chair, stretching out his hand to her. Now, if she came, he could tell her. Then it would be done. Then it would be final. They'd walk upstairs together, talking of Richard. Suddenly, they'd stop and he'd tell her.

"Let's go," he repeated.

She wanted to go. Within her, she could feel his impulses. He saw temptation in her eyes—then the deliberate chill of self-discipline.

"Later," she answered. "It isn't fair on the nursery to make him excited just when they're trying to get him to bed. You know how he splashes and ramps if you go into his bathroom." She smiled. "We can go later, when he's in bed. They will be expecting that."

"They?"

"Miss Kelm. The nursery."

"Too late," he said.

She looked at him, puzzled, and he, that she might not be puzzled or wounded, took her by the shoulders and said, with tender mockery:

> "'*Twould ring the bells of heaven*
> *The loudest peal for years*
> *If Etty lost her senses*
> *And*——"

"I dare say," she answered, "but in running a household the size of ours someone has to keep their senses, haven't they?"

"Why?" he said.

To that she made no reply, but handed him his tea. "O Piers, it is good to have you back. I should have been almost frightened of the ball without you. Richard will be glad too. He wants to go to the Tattoo."

"The Tattoo. Very well." The tea she had made was perfect. "Bissett makes it in the same way," he said, "but with different results. I haven't had such tea since—you last made it."

There was a little silence. Her voice, when she spoke, was studiously at ease.

"Shall you be in England long, Piers?"

Now—could he say what he had to say? He laid down his spoon in his saucer, but all he could say was: "As long as you will make my tea"—a dead saying, spoken without meaning and passed by her with smiling recognition of an arid compliment.

CHAPTER TWO

STANDING at Etty's side at the head of the central staircase, Sparkenbroke struggled not to count his guests or to observe particularly the partings of their hair as they came up to him or the contacts of their hands with his. To count without reason is to count beyond reason; a hundred and seven, a hundred and eight, a hundred and nine—ten, twelve, sixteen, eighteen—the Gutborough twins, twenty —six score, four thirties, sixteen times seven and a half— a hundred and twenty-one, two, three. . . . It was better to observe the partings: how some were wet and narrow, some dry and dusty, some irregularly expansive like a snake whose meal was still an undigested bulge; and how, on the heads of women, seen in plan, they were often remarkably pinker than the forehead, the nose-tip and the dividing breasts to which they pointed. A hairdresser, he thought, sees all heads in plan. Under the hair he learns the skull and, when the head is laid back and the eyes are sealed with herbal pads and the jaw is clamped with bandages, does he also discover the sockets, the stunted nose-bone, the grinning teeth? Under the glove, the limp flesh; under the flesh, the clasping bones; but many do not clasp; they touch and skim with a weary archness not pretty in skeletons. A hundred and seventy-five, six, eight, nine score—and one, and two, and three.

"Yes, I hope to be here for some time. . . .

"Yes, it's called *Tristan and Iseult*. . . .

"I know. And not only Wagner. . . .

"Your daughter?" He turned from the father and took the girl's hand. " 'Your ladyship is nearer to heaven than when I saw you last.' "

"Nearer heaven?"

"By three inches at least."

"Ha, that's good!" her father exclaimed. "I must remember that—'nearer heaven'!"

"But you mustn't repeat it as an original greeting, Tom. All that I have is yours but this—is Hamlet's."

"Prince of Denmark," said Tom informatively, and hoisted his buttocks and his daughter up the stairs.

Each of them, with their partings, nose-tips, upturned faces, smiling teeth, each of them was the centre of a world, a pivot of consciousness. Rowlandson would have drawn them—but first he would have intoxicated them and given them a push and sent them all jumbling down the stairs, snatching at the banisters, grasping at the air, a cascade of flesh and garters—of suspenders, elastic belts. Max would have drawn them in staircase ritual, the procession of protracted affability, sloping shoulders, melting legs, bottles of hock on legs of liquorice, stamped, all of them, with Max's prevailing impression that the human body is liquescent and the human head soft and slippery, like a peeled egg to which hair has become freakishly attached. Caran d'Ache would have drawn them, a rivulet of pebbles, indistinguishable except in the graded preparation of their smiles—on the lowest step, a blank; on the third, a hint; on the seventh, a flicker; on the tenth, a hesitant slit; on the fifteenth, an experimental gash; on the twentieth, teeth. And each satirist of the pen would have set in the midst of his cartoon their host—their admirable, elegant host, aware—and aware with pleasure—that his presence was the flutter of the evening, drinking up their curiosity, their flattery and homage, coining phrases for them to repeat, and yet despising and hating them—why? —was there any good reason that he, who acquiesced in this life not his own, should despise them whose life it was? Dr. Celli, the man of science, would have provided an answer and suggested a remedy. Better sleep in sin than lie awake hating mankind. Sleep? But I shall sleep like a log! he heard his own voice saying, and Celli's sigh as he answered: Lightness of heart! Everything depends on

that. When I was young, I wanted to be sure I was
right. Now I take what I want, if I can get it—and I
sleep well.

Thinking of Celli and of their drive together into Pisa,
he began to seek in his mind, while the throng of guests
passed him on their way upstairs, for the circumstances
that had given to that drive and its trivial conversation a
memorable significance, and he heard the rain falling on
the vine and saw a beam of light, from between the
curtains of the Long Room, slant across the rain. While I
was driving that car into Pisa and back, what were you
thinking of? Of Nicodemus, her voice answered, and at the
sound of her voice the people on the stairs and the faces
looking down from the gallery, the same people, the same
faces that he had encountered everywhere during the past
month in London, became dummies. He saw himself
among the dummies, welcoming them—Etty and himself,
like the wooden figures of man and wife on a German
clock, stretching out automatic hands.

Soon afterwards he went upstairs to open the ball with
Merioneth's young wife, doubly entitled by her rank and
by her being an April bride. She had been to Corfu.

"To Corfu? Did you swim there in little bays backed
by olive-trees?"

She looked up from his shoulder. "Why? Do you know
it?"

"No. But there's a young painter, a friend of mine,
who said—oh, well, no matter."

"What did he say?"

"That he chose his own bay and swam naked."

"So did I," she answered.

"And Merioneth?"

"He doesn't swim."

"What does he do?"

"Oh," she said, "he sits about."

"So you swam alone? It seems a waste."

"Most things are."

"A waste? Aren't you very young to say that?"

"Perhaps that's why."

It would be pleasanter, he thought, to dance in silence. He had no wish to supply the deficiencies of Merioneth, but his curiosity provoked him to ask of the red Velasquez they had in the country.

"Why not come to see it?"

"That's charming of you. But when I go back to Sparkenbroke I want to stay there a long time."

"To write?"

"To live. . . . There's water I can swim in."

"We have water."

"Well," he answered as the music ceased, "having chosen one's lake, one must swim in it."

"Isn't that rather a puritan sentiment?"

"Doesn't this tempt you to puritanism?"

"What?"

"*This!*" The curling gesture of his hand included the room. He wanted to be rid of her because, though beautiful and young, she had no power over him, and it was not until he found she could teach him something of the skill and jargon of dog-breeding that his interest was kindled.

"But why do you ask? Why do you want to know about dogs?" she asked. "They don't mean anything to you."

"First, because I'm ignorant; I want facts; I want new words and you can give them to me. Secondly, because dogs do mean something to you."

"Much more than Velasquez."

"That's what I wanted!" he cried. "Now you are real. Tell me why you'd rather breed a good dog than paint a good picture."

"Because it's what *I* can do."

"It won't make you immortal."

"Who wants to be immortal? I don't. Besides, it will, in an anonymous way, and that's the way I like."

Suddenly, while she was telling him about her kennels, she stopped and said: "I like you now. I didn't. You were exciting, but I didn't *like* you."

"We like the people we are with when we like ourselves," he answered, "and hate them when we hate ourselves. You happen to like yourself in relation to dogs."

"And you," she said, "though dogs bore you——"

"Nothing bores me that touches a human being on the quick. You'd die in defence of your kennels."

She smiled. "At any rate, you have enough imagination to imagine it. If you talked to me about poetry, I should be blank."

"No."

"But I should."

"No. I have enough imagination to make you imagine it."

"Is that why people fall in love with you?"

"Do they?" he said.

But she was no longer called upon to die in defence of her kennels. At the opening of the next dance, she was taken by a less exacting partner, who asked whether she had seen Helen Wills beat Señorita d'Alvarez at Wimbledon that afternoon, and Sparkenbroke walked away from the music through the long, communicating drawing-rooms, pausing, as he went, to speak to such guests as approached him. The night stretched ahead, an unending prospect of heat and noise, a bleak futility. He remembered days in which he had enjoyed such entertainments and other days in which he had raged against them and fled. Now he was without pleasure or anger, afflicted by his own emotional deadness as by a paralysis of the soul. Even his interest in the girl's dogs had been the working of a mechanism in him—the mechanism of sympathy with *une femme incomprise*. Because it's what *I* can do! she had said, and it had been easy to persuade her that the breeding of dogs was a sacred expression of her individuality, her special virtue, the activity that distinguished her (for those who had imagination enough!) from all other women. How tactfully he had conceded her equivalence with Velasquez! How soon, if he consented to swim in Merioneth's lake, he would be solemnly discussing, in her hours of ease, the temperament of bitches. To flatter where others flatter is the game of a fool. Discover in a courtesan her little, secret vanity of innocence and the open air; in a woman of the world, her private flirtation with the occult; in a cheat, her streak of honesty; in a duchess, dogs—discover these, play upon them, exalt them, and are you not that creature of miraculous insight, a lover with eyes to see where the cruel world is blind? But I have wasted my time, he thought. I have played the opening without inclination to finish the game. He turned away from his place by the ballroom door, whence he had observed her while she danced, and swung off through the drawing-rooms again, his eye on the dawdling clocks.

In the picture-gallery he encountered Etty—tired, watchful, gracious, discreetly proud, and while they spoke together he knew that she was hungry for his praises of this entertainment which, with so elaborate a care, she had devised. "Isn't it the kind of foolishness that would please you?" she had written. "A ball in Chelmouth House again, your music and your ghosts?" She had devised it for him —and suddenly he knew that to her also it was laborious duty, not pleasure or vanity or pride. He spoke its praises. It wounded him to see the relief, the springing gladness of her face.

"Was it worth coming back for?"

"My dear, it's magnificent." And he forced himself to add: " 'The kind of foolishness that pleases me.' "

For a moment she was puzzled by the echo; then recognized her own words.

"How did you remember that?"

"Why should you suppose I forget your letters?"

She smiled slowly, with tentative happiness. "I'm only sorry," she said, "that it couldn't have been a month ago, on the day of the Oaks," and with a little clasp of his arm she left him for her guests.

At the end of a long corridor leading out of the picture-gallery was a panelled room that overlooked the garden. Etty had assigned it to him when she had led him round his own house on the day after his coming from Italy. I expect this is the room you'd like as your own. She had removed their tenant's accretion—as much as she could certainly identify. The room was as it had been in his father's time, but stripped of much that had made it his father's: the pipes, the tobacco-jars, the brass stand bulging with newspapers, the hats—for his father had had a mania for hats; had worn them through the house and cast them down, in a profusion that defied his valet, wherever for a little while he had come to rest. Without the hats, the newspapers, the—what else? what else? Sparkenbroke thought, his eyes sweeping the room—the birdcage! There in the ceiling was the eye from which the cage had hung, always swaying a little, over a circle of husks. "Last night I flew into the tree of death. . . ." Then it was of his father's birdcage, now gone with the boyhood that had known it, and of this tree whose branches stretched out to the window-panes, that the verse had long after-wards been written.

He stared at the room, searching it for the past, locked the door and switched off the light. What he had expected to find here he did not know. He had come down the corridor in haste, almost running as soon as the door from the picture-gallery had swung behind him, and now, as he kneeled in the window-seat, and bars of light from the illuminated garden coiled over his extended arms, he found his hands clenched, finger-nails driven against the mound of thumb, and only by an exercise of will could he relax them. One of the long, narrow windows was open. He leaned out, thirsty for air. Near to him, in the upper branches of a chestnut, an electric lamp had been set at such an angle that the white under-side of its reflector was partly visible and a naked shaft from its bulbs lay up-ward. Protecting himself from its glare by an arm crooked over his forehead, he looked down under the rimmed dark-ness of his sleeve. The trees' lower branches were puffy with a high, whitened green; the flowers shone as though certain blooms or, within each bloom, certain petals, had been dipped in a blue phosphorescence; and the lawn itself was sliced by revolving and crossing sectors of shadow cast by the human figures that moved on it. As the in-fluence of one ground-light receded and the beam of another was cut, the emphasis of these shadows changed, and their extent also, each flow of darkness swelling and contracting continually so that the intervening spaces of light and the glowing dresses of women became alive with the deep rhythmical animation of sea-anemones, and the patterned lawn seemed to breathe.

Beneath the vibration of music, there was, among the chestnut boughs, an interior whispering, not projected sound but a stress secretly audible like the throbbing of a human pulse; and from this profound whisper, hushed and perpetual, aloof and secret language of the tree, from the innermost stirring of leaf-edges in a foliage that appeared to lie motionless on the night, there came to Sparkenbroke an entry into the tree itself, a knowledge of it, even of its communication between earth and air and of its ascending essence. Yet there remained a part of him in the window observing it; and behind me, he said, a bird is in its cage; the window is open and the door of the cage; but the bird is on its swing; and he turned from the window into the blackness of the room to remember that many years ago he had indeed found the cage-door open, nothing but a stroke of the wings between bird and tree, and the bird idly swinging. In the morning the bird was gone, the cage empty, and, though he was told that the poor bird, accustomed to confinement, must perish of its liberty, and that he had been cruel, not kind, to leave the door open, the reproof had not touched him. His imagination had tightened to the leap of the bird's heart when it grasped its freedom, he had felt the leg-spring, the wing-beat, the rush of air, the sway and passion of lighting on the bough. There, clinging, he had been mottled by the shadow of the leaves. Under his wings, lifting and desiring, soft feathers had turned over in the threaded currents of the wind. In the needly darkness, he had huddled himself and breathed and looked out, entranced; then, suddenly, had left the tree also, and cast himself upon the rings of the air.

As within words thought lies speechless, so within thought itself is a profounder action which thought cannot translate, and within this action a stillness where there is neither doing nor saying nor thinking, for all is done and thought. The circle of cause is completed, the ring is made, the creature resumes his essence; and it seemed to him, while he sat in the window-seat, having turned away from the window into the darkness of the room, that his self was lifted from him; he ceased to feel and know in terms of temporal things, yet felt and knew. It was as if, aroused from sleep, at first frightened and alone in a dream's chaos, he had found his head upon the breast of Reason, and had heard, within the equal rhythm of his own pulse, the beating of her heart.

There was a knock on the door. After a little while, Sparkenbroke unlocked and opened it.

"Well? . . . Why do you stand there? What have you seen—a ghost?"

Bissett, hearing him speak, could say: "I thought you'd wish to know, m'lord——" and then, staring, was silent.

"What is it? What is it?" Sparkenbroke cried. "For God's sake, say what you have to say! Are you dumb?"

"No, m'lord . . . I knocked at the door—it's very near time for supper, m'lord. They'll be moving down. I thought——"

"Very well. You were right to tell me."

What he had experienced endured in his mind as the sound of a sea endures though the wind that stirred it be fallen; the beat of vision was in him like the beat of waves, his imagination retaining for a little while, not the substance of things seen, but the awful and certain gladness with which he had partaken in the unity of forms. As he made his way along the corridor, he remembered that, while he had been in the window-seat, the wall before him had not been evenly dark but lined with vertical bars of light and darkness. His memory observed the fact, without as yet revealing its significance; but intuition clung to it, bidding him search there for a truth which, if he could but seize it, would declare his experience to him.

He recalled then that a part of this experience had been

to hear again the sound of Nicodemus's axe, and to live again the instant in which Mary had enabled him to hear it. He had been with Nicodemus in the forest—had been in Nicodemus, aware of many cedar-trees, of their ascending darkness and the light between them, and had been quick with that pang of liberty which the bird had known within his open cage—a sense of being himself identical with his expectation, as if he had been listening to the wind and was the wind, or to footsteps and his were the footsteps.

As he approached the end of the corridor that led to the picture-gallery, he found it easy to account for his experience. There was an evident connexion of shape between the cage and the vertical forms of a cedar wood and the bars of light and shadow that he had seen on the wall; but his need was not to have explanation of these things but to discover them in himself and himself in them. While he struggled for this he struggled in vain. At last he ceased to struggle, and took in the scene before him—the arches and balustrade of the gallery, the can-vases aglow beneath their picture-lamps, the little groups mirrored in the polished floor; and, without process of argument, as though a flower had opened in his head, he knew that, in his father's room, he had been gazing through the bars of the Sparkenbroke Mound, had been in his grave; and all he saw and heard that night was seen and heard thenceforward in the power of that exaltation.

In the past, certain onsets of his disease had raised a shutter from between him and death, but always, then, he had been dazzled by pain or by relief from it. Now his experience, unconfused by physical excitement, had rare completeness and intensity, enabling him to preserve within himself the essence of it during long, crowded hours, though he talked to others and appeared to them unchanged.

At supper, and afterwards in the garden or in the ball-room itself, he moved among his guests, having no wish to shut himself away, for they had not power to disturb him. His feeling was, at first, of extreme separation, as though he were not of the same kind with those he watched; but soon he began to perceive that the difference between himself and them was not of nature but of degree, they also carrying within them the spark of that illumination by which he himself was interfused.

He saw them, and in them all mankind, not as they appeared to be but as they were, and knew, with the breathless pang of entry into a new world, that creatures were to be compared in terms, not of beauty or intellect, the qualities of appearance, but of their being permeable by the creative flux. Nothing had virtue of itself, or in its relationship with other things on the same plane with itself, but only in the degree of its penetration through the unreality of particular aspects to the reality of completed being. To penetrate into reality, to be visited and permeated by it—these appeared to him to be the two complementary and governing impulses of life, and he perceived that the social existence to which he had deliberately returned was a denial of these impulses, their poisoning and atrophy.

Seeing his wife look across at him from an opposite doorway, he knew that, for all her forbearance, her care for him, the life she represented was one that he had outgrown; and, from a chair set in the embrasure of a tall, opened window, he watched the dancers, not now with contempt or pity, with none of the judgments of the intellect, but with awe, for in their differing qualities of spirit he saw represented the values of his own life and his many betrayals of them. These were exiles that had forgotten their place of origin, prisoners in whom the idea of freedom was lost; they were earth so paved with pride and knowledge that sun and rain could not enter them nor they bear fruit. In some there survived a vague intuition of the creative flux without power to acknowledge or accept it; from time to time they were haunted by it as men are haunted by a recurrent dream they cannot interpret. They struggled confusedly if they were young, reading poetry they dared not fully receive, experimenting in love they had not the capacity to accept, dabbling

Q

fearfully in the ecstasies, to become at last the prey of charlatans and pedants. Others were hardened against all heat and all inflowing. In them the natural animal was debased and tamed, the god abandoned. They were social beings, shut, impervious, glazed, barren to angels; having no existence except on the plane of unreality, yielded up to exile from themselves. They had cast away that gift of silence to which alone may be added the wisdom without word or sound, whereby, though the ward of the flesh continue, the prisoner is made absolute in his ghostly kingdom.

While in the tale of their varying imperfection, he read his own, his guests became fewer and the sound of music more articulate in the emptying room. Morning rose from the garden with the scent of earth. Upon the faces of those who looked out from the open windows appeared the stress and subtlety of a double light, bleakly exposing the blur of powder at the men's shoulders and streaking with pit and crevice the grey shadow at the women's throats. From time to time one and another said good-bye to him; the last dance was played; the musicians wiped the sweat from inside their collars. There was a rattle of instrument-cases and music-stands, a tramp of black figures across the naked floor.

"Good-night, m'lord."

"Good-night."

He dragged himself from his chair to speak to the head of the orchestra and praise his music, took him downstairs, drank with him and his musicians, and at last let himself out into the garden.

The mood of exaltation in which he had come from his father's room was gone. He was conscious again of his flesh, his vanities, his lust for applause, the arrogant uses of his powers. Tormented by what seemed to be the unbreakable chain of his hypocrisies, he told himself that his return to London, his wish to be finally reconciled with Etty, his determination to make a normal settlement of his life, had all been false. Had he not come, in obedience to the advice an American had once given him, "to cash in on his fame"? He had enjoyed the notoriety he despised; he had shrunk from his own legend—and encouraged it. Was it any regard for Mary or, even, a wish to avoid fruitless entanglement, that had impelled him to let her go? Had it not been rather fear of a love that would have swept him from his cautious reserves, destroyed the compromises of his life, and perhaps—the idea looked up at him with a grin—have made him ridiculous? The same fear of ridicule, the same refusal of love, the desire to startle the foolish or to placate the dull which he contemned in others he discovered in himself. In the world of fashion we are all contaminated, he said—hard, frivolous, cruel, afraid; and feeling the prison walls close about him in this place, he knew that at all costs he must be free of it.

From within the house the illumination of the garden was switched out; a velvet blackness slid over trees and lawn, muffling the daylight. Above him was the scent of syringa, and presently the whiteness of it appeared again as a bloom upon the dark. He saw the sky beyond it, and the line of a wall powdered with morning, and high up, a single window, yellow-lit, from which a woman looked down, her face like ivory, her hair in stiff plaits against her cheeks, an alarm clock in her hand. He saw the glint of the white metal as she turned it over to re-wind it, the twist of her forearm, and the blank stare of the clock-face as she turned it back.

There was no longer any division in his mind. He knew that everything to which he had returned was valueless to him and he to it. His pose before the world fell away from him, and he ceased to calculate or argue, to weigh ambition with pleasure or to consider his actions in the light of opinion. He imagined himself returned to Lucca, there to live without ambition or commitment, so emptied of his former life that a new life would flow into him, making of him and his art an instrument, as the sun and rain make of the earth an instrument of Nature, achieving purposes to which the earth itself is contributory only in its power to be impregnated. It was of the essence of the life he foresaw and of the liberation he experienced that his action should not be intellectually planned. The nature of genius appeared to him as the power to suffer and admit, for what a man does of his will and intellect he does of himself; he can give no more than is in him; but what he admits is of god or devil and, being poured into him, is poured into the imagination of the world.

Chilled with an icy fire by the descent of this liberty upon him, he returned to the house, and went through darkened corridors, in which guard-lights were burning, towards his rooms. On the way he came to Etty's. The door of her sitting-room was partly opened, and he knew that she was waiting for him. He might have passed; though she heard his footstep, she would not call him; but he had loved her, he imagined the droop of her shoulders, the tightening of her lips at once patient and tormented if he went on without a word, and he entered her room.

Partly undressed and wearing a crimson wrap with a high open collar like the collar worn by men in the Regency, she leaned forward in her chair, stretching out her hands to a wood fire newly kindled.

"My dear, are you cold?"

She gave him a hand to feel, smiling and looking up into his face.

"Early mornings need a fire," he said. "It's the time when ghosts walk and changelings appear," for he, too, was glad of the blaze, the lively crackle of twigs.

Seating himself on a stool at her feet, he picked up a long-handled brush and began to push back into the well beneath the grate the glowing pieces that fell from it. "Piers!" she exclaimed, "the bristles are catching fire," and he rubbed out the sparks against the hearthstone. She was talking of the people who had come to the ball and of how many had been glad that he was entertaining in Chelmouth House again; and Richard, too, had been glad; he was old enough now to feel the tradition he would inherit. "You know," she said, "it's a kind of game I play with him—how, piece by piece, we shall win back the whole estate, in London as well as in Dorset, as it was in your grandfather's time. He wants to know whether we shall have racing-stables again."

"Shall we?"

"I think we might. I don't see why not. In his time, Piers, if not in our own."

"But do we care a damn about racing-stables—you or I or Richard?"

"He knows that his grandfather won the Derby and the Oaks in the same year. . . . And you, Piers? Confess. I know racing has never meant much to you, but has a poet ever led in the winner of the Derby?"

He turned up his head and laughed. "You know me too well, Etty. Extravagant fame and spectacular withdrawals; a developed sensuality and a monkish spirit within; a great landowner and a wanderer on the face of the earth—and, if you like, a cheering mob at Epsom and a secret loathing of them. It was all true. How you must have hated the showman—you, too, sometimes, with the rest of the world!"

"No," she said, "it was part of you."

"It was part of Nelson if it comes to that. Wasn't it, Etty? Remember what the school-books find it convenient to forget—the processions, the laurel-wreaths, his host's wife. He was more than half mountebank and cad, by our standards. However, I admit that I have yet to win the battle of Trafalgar!"

She stared at him. "You say that as if you were attacking yourself, not Nelson."

He smiled. "So I was. That's the blessing of you, Etty. Other people think that my shames are my vanities. When I boast like a fool or chatter about Nelson like a half-wit in a debating society, you know that I——"

"Nothing matters," she said, "if you have come back now. If to-night's a beginning between us, nothing else matters to me."

Again she stretched down her hand to him. He did not take it, and leaned nearer to the fire, seeking the words with which to interrupt her; but before he could speak, she took his head and drew it against her knee.

"You were happy to-night, Piers? And proud—a little?"

He moved his head in the prison of her hands, trembling because the fullness of her heart was communicated to him, and because he knew that, like a traitor, he was already escaped from her life. He did not hear what she was saying. He was remembering her as she had been when most he had needed her, the only human being on earth with the faith and patience to receive him. He remembered her with Richard at her breast; he saw her battling with ledgers and income-tax returns; he recalled, with a dry shudder of the senses, how she, being herself a simple, affectionate lover but without sensual imagination, had tried, with groping experimentalism, to be his, even in his sensuality. He had not dared check her lest he should seem to scorn her failures, and by his suffering at that time was now able to measure her own. How much she had suffered! How indomitably, through the years, she had hoped—for what? For to-night? For the day in which he would return and their life together fall into that evenness which was, for her, safety, a condition of happiness and honour. He had nothing to give her. In his heart, he was already separated from her. She had been no part of his imagining in the garden; his future did not hold her; but over his eyes he felt her fingers close, and between the lighted rims of her fingers the gleam of fire came in.

"And if that is to be so," she was saying, "Richard——" She drew breath and waited. She was waiting for him to speak. "I think, now, Richard's very strong and healthy," she continued in that voice of reticence by which her deepest emotions were denied expression. "I don't fear for him in the ordinary way. Still, we ought to consider everything—war or accidents. There's no one else to inherit. The title would go. I suppose the estates would break up. And after you and Richard there'd be——"

Before she could say the words "no one," he swung round, thrust the stool away, and gathered his feet under him, his body erect, his head thrown back. But the fierceness went out of him. A longing that he might be enabled to communicate and she to receive, appeared in his face. With his forearms rested on her knees, he said:

"You mean that you wish us to have another child?"

"Yes."

"To inherit this? To make sure of it?"

"Yes, Piers. Why is that wrong?"

It is not wrong of this life, her life and mine, he thought, but that life is ended. The man who existed in it no longer exists; but she looks at me and sees the same man whom she has always served and loved. Whatever my mouth says will be for her an insult and a lie.

While silence continued between them, she knew that her hope was dead. She had only to await the pronouncement of its death—the explanation he would give, the vain answers she would make. She found that what she chiefly cared for was to drive back tears from her eyes, for Piers hated weeping, and to keep her body still, not to stand up, not to cry out, not to speak, to confine all movement to the twitching muscle in her side and the rhythmical expansion and contraction of her tongue against the upper walls of her mouth.

He had no other desire than to escape from this silence and to cease torturing her. I should have gone from London at once. I have accustomed her to that kind of cruelty—but not to this! and he saw himself kneeling beside her, dumb because what was now the single truth and necessity of his life could not be expressed to her except as insult and hypocrisy.

Observing her face as the meaning of his silence became clear in her mind, he saw her lower lids tremble under the first impact of terror. The human features, he thought, have a very narrow but a profoundly subtle expressive range. This is the flinching of the soul itself; it is the ruin and cancellation of her life, yet that flicker of the lower lids, that drying of the mouth-corners and simian shrinkage of the face is the expression of a child suddenly aged by trivial disappointment.

"Piers—what are you looking at?"

"Your face."

"My face," she repeated.

"Shall I tell you what I was doing?" he cried. "Shall I tell you? If I can confess that, I can confess anything. I was learning from your misery what a face looks like when it is tormented, what changes it undergoes, how it shrinks like a monkey's face, and the mouth opens a little, and the saliva burns dry. It is true. Your despair, my insults, everything we say and do—some day I shall dip my pen in it."

She had no thought but to calm him.

"You have not insulted me," she said and took his hand. "Tell me, why may we not have another child?"

"This isn't a beginning between us. It is an end."

"You mean that you are going away?"

"But it is an end, an end, an end!" he repeated. "You want to know why. You have a right to know. And if I were to say that I have seen a new life in a vision and that I must lead it, what would you answer? A pretty excuse for running away with another girl! Sparkenbroke's a saint that must always have a new woman in his bed! . . . And I should say: She's part of the new life. Her body is the night of the old day, the morning of the new. Words, words—all true for me, all lies for you, whining and contemptible for the world. Look at me, Etty, and remember me with ridicule; that will be my punishment." He dragged his hand from her and sat back on his heels. "Look at me who haven't the self-control to keep my reasons to myself! Our guests to-night have prescribed a convention for these things. Why can't I stand here coolly and say: 'My dear Etty, I want you to give me my freedom. I ask your licence to commit adultery with another woman.' 'Do you love her so much?' you would say. 'If you love her, you must be free.' I should tell you that Mary is to be your successor. We should be very considerate and gentle to each other. We shouldn't discuss her. We should discuss Richard—the estates, too, but Richard chiefly. You'd be generous on the subject of access. You'd be courteous enough not to speak of money because most of it's yours. Our lawyers would do the rest. . . . Instead of that I ask you to believe that I've undergone a spiritual revolution and that Mary's an aspect of it." He raised his voice in mockery of himself. " 'Her body is the night of the old day, the morning of the new!' What is it—a catch from a *revue* song or a sick psalm?" His fists went up to the sides of his mouth, their pressure distorting it. He rose and, turning from her, leaned against the mantelpiece. "Etty, I've only a half-knowledge of what I have been saying." And he added very slowly, separating word from word: "You married a man with a devil in him, that he cannot cast out."

Even when he spoke of Mary, it seemed to her that he was speaking of something she had long known, and she remembered that she had observed the girl closely since her return with George from Lucca, had made friends with her, had continually talked of her to George, and studied, with an interest then believed to be impersonal, the relationship between them. She had been glad that they were happy; a new tenderness in the girl had told her that at last they were happy even in their bodies.

"Piers," she said, "if you came home for her, why didn't you tell me then?"

"I didn't know, Etty. I didn't come to England for her, but to live at Sparkenbroke and forget her—not forget," he cried, struggling for the truth, "but to outgrow the need of her. I wanted that."

"And now? What has changed, Piers? You are going. You're never coming back. That's all I know. It's like things that happened in childhood. People came and went; you didn't know why; you were given reasons, but they didn't seem to be reasons. If it were just the body I could understand it. I've never been jealous in that way. I'm not jealous of her. I feel as if you were dying—that's all——"

"Dying?" he said.

"Going where you might be lonely and frightened and haunted. I shan't be able to reach you." She began to turn her head with little movements to and fro. "After our years together—not that years matter . . . I've seen you in such agony. . . . Like Richard in agony. . . . You let me help you then." Unable to direct her words, she leaned forward, took his hand and drew him down to her. "As if you were drowning," she said, "and I letting you go."

"It is a kind of death, Etty—an end of the life I have known, the beginning of another. It's not the exchange of you for Mary. It's the beginning of another story with different people—with myself as you know me gone out of it. What the new story will be, I don't know—not, even, that Mary is a part of it, but I know the theme of it," and he began to tell her of his experience that night and that, when he came from his father's room, he had seemed to be raised up from the grave.

"I think," he said, "it comes also to whole peoples—a knowledge that they've outgrown their past, they must destroy even what is dearest to them in their past—the more cruelly because it's most dear. They must die, they say, that they may live again; it's the desire of every revolution; it has ruled me. Nations can't fulfil it. A man must die alone and be born alone. He can do nothing collectively, except act, and, when he begins to translate a spiritual impulse into political action, the impulse is perverted. Nations fail because they cannot first confess.

"Perhaps I shall fail for the same reason," he said after a pause, beginning to speak to her with reliance and affection as he might have spoken, not to the woman he was deserting, but to a friend in whom he had trust. "Did you know, Etty, that my mad shouting at you just now was an attempt to confess? I think that was the meaning of it. I can hear it now, like the shouting of a mob—out for blood in which to wash their hands of the past."

"What is it," she said, "that you have to confess? We are alone in this room. It's the last time we shall be alone."

"I can't confess to you—to you least of all."

"I love you, Piers. That's why I exist."

"That's the reason. That's the reason," he repeated, taking her hands for the first time. "Confession itself is a sin against you. There are silences that must be kept."

"Not by the dying." Her fingers moved within his and she could not speak. "If you were dying bodily," she said at last, "I should have wanted you to die in my arms."

But if he had been able to confess, he would not now have been deserting her, and he could say only: "All my sins are one sin: hardness of heart. Sometimes I think there's no sin but that—to refuse, to shut out. In me it's the unforgivable sin, the one I cannot forgive myself. All my life I have had powers not given to other men, or to very few. I don't mean the power to write but the power to listen. That's the supreme power. I've quenched it in myself, planning, thinking, fearing. What will become of me now, I don't know. If I try to think out my future, at once it becomes impossible and ridiculous. If I go to Lucca, I shall be known there; if Mary is with me, her own life will cling to her and to me; if she's not, I shall be torn by her absence; if I write, my prides, my reputation, the idiom of my dead life will infest the new; if I change my name, the change itself will become a form of notoriety. The intellect turns all spiritual purposes to futility and ridicule. I remember, when I was a boy, I used to go out on to the moors looking for certain birds and for rare grasses. I'd learnt a great deal of them—where to look, and why—but when my reason and patience failed, I found them in another way. I lay down and waited. I forgot the bird I was looking for, and suddenly I'd hear it. I forgot the grass, and suddenly I'd see in my imagination the place where it was. And I know that the time has come for my former life to die. A new life will come because it has been imagined. The new life is there—in what form I don't know—only that the intellect denies it form, yet it's there, waiting for me, a miracle fully imagined—a silence, unbroken even by speculation, an absolute power to hear and accept."

"Piers," she said, stooping over him, "when I am dying I shall hear your voice saying those words. 'A silence, unbroken even by speculation, an absolute power to hear and accept.' But I don't believe it is to be found in any human love, in my own or yours or any other, unless by a miracle."

"Nothing is to be found," he answered, "except by a miracle."

His voice failed, his head sagged under her hands; his weight, leaning against her, increased. The spring went out of his body. She fell upon her knees beside him.

"Once—it was before we married—a winter's afternoon in my father's house—you repeated to me something which, at that time, seemed—I didn't then understand why—seemed to mark—"

He was taut now, watching her. Leaning away from him she was at length able to say:

"To mark, you said, a new beginning of your life. Do you remember?"

"Augustine and Monica. I remember."

"Do you remember the words now?" she asked in a stifled voice. "Will you say them to me?"

He laid his hands upon hers and began to say: " 'If to any the tumult of the flesh were hushed; hushed the images of earth, of waters and of air; hushed also the poles of heaven; yea, were the very soul to be hushed to herself, and by not thinking on self to surmount self; hushed all dreams and imaginary revelations, every tongue and every sign; if all transitory things were hushed utterly . . . if, when their speech had gone out they should suddenly hold their peace, and to the ear which they had aroused to their Maker, He himself should speak, alone, not by them, but by himself, so that we should hear his word, not through any tongue of flesh, nor Angel's voice, nor echo of thunder, nor in the dark riddle of a similitude, but might hear indeed Him, whom in these things we love, himself without these——' "

Sparkenbroke could not continue, nor could he speak more to her. While they had been speaking the fire had died. Their hands were cold. He rose and went from her to the window. Beyond the curtains, morning was bleak and high. It was Sunday, and bells were ringing. Returning, he stood beside her a little while where she knelt, but though she raised her face to his, there was nothing that either dared say or do. He kneeled down and would have kissed her, but she held back, quivering, and hid her face, and, in the darkness of her hands, waited until he was gone.

BOOK VI

THE FOREIGN COUNTRY

SPARKENBROKE

CHAPTER ONE

EVERY morning, a few minutes before eleven o'clock, Felling, the male nurse who attended the Rector, brought him downstairs. With the help of the banisters and, afterwards, of a stick, the old man was able to walk by himself, not lifting his feet except when a staircase compelled him to it but sliding each foot a few careful inches and halting now and then for rest. Felling walked behind him, ready to support his elbows if he should stumble or sway. If the day was cold, the Rector was settled in the library, his back to the light; if fine, he went out to the place on the lawn from which Helen's chair and the feet of her visitors had long ago worn away the grass. Every Sunday on his way to church, where he sometimes preached though he did not conduct the Services, he turned aside to the grave in which Helen's ashes were buried. Mary went with him, he leaning on her arm. At the grave, he took her hand, for he knew that she blamed herself for not having been with Helen when she died. He did not know that this regular taking of her hand had acquired, for her, a different emphasis, or that by it she was reminded of Sparkenbroke.

It was a reminder which she had ceased to fear, for it did not disturb her. It touched her with the wonder of a life that she had put away. Help his work and make him happy. Keep me from pride and longing. Teach me to love him without sin. Though we do not meet, let us not fear to remember. If we meet, be with us then. At first, after her return from Lucca, this prayer had brought tears to her eyes. As the winter passed, she had grown calmer;

she had used it with other prayers, for George and the
Rector, and had added to it a thanksgiving for peace of
mind. During a visit to London, she had come upon a cast
of Ilaria's tomb in the Victoria and Albert Museum.

"That is in the Cathedral at Lucca."

"Oh, is it?" George had answered and he had examined
it with interest.

As they walked out of Gunter's after tea, he had asked
her suddenly: "That doesn't worry you any more?"

"What?"

"Lucca."

She had shaken her head.

"All over?"

"It doesn't worry me any more."

Sometimes, lately, she had forgotten to pray, for she
was happy.

"Piers has finished *Tristan*," George had announced
one morning at breakfast. He had not shown her the
letter, but later in the same day she had seen its envelope
on the small table beside the Rector's chair. She had
touched it and had imagined Piers at his desk, his moving
head and his eyes looking up at her.

"I'm glad Piers has done his book," the Rector had
said. "It will do us both good to read it together."

Often she read to him, books and newspapers, in the
mornings soon after eleven, and in the evenings, in his
own bedroom, before Felling settled him to sleep.

" 'LORD SPARKENBROKE IN LONDON. . . . NEW TREAT-
MENT OF OLD LOVE-STORY. . . . Lord Sparkenbroke
reached England from Italy yesterday. He drove at once
from Victoria to Chelmouth House which, though still
owned by him, has not been occupied by the Tenniel
family since 1905. Lady Sparkenbroke has rented it for
a short season from her husband's tenant, Mr. H. E. S.
Grisby, the head of the well-known firm of textile manu-
facturers, and will give a Ball there. Lord Sparkenbroke
refused to make any statement of his plans. Asked about
his novel, *Tristan and Iseult*, the completion of which was

first exclusively announced in these columns three weeks ago, he pointed to a bag, which his manservant had not let out of his hand, and said: "There it is. If I could tell you in a sentence what it is about, would it have been necessary for poor Bissett to drag a thousand sheets of manuscript across Europe?" Asked why he chose to write of times so distant from our own, he replied——' "

"He must be sick to death of that question," said the Rector. "Why does every newspaper conversation make a man sound a prig or a fool? Piers says it is because things said casually, which ought to be passed over in *oratio obliquâ*, are wrongly isolated and set up in the glaring emphasis of direct speech. There'd be fewer wars if there were no inverted commas. . . . Does it tell us how long he is staying?"

" 'Indefinitely, it says."

"That commits him to nothing."

They continued to discuss him, and while the Rector was telling her of a mis-translation that Piers had made when he was a boy, she watched the leaves of the sycamore and remembered how calm her voice had been while she read of Piers in the newspaper.

If I had gone with him to Florence, she was thinking, that column of the newspaper would now have been filled by something else, and she stared at the crumpled sheet on the ground; the headlines shifted in her view, and she tried to imagine what they would have been. She would not have been here at all. Where? Where? A room with a wall of white plaster appeared in her imagination. She was alone in it. The shutters were closed and the room was dim, but outside the sun was shining with a bright, cruel heat; the air was full of strange smells and the sounds of foreign voices; her body was lulled and sleepy, but her mind could not sleep; she was lonely and afraid, she was thinking of the Rectory as of a safety lost, a companionship abandoned.

But I am at the Rectory; that is Helen's sycamore, and she remembered that Helen was dead. She sat down on the grass beside the old man's chair, with one hand turning the newspaper, with the other, which supported her, feeling the upward heat of the earth.

"I have some things to do in the house." She sprang up. "I'll come out again."

"Will George be in to lunch?"

"He said he thought so."

She looked forward to his coming and, two hours later, ran out into the hall at the sound of his step and the rattle of his stick in the umbrella-stand. She put her arms round his neck and kissed him.

"Bless you," he said, "I'm not much late, am I? Father in from the garden yet?"

As he strode on towards the garden door he felt his hand taken from behind.

"George. . . ." He turned. She did not release his hand. "Take me with you this afternoon."

"On the round?"

"Please!"

"There's nothing I should like better. But why particularly?"

"Not 'particularly.' I thought I'd like the drive. We used to, often—do you remember?"

He nodded, a little surprised by her emphasis, delighted by her vitality. "Yes. Good. Let's do that." He would have kissed her, but her eyes were dulled again. Already she appeared to be thinking of something else.

During the next month Sparkenbroke's name appeared often in the newspaper, always on the sheet that happened to lie uppermost. While she was reading to George's father, her eyes, lifted for a moment from the page, would see the name look up from the folded paper on the shelf beside his bed; or, in the kitchen, she would find, when she raised her hand from the table, that it had been concealing the name printed in the column before her.

Its recurrence did not trouble her, for she had no doubt of herself. In any case Piers was far away; it was probable that he would return to Italy without visiting Sparkenbroke Green, for Richard's being in London took away his chief reason for coming to Dorset; and if he did come, he would keep his pledge. She felt older and wiser than she had been in Lucca—stronger, too. In the evenings, when she knew from what direction George would return from his work, she walked out to meet him and climbed into his car. At night, if it was her turn to read to his father, she went down afterwards to George in the dispensary, as she had done in the early days of their marriage; or, if she went to bed early, she lay awake until he came.

One Saturday evening, she saw that the Rector drew his rug higher over his body while she was reading to him. The movement reminded her of the day on which her own father had died. She put down her book and held out a match to the grate. By its flame, she saw the word Sparkenbroke on a bulge of paper among the kindling, and watched it burn. As soon as the fire was well alight, she continued to read. There's nothing in it, of course, she said to herself. It's only that I happen to notice it when it *is* there. Other names are there as often—the King's, but I don't notice the King's.

"Why have you stopped, my dear? Tired?"

She noticed, as she answered, that the Rector's voice had been louder than usual, and knew suddenly that his question had been asked more than once, twice certainly, perhaps three times. How long had she been silent, the volume of Gibbon idle in her lap? She glanced at the old face; it was expressionless, the eyes almost closed; the lips made no smiling, easy comment on her absent-mindedness. Well, your thoughts were far away! he might have said; but he had abstained.

She began to read again. Soon he would say, as he did each night: Thank you, Mary. Now let us talk for a minute or two before Felling comes in to put me to bed. She determined to keep her attention firmly on the narrative, but wondered, at the same time, whether George also was allowing absent-mindedness in her to pass unreproved. He and his father had, each in his own way, so extraordinary a

forbearance. Both had an air of waiting—the Rector sometimes with impatience—for the world to come to its senses.
Time, George would say, is generally the best remedy.
Men of character cure themselves in the end—like a
patient with a constitution. Keep them warm; give them
rest; don't shout and bother them. Nursing's the key to
medicine—nursing, and the will to live. That phrase,
"the will to live," had an echo in her mind, and, turning
a page of Gibbon, she listened for the echo until she remembered that Piers had spoken to her of the will to die,
and she looked at the two phrases, one on the left, the
other on the right, like the margins of her book. But when
he asked why I had stopped reading, I wasn't thinking of
Piers; I was thinking of the King and how odd it must be
to take out a handful of change from your pocket and see
your own head, or your father's or your grandmother's,
on every coin. I wasn't thinking of Piers. Perhaps he's
reading a book too, with the edge of a page sharp in the
joint of his finger. But to-night there's a ball at Chelmouth
House. It is George who is reading, down in the dispensary.
When I go in, he'll close his book on his finger; his other
hand will twist the loose tag of leather on his chair while
we talk. Then candles. The banister shadows like the
spokes of a wheel. So quiet, she thought, that if I lie still
in bed for a long time it will seem that the sound of dance-
music—for after all sound goes out endlessly, doesn't it?
like the ripples on a pool; and it seemed that her head was
already on her pillow and that there were no walls to
interrupt the long ripples flowing towards her on the air.

"Sleepy?"

"Not really," but the book was sliding from her knee.

To-night he did not discuss *The Decline and Fall* with
her. "Will you pull the bell, my dear? It's a little before
my time, but I'm ready for bed. . . . Thank you for your
reading; it is one of my greatest pleasures; there's a bond
between two people in sharing a masterpiece. One never
forgets it, I think. You will never forget, whenever you
see Gibbon on a shelf, that you and I read him together."

"George and I read aloud too."

"I was thinking of that."

"In Sicily we read *Inglesant*."

"And now?"

"At the moment," she said, "we aren't reading anything together. George is in the middle of Zimmern——"

"*The Greek Commonwealth*. And you?"

"I was reading Keats's *Letters*—but I finished them about three weeks ago."

"And since?"

"Only bits here and there."

"That's all right. It's no good forcing yourself to a book. Go on browsing. In the end, a book will suggest itself. . . . What put you on to Keats's *Letters*?"

"I'm not sure. . . . There's Felling now. He always grunts on the stairs. . . . Oh, yes," she said, "I remember. I began Keats at Lucca."

"With Helen?"

"No, to myself."

In the dispensary, she leaned over the back of George's chair.

"Have you nearly finished Zimmern?"

"One more evening. Why? Do you want him?"

"Couldn't we read a book together again?"

"We can do that without waiting for Zimmern."

"In Sicily, do you remember, we used to go up to our rooms in that funny little hotel and read before we went to sleep?—or until you did!"

He closed *The Greek Commonwealth*. "Let's begin to-night," and they wandered about the house together holding a candle to the shelves. "Yes," he said, laughing, "it's all very well, but we must have a book! You can't royally reject all literature."

She stood up from the bookcase into which she had been peering and handed the candle to him: "I know," she said. "*Inglesant*."

"Again?"

"Not all of it, perhaps. The Little Gidding part."

"You always loved Nicholas Ferrar!"

"I imagined him with your face."

"Mine, but——"

"I know. Not really like. . . . Still, I did." She began to go upstairs. "Because I loved him." And before he could answer, she added: "*Inglesant's* in the low shelf in the dining-room, I think. You find him, while I undress. . . . No. I don't want the candle. I can feel my way. Besides, there's a night-light on the landing. Hold yours for a moment till I get there." And she whispered from above: "All right, George. Now I can see."

CHAPTER TWO

PROBABLY, she thought, as she came out of church next evening, he came over to London chiefly for the ball; now it's over, he will soon go abroad again; and she felt that the influence which had lately disturbed the waters of her life had passed on like a wind, leaving them to their former tranquillity. She hoped that she would never become so old or set as to reprove herself for having loved him or to forget the manner of it; she had been alive then as she would not be again; but she was glad that the stress of that love was now in the past.

So far in the past was it and so gentle her mind's composure this July evening, that she was able without misgiving, with indeed a strengthened assurance, to turn aside into the graveyard, to read again the inscription on the Sparkenbroke Mound, and, wandering on to the wooden bridge, go home by way of Derry's Wood and the drop into the Ancaster road. When she reached the cross-roads she saw George climbing the hill from the village. He had, she knew, been visiting Mrs. Geddes. There was no more that he or any man could do for her, but he was fond of her, admiring her humour and patience, and he indulged her whim, shared by her frightened family, that she could not safely prepare for the night until the doctor had visited her.

Mary waved to him. He took off his hat and stood at the Rectory gate, talking to Caesar, the cocker-spaniel he had bought for her when they returned from Italy. "Look! Look who's coming!" he said, pointing up the hill with his stick; but Caesar took this to be an invitation to carry the stick and began to angle for possession of it. When at last he discovered Mary's approach, he bounded in welcome of her, not advancing up the hill, but padding his feathered paws from side to side, crouching, and swinging his great ears. His shadow, cast by the evening sun, bounded with him; he saw it, was puzzled, stiffened, was still, and leapt away from it. George began to laugh, and she thought: What a good laugh he has! I've never heard him laugh *at* anyone—not even at Caesar! She took his arm and they went on together towards the white bridge.

"Do you know Derry's Stream is almost dry?"

"Well, our own stream isn't exactly a torrent," he said, and they stopped to listen to it and to watch the swoop of bats across the white face of the Rectory.

"Sometimes," she said, "I feel almost as if I'd been brought up here. You were lucky, George."

"I am. . . . But it was a good guess of mine about you. That first day, when I met you and your father in Chelmouth, I thought you were the kind of person that grew roots."

"But you weren't planning to marry me then, were you?"

He hesitated. "Do you know, I'm not sure that I can answer that truthfully. It seems absurd, but I believe it did cross my mind. But you were engaged."

"Peter!" she said, but it was Piers's face she saw before her. Merton's Passage, the book-shop—what was the name of the book she had picked up from the tray? Hazlitt: *Liber Amoris*. To this day she hadn't read it; perhaps it was there still. "I wonder what has become of Peter."

"He married. I saw it announced."

"But why didn't you tell me? You didn't imagine I still had dreams of him?"

"No," he answered, moving off to the house, "I didn't imagine you still had dreams of him."

Because it was Sunday night, the Rector, to vary his routine, came into the dining-room for supper. Afterwards there was no reading aloud to him, for he would play chess with Mr. Ryman, who, having taken duty in church, had come in for his bottle of claret and his game. "Let's walk a bit," George said, "and turn in early. Caesar will be glad of it too. It's one of the evenings to remember when you're so old you can't see or smell or feel or taste or hear any more. The hedgerows have a scent that makes your heart turn over." On their way through the garden. he stopped and took her hands and gazed at her.

"I used to be frightened of that," he said.

"Of what, my dear?" She spoke with trembling gentleness, for she saw that he was deeply moved.

"That you were—more than normally—beautiful. It seemed incredible that so much—in that way—should have been given to me. I mean," he added hastily, lest he should seem to be squandering himself in false modesty, "I mean that in other ways—affection, loyalty, understanding, all that—I felt I had something to give in return for what you gave me. But you see—" He broke off and did not continue until they were walking up the hill towards Sparkenbroke Cross. "You see—I take no credit for it, but it's true—I didn't happen to be a very sensual man. I liked the look of a pretty girl but not more than her pretty frock and less than a flower. I didn't mean to marry, I didn't want to, I wasn't even lonely—or didn't know I was. I didn't think of women's bodies much except to mend them when they broke— seldom, anyhow, and not intensely. And then—I don't know why I'm talking to-night."

"Because I want to listen."

"Well," he said, "then there was you. For me, it was like being the lover of some princess in an Arabian Night. I seemed to have wandered clean out of my own story. I do still when I look at you. But it frightened me then, and now——"

"It needn't, George."

"I know. . . . I think," he said, smiling suddenly, "with all your faults you must be the least vain woman in the world."

"About my face?"

"Do you ever look into a mirror, except to do your hair?"

"Not much. That's true. Not to stare at myself. You see, in a sense, I was made in much the same way as you—a kind of converse of you. I didn't think of men looking at me—as you said—'very intensely.' But I did look into a mirror once," she continued, borne out of his presence by the sudden flow of her thought and seeing herself at her dressing-table in Lucca with her smudged Journal beneath her hand. "I remember once looking into a mirror when I was crying, to see what my face looked like when I cried!"

"Crying?" he repeated.

But she did not answer, and they walked on beside the little stream that divided road from churchyard until they came to a stretch of road that was still light, there being no trees to darken it.

"You mustn't ever be afraid," she said, and added very softly and without emphasis, as if she were reading the words from some page spread before her: "Never—never—never." After another long pause, she said: "I'm happy too. Not just for your sake—for my own."

They did not turn back until night had almost come. They had to call the dog who had gone on ahead, beyond their sight. "There ought to be a moon," George said, but though the evening had been clear when they set out and the air had still a buoyancy and freshness that promised a fine night, the moon was retired. As they walked home, they talked of their plans for the autumn. A year would then have passed since George's holiday in Sicily, and she wondered how, without neglect of his father, it could be made possible that he and she might leave the Rectory together for more than a few days. Somehow it must be arranged; even if it could not, she would be content; and seeing that George was troubled lest he and his father should seem to be holding her prisoner, she ceased to talk of foreign journeys and said they would make their own holiday in Sparkenbroke Green itself if he would hand over his practice for a fortnight or three weeks. "Perhaps," he said. "I'll see what can be done."

It was not of the autumn he was thinking, but that to-night, in less than an hour, so soon that the pliancy of her was already beneath the touch of his mind, she would be lying with him. She knew it by his quietness, and by his shivering response, the sudden grip of his fingers, when she took his hand. He held her body to him and kissed her. How happy she was, loving him as she had not loved him in the past, glad now of his touch, his eagerness, the spring of youth in him that she evoked! The great wrought-iron gates of Sparkenbroke House, through which he had driven her on her first visit there, were left behind, the trees of the churchyard darkened the way before them, and, at the corner of Derry's Wood, at the cross-roads, seeing some object glint in the road at his feet, he stooped to pick it up.

"Careful, George. There's a car coming."

He stood back to the side of the road, his head bent to examine what he held in the cup of his hand. "Only a stone after all," he said, and tossed it into the hedge. A bird that had been sleeping there rose into the darkness.

She took his arm at once and led him downhill towards the Rectory. She was listening to the car as it swung on in the direction of Ancaster. The sound of its movement was quieted suddenly. It had stopped, not at the stile by which she had come from Derry's Wood that evening, but at the farther gate. Bissett would climb down and open the gate. Soon he would be carrying their suit-cases across the wooden bridge to the cottage. In the windows, light would appear.

It would have been easy to say: that was Piers, I think; but she said nothing. The hall was dark when they entered it. While George was lighting a candle, she heard Caesar padding over the linoleum which led him to the scullery where he slept. His basket creaked as he settled in it. The candle-flame drew up.

They went upstairs together and listened at the Rector's door, but he was asleep.

"I want to get one or two things ready for the morning.
I'll follow you," George said, and, in gratitude for the unspoken promise that she had seemed to give while they
were walking home, he would have kissed her again. The
hand in which she held her candle was jerked by his moving arm and the wax overflowed. He stood back, laughing
at what he supposed to have been his own clumsiness.

In their bedroom she wished to be solitary, but stifled
her wish. Soon George would come up. She would say
something at once as he entered, that no silence should
fall between them. What should she say? Did you know
you woke a bird when you threw your stone into the hedge?
I wonder who won at chess to-night? Ought we to have
been back, I wonder, to see Mr. Ryman before he went?
She spoke these questions with her lips, but silently, looking at herself in the mirror and watching her lips move.

In the morning, she wished above all else to tell George
that Piers was in Derry's Cottage.

On Sunday evening, it would have been natural, and
consistent with her happy mood, to have said at once: Did
you see? Piers was in that car! Her silence had not been a
reasoned but an intuitive lie. It had the more clearly revealed her own secrets to her, and she desired now, by
confession, to annul them in her mind. While she gave
George his breakfast, her lips moved continually to speak.
But, my dear, why didn't you tell me at the time? George
would say, or, perhaps, to spare her, would say nothing.
Still I must tell him, I must tell him, she said to herself.
If only I can tell him, all will be well. She followed him
out to his car and he started the engine. His foot was on
the accelerator when she began to speak, and he did not
hear. She watched him go. Though he turned round, she
could not wave, for she felt that this also would be to lie.

How absurd! It can make no difference. What am I
crying about?

Before going to make up the laundry-list, she went into
George's dispensary. Here she changed the blotting-
paper on his table and, taking the roses from his bowl,

clipped their stems. While the fragments were falling into the waste-paper basket, each with a little clack in answer to the snip of her scissors, she began to remember, as though he were dead, the happiness that he and she had known together, and there passed through her body that shudder of failure and loneliness which cries, through all partings: Why did I not love him more, while there was time?

The day being overcast, the Rector spent the morning in his library. She went to him there at a quarter past eleven and read *The Times* aloud.

Soon he checked her, saying with a glance at her grave, abstracted expression that, after all, the chief value of a political newspaper, earnestly advocating this or that, was to remind one of the maxim of Descartes that nothing was altogether within our power except our thoughts. " '*Ma troisième maxime était de tâcher toujours plutôt à me vaincre que la fortune et à changer mes désirs que l'ordre du monde.*' A good motto for the desk of a politician! But my accent is vile," he exclaimed. "You shall be spared it; but if you would give me Descartes, I might read a little to myself. It's on the window-ledge."

From the window she saw Piers coming down through the orchard. The branches intervened and his face was seldom visible.

"Piers is in the garden," she said, but so quietly that she had to walk across the room and repeat it: "Piers is in the garden."

"Piers," he answered, and stirred, as though listening for a footstep. Then, with authority: "Go and meet him, Mary."

The front door stood open. From the hall, she was looking beyond him into the light.

"Mary?"

He came near but did not touch her. The absence of touch, his nearness, the hush between them, enwrapped her as though she were in the arms of a ghost. At last she said dully:

"I saw you from the window. . . . He's in the library, waiting." She thought she had begun to move towards the library, but her limbs were still.

On the table in the hall was a large bowl, round which blue Chinese warriors were climbing a rocky path. She watched them, remembering that, behind the bowl, they would reach the summit of a mountain.

He took her hands. She yielded them but did not move. She was waiting for his eyes, and, when his head was lifted again, her long gaze continued until, suddenly, she whispered: "How changed you are! . . . Oh, Piers, why did you come? I was so happy yesterday!"

"For you."

She did not answer, but little sounds came from her as though her heart would break. He led her into a room of which the door stood open, and she saw that she was in the dispensary, seated on an upright chair at the end of the table. At her feet was the waste-paper basket; a thorny clipping of rose-stem clung to its edge. From another chair, on the arm of which he was sitting, Piers leaned across the table and took a pair of scissors into his hand. She saw that they were wet, and would rust.

"What did you mean—'changed'?" he said. "How am I changed?"

She looked at him and answered: "New. In some way —new. Happy."

"Because I'm near you."

She shook her head. "Not that. Something else has changed—a wonderful change." She stood up, her body like iron; then, passing her hands across her eyes, sat down and smiled suddenly: "Perhaps it was seeing you like that —through the window. It's as if you'd risen from the dead," and her cheeks flushed as though she were ashamed of what she had said.

He began to tell her of his last days in Lucca and of his last hours in Chelmouth House, wishing her to understand why he had come for her.

"If we go now," he said, "perhaps we shall never return to England. From the point of view of men we respect—George and his father—we shall have betrayed everyone who loved and trusted us. We have no answer that can have any meaning for them. If they forgive us, it will be as men forgive the dead."

She listened in such a way that he could not be certain she was listening. Her face had become pale; her lips were dry, her eyes open and shining. Sometimes she folded or unfolded her hands.

When he was silent, her gaze moved wildly around the room. "I love this place—and all the people in it." Then, looking steadfastly at him, she added in a tone of shame and astonishment: "But it makes no difference. None. With you—there's some other blood in me." Then, in anguish: "What will become of them? Last night—it's true—it's true, Piers—he was my lover; he didn't know I'd seen you. Afterwards—long afterwards—I lighted the candle. He was asleep. . . . Do you know? Do you understand that? It's like poisoning him in his sleep."

She stood up and he took her in his arms.

"This is his room," she said.

"My dear, I know."

"It was here— Oh, Piers, shut him out! Shut everything out! I want to die in everything I am, except in you." She began to kiss him, with kisses that feared to cease. Then: "Is it now?"

"Now?"

"That I'm to come?"

"Yes."

"Without seeing him? . . . To-night, where shall we be?"

"Away from here."

"Am I—to write—something?" She looked at the desk.

"What do you want to write?"

"For him. I must. He'd wander about the house, not knowing. . . . Helpless. Like a dog people leave behind."

But as soon as Piers touched her she forgot the desk, and, listening to his voice through the darkness of her closed eyes, feeling his breath upon her as he spoke, and, now and then, even the contact of his lips, she sighed in

R

terrified memory of his absence—a low, tormented sigh.

"I love you. I love you," she said again and again; then, in passionate entreaty, that she might persuade herself: "You. You only. It's true. Without you— And you, too," she added slowly, "are giving up everything."

For a little while they were silent. If they moved or spoke, time would seize them. They would know again the place they were in and what they must do; one would speak, the other answer; from the wordless security of loving and being loved, they would move out into the peril of words; and even beneath his lips, she remembered how, in this room, she had asked George that they should read *Inglesant* together, and she said aloud: "We shall never finish it. He will never open it again." It was lying on the table in their bedroom. He would stare at it and turn it over.

"My darling, what will he never open again?"

She did not know she had spoken aloud or understand Sparkenbroke's question. She remembered only that once, when she was a schoolgirl, she had made a vow that she would never hurt anyone, man or beast, as long as she lived. It had seemed to her then that she had discovered the whole secret of life, and she had written the vow on a leaf of her Bible and the date on which it was made.

"Did I leave a book at Lucca?"

"A book?" He turned up her face to his and saw distraction there. "What book? Do you mean your Bible?"

"I don't know! I don't know!" she cried. "Take me away. Far away. I wish—I've forgotten——" She hid her face in him. "Soon," she whispered. "Soon, soon, Piers!"

The repetition of that word, fluttering and muffled, the weight of her body against his own and the movement of her breath, enraptured him. The surrender of flesh and spirit was in them. All the experience of his past life warned him to take her now, and he imagined the Rector in his chair, waiting. They would be gone. In the end, after George's return, someone would come up to the cottage and knock; there would be no answer. To-night, she would look into his eyes in the terror and outpouring of an unendurable bliss; she would become unconscious, her bare shoulders limp, her arms fallen away, her throat slackened; her lips would move while unconsciousness advanced, by dreaming, into sleep.

He wished to look at the beauty of her face, and put her from him that he might see her. She stood at a little distance, gazing back. Suddenly a tremor convulsed her body and, through her open eyes, still regarding him, tears welled up and overflowed. Like a child, she snatched at them once with the knuckles of her right hand, then ceased to care, and stood in agony, until at last she uttered a cry so thin, so nearly soundless, that it was not hers, but the remote scream of her childhood lost in the wilderness of her mind; and she fell upon her knees, her face covered.

"Mary," he said, "I'm torturing you."

"Not you. Not you. Don't you see?" she whispered. "He'll never feel or live again."

"But you?"

"I?"

It was as though he had spoken a stranger's name that she failed to recognize.

"You must choose, Mary."

"Oh!" she whispered. "I have chosen. Long, long ago. In Derry's Wood. It was you who chose."

He drew her up from the ground, and held and watched her, remembering that once, in Lucca, he had tried to scorn himself for not having taken her when he might. But his happiness had been greater than his scorn and he had loved her the more, and in a new way, his compassion being poured out in her. The same compassion flowed in him now. He thought: perhaps it's true—we love those to whom we have given, not those from whom we take what we need.

If he hadn't come, she would have continued in the assurance of her life without him—and if he were to go, now, out of her life? It seemed, for a moment, an impulse of passionate generosity—to go, to leave her in peace. The violence of that abandonment tempted him—the theatre was in it—so magnificent a self-sacrifice—so noble an exit, the orchestra clashing its approval! But the idea was false. Even if it were possible, such withdrawal could not heal her; she would live with an open wound of desire and its humiliation. He would return, as he had returned to-day; she was in his spirit and in his blood, close to him now, her body warm under his hands; if he went violently, it would be in the pride of a lying abstinence. Even in compassion, then, he could play a part!

The impulse came and went. He rejoiced that it was gone, and, looking through his desire at Mary herself, whom he loved, he began to tremble, for he saw that what he must do was simple, with no light of the theatre to deck it out—he must allow her to decide in his absence. In this house, in George's company and beyond his own influence, she must be resolved, so that, if she came to him, it might be in the singleness of imagination, bringing him her innocencies—not division and hunger and shame.

"Mary," he said, "will you do what I tell you? Will you wait?"

"Wait!" she said. "Here?"

"Do nothing to-day or to-morrow. We will go in to the Rector now. I'll wait until George comes back. After that, I shan't come near the Rectory or see you."

She was frightened. Her hands slid down from his shoulders and gripped his arms.

"But, Piers, you said—to-night we shouldn't be here, and now——" She broke off and, having looked into his face, said: "Tell me what to do."

He began to speak in a rapid, decisive tone. "On Wednesday night at ten I shall bring the car to the stone bridge leading to the church. You can walk there—a small suit-case, enough for one night."

She let her arms fall and did not speak.

"Can you be alone? Can you get clear of the house?"

"Yes."

"If you are there, we start for Italy at once. If not——"

"The day after to-morrow," she said, and added: "A minute ago I believed I should never spend an evening in this room again."

CHAPTER THREE

ALL Wednesday she was heavy with the aching knowledge that what she did was being done for the last time. This house, which had been her refuge, held no memories, except of her own failures and weaknesses, that were not gentle within her. It is a kind house, she thought, and has given me nothing but kindness. In it she had rebuilt her life.

I am making my own decision, she said to herself, and it's softness and foolishness to cry for what I'm leaving behind; if I had children, it would be different, there'd be reason in it; but the house won't feel my going. I'm treating it as if it were alive. But when she had closed the linen cupboard and had walked a part of the way to her and George's bedroom with clean sheets over her arm, she hesitated and returned. Looking into the cupboard, she let the scent of it come to her. The shelves ought to have had new labels since I altered the arrangement of them; no one will ever find anything, she thought; and because it seemed lazy to neglect the labels but intolerable now to write them, she stared with burning eyes at the heaps of linen.

Forgetting that she was standing before the open cupboard, she began to struggle in her mind with the letter she must leave behind for George: George dear, I'm going away after all. I ought to have told you but I couldn't. You'll understand. You've understood so much for me . . . for my sake . . . my dear, you've been kind, kinder than ever I've deserved, and Father too. Give him my love. He knows and God knows I'm not wanton or cruel,

though. . . . Please, please. . . . I'm going because I must.
I can't help it. I must. You know how sometimes in a
dream one goes on because one must. . . . But I love you.
I love you both—you and Father. It's not because I don't
love you. . . .

She shut the cupboard, went into their bedroom and
began to put clean sheets on their beds. She wound
George's undersheet tightly round the bolster and tugged
at it—her own way of making it smooth and taut. George
would slide very quietly into bed and say, like a boy, smiling at her: Clean sheets to-night. Wednesday. It used to
be Mondays in Helen's day. Imagining him thus, his
pyjama-collar turned up, his hair ruffled, his face content
as he leaned over to blow the candle out, she remembered
that it was when he came upstairs to-night that he would
know she was gone. Hullo! You awake? he would whisper,
peering round the door. You didn't come to the dispensary.
There would be no answer. He would take away from
the candle-flame the hand with which he always carefully
shaded it until he knew that she was awake, and, seeing
her bed empty, would stand there, puzzled; he'd pull at
his ear; then he'd see her letter and plunge his finger into
the flap and sit down to read. Controlling himself. On the
edge of the bed.

She would be in the car, the hedgerows billowing past
her under the headlights. Everything would be over, for
ever decided; and she would be pitilessly happy, with a
rapture of expectancy in her body and cries of fulfilment
ringing within her. She would not then remember this
room or George with her letter, crumpling it. To be with
Piers whitened memory.

Fortified and blinded by this eagerness of sense, this
yearning of her imagination for the supreme loss, called
passion, by which for a little while all other losses are
cancelled, she took out the suit-case that George had
bought for her. One of its fastenings was broken; she
would need a strap or cord. Before kneeling down to pack
on the narrow rug at his bedside, she locked the door,
and, seeing herself reflected with her hand upon the key,

became for an instant a spectator at her own play—the spectator being herself as she had been before her values were confused, a girl who distinguished good from evil with an absolute assurance. Though she was aware now that experience blurs the distinctions of youth and had told herself a thousand times that goodness was conditional and relative, the dramatic intuition—or prejudice—of childhood survived in her, and the woman locking her door seemed infatuated and sinful, with acknowledgment of sin in her eyes.

She knelt down beside her suit-case. If you are not doing wrong, why have you locked the door? she asked of the woman whose hands were smoothing out tissue paper and whose tears fell upon her hands. It's wonderful how you always keep tissue-paper, George had said when they were packing for their holiday in Sicily. I love the rustle of it. That means holidays—yours and mine now. She heard him add: Odd how little things get to mean so much. She had looked up then, smiling.

Lazy! You go and pack your own things. Or do you want me to pack for you?

You pack for me.... Will you? I'll put out what I need on the bed.

And then I suppose you'll sit and watch me?

Yes. He came to his knees clumsily on the floor and kissed her. I'll watch you. Why not?

Every word. She heard them all again, felt him standing over her, looked up, as she had then—but now into an empty room and at the arc of sunlight thrown by the mirror's bevel on to the wall. Swerving on her knees, she curved her arm across her eyes as though warding off a blow and flung her face down against the coverlet.

Oh God, help me. Oh God, help me now. You know that this isn't ugliness and lust in me. You know I love them—both, I love them. With my whole heart. Both, with my whole heart. You know that is possible, for you made me.

And after a time in which thought was silent, she wondered whether the pressure of the coverlet would leave a pattern on her forehead, and said: Oh God, I can't kill either of them. I can't choose. Make me do what is right.

It startled her to find that she had not used "Thou" in speaking to God. Her prayer seemed hysterical and contemptible—not the prayer of a sane woman, scarcely a prayer at all. God had not listened to it. But she needed to pray and, reaching out for help into her childhood, she made her body erect and brought her clasped hands near to her breast, and began to say audibly: "Our Father, which art in heaven, Hallowed be Thy Name. Thy kingdom come. Thy will be done in earth, as it is in heaven. Give us this day our daily bread. And forgive us our trespasses, as we——" The words had calmed her, but when she saw that she was praying to be forgiven for sins that she was hot to commit, she could pray no more. God had hemmed her in. Opening her eyes, she let her hands fall; then swerved again, as though hunted, and, seeking to escape God's pursuit of her, said: "Help me, Jesus. O Christ, guide me."

She felt coldly that her prayers were lies, for she had known already what guidance she would accept, and she continued her packing. Afterwards, at her dressing-table, she wrote her letter in pencil. The strange woman she had become since prayer had shrivelled in her found the letter surprisingly easy to begin.

"DEAR GEORGE,

I am going away with Piers. Lady Sparkenbroke will divorce him probably and then we shall marry, I expect. I don't know what to say, my dear (she added '-est') my dearest. A letter like this is all hopeless. Nothing's your fault. Don't think it is. Don't ever think this is because I don't love you. I do—in our own way. But don't wait for me or forgive me or be kind again. It's all hopeless now. Give my love to Father and thank him from me— for everything. Bless you, dear one.   M."

Without sticking down the envelope, for perhaps she would read the letter again, she hid it among the handkerchiefs in her top drawer, thinking: later I'll put it somewhere where he'll find it; when I come up for the suitcase, just before I go, I'll do it then. A small table, on which spare candlesticks were kept and a night-light for the landing, stood against the wall outside their bedroom door. She would put her letter there, leaning it against the saucer that contained the night-light. It was a place in which messages were often left for Joanna. He wouldn't miss it there.

Behind the handkerchiefs was lying the small oval locket, containing her hair as a child, which she had formerly carried as an amulet. She would take it with her, and slid it into the black velvet pouch she was carrying.

In the evening she took the Rector's supper-tray from Joanna's hands and carried it up herself. She was reluctant to leave him, for she would not see him again; but I shall, she added with a tremor. I must come up to say goodnight to him as usual or he will ask where I am and Joanna will come running to my bedroom door and say: You've forgotten the Rector, Ma'am. She would knock then and come in, having received no answer.

Mary could not prevent such fragmentary scenes, in the common life of the household, from playing themselves in her mind, and the Rector, looking up from his toast, said, with a thrust for the truth he read in her face:

"What are you unhappy about, child?"

"Unhappy, Father? I'm not unhappy."

"So . . ."

Alarmed, she dropped beside him on her knees and took his hand. "Really, I'm not. Why?"

He would not look at her. His hand was stiff and unresponsive. He knew she was lying.

"Then, my dear, if you're not unhappy, let me drink my broth while it's hot."

Downstairs, there was rabbit for their evening meal.

"I'm not squeamish about eating other things," George said, "except small birds. But I always have a conscience about rabbits."

"Yes," she answered. "I feel sorry for rabbits too. They are nice little beasts."

She smiled, hearing their conversation from some place outside themselves, and wondering—with an impulse to defend this domestic privacy—what Piers would have thought of it. That's the trouble with marriage, he had said once. People let their minds slop about in carpet-slippers. Oh well, she thought, it was a relief sometimes. Things were silly if they were silly at heart—not otherwise; and if now and then, when they were alone, she and George talked almost like children— Did other people, grave solemn people, talk like that secretly? Had every marriage its own code, its own ridiculous, beloved phrases of nonsense and tenderness? When Joanna was gone from the room, she asked George this.

He held out his plate for more potato and said:

> *Uxor vivamus ut viximus et teneamus*
> *nomina quae primo sumpsimus in thalamo.*

"Which means?" she asked.

But he shook his head, smiling. "Not to-night," he answered. "I'm sorry. A man who quotes and refuses to translate deserves to be shot, I know."

He was silent, as he often was when tired at the end of a long day. Sometimes she had teased him for this habit of silence, and she was blaming herself for having been unjust when she understood suddenly that George's silence this evening was different from silences that had their origin in weariness. They had, in the past, irritated her because she had thought that she was excluded from them. He would eat his meals, and afterwards sit and smoke, his mind moving slowly, she had imagined, over recollections of the day's work, or an article he had read in the *Lancet*, or anxieties for a dozen trifles of routine. It was a shock to discover that to-night his silence was possessed by her. There was a shy, watchful distress in his eyes which, when they looked at her, seemed to say: why can't we talk to each other now? And his eyes were not long absent from her.

"What have you been doing all day?" she asked, and,

while she stared at the heavy base of the lamp and at the indentations made by its claws in the white table-cloth, he gave her an account of his visits, timing them hour by hour as he had timed them in his own mind. He might have been reading from his appointment-book. He gave her none of those tales of small adventure from the tone of which she had always known whether his day had been happy. "I was at the mill by 4.30," he said. "The daughter there kept me talking. She wants the old man's treatment changed. She always does; she has no patience. So I was late back to the village. Mrs. Geddes doesn't alter. She won't now until the end. One more attack will finish her. Weeks perhaps. Or to-morrow. Any time now."

"Poor old thing, she's patient."

"Yes, she's patient enough."

After that, silence. Joanna came in with the pudding—a steamed pudding with treacle—which Mary had ordered because he liked it best. When he had his helping and they were alone again, he let his spoon and fork lie at the side of his plate.

"I remember," he said. "They used to give me this on the last day of the holidays. It made me choke."

"But you like it?"

"Oh yes, I like it. It's my favourite. Always has been. But it made me choke just the same. When you're a child, it's people being kind makes you blubber more often than the other thing. The same when you're older."

This relieved her. If he had known her intention, he wouldn't have spoken of "the last day of the holidays"; he was too hard-set against self-pity to blow upon her with such a side-wind of sentiment. He did not know; he had not even a defined suspicion.

In the parlour, while the coffee-machine was bubbling, he dragged himself out of silence, saying at random: "Oh, I never told you. Yesterday I gave Arkell a lift on the way back from Chelmouth and he began to twit me about that story of Sparkenbroke's, *The House of Glasbury*."

"Why twit—*you*?"

He laughed. "You don't see it either then? That's all

right. Nor did I. But Arkell would have it that Piers had put me into the book."

"You! What nonsense! I'm sure— Why do you sometimes call him Piers and sometimes Sparkenbroke?"

He shrugged his shoulders. "I don't know. According to whether I'm thinking of him as a man or a writer, I dare say. . . . You remember," he continued, returning doggedly to his point, "you remember, in that solicitor's office, the elder Glasbury—not the father that dies—the elder of the two sons, Henry wasn't it?"

"Yes," she said. "Henry Glasbury." The coffee cup she was holding clinked in its saucer. When he had taken it from her, he took her hand and held it, not in affection only, not chiefly in affection, but in curiosity and seeking, as though he hoped to discover, through the physical contact, an outline of the shapes forming in his head. And Mary, to whom fear was communicated by his touch, said within her: He's afraid. He doesn't yet know what he's afraid of. And he goes on talking of Piers while he waits to find out. She didn't want him to talk of Piers now.

But on he went: "Arkell said that fellow—Henry—was me."

"But why?"

"Oh, dull and dutiful, I suppose."

"George, how ridiculous!"

"Arkell would have it. Same coloured eyes; same trick of pulling at his ear when he wasn't sure of a thing; and, yes—the same way that I have of getting the collar of my coat turned up behind. He had it all pat."

"But, George, you don't believe it, do you? Piers may have put those things in; they may have been in his mind; but, when he was writing, he didn't know where they came from. Isn't that obvious? If he'd been thinking of you, they're the very things he'd have left out. He'd have given you *different* coloured eyes. Authors do. Don't you see that——"

Surprised by the nervous speed and unnecessary vehemence of her own speech, she broke off, and looked at George, wondering if he also was surprised.

"Well," he was saying, "it doesn't make great odds either way. Henry Glasbury, as I remember, wasn't a bad fellow." He smiled and added: "Though he did marry a girl too young for him, didn't he?" And without waiting for an answer to that, he threw in: "Anyhow, Mr. H. G. will be remembered long after I'm gone up the hill. He'll do as a monument."

They drank their coffee in the parlour. George had been speaking so quietly and with so much of his peculiar sedateness of humour that a fitful confidence returned to her and, though she had forbidden herself to look at the clock, she glanced at it without turning her head. In twenty minutes, at half-past eight, he would go upstairs to read *Esmond* to his father, for to-night it was his turn to read aloud. An hour later he would come down and put in his head, saying: He's ready for you, and go off to his own room. You won't be reading late? she would remember to say. Oh no, he would answer. About an hour. Shall you look in or go straight to bed? After that she would go up to the Rector's room; then to her own for the suit-case; then into the hall, calling the dog. Caesar! Caesar! she would call. Hearing the front door open and shut, they would suppose that she had taken Caesar for his walk. She would let Caesar in again and be gone.

It was so clear in her mind, that she imagined the dog looking back at her in surprise when she thrust him into the house again and did not follow. Perhaps he would bark. But they would quiet him, thinking that she had already gone up to bed. The house would be silent. George would be in his den, book on knee, his curly pipe smoking against his chin, his fingers folding and unfolding on the stem of his reading lamp, and she would be crossing the orchard by the path near the hedge.

So far had this swift imagining carried her out of herself that she forgot the tension of George's silence. It was as if she had been tracing in her mind the escape of another woman, not personally linked with the man who was now coaxing tobacco into the bowl of his pipe; and, filled with a remote arrogance of adventure, it was she that could not resist speaking of Piers.

"You do think his works will live, then?"

"I'm no judge, dearest."

"No, but—you must have a feeling about it. I mean, if you had to bet whether a hundred years hence——"

"A hundred years," George said. "That's a long time. Novels go out of fashion, and poems too. Still, if I had to bet on anyone—yes, I'd bet on him."

She had wanted this reassurance. She had wanted it from him. It was as if he had said: Well, I grant you it's a great man you're throwing your life away for. And she wanted more, feeling intuitively that, if one were reckoning in centuries, George's opinion was more valuable than most, being less affected by fashion.

"Why would you bet on him?" she asked.

He considered. "Well," he said slowly, "Sparkenbroke doesn't paddle in manners, and, though he sneers in his talk, he doesn't sneer in his writing. People in cities where there aren't any graveyards, forget they are going to die; that's why they live in cities and like to do everything in droves. They are afraid of the country and afraid of being alone; it makes 'em think; and when they write, they've nothing to say—except to sneer at the woman in the other drawing-room or the poor devil on the other omnibus. A hundred years hence won't give a damn for our sneers. Hatred lives sometimes, there's blood in that; and indignation lives; but not sneers. You can't sneer at a man if you know how little time he has to learn sense or at a girl with death waiting for her round the next corner. You can't be pitiless if you know how pitiless Nature is. Hardy knows and Housman; they'll live. And Sparkenbroke. . . . There's a line I've heard him quote. I remember he said it once when he was a boy—quite suddenly—we were out on the moor, Ancaster way. About a chariot."

Mary said:

> *"But at my back I always hear*
> *Time's winged chariot hurrying near."*

George nodded. "That's it. If a poet can't hear that, no one will hear *him* for long. Sparkenbroke hears it—almost too much."

She wanted to argue, even against Piers now, for it was this in him that frightened her.

"But death," she said; "people can't always be writing about death. Not always darkness. There must be light too."

"Don't you think it's knowledge of the dark makes the sunshine good?" he said. "Makes it precious. It's that makes it shine. Just as it's the possibility of sound that makes silence intense. Without that chariot there is no silence. That's what's the matter with the sneerers," he concluded. "They glitter and chinkle all right. But they have no silence, no light, no heat."

She thought how peaceful and pleasant this discussion would have been if the poison of finality had not been in it. Lying in darkness, they would, perhaps, have continued it when George came up to bed. To talk after lights-out was among their happiest domestic vices, continually resolved against, for he must rise early, but steadily persisted in. Once eager on the trail of a subject, he pursued it well and plainly, always a little ahead of her—which she liked—but always on her level. None of the plunges of genius, or the angers, or the incomprehensible scorns. With an impulse of friendly gratitude, she took his hand from the arm of his chair and held it between hers; then saw herself holding it and, stung by what presented itself to her as a cruel hypocrisy, let it go. Even friendship between them was made impossible by her resolve to betray him, and, though she tried to say now, as she had said often before, why should any man claim all of me—even the possession of my body? the bitter plea did not avail against the loyalties, the virginal singleness, bred in her long ago. Argument would not quiet her intuition. That she dared no longer touch his hand was enough; and suddenly, beyond all control, her face was convulsed, her eyes opened wide and were filled with tears. She turned away her head and body. In an instant, she was by the fireplace, her back to him, mistress of herself. Perhaps he had seen nothing, and she said dully: "I expect you're right. I think Piers's work will live."

He did not answer, but his silence was not long, for the telephone began to ring. He picked up the receiver.

"Yes. . . . Speaking. . . . This is Dr. Hardy. . . . Where are you speaking from? What? Chelmouth? I see. . . ."

He was listening. From where she stood she could hear the distant mutter of the ear-piece. At last, he said:

"I'm very sorry, Miss Dempster. I can't come out to-night—I'm laid up myself. . . . I said: I'm laid up myself. In bed. . . . Oh, nothing much. Precautionary more than anything. I hope to be about again to-morrow. . . . I'm sorry. Give her another hot compress; that should relieve it. Perhaps she'll fall off to sleep. If so, don't disturb her for the medicine. Nothing like sleep. . . . Well, if you have any difficulty, perhaps you'd ring up Dr. Staniforth. He's in the town, not more than a few streets away from you. . . . Thank you; it's good of you to say so. I'm sorry too. Don't like disappointing a patient, but to-night . . . Wait. I'll give you Staniforth's number: Chelmouth 746. . . ." Another pause. "Good-night."

She was gazing at him now. "But George, you're not ill. You're not laid up."

"No, I'm not ill."

"I've never known you refuse a patient before."

"I never have." He rose and touched her shoulder. "But I'm not going out to-night."

There was nothing she could answer.

"It's time for Father and *Esmond*," he said and, going to the open window, knocked out his pipe against the sill.

George went upstairs slowly, blaming himself for the unreasoning impulse that had made him refuse to visit Mrs. Dempster in Chelmouth.

He sat down beside his father, found the place they had reached, and began to read. Mary's alone downstairs, he thought. He tried to imagine that she also was sitting quietly with a book in her lap, but his imagination would not accept so much repose in her. He saw her kneeling on the hearth-rug, her arms straight, her fingers inter-twined, her face hidden from him because there were tears in her eyes, and he understood that he was not im-agining, but remembering what he had seen.

"Tired?" his father said.

"Not particularly; why?"

"You were reading slowly, I thought. Don't read if it tires you. Let's talk a bit. Thackeray won't be in a hurry for us. The giants always wait."

George continued to read at amended pace. On Sunday night, he remembered, when he went up to his bedroom after their walk together, he had found her kneeling on her bed, naked, a night-dress spread out before her. I'd put it on, she had said in explanation, but it's torn. I doubt whether it will mend. You'll catch cold, he answered, and she, rising on her knees, had stretched up her arms, twisting towards the open window, curving her back. Cold? On a night like this! When he had sat down on the edge of her bed and moved his arm, meaning to kiss her, she had jumped to the floor and padded across to the green-painted chest of drawers, foraging for some-thing to put on. He had watched her stooping there—the heels, from which a little flush, in the form of a sharp arrow-head, ran up the Achilles tendon; the whiteness of the plane behind her knees; the sheen of her flank, still coloured by the pressure of her feet under her while she knelt—and he had felt then, as though it were a thin knife plunged into his admiration, the peril of so much beauty, his marriage seeming to him a dream ill-matched with the plain texture of his life. But this stroke of fear had been no more than a momentary accent on a general unease that his reason and loyalty condemned. During the intervening days, he had gone peacefully about his work, and this evening had returned without much thought except of old Mrs. Geddes for whom there was no more to be done. On his way downstairs to supper he had visited his father's room, and it was his father who had said: George what's wrong with that girl of ours? She didn't tell the truth to

me just now. Said she wasn't unhappy. She doesn't
commonly lie. It had seemed best to laugh at this. Well,
my boy, you know her better than I—at least I suppose
you do. "Unhappy" may be too strong. But there's something on her mind.

That, too, he had laughed away; but his father was
shrewd. All the evening he had felt the ground shifting
under him. Then he had seen, or imagined, tears.

He devoted himself now with determination to the
book he was reading and, for the first time that night, its
words made their mark.

"'. . . Wings!—why not say crutches?'" he read.
"'There is but eight years' difference between us, to be
sure; but in life I am thirty years older. How could I even
hope to please such a sweet creature as that, with my
rough ways and glum face? Say that I have merit ever so
much . . .'"

He continued to read but the words' meaning slid away,
his mind having leapt towards an explanation of all that
had been mysterious—of her denial that she was unhappy,
of the reserve, the fitfulness of her manner—yes, even of
her having so abruptly taken his hand between hers and
as abruptly dropped it, concealing her tears. An exultant
certainty drove out the perils from his mind. How we shall
laugh when all's known!

"'The next day,'" his voice continued, "'although
Esmond gave no sign of what was going on in his mind,
but strove to be more than ordinarily gay and cheerful
when he met his friends at the morning meal, his dear
mistress, whose clear eyes——'"

He stopped in mid-sentence.

"Father . . ."

"George Eliot called it 'the most uncomfortable book
you can imagine,'" the Rector said tranquilly, "and much
as I love it there are moments when——"

"Father, I believe I know what was the trouble."

The white eyebrows came up. The eyes beneath them
slowly, and with reluctance, forsook Thackeray.

"The trouble?"

"About Mary. Perhaps she's to have a child. I think she was trying to tell me that."

"Why not tell you, then?"

But George had closed the book and sprung from his chair before he remembered that his father was entitled to be read to for another quarter of an hour. He began to find his place again.

The corner of the Rector's mouth turned a little. "Go on, boy, if you'd be with her. I shall be glad enough of a granddaughter if you can bring me one."

"A grandson," said George.

"I shan't be able to wait for him," the old man answered. "I'd have a granddaughter first, so that she take after her mother."

"I'll go down and ask her. Now."

The drawn face, that had been smiling, straightened. "Slow, boy. Go slow."

"But if——"

"Let her tell *you*, George. . . . It mayn't be."

"I'm pretty sure——"

"So. So. But let her tell you. She'll want that. Women don't like to be guessed by us foolish men."

George took his father's advice, partly because experience had taught him to respect it, partly because he was learning that evening to distrust his own impulses. His refusal to go to Chelmouth troubled him; it had been extravagant and unreasonable; he was not accustomed to extravagant unreason in his professional life. Just a whim, he said as he came downstairs, choosing a word which, because it was ordinarily associated with women, would, he hoped, sting him into masculine good sense.

Entering the parlour and seeing his wife's start of surprise—"You're ten minutes early!" she exclaimed— he was at once aware that his hope of a son was a whim likewise, wanting substance. I suppose my mind threw it up as compensation, he said to himself, and a foolish, witless phrase formed itself to torment him: "The wish was father to the child." And yet, he thought stubbornly, it may be true. You never knew with pregnant women. They could be glad and miserable at the same time, rejoicing amid terrors. That, at any rate, was fact. He clung to it, for it shored up his crumbling expectation, and sat down, waiting for her to tell him, knowing in his heart that she had nothing to tell.

She had nothing to tell and, it seemed, nothing to say.

"I wonder how old Mrs. Geddes is."

"Oh," he answered, "she doesn't change."

A little breeze was flicking the blind cord at the open window.

"Is there a draught?" he said. "Would you like it shut?"

"No, I don't think so. It's a warm night."

"I thought you shivered."

She moved her head but did not reply. There was a book beside her. She opened it at hazard and stared at it, but she was not reading. She looked up, moved her lips as if about to speak, then looked down again. He wondered how he could make it easy for her to say what she had to say.

Often in the past their ability to be peacefully silent in each other's company had seemed good to him, an evidence that their relationship was tranquil and unexacting; but to-night there was no quiet in their speechlessness. Perhaps, he thought, if I were to talk of something vague, something inconsequential, no matter what, that might lead her on, and he told her of George Eliot's saying that *Esmond* was an uncomfortable book. She tried to join in a discussion of *Esmond*, but her mind was not in it. She looked at the clock, stirring uneasily and turning her finger-tips into the arms of her chair. Even as he suggested that Thackeray wasn't a Victorian at all in spirit, but an eighteenth-century man, his thought broke in upon him with the cold shuddering clangour of a bell, saying, first: She is afraid; then, with sharp, repeated reverberation: She isn't there. She isn't there. What his thought intended by these phrases or whence they came, he did not know. They were hushed instantly by a great tenderness and pity for her—as though she were in a prison and

separated from him by a wall of glass. With no more than
a hesitation in his speech, he struggled on into talk of
Thackeray.

"Isn't it time I went up to Father," she said.

"Yes; so it is; after half-past."

She rose. "Aren't you going to your room to read?"
And as though he were already following her, she added:
"Shall I put this lamp out?"

"Not yet," he said. "I think I'll sit here for a moment.
Call me as you come away from Father. I'll be off to bed
early to-night. A bit tired, I suppose."

At that she stiffened. Her eyes moved to right and
left, rapidly, as though she were seeking an escape. Her
lips opened and closed.

"My dearest," he said, "what is it? For God's sake——"
He closed up to her, thinking she would fall. "Sit down,"
he said.

She might have obeyed him, and he thought: It's
coming now—whatever it is; but at that instant there
was a loud, agitated knocking at the front door. Her
body shook, and a sigh—the thin, moaning sigh of one
who returns to consciousness—came from her; then with
passionate activity she went to open the door.

There was a small boy on the step, hatless, with upturned hair. She stepped back from him and leaned
against the wall, her hands loose at her sides.

"Please can Doctor come on up to Gran's house quick?"

George walked down on him: "Come in. I can't see.
Who are you?"

"Bertie, sir."

"What—Geddes?"

"Yes, sir. Please, sir, Mother said can you come on up
to Gran's house quick."

"What is it?"

"She's took bad, sir." The boy gulped for breath. "I
seen it meself. Blood from 'er mouf—awful. I was up
in 'er room, sayin' g'night, right by the bed I was, sir.
And Mother said: 'Tell Doctor. Go say, Can 'e come on
up to——' "

"All right, boy, I'll come. . . . I must go, Mary."

"Yes."

"But you?"

She smiled slowly. Her eyes shone.

"I? I'm all right, George."

"You'll go to bed?"

She nodded.

"Promise?"

"Yes."

He took her hand. To feel her pulse, she thought; but he kissed it.

"I see it meself, sir, I——"

She closed the door behind them.

CHAPTER FOUR

SHE was calm now.

It had been understood between her and Piers that
if chance barred them to-night they should warn each
other; there would be time enough for warning, they
had supposed, and no provision had been made against
hindrance at the last. George's decision to stay with her
had broken her plan. While she had stood, rigid, at the
door of the parlour, her mind had frozen over. Even her
will to invent, to lie, to struggle, had died.

She had seen herself as an old woman, George's wife,
complacent in long affection, going out of this parlour
on some distant evening, pausing where now she stood.
Shall I put this lamp out? she would ask—or perhaps
they'd have electric light by then. Her heart would
range Italy for the sunlight she had shut out and
ache for the passion she had not spent; would ache in a
dull, stupefied vanity of self-reproach because to-night
she had neither chosen nor renounced these things but,
in a paralysis of mind, had allowed them to slide from
her.

"Sit down," George had said, and she had moved to
obey, thinking: Now tell him the truth. Be honest. Ask
him to let you go. But she had known that if, in speech
with him, she had attempted to break the cord that
bound them, she would have frayed but not have broken
it. He would have let her go and she would not have gone.
Therefore she would not speak, and had seen the future
closing in upon her frustrate silence.

But she was calm now, her plan re-formed. She went

to the Rector's door, where Felling admitted her and withdrew. The invalid was in bed but straightly propped, it being too early for him to sleep.

"Well, my dear, on your way to bed?"

"Yes," and, not wishing to delay now, she stooped to kiss him. As she did so, her hand, gripping the velvet bag she carried, felt the hard oval of the locket that she had intended to take away with her. "Look, Father," she said suddenly, "I have a present for you."

"For me? But it's not my birthday."

"No. But why should I want to give you things only on your birthday? Perhaps I shan't then. I do now." She put the locket in his hands. "Did I ever show it to you?" And she told him what it contained.

"Your hair as a child," he repeated. "Bless you." He too kissed her hand, not yet wishing to lift his face.

"I suppose it's foolish to give you a locket," she said. "What shall you do with it?"

"Sleep happy and proud. Isn't that enough?" And he added swiftly: "I'll give you something in return."

"No, Father, no."

"Yes. Gift for gift. Let us observe the tradition. . . . But you must fetch it yourself, my dear. There, in that little cupboard on the wall. It's unlocked. On the lower shelf. Do you see a small brown octavo?"

She brought it to him and he stroked it with a slow hand.

"It's Theocritus," he said. "But that's not all. They'll fight for this at Sotheby's some day. . . . When Piers was going to Gallipoli, he wanted to give me a present. Give me the Theocritus we read together, I said. But I used it at Eton too, he answered. It's battered and scored over. But I should like it, I told him—and here it is." He smiled. "Look how it's scored over. My pencil, too; the snaky lines are mine; but look at the margin of page forty-two. He wrote that at school. I asked him how. In class, he answered—a jingle that filled the margin. Listen. It may be a jingle, but it says what it wants to say.

Since I, a fool,
Am put to school
    By God,
He'll let me run
Into the sun
    And 'scape His rod
When school is done.

There," the old man said. "Take it, and show it to the world some day. They may forgive the man for the sake of the schoolboy's rhyme."

She took the book and kissed him again. When she went out, her locket was re-gathered into his hand.

When she reached her bedroom she was in haste. Her letter to George had become enfolded among her handkerchiefs, but, finding it at last, she touched its flap with her tongue, closed it and, going out, leaned the envelope against the saucer of the night-light. She returned then to the room.

Suit-case in hand, she said: What shall I do with the book? and laid it on the dressing-table; but the Rector would learn that his gift had been rejected; she could not leave it; and she carried it in the press of her arm.

The hall was empty. She went down into it and called the dog. A door-handle turned, for a moment Joanna's voice was to be heard, and Caesar came skiddingly over the linoleum of the kitchen passage. She let him out and followed. So often had these actions been rehearsed in her mind that they seemed to have been performed before, and she felt that she was repeating them now under compulsion of the past.

Not until the dog was in the house again and the door re-shut was she roused to a sense of present responsibility for her undertaking. What stirred this active consciousness at last, telling her that she was not an automaton being watched but a woman who must move cautiously from the gravel to the muffling of the lawn, was a clash between the reality of the scene and her imagining of it. Piers had said: There'll be a moon. She had thought of a night brilliantly illumined, but the sky was lightly clouded, the moon a pewter haze, and as she went up through the orchard she rocked unsteadily over the rough darknesses at her feet.

The weight of her little bag increased and she could not swing her left arm because Theocritus was clipped by it. She stopped, adjusted the book so that she might carry it in her hand and went forward again, thinking: why not leave it in the rough grass at the foot of an apple-tree? No one would find it there. But Piers would laugh when she told him what she had brought with her. They would be under the elm in the churchyard; beyond the bridge the car's engine would be turning over with soft, regular expectancy. As he stood away from their kiss, a silence would fall between them, and out of her breathlessness she would say: Look what I've brought—your Theocritus! His fingers would close upon it, and upon hers, in the dark, and he would say: Theocritus! My dear—why? When she said the verses to him, he would laugh, glad to hear himself quoted, glad that she had quoted him, and these verses would become a seal between them to be spoken often again in remembrance of to-night—in Lucca, perhaps, in— But could she remember them? "Since I, a fool—" She could not, and her mind fled from them to Lucca, to the delight of waking there, seeing the day's sunshine blaze through the green shutter-bars and streak her bare arm when she stretched it out. She slid from the bed and, pushing open the shutters a few inches so that they were still unseparated but disclosed at their base a triangle of light, she looked down into the garden and at the rampart beyond. All day! she thought, spreading the hours before her imagination, but it's early yet, and, drawing in the shutters again so that the triangular gleam no longer struck downward on to her feet, she stepped back and looked at Piers. He was curled up into his pillow, a hand holding his throat; but when, returned to bed, she lifted his hand away from his throat, his eyes opened and he recognized her—with a slow access of wonder until recognition was complete, and life sprang into his eyes, and his hand swept her body, gathering her, as though by touch his vision must be confirmed.

But are we going to Lucca? she said. He didn't tell me his plans—only that we should go away at once, out of England. Perhaps to-night we shall be in Southampton; and, never having been to Southampton, she imagined their car threading its way among trams. But perhaps it will be very early morning when we get there; there will be no trams, but only empty streets and ships looking up over the edges of wharves. They would go to a hotel. It would be grey and asleep, with the air that sleeping buildings have of being settled into the earth; defiantly closed. But a porter would admit them at last. While the car was being put away, she would stand in a bedroom, still with her coat on, a white unshaded bulb blazing at her from beneath its useless canopy of white china. Then Piers would come. She would have to undress while he was in the room. Or perhaps to-night they would have two rooms. Hers would have lace curtains with brass rings, and at the foot of the bed a curly sofa of red plush. In the morning, when they had breakfast, there would be strong, bitter Indian tea, drunk out of thick cups with blue edges and the name of the hotel on them in blue and gold. She tried to read the name of the hotel, but could see only a device like a wheatsheaf, which turned red as she peered at it, and the word: Southampton. It would be late, for in England Piers always breakfasted late, and George would be already in Chelmouth unless, after his refusal to go to her, Mrs. Dempster . . . George, she said, I've never broken into your practice before; I hate myself for that. . . . Oh, George, my dear, Mrs. Ferris telephoned to say that Bob wouldn't be home. So the Saturday morning appointment is cancelled. I didn't cross it off in the book. Should she telegraph to George from Southampton? Hardy, Sparkenbroke Green. Cancel Ferris appointment Saturday Mary. Better leave it, Piers would say, but if she could she would send a telegram. If she did not, George would go to the Ferris's at eleven on Saturday by this road.

She was on the road now, hearing the stream lisping over the pebbles. It had a soothing, creamy sound. How often during the past year she and George had walked beside it at night before going to bed. For the last month or two, these evening strolls had been rare. Their custom of visiting the Rector in turn before he slept, had changed their evening habit. But I've missed the walks, she thought. I enjoyed our walk last Sunday, and George enjoyed it too. Last night, when he came to bed, he said: When are we going to have a night-cap walk again? Standing now on the church bridge she answered in surprise: Never, I suppose. It seemed strange that the woman whose bag was resting on the parapet should have power to end a custom so firmly established and so intimate.

There was now moon enough to light the dial of her watch and she saw that she was early. Entering the grave-yard, she leaned against the elm and closed her eyes. She remembered the stream at Ponte a Moriano; it had gone from her life that afternoon, long ago, in which Piers had driven her to Bagni di Lucca; soon she would visit it again. It was when her eyes were shut that she could best imagine that Piers was with her, and she needed him now. She was very tired and she needed him. If she waited with her eyes shut, he would come out of the darkness and touch her. Then she would be alive, life would spring up like water spurting from the earth, the battle in her would cease. With eyelids pressed together and the bark hard against her shoulder-blades, she waited for his touch, thinking: He has seen me. He is coming nearer and nearer without sound. In an instant he will touch me. Now. . . . She opened her eyes, believing that she would find herself in the shadow of his face, but except the elbow of a drooping branch nothing cut the ribbon of sky between the hedge-rim and the elm's dense curtain.

I am mad, she said; there was no sound of a car, nothing but the stream and the soft shifting of the leaves everywhere, as though the dead in their tombs were breathing. And she thought: Who am I, standing out here in the night, my eyes shut, waiting for a body to inflame my body? She was ashamed; her spirit failed her; and suddenly she was defiantly contemptuous of the woman that had been ashamed, and said: This is my life. Without his love, I am half dead. Without this wickedness, I have no virtue. And I am committed. I have come away. I can never go back. She spurred herself with the strength of this finality. I am here, she said, under this tree, and she touched it with the knuckle of the hand that grasped Theocritus.

But she was not yet committed, for she was early and Piers had not come. Even now I might go back and let myself into the house, and she saw herself returning down the road by which she had come, watching the clumsy moon-shadow of herself and of her suit-case at her side. Her anger was kindled against the coward who would walk home to her prison and lie down upon her bed in terror of her own rapture. Are you awake? George would ask, and soon he would be telling her that Mrs. Geddes was dead. She would have submitted to the placid eternity of life in his house.

But she picked up her suit-case. She came into the open, away from the shadow of the elm, and there stopped, for a car was approaching. Now she knew her mind. The responsibility of judgment was lifted from her. Soon, soon, she would be leaning back in her seat watching the needle of the speedometer, knowing that all was done, remembering the elm vaguely as a nightmare from which she was awakened. She was already in Piers's keeping. He might do with her what he would. He might be cruel to her if he would. She would move when he told her to move; be still when he told her to be still. Her spirit lay down in a rapture of obedience because to obey was to be undivided.

As the car came near, she moved a step down the slope. Its headlights pierced the hedge with a rain of brilliant arrows; its tires hissed and sucked, and it was gone.

Blackness fell upon her. She turned her head violently, looking this way and that in the darkness, then stared at the hedge, which had changed into a solid wall, and seemed to be mounting the sky. As it shrank again and above it an area of moonlight reappeared, she heard, as though she were listening to one asleep beside her in darkness, her own throat dragging for breath. Slowly she began to understand that it was she who stood in the churchyard, and had been in the act of leaving it. An instant ago her destiny had been clear; she had been a god because she had been naked of doubt; now the dreadful patterns of irresolution had begun to wind themselves upon her. A reasonable self was persuading her that the passing of this car was an irrelevant accident. Soon, this persuasion continued, Piers will be here, but she could not heed it, and knew in her heart that, when he came, he would not find her. Where she would be she did not know. Not at home. Not waiting here. With her intelligence she desired nothing and expected nothing, and she went out of the churchyard, not by the bridge, but westward, by the bridle-path leading through the woods.

This path, where it debouched upon the churchyard, widened as a river widens to its estuary. She walked up a grassy triangle of light towards its apex, whence the path itself visibly extended a few yards until a turn of its course nipped it in darkness. She was conscious of no further purpose than that she should reach this apex and ascend as much of the path as she could now see. Her attention was, therefore, bent upon the rivulet of frosted light, and she suffered a stroke of anguish, as though a place of refuge had been closed against her, when it vanished, the trees, or some other hovering blackness, having eaten it up. But soon the interposed mass was withdrawn; she did not perceive that a human figure had crossed her way or know that she was being watched.

She walked some distance along the path before she remembered whither it led. Soon it would fork; its branch to the right was an approach to Derry's Cottage; that on the left would take her, by way of the wooden bridge, across Derry's Stream on to the road from Ancaster. The thought that she would then be close to the Rectory, and, if she walked to the cross-roads, within sight of it, caused her to halt, dazed by her discovery that a world from which she felt herself to be cut off was physically so near that by taking a few hundred paces she might re-enter it. She would never re-enter it, for she belonged to it no more; she saw it in imagination as if she were already a spirit unreceived, errant among familiar scenes with which she had no vital contact. As she moved forward again, the church clock began to strike. She counted ten strokes and said aloud: "Ten o'clock." It was at ten o'clock that Piers was to have met her; but the remembrance was without power, and she was not tempted to turn back.

Cut off from past and future, seemingly frozen in the intolerable instant, the imagination yields itself, like a ship in irons, to any breeze that will give it movement. To this submission she was now come.

As she followed the arm of the path that led to the wooden bridge by which she and Sparkenbroke had first met, she saw that she would die there, arriving at this conclusion by no process of argument, but by vision of her death enacted. She saw herself swinging by the neck from the willow-tree, her head forward, her body languidly revolving as the cord twisted or untwisted itself. The vision did not frighten or surprise her when it appeared in her mind. She was observant of it.

A little later she became interested in the accomplishment of her design, wondering how the woman whose body was twisting to and fro had contrived her hanging. Derry's Stream was almost dried up at that season; there was a sufficient drop between its banks; and the cord binding her suit-case, which had been so much too long and heavy for its original purpose, was the cord knotted by the dead woman round her throat. Mary put down her suit-case, felt the cord, rolling it between finger and thumb, and went forward. When the cord was taken off, the suit-case would spring open; by the morning its contents would be wet with dew; the cardboard box of powder would be sodden, and the tissue-paper have lost its crispness. But the paper would dry if it were weighted with stones and stretched in the sun; even the powder, spread thinly on the lid of a cardboard dress-box, could be dried by the parlour fire.

The girl kneeling on the hearth, who shook the powder to and fro with the gentle motion of one sieving fine earth, looked up saying that suicide was a thing that only the hysterical accomplished. Even in extremity, one's character stood firm if one had character; one went up to the edge, perhaps, but not over it; and Mary, hearing this, perceived that death by hanging was a denial of her knowledge of herself, and that she would not accomplish it. Her body would not revolve nor her head droop forward; she would approach the bank but not leap from it; the cord that she was now scraping with her finger-nail would never tighten about her throat. Nevertheless her imagining of herself dead had the quality of a remembered past. The two currents flowed through her mind not in opposition but independently.

Derry's Stream had little water in it. Though its trickle was audible, she could see no glint when she leaned out from the overhung bank. The smell of earth was fresh in her nostrils as though it were newly dug. Across her palm the cord was lying; the suit-case had sprung open at the locks. She thrust in her arm to be sure that the cardboard powder-box was in its place, as in a dream one touches a stick or a wall to be assured that one is not dreaming. Everything, she understood, was being accomplished as she had foreseen, but she was still aware that she was not about to die.

One end of the cord she tied firmly round her neck, adjusting the knot until it was beneath her left ear, this being, she believed, the correct position of it. She supposed that she must have read somewhere of a hanging, and paused in an attempt to remember where she had read of it. In adjusting the noose and tightening it, she was very clumsy. She was afraid that she had hurt her neck, perhaps scarred it; the cord had been rough and she had jerked at it impatiently until it slipped, chafing her skin. Piers would say she had a red collar and ask why. Then she would tell him how difficult it had been, and how much more difficult to slide the other loop out along the branch of the willow without falling into the water.

The rope, between its two attachments to the tree and to her neck, lay across her arm, and, though she knew that to commit suicide was a phrase not applicable to her, she walked to the edge of the stream and into the air beyond it.

As she fell, she was possessed by the impossibility of what she had done. When they found her, she would be laid out on her bed at home and George would gaze at her. After one had fallen through the air a little while, one's body ceased to have weight; feeling stopped, except of an upward rushing of the eyes and a sense of time extending and extending like a viscous rope. The rope would cease to be viscous; it would harden suddenly and her head jerk forward.

A blow fell upon her head behind the ear, and arrows of light spurted from her eyes; her shoes were wet and stones were pressing under the soles. When she moved her feet, water lapped over her insteps. She moved them again desperately, this way and that, crying out through the pillow of suffocation that enwrapped her head, and the earth rose up at last under her heels through the water. She had foothold, and the willow, when she looked up, leaned across the sky.

By its branches, by earthy roots, by the thrust of her hands into stony crevices, she dragged herself, with a strength not hers, up the bank, and there lay still, perhaps for a long time, until she became aware of a blade of grass in her nostril and of dust upon her lips. The rope was too long, she said, and repeated aloud, as though she were explaining her failure: "It was too long, I think." Then she rose to her knees and undid the cord at her neck; rose to her feet and detached it from the bough; coiled it round her bag and looked about her. No trace remained of what she had done. Kneeling beside her bag, she inquired with slow curiosity of the place where her body should have been hanging, and shut her eyes. Her knee touched something flat and hard which she picked up and enclosed within the press of her arm. After another pause, she rose, lifted her suit-case, crossed the bridge and the wood beyond it. The road was empty, a shining dome between black gutters. She went down it and let herself into the house.

In her room she emptied her suit-case and put it away, then undressed, concealing her shoes and stockings that were wet and hanging her frock at the back of the cupboard that Joanna might not come upon it until, in the morning, she herself had brushed the earth away. Was she now to sleep? Piers was at the elm, waiting. How long would he wait? In her bed, she leaned up on her elbow and, drawing Theocritus towards her, gazed at the Greek characters and the boy's handwriting in the margin of page forty-two.

The front door opened and closed. George's cautious footstep was on the stair. She blew out her candle, lay down and shut her eyes.

CHAPTER FIVE

EVEN while he and Mary had been together in the room that was called the dispensary, Sparkenbroke had felt the pulse of new imagination beat within him and had known that he would write again. No project was formed; his imagination had opened its eyes and had as yet seen nothing; but its eyes were open, its expectation was alive. In the library, to which she took him, he had talked with the Rector; George had come in and the conversation been continued; through it all, he had been aware of that inward stir and eagerness, that quickening of all his faculties, which was, in him, a presage. On the rug before the empty grate, Mary had neither watched them nor listened to their talk. She had been still, her head bent, her weight on her arm.

When he reached the cottage, Sparkenbroke had sat down in the living-room, and there remained until Bissett, who had been out for provisions, returned. His mood of intense quietness long continued. His thought of her was without the shape of desire, and his imagining of the work he must do formless, untroubled, not wracked by words or persons.

That night he slept peacefully. Next morning, refreshed, his mind lay open. He went down through the wood to the churchyard and admitted himself to the Mound, not in distress or for refuge as he had in the past, but with a sense of having outgrown even this that had been his necessity, for the life from which the necessity had sprung was itself receding from him. It had already so far receded that, though the wood, the stream, the cottage itself, were deeply familiar and beloved, he felt no melancholy in parting from them. To-morrow I shall be here; after that, not again; but he was aware only of having put a burden of experience from him. A painting that had failed was lifted down, a new canvas was given him, and, with it, not indeed the picture to be painted, not yet its colour or design, but a new apprehension of the art of painting. It was as if one had said within him: Yesterday you had sight, hearing, touch—all these senses, your attributes, your powers. They were your arms and are outworn. Lay them down. To-day live only in this security, that to-morrow you shall be armed anew. Not a bird in the air nor a leaf on the tree, nothing small or great, not love itself, is as you have believed it, separable, inconstant, mortal, but in each there is a celestial tongue, that you shall hear speak.

In the evening, a little before dusk, while he was washing in cold water, he received warning that a paroxysm was about to seize him. A stiffness of neck and shoulder was followed by a deep aching within the left arm, and, after a little interval, by an agony within the leg as though a wedge were being driven into the bone's marrow and the bone itself split. He had dragged himself from the wash-stand to his bed and covered himself, for he was half-naked, his body still wet and now bitterly cold. As the pain increased, the leg stiffened; his back arched; his arm, beyond his will, was twisted under his back, and he cried out, for his ampoules of amyl nitrite were in the coat he had taken off. Bissett, hastening in, put one of these into a handkerchief and the handkerchief within the grip of his hand. He crushed it and inhaled. For a little while it gave relief. His body was loosened from its contortion and he lay against pillows, struggling for breath, asking that he might escape the greater paroxysm of the body itself.

But the agony swept upon him afresh. There appeared in his mind an image of his chest as a bony shell within which the organs of his body were being compressed by cords. The organs themselves had individuality and voices; he heard them cry out, saw them twist and spurt, emptying their blood-red to a pearly and sweating grey. Far off, within the divisions of his fingers, were folds of linen; he raised them up; a handkerchief was twined against his nostrils, which sucked in its fumes. They had the smell of comfort, but a gust of torment swept them away, and he saw Bissett laying hot compresses on the bony shell, which heat could not penetrate. He heard Bissett speak, and cried out: "No. Not to the Rectory. Not now. Not until I am dead," and he gathered his knuckles into the softness of his throat.

When at last the pulse of agony weakened, he asked for water, and, having drunk, said:

"The nitrite was no good, Bissett."

"No, m'lord."

He turned on his pillow and covered his face with his hands. "Thank God for a rest!"

"Thank God it's over, m'lord."

"It's not over. It will come again. I know when it is incomplete. . . . You wanted to go to the Rectory?"

"Well, there's only morphia, m'lord, if the nitrite won't serve. We haven't any morphia."

"I know. But you are not to go, you are not to leave me. If it comes again—even if I scream for morphia—then you are to disobey me, not leave my sight."

"But I could go now, m'lord, to have the Doctor handy."

"No. He is not to be told. Do you understand? The Rectory is not to be told."

"Yes, m'lord."

"Swear it—in no circumstances, in no extreme, unless I am dead. Swear it."

"As you please, m'lord."

For a long time Sparkenbroke was silent, then said: "Bring a book, a newspaper, what you like; sit, and smoke. I shan't talk much or need anything. Until night shuts down I want something alive in the room."

At the last phrase, Bissett threw a quick, searching glance at the figure on the bed. By it he knew that there

were now more enemies to fight than pain. He went
upstairs for his book and, returning to Sparkenbroke's
room, sat down on an upright chair to read.

"You'll need a lamp, Bissett."

"Very soon I shall, m'lord."

The slow, heavy ticking of a clock came in from the
living-room next door, and, through the open window,
the songless evening twitter of birds. The sound of
breathing from the bed varied in pace and volume. Once
it ceased, and Bissett looked up, observant for the death-
like torpor into which, he knew, Sparkenbroke might fall.

"Do you remember, Bissett, climbing trees when you
were a boy?"

"That I do, m'lord—after apples."

"But not after apples? After nothing? For the sake of
the tree—of being in it?"

"Sometimes I expect it was like that." The answer
had a doubtful vagueness as though it had been spoken
to humour a child.

"But no particular tree?"

"Not particular; no, m'lord."

This was the track that Bissett knew too well. It had
taken him long to understand that, on these occasions,
his master's thought converged on the burying-place.
Through all his words, Sparkenbroke would make long,
tortuous approaches to—to what? In Italy, he would
speak of England, of villages, of churches; then of mothers
and children, of being born, of whether a child *was* before
its birth; then of sleep, of streams, of falling asleep in a
boat and waking in it again; then, as he had this evening,
of climbing trees and of their roots—how far they
stretched underground and how powerfully, breaking
through whatever stood in their way. It was all connected,
Bissett knew, with the Mound or with something that it
stood for in his lordship's mind. It was deeper than anyone
would think. There were the trees, mostly elms, standing
round the graveyard, and there was the stream, running
beside it; one could put two and two together; but there
were clocks, too, and setting their hands, and moving the

regulator to make them go faster or slower—Bissett had
learned that clocks were best tended out of his master's
presence when these moods were on him.

Sparkenbroke began suddenly to speak of what a woman
felt while she was giving suck.

"As to that, m'lord, I'm sure I don't know. But my
brother tells me his wife speaks of it as a pleasurable
sensation."

The man on the bed began to laugh, a broken, gasping
laugh. "Thank you, Bissett, you are my sanity. You put
everything in its place. She doesn't see herself as the
resurrection of the dead, does she?—and that's to her
credit. She'd give bad milk if she did."

Daylight was gone.

"Would the lamp try your eyes, m'lord?"

"No. Light it. And draw the curtains. . . . What are
you looking at?"

"Looking at, m'lord?"

"Out there—through the window."

"Nothing, m'lord."

"Thinking then?" And, seeming to know that his
servant's thought had been of him and to guess the quality
of it, Sparkenbroke said: "We're unlike master and servant,
Bissett."

"By the modern reckoning we are, m'lord."

"The modern reckoning?"

"Well, m'lord, from what I read, master and servant
knew each other pretty well a hundred years ago."

Sparkenbroke smiled. "It was my father's generation
broke the tradition. They treated even their personal
servants as if they were panes of glass. . . . Did you bring
the chessmen down from the House?"

"No, m'lord. I'd fetch them if a game would ease you."

Sparkenbroke shook his head. "I'm beyond that to-
night. But bring them to Italy."

"To Italy?"

"To-morrow, Wednesday, ten at night—we leave here."

"Leave? M'lord, you can't do it. You can't. You'll
never be fit."

"There will be a lady with us," Sparkenbroke went on. "You understand? I am pledged to it."

"But, m'lord, you're ill. Some other time——"

"No other time. It must be now. . . . She wouldn't come at any other time."

"Well, m'lord, it's our experience of women they'll always come if they mean to. The more if they've missed something—they'll come to see what they've missed."

Sparkenbroke jerked himself up in his bed. "I have spoken of the Rectory. You understand who she is?"

"I do now, m'lord."

"Very well. . . . We shall not come back here. Her ladyship holds the estate; she will continue to hold it for my son. This is the end—if you come."

"You can't leave the place, m'lord. Not cut yourself off from it. It's necessary to you—at times. It's not for me to say. But I've watched. I do know, m'lord, as well as your lordship——"

"It is not the place that's necessary, but what I find in it. . . . I have found it elsewhere." Sparkenbroke gazed at him. "I understand you. I know what you wish to say." And he added with violence: "But I tell you I have found it elsewhere. I believe that."

The clock in the living-room chimed the hour.

"Cut out the chime. I may sleep before day."

Bissett went to the clock, returned and sat down again to his book, holding it out in one hand towards the lamp.

"What's that you're reading, Bissett?"

He turned the book over as if he did not already know its title. "*Cloister and the Hearth*, m'lord."

"What—again? You were reading it a year ago in Italy."

"I used to read it as a boy, m'lord. It's an old favourite, you might say. I don't get tired of it."

Sparkenbroke glanced at him with keenness and with a kind of gratitude. "That's a good epitaph for Charles Reade," he said. "Peace be to him. Read aloud. . . No, no. . . . Straight on—from where you are. Aloud!"

Bissett read at once, fast and loudly: " 'She was soon at Margaret Van Eyck's house. Reicht took her into a room, and said, "Bide a minute; she is at her ori*s*ons." There was——' "

"Orisons."

" 'Orisons. There was a young woman in the room seated pensively by the stove; but she rose and courteously made way for the visitor. "Thank you, young lady; the winter nights are cold, and your stove is a treat." Catherine then, while warming her hands, inspected her companion furtively from head to foot, both inclusive. The young person wore an ordinary wimple, but her gown was trimmed with fur, which was, in those days, almost a sign of superior rank and wealth. But what struck Catherine was the candour and modesty of the face. She felt sure of sympathy from so good a countenance, and began to gossip.' "

"There, you see, that's their strength," Sparkenbroke exclaimed. "They stumble about through their 'both inclusives' and their 'young persons' and their 'which was in those days . . .' until you'd swear they hadn't a blue pencil in their kit. Then, suddenly, they take a short cut where we should waste a page in subtle avoidances. 'The candour and modesty of the face. She felt sure of sympathy from so good a countenance, and began to gossip.' It's all said in a dozen words and they plunge on into their story. Clumsy as a cart-horse in a pond, but they go straight through. We loiter to watch the bubbles. . . . And you say: 'I don't get tired of it.' My God, you make me envious. You must know it by heart."

"In a manner of speaking, I do, m'lord. But it comes fresh each time." The reader ran his tongue over his lips and was about to continue.

"All right, Bissett, I'm easier now—and tired. Charles Reade drove away the vulture. . . . But this may be a bad night for us. You'd better get some sleep while you may."

"Good-night, m'lord."

"Pray God. . . . Good-night to you."

Near morning, Sparkenbroke fell asleep. His last thought before he slept and his first in waking sprang from his deep assurance that, for all the suffering he had endured, the force of this attack was not spent. When Bissett asked again that he might be allowed to go to the Rectory, he forbade him.

"Listen. I know my own disease. You needn't be afraid that I shall die of any attack in which morphia might have time to save me. There's another form of attack—a single pang and all's done. I shall go that way, if I go at all. At least, I feel so."

He turned on his side and lay with little movement and with his eyes shut until far into the afternoon. He then raised himself on his elbow and asked for pillows. "And I want paper and ink." When they were at his side, he said: "I shall dress at eight. Supper at a quarter to nine. Have you packed what is necessary?"

"Enough, m'lord, to travel light."

"Good. The rest can follow. . . . Where is the car? At the House?"

"Yes, m'lord."

"I had meant to go up there again and drive down past the lodge, but I won't risk the climb over the terraces. . . . You go, Bissett. Bring the car to the church and——" But in Bissett's presence, to doubt her coming, to perceive in his heart slowly that she would not come, to wait, listening for her step, to hear it and to know that there was nothing to hear—better alone. "Not to the church," he said. "Bring it to the gate—not the stile near the cross-roads, but the gate higher up that leads from the wood to the Ancaster road. Wait in the car, at any rate until half-past eleven. If we haven't turned up then, you can come back to the cottage; sleep if you like. We can walk up from the churchyard through the wood and find you here. And understand, Bissett, in no circumstances follow me. She may be delayed— God knows how long." His eyes moved away from Bissett's face. "She may not come. If not, I shan't wish for company."

"MY DEAR MARY,

This, I hope, is a letter to the waste-paper basket—
or one that we shall read together in Lucca. If it comes
to you alone, it will come as a warning that I am dead.
I had an attack last night. What brought it on I don't
know—cold water, I think; it gives me a doubt of driving
through Pisa to swim. I feel now, though I am in no pain,
that the storm hasn't blown over. I don't want you to
come to the elm and find no one there. It may be ridiculous, but it is necessary, to write this. If anything should
go wrong, Bissett will put it into your own hands. Let it
be, not my farewell only, but still my welcome to you.

Was I a fool not to take you when you would have
come? It was more than forty-eight hours ago—we might
have been in Italy now, unless, as perhaps we should,
we had chosen to loiter in France. Once, I should not
have hesitated. But I want you to come of your own will,
not mine; to be given, not seized; above all, to have
become, by a final imaginative act, single-minded.
Though, while I was with you, you assented, the imaginative act was not complete; a part of you was bound by
your reason and loyalty in this place, and I would not
over-ride them. I hope I should not even now, for I love
you not in the body only, or in the mind only, but in the
core of my imagination. In you, if you also are single-
hearted, I may die to my former self. I love you for this
mystery, and for the simplicity of your own life within
it, and for the sensation I have of being, in your presence,
always in the tension of a dream, and yet, within the
dream, at ease. Before the world, and in the masks we
present to the world, we are widely separated, but when
we are alone together I feel myself a liberated being
with natural entry into all created things, and, in you,
security and flight; so that towards each other we can do
no wrong or be in peril of misunderstanding. With
you, the one believable innocence among all the false
innocencies of life, I come as near to absolute communication with another human being as I shall in this
world.

If I have thee, it is to lock thy face
In visionary masks, and gaze thereon,
Until this ecstasy acquire the grace,
If but an hour, of contemplation.

If I seek love, it is to plunge therein
And, being darkened, sink to former light.
It is, with clay, from blindness to have sight;
In death, an end or resurrection win.

O perilous one, now is no loss but thee.
If thou art silent, music all is done.
The thrush is silent also and the tree
Muted in the wood,
The stream dead;
In peace no melody, in battle none.

I send you these verses which, if you receive them, are my last. They came into my mind this afternoon—a succession of moods—an autobiography, perhaps.   S."

A little before ten o'clock he left the cottage. At first the wood was close and dark, but ahead the milkiness of the bridle-path appeared and soon he entered it. The earth being now dimly illuminated, he could advance more quickly, and he thought: perhaps she will be early, perhaps she is already there. Soon she and I shall return by this place and I shall say: this was the place—look, I snapped off this branch as I came down. A turning in the ride brought him to the point from which view of the church-yard lay open, and he stopped, for there had been movement under the elm.

He was not at once certain that a human figure had stirred, for the outline of the elm-trunk could not easily be distinguished from the distant foliage that was its background; but, through the branches, needles of light fell vertically, and across these he saw her darkness move. Now she was not to be mistaken. She stooped, raised herself again, took a couple of steps forward, which brought her beyond the deep shadow of the trees, and set down the thing she was carrying. Set it down, lifted it again, moved and halted. He watched without curiosity, in sole delight, in the bliss of his eyes, in joy that she was there—a joy which, deliberately, he prolonged, held back against the trees. He did not ask himself why she moved as she did. She was alive, waiting for him; his joy told him how great his fear had been that she might not come; he shut his eyes, imagining her absence, and opened them upon the miracle of her being there.

She was moving again, lifting, advancing, setting down. It was not until her head was turned in his direction that he understood these to be the movements of anguish. Her figure was illuminated by gleams too uncertain for him to have distinguished, precisely, the turning of her head. He had believed himself to be looking at her back when, suddenly, her face had appeared, vanished, and appeared again. She is turning her head, she is looking this way and that, she is afraid! Her stricken confusion was communicated to him; he felt the cramp of her fingers on the handle of her suit-case and the imprisoned wildness of her heart.

A car approached from the eastward. In the tautening of her body, its locked rigidity, her mind became visible. It is for my car she is listening—and now she listens no more. Her face, an oval pallor, was turned to him again and began to approach with the swaying persistence of an automaton. In the place where he stood he was visible, and he crossed the bridle-path into the opposite darkness. She had come, but in doubt; had stood, her life divided; and now was going, her decision made. I shall not see her again, these are the last instants—her footstep crackling on a twig, her shadow rocking on the grass.

Unless, as I crossed the path, she saw me, and is coming to me; unless I go out and touch and claim her. As she comes near, he thought, I will go out gently, not to frighten her by sudden appearance. With a little cry she will surrender, her cheek salt, her hands cold, leaning against me, her will mine. I will go out, and take her, for her destiny is in a puff of wind; but he did not move. It is her own will, her life; it is her decision; she is going from me, she is in flight from the place where we should have met. It is not yet ten o'clock.

Her eyes looked directly ahead of her. Her face was lifted up, and she swayed on the uneven ground under the burden she carried. Her advance was very slow, but she made haste, her lips parted, her body inclined forward against the slope.

When she had passed, he looked after her. The cord binding her suit-case dragged its end across the ground, sliding and darting, the shadow of a lizard in the moon. Presently the bridle-path curved to the right and she was gone.

CHAPTER SIX

EVEN the sound of her was gone. The wood had fallen asleep and, in the clearing before the Mound, the elm under which she had stood did not remember her. The air that had been full of her agony was the calm air of night that birds and cattle were breathing. There were no sounds anywhere but of the stream and of the church clock striking the hour.

Her being gone had for him the appearance not of loss, which is to be measured and thought of in terms of a remaining poverty, but of transmutation. In her, while the nature of men clung to him, his imagination had been incarnated. From it the necessity of the flesh was now withdrawn, and he, passing through her absence, as a guest passes from an outer to an inner room in the same house, began to enter directly into that presence which had caused him to love her.

He stood near the elm, in the place where his father had laid him when he was a boy, remembering his father's eyes, and the charged silence from which he had summoned him. Opening the gate of the Mound, he went in, not in the hope of renewal before the world that had brought him often to this place, nor in the desire of visions or manifest powers, nor in the tumult of spirit which cries: Speak, yet cannot hear for its own outcrying, nor in the ambition of knowledge, nor in the pride of angels, but in certitude of that divine presence which, formerly apprehended as but the mediate essence of created things, was now immediate and everlasting, an absolute singleness exempt from the division of forms.

In this he stood, at first in wonder, for it was external to him and he as yet armoured in the body, himself, alone; but, by the last pang of the body, it came into him, as the sun into a candle, so ravishing and including him that wonder laid down its arms and imagination its images.

CHAPTER SEVEN

WITHIN an hour of Sparkenbroke's death, George returned from the village. Looking up as he crossed the
white-railed bridge, he saw light within the curtains of
his bedroom. His relief in seeing it—the secure, the
familiar, the sane—discovered his fears to him. He stopped
and twisted his boot on the gravel, in shame that so
vaguely, so deeply, he had mistrusted her. What had he
feared—that he would lose her? that her place would be
empty? Not that—and yet he had feared.

It seemed now a remote fear, causeless and unjust.
Since the first morning, Piers hadn't been near them.
That was two days, almost three days, ago. Even then she
had sat on the hearth-rug in the library, unmoved, disregarding him, not joining in their talk or listening to it.
And this evening, when they had spoken of *The House of
Glasbury*, it had been he, not she, who had begun the discussion. I was suspecting her then, cross-examining her,
laying traps, making it harder for her. Of course it's hard
for her, must be, with Piers about, the past being as it is.
But she came home from Lucca. I took the risk then and
she came through it. She came home—and we've been
happier than ever in the past. To-night, for no reason, I—
He put his key in the door. It was over. She was safe, in
her bed, reading, waiting for him.

As he climbed the stairs with his candle, he saw a
pencilling of light shine under her door, and, suddenly,
be extinguished. She has given me up, he thought, and is
settling down to sleep. Against the night-light was a
letter, his name upon it; she hadn't known, of course, how

long he might be. As he took it up, the envelope, with a
little snap of gum, flew open. He took out the enclosed
sheet and would have read it; but as she's awake, he
thought, she can tell me herself, if it's anything worth telling; and he let himself into the room, the letter held between his fingers and the candle-bowl.

"Afraid I'm late," he said. "That poor old woman——"
She did not stir or answer.

"Mary, are you asleep?"

Was it possible that she had fallen asleep so swiftly?
Her breathing was soft and regular, her lips were a little
parted, her lashes spread. He came near to her and
watched. Was it a game she was playing? On the bed-table
was a small volume in old leather. He lifted the cover—
Theocritus. Theocritus!—but she doesn't read Greek.

"Mary, my dearest, are you awake?"

The shadow beneath her eyelashes quivered and he
knew that she was awake. Was she angry with him? Was
this her reproof? Not that; she was incapable of the
trickery of pique; she wasn't a fool; and suddenly, because
he understood nothing except that in this long, silent pretence, she was lying to him, he was filled with terror and
pity, for she would not thus lie madly without cause.

A corner of the letter she had written stood out from
beneath the candle-bowl. He drew it down and read it,
and saw the great curve of the bowl-shadow leap up bed
and wall. She has come back, she is safe, she has forgotten
her letter; in the morning she herself must find it, believing that it has not been read. Without ceasing to watch her
eyes, he slid the letter into its envelope and, having closed
it, reached out through the open doorway, and returned
it to its place.

In silence he prepared for bed, withdrawing the light
from her. Might he not go now and take her in his arms
and comfort her, breaking her frozen secret? But he would
not allow himself, at her cost, the passion of forgiveness.
She has come back; she has chosen; she is safe, he repeated
again and again; at last the thing has worked itself out; and
it seemed to him that their life together depended upon

his power to accept these facts and to let the night pass and the day come.

At last, in this acceptance, going to his own bed, he lifted the candle that he might see her again. Her head had fallen over on her pillow; she sighed; perhaps, even, she was asleep. She has come back, he thought, she has chosen, and, wondering what her suffering had been, he saw on her flesh the dark stain of the rope. Then he might have cried out and awakened her; but he did not, for George was a man who always knew when to hold his tongue.

1932–1936

THE END

his power to accept these facts and to let the night pass and the day come.

At last, in this acceptance, going to his own bed, he lifted the candle that he might see her again. Her head had fallen over on her pillow; she sighed, perhaps, even, she was asleep. She has come back, he thought; she has chosen, and, wondering what her suffering had been, he saw on her flesh the dark stain of the rope. Then he might have cried out and awakened her; but he did not, for George was a man who always knew when to hold his tongue.

1924–1926

THE END